REGENCY
Proposal

Ann
Lethbridge

MILLS
BOON

First Published in Great Britain 2017
By Mills & Boon, an imprint of HarperCollins*Publishers*
1 London Bridge Street, London, SE1 9GF

REGENCY GAMBLE © 2017 Harlequin Books S.A.

The Laird's Forbidden Lady © 2012 Michèle Ann Young
Haunted by the Earl's Touch © 2013 Michèle Ann Young

ISBN: 978-0-263-92379-7

52-0417

Our policy is to use papers that are natural, renewable and recyclable products and made from wood grown in sustainable forests. The logging and manufacturing processes conform to the legal environmental regulations of the country of origin.

Printed and bound by
CPI Group (UK) Ltd, Croydon, CR0 4YY

A REGENCY

Collection

The Laird's
Forbidden Lady

Lots of people are involved in getting a story on to the shelves or up on line, and I am grateful for all their hard work. This book I am dedicating to my amazing editor, Joanne Grant. Thank you for your patience and for your invaluable guidance with this project. Without you it would never have come to fruition.

In her youth, award-winning author **Ann Lethbridge** re-imagined the Regency romances she read—and now she loves writing her own. Now living in Canada, Ann visits Britain every year, where family members understand—or so they say—her need to poke around every antiquity within a hundred miles. Learn more about Ann or contact her at www.annlethbridge.com. She loves hearing from readers.

Chapter One

Scotland—1818

Why had she ever thought returning to Scotland a good idea? Lady Selina Albright eyed the wrought-iron candelabra suspended from ancient oak beams and the grey stone walls covered with ragged tapestries, great swords and rusting pikes, and suppressed the urge to flee.

Having run from two eminently eligible bridegrooms, one more would put her beyond the pale. Not even her father's considerable influence would prevent her from being gazetted a jilt.

And besides, this one was her choice. Finally.

All around her, dark-coated gentlemen and sumptuously gowned women, their jewels flashing with every movement, filled Carrick Castle's medieval banqueting hall.

'I hadn't expected it to be such a squeeze,' observed Chrissie, Lady Albright, her father's wife of only a year and the reason Selina had agreed to this trip.

Not that she would ever have been so unkind as to tell Chrissie the truth.

'He must have invited every member of the Scottish

nobility,' Selina said. 'At any moment I expect to see Banquo's ghost or three witches hunched over a cauldron.' A shiver ran down her spine. 'I should have waited in London for the end of Algernon's tour of duty.'

She glanced across the huge chamber to where Lieutenant the Right Honourable Algernon Dunstan, conversed with another officer in front of the enormous hearth decorated with stag antlers. Fair-haired and slender, he looked dashing in his red militia uniform. Not quite the brilliant catch her father had expected, but he was a young man of good family with a kindly disposition. The kind of man who would make a pleasant husband.

He caught her eyeing him and bowed.

She inclined her head and smiled. He was the reason she was here: to bring him up to the mark and get her out of her father's house, where she felt decidedly underfoot.

'I think it is all very romantic,' Chrissie said, looking around her with wide-eyed appreciation. 'I feel as if I have been transported between the covers of *Waverly*. Is Dunross Keep equally enchanting?'

'Dunross is about as romantic as an open boat on the North Sea in winter.' It was hard to imagine she'd fallen in love with the keep when she first saw it some ten years before. She'd been a foolish impressionable child, she supposed. 'Nowhere near as grand as this and as cold and damp in summer as it is no doubt freezing in winter. Did Father tell you the local people hate us because we are English? They think of us as usurpers, you know.' For some obscure reason her father, the lord of the manor, wished to visit there next—something he had not told her before they left London and the real reason she was regretting her agreement to accompany him. Dunross was the last place in the world she wished to visit.

'Oh, my word,' Chrissie gasped. 'Who is that?'

Selina followed the direction of her gaze.

A hard thump of her heart against her ribs was a painful recognition of the tall man in Highland dress framed within the stone arched entry. Ian Gilvry. The self-proclaimed Laird of Dunross.

The reason she hated Scotland. A knot formed in her stomach and made it hard to breathe as her gaze took him in.

He was not the gangling youth she remembered, though she would have known him anywhere. He was virile and brawny and, despite his green-and-red kilt, exceedingly male.

His features were far too harsh and dark to be called handsome in the drawing rooms of London, and the frill of white lace at his wrists and throat did nothing to soften his aura of danger. The raw vitality he exuded drew and held every female eye in the room. Including her own.

He was the last man she had expected or wanted to see at Lord Carrick's drum. Hopefully, he wasn't here to make trouble.

His gaze swept the room and, to her chagrin, her heart raced as she waited for some acknowledgement of her presence in his sky-blue eyes. When his gaze reached her and halted, she couldn't breathe. Her heart tumbled over.

An expression of horror flickered across his face, then his gaze moved on. The sting of rejection lashed her anew. Ridiculous. She cared not one whit for Ian Gilvry's opinion. He might have been the first man, or rather boy, to kiss her, but it had been a clumsy attempt and not worth thinking about. Especially not when their families were at daggers drawn.

'Who is he?' Chrissie whispered.

'Ian Gilvry of Dunross,' she murmured. No further explanations were needed.

Chrissie looked down her nose. 'That is Ian Gilvry? What is he doing here? I thought only the real nobility were invited.'

Selina winced at the sudden urge to protest the scornful tone. 'He is a distant cousin to Lord Carrick. On his mother's side.'

'That costume is positively indecent in polite company.' Chrissie sniffed, clearly reflecting her husband's opinion of all things Gilvry. On anyone else Chrissie would have declared it romantic. 'He looks positively barbaric.'

He did. Deliciously so.

Oh, that was not the way she should be thinking about a man who held her and her family in contempt.

'It is the traditional garb of the Highlands.'

'I am surprised you would defend him,' Chrissie said with a little toss of her head.

She felt herself colour. 'I am stating a fact.' When Chrissie stared at her with raised brows, she realised she'd spoken more sharply than she intended. She shrugged.

From the corner of her eye, she watched Ian stroll across the room to greet a friend with a smile that lit his face and transformed him from stern to charming.

What, was she still fooled by his smile? Hardly. She didn't give tuppence for Ian Gilvry or his brothers. They were proud, arrogant men who would stop at nothing to put her father off land they considered their own.

As if sensing her watching, he glanced her way. Their gazes clashed for no more than a second. Heat flooded her cheeks. She swiftly turned away.

'Look, Sel,' Chrissie said, 'there is Lady Carrick.

Your father particularly asked me to get to know her better and this is the first time she has not been surrounded by crowds of people. Will you be all right here by yourself?'

Selina swallowed a sharp retort. Chrissie was being her usual sweet self and she had promised herself she would vanquish her annoyance at the young woman's attempt to play the mother. 'I am perfectly content to remain here and await your return.' She gave an airy wave of her fan and hoped Chrissie would not see the effort it cost her not to show her impatience.

Chrissie bustled away with a wifely determination that brought a genuine smile to Selina's lips and a warm feeling to her chilly heart. She hadn't expected to like her father's new wife, but they rubbed along quite well, most of the time.

Unfortunately, Chrissie's unflagging solicitude and her unfailing kindness made Selina feel increasingly like a guest in her father's house. It had become a source of increasing irritation since her accident had kept her confined to the house for so many months. With time for reflection, she had decided it really was time she found her own place in the world. And the only option available was to become a wife.

Unintentionally, her gaze slid once again in Ian's direction. He seemed to be circling the room, going from group to group, drawing closer to where she sat by the minute. Her heart picked up speed. Her mouth dried. Surely he would not have the unmitigated gall to approach her? She eased her grip on her fan and kept her gaze moving in case someone noticed her interest.

And here came Dunstan to ensure she was all right on her own. He bounded up to her like a puppy who had found his new bone, after misplacing it for a while.

She wasn't sure whether to pat him on the head to keep him happy, or throw him a stick to send him scampering off. Neither was appropriate, of course. Not if she wanted to keep him.

The third son of a powerful earl, he was a perfect match for the daughter of a baron, though at one time she'd been on the brink of landing the rakish heir to an earldom, had even been so bold as to follow him to Lisbon. But when he'd come up to the mark, she'd panicked and run. When it had happened again, with a viscount, she'd been labelled a jilt and become an object of fascination for gentlemen who liked a challenge. Or at least she had until her accident made her an object of pity.

She'd been right to flee that first time, though. Her suitor had later proved himself an intractable husband, according to gossip.

Dunstan was a whole other prospect. He would make the perfect husband. Malleable. Kind. And definitely besotted. She would have no trouble twisting him around her finger. She just wished he'd been stationed at Bath or Brighton instead of the wilds of Scotland. She smiled in welcome as he arrived at her chair.

'May I say how lovely you look this evening?' he said eagerly.

'Thank you, Lieutenant Dunstan, you are too kind.'

His eyes flickered down to her bosom and then up to her face. Desire shone in his eyes as he pressed the back of her gloved hand to his lips.

A public demonstration of possession.

Again the urge to run beat in her blood, but that would be cowardly. She gestured for him to take the chair vacated by Chrissie. 'Lord Carrick's castle is a thing of wonder, don't you think?'

Again her roving gaze fell upon Ian. He was much

closer now. Too close. Oh, why was he here of all places? She could not concentrate upon a thing Dunstan was saying. She shifted in her chair, turning to focus all her attention on the man at her side. But she could still feel Ian's presence, like a dark shadow looming in the corner of a room.

She forced a smile at Dunstan, who blinked.

'I think you will like Pater's seat in Surrey,' he said. 'I am to go on leave at the end of the month. I hope you and your father will do us the honour of a visit?'

Perfect. A man only interested in flirtation did not ask a woman to meet his parents. And it seemed he was no more enamoured of Scotland than she. 'We will be delighted, I am sure. And I hope we will see you at Dunross Keep before you depart for England?' It was to be her dowry. Her contribution to a convenient arrangement. He might as well see what he was getting.

'It will be a pleasure since I will have business in the area.'

'Military business?'

'Indeed,' he said heavily, his tone full of importance. But since he did not volunteer to say more, she let the matter slide. 'There are a great many people here I don't know,' she said brightly. 'I am sure you know all those of significance. I would be grateful for your insights.' If she'd learned one thing in her years on the town, it was how to make a man feel important.

The rather proud smile as he glanced around the room gave her a pang of guilt, but he seemed to enjoy the opportunity to show off his knowledge.

'The couple talking to your father is the local constable and his wife. Colonel Berwick fought at Waterloo with the Black Watch.'

'A brave man, then.' Selina memorised the soldier's

face. A good wife paid attention to those who could aid her husband. And she would be a good wife. She was determined to keep her part of the bargain.

'An unruly Highlander, more like,' Dunstan grumbled. 'They give the regiment no end of trouble.' He was now staring at Ian.

Her blood ran cold. It was as if a chill wind had swept through the room. 'What sort of trouble?'

'Illegal whisky stills. Smuggling.' His gaze narrowed.

If Ian was engaged in smuggling, he was more of a fool than she ever imagined. Without thinking, she noted the way his plaid grazed the tops of his socks as he sauntered with lithe grace to a group of guests not far from her chair.

Her heart hammered so loud she was sure Dunstan must hear it. Would he speak to her? Surely not. What would she say if he did? His words at their last meeting some nine years before had been horrid. Crushing. But more recently he had responded to a written request to call his brother home with a surprising alacrity. For that at least she owed him a debt of gratitude.

Now was not the time, however. With luck, Ian would pass on by.

Luck, as ever, was not her friend.

Annoyance crossed Dunstan's face when Ian paused in front of them. Ever the gentleman though, Dunstan gestured to Selina. 'Ian Gilvry, allow me to introduce you to Lady Selina Albright.'

Ian bowed. 'Lady Selina, it is indeed an honour to once more make your acquaintance.'

The butter-soft burr of his highland brogue made her skin tingle the way the touch of his lips to hers once had. Or was it the feel of his hand on hers and the sensation of warm breath she could not possibly feel through her glove? Or was it merely his acknowledgement of recollection?

Heat flashed in her cheeks. He was the only man who had ever had the power to disturb her equilibrium. Years of careful training stood her in good stead, however, and she gave him her most brilliant smile. 'Why, Mr Gilvry, I hardly recognised you after all these years.'

Bright blue eyes regarded her coldly. His mouth curved in a bitter smile. What did he have to be bitter about? It was her pride she'd ground into the dust by asking for his help for Alice. But the Gilvrys and the Albrights had always been enemies. Perhaps she was reading more into his expression than she should.

'You have also changed a good deal, Lady Selina.'

His tone said he spoke out of mere politeness. Something to say.

Dunstan frowned, then his brow cleared. 'Ah, right. You spent some time at Dunross Keep as a girl. You must have met then.'

'Briefly,' she said.

'Once or twice,' Ian said at the same moment.

She snatched her hand back. 'No rocks in your pockets today, I hope?'

An unwilling smile curved his full lips. 'None today, my lady,' he said smoothly.

She arched a brow. 'And how is all at Dunross? Your mother is well?'

His eyes darkened to stormy grey. 'As well as may be expected under the circumstances.' A muscle jumped in his jaw. 'I understand you are to honour Dunross Keep shortly.'

Gossip abounded. But then the self-professed Laird of Dunross would know everything about the demesne he claimed as his, when it really belonged to her father.

She lifted her chin, meeting his gaze without flinching. 'I believe it is on our list of quaint points of interest.' She smiled sweetly.

He stiffened slightly. Resentment flashed across his face, before it once more smoothed to bland indifference. 'Do you have many quaint places on your list?'

'A few. It is *de rigueur* to be in love with Scotland since *Waverly* came out. You have read Sir Walter Scott, I assume?'

This time real anger flashed in his eyes. 'Why would I?'

Dunstan tugged at his collar. 'I will also be visiting Dunross.'

'How pleasant for you,' Ian replied, his gaze never leaving Selina's face. 'I am delighted you *Sassenachs* find us poor Scots of such interest.'

'La, sir, you make yourself sound like insects beneath a lens.'

He gave a hard laugh. '*Touché*, Lady Selina.'

This was getting out of hand. She turned to Dunstan. 'Lady Albright is in alt with the country. And knowing Scotland as well as I do gives it a special charm.'

'Some say familiarity breeds contempt,' Ian said, before Dunstan could respond.

She raised a brow.

'No need to be churlish, Gilvry,' Dunstan muttered.

The orchestra struck up a reel. Ian inclined his head. 'I see I should make amends. May I request this next dance, Lady Selina?'

The air left her lungs in a rush. That she had not expected. For a moment, she almost said yes. It might be her only opportunity to speak with him alone, to proffer her thanks for the service he'd rendered her friend. A dance was about as private as she'd ever dared be with Ian Gilvry. But dancing was out of the question. Did he know that? Was he taunting her, knowing full well she could not dance? It would be the sort of thing a Gilvry would take pleasure in. 'I do not dance tonight, Mr Gilvry.'

His eyes remained wintry, giving no hint of his thoughts. 'You will excuse me, then,' he said softly. 'I promised Miss Campbell I would lead her out at the first opportunity.' He executed the slightest of bows, an arrogant inflection of his neck that said he bowed to no man or woman, and strode off, his kilt swinging with each long stride, his wide shoulders square.

The feel of her arms clinging to those shoulders for dear life teased at her memory. Although on that long-ago afternoon, they'd not been quite so breathtakingly broad.

She dragged her thoughts back to the present and watched Chrissie and her father take to the floor in another set. Despite the differences in their ages, they made a handsome couple. And she couldn't help but feel glad for his happiness, even if it did mean she must depart his home.

Her gaze wandered to Ian and Miss Campbell. His whole attention was focused on his partner's face. The girl blushed in response to a murmured word and a flash of a smile.

Something tightened in her chest. Jealousy? Certainly not. A pang of envy? Perhaps. It wasn't surprising. Not because the girl was dancing with Ian Gilvry—about that she surely didn't give a hoot. No. It was the dancing she missed.

A wry smile tugged at her lips. She was lucky it was only dancing she'd lost as a result of her recklessness. She could have lost her life.

She gave Dunstan her most brilliant smile. 'I gather your colonel gave strict instructions with respect to entertaining the single ladies tonight and since I do not dance, I shall not keep you from your duty.'

His expression held relief. 'You are gracious to be so understanding, my lady.'

'A soldier's duty must come first.' And she really needed to be rid of him for a while. Her heart still raced uncomfortably fast after sparring with Ian.

'I will escort you to supper, of course.'

'I look forward to it. In the meantime, do not worry about me. I am well entertained.'

He bowed and departed and was soon leading out a handsome young matron. Strangely enough, Selina didn't feel a smidgeon of envy as she watched him. Nor would she, she was sure, when he continued to dance with other ladies after they were married. It was the way of their world.

As the music finished, Lord Carrick took up a position on the dais in front of the orchestra.

'Ladies and gentlemen, I have a special treat for you before supper. If you will please follow me out onto the terrace.' A buzz of excitement circled the room and people moved towards the French doors at the far end of the hall.

Ian Gilvry, she noticed, left by way of the arch through which he had entered.

With no choice but to follow the rest of the company, she pushed to her feet.

Chrissie and her father joined her. 'What is going on?'

'I have no idea,' Selina said.

A woman standing nearby turned to them. 'It is a contest. The local lads will compete for a prize for our entertainment.'

'Not boxing,' Chrissie said with a shudder.

'Och, no. Something better. Wait and see.' She disappeared into the crowd.

The Albright party joined Lord Carrick, who indicated they should sit in the front row and guided Selina to a chair beside Chrissie.

Chrissie gave her a sweet smile. 'How are you feeling?'

'Excited about the coming spectacle,' she said, deliberately misunderstanding Chrissie's true meaning.

Chrissie leaned closer and whispered something in her husband's ear. Her father smiled down fondly, murmuring something that made Chrissie giggle.

Feeling like an intruder, Selina averted her gaze and pretended not to notice.

Lit by torches and a full moon, the flagged courtyard looked positively medieval. Lord Carrick seated himself on a thronelike canopied chair carved with symbols of his clan. Clearly he was to be judge and jury of the coming contest.

To the skirling sound of bagpipes five kilted men marched into the open area from beneath a shadowing arch, holding swords across their chests. Among them, taller than all of them, was Ian. Two of his three brothers accompanied him.

The men bent and laid their swords on the flagstones crossed at right angles. The music ceased.

Lord Carrick rose to his feet and the five men bowed. Their chief signalled for them to begin and the piper played the opening bars. The men were going to dance for a purse.

It was a magnificent sight. Strong young men in their plaids and white lace leaping lightly over their swords, jumping higher and faster in ever more complex patterns. Ian's heavy kilt swung high, revealing strongly muscled thighs and…nothing more. Too bad.

That thought brought heat to Selina's cheeks. How could she be so wicked?

But the sight of Ian dancing, the controlled wildness in his movement, the demonstration of his male strength and grace, called to something primal inside her. The iron control in the lightness of his feet caused her to hold her breath in awe and fear. A man touched his sword, knocking it askew with a clatter. He ceased dancing immediately, bowed and walked away defeated. She could scarcely bear to watch in case Ian also failed, yet could not look away.

The music's tempo increased. Another man dropped out. And another, until only two of the older Gilvry brothers remained.

Ian and Niall. Of Andrew there was no sign. Ian leapt without effort, his feet so close to the blades he barely moved from the centre of the cross. What held her transfixed was his intensity, the hot blood of battle expressed in the position of his arms, the proud angle of his head and the fire in his defiant eyes.

Impossible as it seemed, she felt their eyes lock and in that moment, it was as if he danced only for her.

Nay, not for her, she realised. At her, rejecting all she stood for. War declared. The final leaps caused an indrawn breath from the assembled company. Yet they landed lightly, clear of the swords, each man holding position until the last note died away.

The connection snapped.

In unison the two men bowed and stood stiffly, waiting for their chief's judgement while their audience applauded and cheered.

Even Chrissie and Father leaped to their feet, clapping.

Selina had no doubt Ian would win. Yet she still felt anxious until his chieftain beckoned him forwards. He ran lightly up the terrace steps, shook the Carrick's hand and took the purse presented with an incline of his head. He did not once glance her way.

There had been no connection between them. He probably couldn't see her on the terrace in the dark. It had all been her imagination. It wasn't the first time she'd been mistaken in his interest. The only connection they had was one of mutual dislike.

Deep inside she felt a twinge of sadness. Perhaps because whoever he had danced for, he had expressed himself through movement—a freedom and grace she could never accomplish.

The two men spoke a few words, then Ian ran back down the steps and walked away. Only when he was out of sight did the sorrow inside her lessen.

She thought she had resigned herself to the future she'd charted, but for some reason, now she felt thoroughly unsettled. She rose to her feet with a slight wince.

'Is your leg paining you?' Chrissies asked.

Dash it all, the woman watched her like a hawk. 'I am just a little stiff from sitting, that is all.' And from the tension of watching Ian.

Chapter Two

Ian joined his clansmen clustered around the piper in the shadows of the gate leading out of the courtyard to the kitchens. His breathing had slowed, but his blood still ran hot—battle fever aroused by the music. There had been a time when he danced for the pure joy of it. Now he felt like little more than a performing bear on a chain performing for these *Sassenachs*. He swallowed the anger. It had pleased Carrick and the coin would bring much-needed relief to his people. Lord Carrick could easily have spent his money on entertainment elsewhere.

He emptied the prize purse into his palm, first paying the piper his due, then dividing the spoils equally. 'Well done, lads.'

'What is that?' Logan, his youngest brother, asked, gesturing to the other pouch Carrick had slipped into Ian's palm.

'You've sharp eyes, young Logan,' Ian grumbled. 'Carrick wants us to make another run to France.'

'I thought we had all the salt we need,' Niall said, glancing up from the pamphlet he'd been reading by the light of the torch.

'He wants brandy,' Ian said. 'He will have used up most of his supply by the end of this ball.'

'Brandy is asking for trouble,' Niall said. 'It is bad enough running the whisky over the border to England.

Ian quelled him with a glance. 'How could I refuse after all he has done for us? Besides, his money will help pay for this autumn's barley.'

Niall shook his head. 'Admit it, you like the danger.'

Did he? Long ago, he'd wanted to be a soldier, but when his father died, he'd shouldered the duties of Laird without a second thought. It was his responsibility.

Straying from that duty had never resulted in anything but trouble, for him or his family. And smuggling was a necessary evil. Part of the job, if he wanted the clan to survive. And he did, desperately. It was all he thought of, day and night.

'What say we go down to the tavern and celebrate?' Tammy McNab said, jingling the coin in his hand.

Ian jabbed at Tammy's shoulder. 'Would you spend your money on drink when your babes are hungry?'

A red-haired man of twenty-five who already had three children to his name, Tammy hung his head. 'Just thought to have a wee bit of fun.'

'Why pay for it, when Carrick has food and drink for you all in the servants' hall?' Ian said.

Tammy cheered instantly. 'You'll be coming too, Laird?'

Ian shook his head. 'I've a ship's captain to meet now I have this new errand. Enjoy yourself on Lord Carrick's coin. You've earned it.'

The men moved off towards the servants' entrance in the low-slung thatched buildings abutting the castle. Ian turned to leave by the drawbridge. Logan caught his shoulder. 'Did you see who was watching? The Albrights. I'd recognise Lady Selina anywhere.'

Because she was just so damned lovely. Even lovelier as a woman than she had been as a child of sixteen. And just as much trouble as she had been then, too.

'I met her inside.' He curled his lip. 'I asked her to dance as Carrick ordered. She refused me.' He hadn't known whether to be glad or insulted.

During the sword dance, he had felt the intensity of her gaze. Had lost himself in her beauty in the final bars, drawing strength from her shining eyes and parted lips. He'd gone back in time, dancing for the girl who had roamed freely among the heather that long-ago summer. He'd been enchanted by her pretty face and spirit, until he came to his senses and remembered just whose daughter she was.

Something he'd do well to remember now, too. Selina Albright had caused his family nothing but trouble. And he, like a fool, had helped.

'I'm no surprised she wouldna dance with you, Ian.'

He stiffened. 'Aye. Albrights have always been a touch above the Gilvry clan.'

'She might think so, but I doubt she can dance, not with that limp.'

Stunned by a sudden stab of dismay, Ian whipped his head around. His eyes narrowed as he watched the progress of the dark beauty in the white gown as she crossed the terrace on her father's arm, the hesitation in her step cruelly obvious in the torchlight.

She had refused him for a reason different from the one he'd assumed. He felt an odd surge of relief.

He turned and pushed Logan after the others. He called Niall back and lowered his voice. 'Keep an eye on young Logan. He's developing an eye for the ladies and Carrick has too many of them in his kitchen.'

Niall sighed. 'You are as bad as our mother, always worrying about the lad. You'll make him worse.'

'Our mother has lost one son.' Because he'd let his fondness for a pretty face overrule good sense. 'I don't plan to let her lose another.'

'Then perhaps you should think twice about smuggling.'

'Now who's worrying too much?' Ian snatched the paper from Niall's hand. 'You can read this later.'

'Give it back,' Niall said, his voice dangerously low.

Ian tossed it to him with a grin. 'Keep it in your pocket, then, and concentrate on what is going on around you for once.'

Niall grimaced, his eyes turning serious. 'Make this trip to France the last one, brother, or we'll all find ourselves at the end of a rope.'

Ian clapped his brother on the shoulder with a confidence that seemed to stick in the back of his throat. 'It will be fine.'

Against his will, he looked back at the terrace, his gaze seeking the girl whose eyes spoke to him in unexpected ways. She was gone. Just as well. He had work to do.

Topaz needed no urging to canter. Selina guided her off the road and across open ground, exhilarated by the speed and the edge of chill on the breeze against her cheeks. At last she could breathe. And on horseback she could forget her incapacity.

The scent of heather filled her nostrils. Sweet, like the honey they made from the bees in this part of the country, yet earthy, too. She filled her gaze with the beauty of hills of smoky purple. Wild, unforgiving terrain, but so grand it made your heart ache.

She'd forgotten how easily the child in her had fallen in love with this place the first time she had seen it. Forgotten deliberately. Remembering only brought back the pain of loneliness and betrayal. Something she would never suffer again.

She smiled at herself. Such maudlin thoughts had no place in her mind on such a glorious day. Live for the now, plan for the future and let the past belong to the devil. Lord knew there were enough mistakes in her past well worth forgetting.

Thirty minutes later she was wishing she'd stayed on the track. After months of inactivity, her muscles were complaining at being forced to keep her steady in the saddle when as a girl she'd ridden the rough terrain astride, without effort. Riding astride was not an option for the woman she'd become. She rubbed at her thigh with a grimace at the reminder she was lucky to be riding at all. Lucky she hadn't killed herself or someone else. She slowed the animal to a walk and turned him around.

A black-and-white collie flashed out of the heather. Barking, it snapped at Topaz's heels. The horse reared. Off balance, Selina clung to his mane.

The animal landed with a thud on its forefeet, jolting her again. 'Steady, boy,' she cried out, fighting with the reins as he tossed his head and spun around, trying to watch the dog. He kicked out with a back hoof. Dislodged by the jolt, Selina had no choice but to free her foot and let herself slide to the ground.

She landed on her rump with a groan. 'Blasted dog,' she yelled. She stared up at the wild-eyed Topaz. Dash it. She'd never be able to mount him again. She'd have to lead him home. Her first chance to ride in months had ended in disaster.

She stretched out an arm to catch Topaz's reins. 'It's all right, boy,' she said softly. The nervous gelding tossed its head and pranced farther away.

Double blast.

Her thigh throbbed a protest. Surely she hadn't broken it again? The thought made her stomach roil. No. She hadn't heard that horrid snapping sound and it was her rear end that was bruised, and her pride, not her leg. Breathe. Calm down. All she had to do was get up and catch Topaz. It was a long walk home, but she could do it.

She forced herself to her knees.

'Lady Selina! Is that you?'

Inwardly, she groaned. Of all the bad luck—it would have to be that well-remembered deep voice she heard. She looked up.

Kilted and wild-looking, his black hair ruffled by the breeze, Ian Gilvry looked completely at home among the heather-clad hills as he strode towards her. He always had.

To a girl of sixteen, he'd seemed heroic and romantic. Especially since the first time they met he'd carried her home and then kissed her, a shy fumbling thing when he set her down at the gate. Utterly besotted, she'd plotted every which way to meet up with him again. And again.

In her innocence, she'd assumed he liked her.

'Are you hurt?' he said when he came close, concern showing on his face, a large suntanned hand reaching out to pull her to her feet.

She ignored it and sank back down into the springy heather, primly covering her feet with her riding habit. 'I'm fine.'

He drew back, putting his hands on lean hips, his head tilted. 'You fell off your horse?'

She glanced at Topaz, who was now happily cropping at the grass just out of reach. 'I dismounted rather more quickly than I expected. The horse was terrified of your dog.'

The smile on his finely drawn lips broadened. 'What, an excellent horsewoman such as yourself put to grass by a wee dog?'

'The dog should be leashed. The horse could have been injured and that would have cost you a pretty penny.' What was she doing? She had no wish to enter into verbal sparring with the man. She should just get up and walk away.

His eyes, as blue as the sky above his head, narrowed. 'Gill is still in training. I apologise if he upset your animal.'

Her jaw dropped. Gilvrys didn't apologise to Albrights. It was a point of honour.

'Apology accepted.' She stared off into the distance, willing him to leave.

'Allow me help you back on your horse,' he said, his voice no more than a murmur.

Kind. Full of pity. Like everyone else. She gritted her teeth in frustration.

A year ago, it would have been easy to leap to her feet and let him toss her up in the saddle. Right now, getting back on that horse and trying to control him with her aching muscles was out of the question. She should not have ridden so far.

She gave him her brightest smile and had the satisfaction of seeing his eyes glaze a little. 'I think I will stay here and enjoy the scenery for a while. No need to trouble yourself.'

Dark brows drew down. He muttered something under his breath in Gaelic. A curse, no doubt. She felt like cursing, too.

'Then I bid you good day, Lady Selina. Come, Gilly.' He gave her a stiff little bow and strode up the hill.

The dog lay down at her side.

'Go,' she said and gave it a push.

It stared at her with soft brown, laughing eyes.

Ian whistled without looking back. The dog remained where it was.

With a heavy sigh, Ian turned, walked back, pulling a rope from his jacket pocket. 'Once more I must apologise for my dog's bad manners.' He looped the knotted rope over the animal's head and gave a sharp tug.

The dog pulled back with a whine. It pushed its nose under her hand where it rested on her thigh.

'Go,' she said, desperate for them both to be gone, so she could limp home with a shred of her pride intact.

His blue eyes suddenly sharpened. 'Can you get up?'

He knew. Of course he did. He'd seen her at the Carricks' ball. 'I'm not ready to leave. Why don't you and your dog just go away?' She certainly wasn't going to give him the satisfaction of watching her hobble after her horse.

Ian stared down at the petite dark-eyed beauty sitting at his feet in the heather and didn't believe a word coming out of her mouth. The tautness around her mouth spoke of pain and more than a dash of humiliation.

'I'll go when I've seen you safely home.' He stuck out his hand to help her up.

She gave an impatient sigh, placed her small hand in his and he tugged. The quick indrawn breath of pain as she rose caused a painful twinge low in his gut. Damn stubborn female. He gently lowered her back down and crouched down beside her. 'I knew you were hurt.'

He glanced down at where her riding habit had rucked up over her ankles, showing a pair of sturdy riding boots. 'Is it your leg?'

Her cheeks flushed red. 'Partly, if you must know. But mostly it is because this is the first time I have ridden in a very long time. I stayed out too long. I am sure I will be fine in a little while, but I thank you for your concern, Mr Gilvry.'

Once he'd been plain Ian and she'd been a hoyden who one summer had roamed the hills around Dunross and fought a running battle with his younger brothers, the Gilvrys and the Albrights being mortal enemies.

He'd been away at his Uncle Carrick's most of that summer. He'd returned home for a few days before he went back to school in Edinburgh and met her by accident late one summer afternoon. He hadn't known who she was at first, and he'd come to her rescue when she twisted her ankle in a rabbit hole and carried her home.

Along with her pretty face and burgeoning womanhood, he'd found her *joie de vivre* and her artless chatter captivating. She'd treated him like a man, not a boy, and there had been hero worship in those warm brown eyes—a welcome change from schoolbooks and lessons in stewardship.

They'd met several times after that, until they'd been discovered at Balnaen Cove by his brothers. That had not gone well.

'So it seems I must carry you home again,' he said, wondering if she also remembered, then wanted to kick himself as shadows darkened her sherry-brown eyes. Of course she remembered. But no doubt she remembered his harsh words, too.

Like a fool, he'd tried to make up for his cruelty, the next time she asked for help, even though years had passed. Too soft-hearted, his grandfather had always said. Drew had paid the price for that bit of softness. Well, he wasn't soft-hearted any more. Too many people relied on him now.

But nor could he in all conscience leave her here. He reached for her again.

'It wouldn't be seemly,' she said, batting his hand away. 'I can manage perfectly well by myself. I just need a moment or two.'

The lass always did have spirit to the backbone. And now she was utterly lovely. She looked like a feast for a starving man laid out in the heather.

He shook his head at himself. He did not have the time or the inclination for romping in the heather. He'd always left that to Drew. And because of Ian's weakness over this female, Drew was no more.

A good Gilvry would leave her here and let Albright have the worry of a missing child, but a true Highland gentleman would never leave a woman in distress. Not even his worst enemy's daughter. He glowered. 'You know I can't leave you here. And nor can I let you walk home in pain.'

'I will manage, thank you.'

He put his hands on his hips and grinned at her. 'Then climb aboard your flea-ridden nag and ride away.'

'When I'm ready,' she muttered.

Ian sank cross-legged beside her. The faint scent of roses filled his nostrils. Roses and heather. Never had he inhaled such a heady combination, although he suspected it was more to do with her than the perfume of the surrounding vegetation.

He folded his arms across his chest. 'And I will sit here until you do. Or until you come to your senses.'

She rolled away from him onto her knees, presenting a view of her curvaceous bottom that sent a jolt of lust to his groin. Thank God for his plaid and his sporran or she'd be thinking him no better than an animal.

Gilly ran around her and licked her chin. She pushed him away, struggling with her skirts and the dog. With a small grunt, she got to her feet and took a couple of halting steps towards her horse.

Ian sprang up, putting a hand beneath her elbow. 'Ach, lass, will your pride no let me help you?'

She lowered her head, until all he could see was the top of her dark green velvet bonnet and the silk primroses adorning its green ribbon. 'It seems I have no choice,' she said in a low defeated voice. 'I cannot ride any more today.'

The anguish in the admission knocked the wind from his lungs. Damn it to hell. 'This is all my fault. I should never have let the dog off the leash.'

Her head shot up. Dark brown eyes, soft as velvet, met his. 'The fault is mine. I should not have left the track.'

'Well, it looks as if there is only one answer to our dilemma.' He put an arm around her shoulders and one carefully beneath her knees and scooped her up.

She gasped. 'Put me down. I will not let you carry me all the way to Dunross.'

'I don't intend to,' he said, looking down into those soul-deep brown eyes and feeling as if he might drown. This was not a reaction he should be having, not to this woman.

He gritted his teeth and grabbed her horse's bridle. The dog followed closely at his heels like the best-trained dog in Scotland. Naturally.

'Then where are we going?'

For no apparent reason the fear in her voice caused him a pang in his chest, though he was damned if he'd let her see it. 'To find a less objectionable mode of transport.'

At that she laughed. It was as if the sun had come out from behind a cloud and he couldn't keep from smiling, just a little.

Chapter Three

Selina held herself stiffly, trying to maintain some sort of distance between her and his chest. Impossible, when she was in his arms. Strong arms wrapped around her back and under her knees. The steady beat of his heart vibrated against her ribs. A feeling of being safe made her want to slide her arm around his neck and rest her head against his brawny shoulder.

Safe? With him? Had she banged her head when she fell?

The Gilvrys were wild and unruly. The last time she had seen him he'd ganged up on her with his brothers, calling her *Sassenach* and thief. And he now was their leader. A man who would do anything to be rid of her father from land he considered his. While she could not refuse his help, she must not trust his motives.

At the bottom of the hill they came across a winding cart track. His steps lengthened as he followed the deep wheel ruts round a sweeping corner to where a long narrow loch glistened like beaten steel in the weak sun. Beside it lay a collection of rough stone buildings.

The old water mill. It looked different—not so derelict—

and the pagoda-looking chimney at one end looked new. 'I didn't think you Gilvrys worked the mill any more.'

'My father didn't. I do.'

'And added a chimney?'

'Aye.'

Talk about taciturn. 'Why does the mill need a chimney?'

He hesitated, his expression becoming carefully neutral. 'To keep the miller warm in the winter.'

A lie. Though it sounded logical enough. What did it matter that he didn't care to tell her the truth? She didn't care what the Gilvrys did with their old falling-down mill.

He carried her into the barn and set her down on a hay bale. Immediately, she felt the loss of the strength around her body, and his seductive warmth, whereas he looked glad to be rid of her. Had she not a smidgeon of pride?

Apparently some part of her did not. The childish naïve part that had admired him from the first moment she saw him. The part of her she'd long ago buried.

Silently, he tied Topaz to a post, while Gilly curled up at her feet.

Her thigh wasn't hurting nearly as much as before. She'd given it a jolt and the bones that had knit badly had decided to protest the rough treatment. But even though the ache had subsided, she doubted she had the strength to manage her horse. She would have to settle for his alternative mode of transport.

The only occupant of the barn was a small dun-coloured pony, which he led from its stall and proceeded to hitch to a flat-bedded wagon.

'Your chariot awaits, my lady,' he said wryly.

She rose to her feet, but he gave her no chance to

walk, simply scooping her up and depositing her on some empty sacks he'd laid across the bare boards.

He was unbelievably strong, so unlike most of the gentlemen of the *ton* who defined themselves by their clothes, not their manly attributes. So unlike the elegant Dunstan.

Oh, now that really was being disloyal.

She shifted until her back was supported against the wooden boards along the side. The smell of barley wafted up. A sweet dusty smell.

He frowned. 'There are no blankets, but I can give you my coat.'

No. She would not go home wrapped in his coat. It was bad enough she had to suffer his help. Wasn't it?

'This will do.' She picked up a couple of the sacks and covered her legs with one and put the other around her shoulders. She flashed a smile and fluttered her lashes in parody. 'How do I look?'

'Like a tinker's wife,' he said, a twinkle appearing in the depths of his eyes, making him look more attractive than ever. A twinkle she knew better than to trust.

She kept her voice light and breathy, her smile bright. 'The first stare of tinker fashion, though, surely?'

The corner of his mouth tipped up as if it wanted to smile more than was seemly. 'Top of the trees, my lady.'

Something about his bantering tone made her feel warm and her smile softened.

They grinned at each other the way they had on those long-ago summer afternoons, before he had turned his back on her so cruelly.

His gaze dropped to her mouth.

Her heart lurched. Her breath caught. Many men had looked at her with heat since her come out. Not once in that time had her heart tumbled over in such a ridiculous fashion. She broke hearts. Men did not touch hers. Ever. That was the way to get hurt.

And besides, she was as good as betrothed to a very worthy man who was utterly besotted.

She turned her face away. 'We should go.'

'Aye. I'll tie your horse on behind.'

She swallowed against the feeling of loss as he walked away, trying to blot out her stupid reactions to his smile by thinking about Father and his reaction when he learned she'd been carted home by a man he despised. Father would not be pleased.

Horse dealt with, Ian leapt easily into the driver's seat with such agility, he made her feel more clumsy and awkward than she usually did these days.

He half turned in the seat, one foot resting against the footboard, his plaid falling away to reveal his knee and the start of a firm muscled calf dusted with dark hair before it disappeared in his sock. So very male. So very intriguing. So very out of bounds. She forced her gaze away.

'The track is rough,' he said. 'I will take it as easy as I can.'

'I'm not an invalid.'

'I never said you were.' He clicked his tongue and the pony started walking. Gilly jumped up over the side of the cart and landed beside her. He lay against her legs.

'Off,' Ian said.

The dog flattened his ears, but didn't move.

'Leave him,' Selina said. 'He's keeping me warm.'

'Lucky him,' he muttered.

Her jaw dropped. Had he really said what she thought she heard? Or was he being sarcastic? He was staring morosely at the road ahead.

'What happened to your leg?' he asked. 'I saw you walking at the ball.'

So much for her efforts to glide smoothly. 'My carriage tipped over and fell on me.'

He winced. 'I hope the idiot driver was suitably punished.'

'I was. I broke my leg.'

His cheekbones flushed red. 'Oh. I didna' mean—'

'The accident was my fault. I was driving too fast and not looking where I was going.' Thinking about her recent male conquest if the truth be told. 'I was lucky I was the only one hurt by my stupidity. It doesn't hurt much any more, but the bones didn't set quite right.'

'I'm sorry.' He sounded sorry. But then once he'd sounded as if he liked her, until his brothers caught them together.

Sassenach. Thief. The taunts danced in her head. The war between the Scots and the English might be over, but their families would battle until no one remained to swing a verbal sword.

The track had joined the main road where the jolts were less and their pace improved. Soon they were driving through Dunross village where a group of ragged boys were kicking a pig's bladder back and forth across the lane. When they saw the cart, they came running over. 'Laird, Laird,' one of the boys shouted, then said something in Gaelic.

Ian replied in the same language. He half turned to her. 'They want me to play with them.'

One of them spotted her in the cart and his eyes rounded in his grimy face. He pointed at her and yelled something. The boys all sniggered.

Ian grinned and replied, clearly in the negative.

She squared her shoulders, set her face in untroubled calm while inside she curled in a tight ball. 'What did he say?'

Ian laughed. 'Boys. They have one-track minds. They want to know if you are my woman. I told them, no, that you are a lady and to be treated with respect.'

She relaxed, looking back and seeing the boys had returned to their game. 'Shouldn't the children be in school?'

'Aye.'

Could he not say more than one word at a time? 'You call yourself Laird—why do you not convince their families to give them an education?'

He glanced back at her, his brows lowered, his eyes hard. 'They call me Laird, because that is what I am. The nearest school is fifteen miles hence.'

'Why not start a school in the village?'

'Where?' He sounded frustrated.

She subsided into silence. Father should be the one to open a school. He owned almost everything except the old mill and the Gilvrys' farmland.

'I will speak to my father about setting up a school. Perhaps in the church hall.'

Now he looked surprised, and heaven help her, pleased. 'It would be a grand thing for the families hereabouts,' he said. 'There are children up in the glens who would come, too, when they weren't needed for chores. It would give them a future.'

She cast him a sly smile. 'And keep them out of mischief.'

He chuckled. 'Perhaps, my lady. Me and my brothers got up to all sorts of mischief, despite having a tutor. But it is true that we had less time to get into trouble.'

A feeling of warmth stole through her, the feeling

they had begun to talk like friends again, rather than enemies. She liked the way it felt.

As they approached the tavern in the centre of the village a youngish man sweeping the cobbles doffed his hat at their approach. He grinned at Ian. 'Good day to you, Laird.'

Ian acknowledged the greeting with a nod.

Then the man's gaze fell on Selina and all traces of good humour disappeared from his ruddy face. He spat on the ground. 'That's Albright's get. You should be dropping her in the nearest peat bog and letting her drown, not driving her around the countryside. It would serve Albright well to see what it is like to lose something.'

'Enough, Willy Gair,' Ian said. 'You know that is not the Highland way of it.'

The young man glared at him. 'Highlanders look after their ane, not the English who have no business here. You are a traitor to your clan, Ian Gilvry, if you have aught to do with them up at the keep.' He started towards them, giving Selina a look filled with such hatred that her mouth dried and her heart picked up speed.

'I'll speak to you later, Willy,' Ian said grimly and urged the pony into a trot.

She bit her lip. Nothing had changed over the years. 'Why is he so angry?'

'He was evicted last month,' Ian said flatly. 'His family had been crofters on Dunross land for generations. When he couldn't pay the rent, he had to leave. He is one of the lucky ones. His brother-in-law owns the inn and is able to give him a little work and a roof over his head.'

'Father said nothing about evictions.'

His expression said how would she know what her father did.

'Why would he?'

'Sheep.'

Another one-word answer that was as clear as mud. Clearly he wasn't going to say more. Well, she would just have to ask her father.

'Almost there,' Ian announced.

Beyond him, Dunross Keep jutted up into the blue sky.

The last time he'd carried her home he'd been nothing but a gangly boy, but to her he'd seemed like a knight in shining armour, and she his lady. Childish romantic nonsense.

He turned his head slightly, still looking ahead. 'Angus McIver is heading this way on foot.'

She winced. 'I said I'd be back in an hour.' She raised herself up and peered over his shoulder. A severe-looking Angus with a knobby walking stick was striding towards them. She waved.

Ian's lips pressed tight. He drew the cart up when he came abreast of the big Scot.

'My Lady. Laird.' Angus touched the bonnet perched on his head. 'Thank ye for bringing the lassie home.'

Selina let go a breath. No yelling. No harsh words. A simple grim politeness, but then the Highlanders were known for their impeccable manners. Some of them.

Jaw set, Ian nodded. 'I'll drive her in.'

'Best not. I'll take her and the horse in through the gate.'

'Angus,' she gasped.

'I've no wish to enter the keep,' Ian said harshly. He clicked his tongue and the horse moved onwards. 'Not while it belongs to another.'

The whip of his words caught her on the raw. She

was wrong about him. He resented her just as much as he always had.

And there was something she'd been putting off saying. She'd forgotten until just now. She'd have to hurry if she didn't want Angus to overhear.

'I never thanked you for calling your brother Andrew home after I wrote to you.'

He stiffened, his face turning granite hard.

'My friend, she is happily married now. It…it all turned out for the best.'

'Did it now?'

'It was good of you.' His granite expression made it hard to continue. 'I just wanted to thank you.'

His lips twisted into a bitter line. 'And one good turn deserves another. You'll no mention the changes at the mill to your father.' The cart lurched to a halt beside the stone arch.

Her stomach dipped. It was hardly the kind of response to her thanks she'd expected. He was waiting for her answer. She straightened her shoulders. 'No. I won't say a thing.'

Then Angus was there, reaching into the back of the wagon to help her down.

The dog lifted his lip and growled low in his throat.

Selina laughed, albeit the sound a little brittle, but true to form, and Angus noticed nothing. 'You'll have to get past my protector, Mr McIver.'

Angus glanced up at Ian. How odd. She'd meant the dog.

'Gilly,' Ian growled. 'Down.'

The dog put its ears down and thumped its tail, sending up a puff of dust. Angus lifted her down.

'Can ye walk, lass?' He handed her his stick. A solid, gnarled length of hawthorn.

She gave him a grateful smile. 'This will certainly help.'

The old Scot untied Topaz, grasped him by the bridle. Together they walked towards the gate

At the sound of the cart pulling away, she glanced back and met Ian's dark gaze. He nodded, a slight movement of his head, yet it seemed to say *I trust you not to betray me.*

And she wouldn't. She never had.

Her heart was pounding as if she had run a mile, when really she had only walked the few steps from the manse. It was excitement causing her heart to beat faster, not the fear of seeing Ian again. Or the prospect of seeing his pleasure at the news she brought.

Dry-mouthed, she knocked on the door of his house. One of the few not owned by her father. Some long time ago, Ian's grandfather had married well, giving the family the house, some land and the mill, according to her father. And they'd been a thorn in the side of every Albright since.

If they would just work together... Perhaps they could now, if Ian's pride would let him accept her offer. Half-afraid she might turn and run, she knocked again. Breath held, she listened to the sound of footsteps on the other side.

The door swung back and Ian stared at her, his mouth dropping open. He was in his shirtsleeves and waistcoat. His throat was bare, where he had not donned a cravat. He looked thoroughly rakish and disreputable. Inside she winced. Clearly, she should have warned him of her intended visit.

He rubbed at his chin with an ink-stained thumb as he clearly tried to recover from his surprise. 'Lady Selina?' He glanced over his shoulder, then stepped outside to join her on the front step, pulling the door almost closed behind him, as if he did not want whoever was inside to know she was there.

Heat rushed to her cheeks. A bright smile formed on her lips. It always did when she was nervous. She nodded regally. 'Good afternoon, Mr Gilvry.'

The wary look on his face remained. 'What are you doing here?'

'I have something to show you.'

'What sort of something?'

Always suspicious. She pulled the key from her reticule. 'This.'

'Who is it, Ian?' a woman's voice called from inside the house.

'No one, Ma,' he called back. 'Wait here a moment,' he said to Selina. He shot back inside and closed the door.

He definitely didn't want whoever was inside to know who had called. Most likely she was his mother. The minister had told her and Chrissie that Mrs Gilvry had been ill for some time. Selina walked down the short garden path to the lane. She didn't want her presence to cause him any embarrassment. Nor did she want to be caught on his front step by one of his younger brothers.

A few moments passed before he joined her, properly dressed in his coat with a belcher knotted at his throat.

'I'm sorry for keeping you waiting,' he said politely.

'Not at all.'

'What is this about?'

The way he said 'about' made her toes curl in her sensible half-boots. 'It is a surprise.'

'A pleasant one, I hope?'

She cast him a glance from under the brim of her chip-straw bonnet. 'I believe even you will think so.'

They walked in silence for a few minutes, towards the manse, then she turned onto a narrow lane with stone walls on either side that led around the back of the church.

Excitement bubbled up in her chest again. He had to be pleased. He could not turn down this gift of hers. Well, hers and Chrissie's. They had plotted it all out for two days, talking and explaining, until Father had thrown his hands in the air and told them to do just as they pleased, because they were going to anyway, with or without his permission.

Chrissie had happily left to her the duty of telling the Laird of their intention.

She stopped at a gap in the wall. The track to the ancient building before them was overgrown with weeds.

'The tithe barn?' he said. 'Is this your surprise?'

'Yes.' She picked up her pace and instead of going in by the double-wooden barn doors, she made her way to a small door at the far end, carefully avoiding thistles and stinging nettles, some of which grew as high as her shoulders. She unlocked the door and threw it wide open, revealing a dusty empty room with a counting desk and a set of wooden shelves with pigeon holes against one wall.

'It hasn't been used for years,' she said.

'A tithe of nothing is nothing,' Ian said. 'The vicar takes his due from the collection plate. What is it you wanted me to see?'

'Wouldn't this make the most perfect place to hold a school for the local children?'

His eyes widened. 'Are you telling me the vicar agreed we could use this building for a school?'

'The barn is on Father's land.' She bit her lip. She should not have mentioned who owned the land. 'He has agreed it can be used for a school.'

He stepped inside and turned in a circle, glancing up at the roof and staring at walls, much as she had done the previous day. He swung around to face her. He didn't look particularly pleased, but nor did he look annoyed.

'You don't think it would work?' she asked, fighting her disappointment with a smile.

'It is a fine room. We could build trestle tables, find some stools.'

'There are funds set aside by Lady Albright for a teacher. We could send to Edinburgh. What to do you think? Will you support the idea?' she asked. 'The clan members won't send their children if you speak against it.'

He stared at her. 'Why this concern now? We don't need your charity.'

His suspicions were like a blade sliding between her ribs. 'Would you prefer the children to run wild, with no chance for an education?'

He stepped closer, too close, looking down at her, his eyes flaring hot. Anger, she thought. Then wasn't so sure. The blue in his gaze was so intense, the heat so bright with his body only inches from hers, it crashed against her cool skin. Her heart banged against her ribs, the sound loud in her ears. Breathing became difficult, as if the only air in the room belonged to him.

The strangest sense that he was going to kiss her tugged at her, drawing her closer; she could swear her body was leaning into his with a wild kind of longing.

He jerked back. She could have sworn she gasped at the shock of it, yet her ears heard no sound. It was all in her imagination, the connection, the physical pull.

'It won't make them think any better of your father,' he said, his voice harsher than usual, his breathing less steady than before.

She shrugged, feigning indifference to the obviously dismissive words. 'I didn't expect it would.'

'Niall will teach them. Two mornings a week.'

Did this mean he supported the idea, after all? 'He can apply to the vicar with respect to his pay.'

'He will not require payment.'

Apparently, his pride would not permit Albright money to be spent, but he would begrudgingly accept the loan of the building.

'Are you sure Niall would be willing to work for no pay?'

'The children will not come to a stranger. And they need someone who speaks the Gaelic.'

'The children would obey you.'

A small smile curved on his lips. 'Aye.' He brushed by her and out of the door. He stopped and looked back. 'Thank your father for the use of the barn. I'll have Will Gair set to making some tables and trestles. Him, your father can pay.'

No wonder he looked so pleased with himself. He had found a way for Father to right what he saw as a wrong. 'You are welcome, Mr Gilvry.'

His cheeks flushed a little red. 'Thank you, Lady Selina.' He strode away.

A proud man, but even so she had managed him quite nicely. And so what if he took it upon himself to provide the teacher and charge her father for the furniture? The children would have their schooling.

That was all that mattered. A feeling of satisfaction filled her. A sense of a job well done, despite his reaction. Perhaps the people of Dunross would recognise her father's generosity, even if their Laird would not.

And as for thinking he was going to kiss her, well… that was all in her imagination. More likely, he had wanted to tell her to go to hell, but had put the welfare of his people ahead of his own preferences.

Two days later, a fine drizzle hung over the hilly landscape like mist. It was almost as if the clouds, having brushed against the heather-clad hills, wanted to linger. There was no thinking about setting foot out of doors, not even in the carriage, so Selina stretched out on the sofa in the drawing room with a book to while away the hours until supper.

The drawing-room door opened and Chrissie bounced in. 'You will never guess who is here.'

Selina put down her book. 'Who?'

'Lieutenant Dunstan.'

Her heart took an unpleasant dive. She hadn't expected him quite so soon. But the sooner the better, surely?

'Is he here to see me?'

'He is with your father in his study.' Chrissie clasped her hands together. 'I am sure he is here to propose.'

Good news—then why did she feel a kind of panic? She wanted this. It had been all her idea. A new beginning after her accident. 'Did Father send for me?'

Chrissie frowned. 'No. But I am sure he will want to see you when they have concluded their business.'

Chrissie was as anxious for the marriage as Selina was herself. She hadn't said anything, but she and Selina had occasionally disagreed on household matters. Until Father had finally told Selina it was no longer her concern.

It had been a painful truth.

She swung her feet to the ground and set her book aside. She patted her hair and smoothed her skirts, a pomona-green muslin. 'Should I change, do you think?'

'You look lovely,' Chrissie said with a smile. 'You always do.'

'Thank you.' Before her accident, she had taken her appearance for granted. More recently, she had felt unsure. She took a deep breath and tried to keep her steps as even as possible.

The antechamber to the study was empty. Mr Brunelle, her father's secretary, must be inside with her father, taking notes, recording agreements. Should she knock and go in, or wait for them to come out?

As she dithered, the door to the study opened. She pinned a smile on her face.

'Lady Selina!' The lieutenant sounded surprised.

She glanced at her father.

He frowned. 'Did you want something, daughter?'

Blast. It seemed she wasn't expected, or wanted, which meant they had not been discussing the betrothal after all. A feeling of relief swept through her, even as she realised they were waiting for some sort of explanation.

Heat bloomed in her cheeks as her mind raced. 'I heard Lieutenant Dunstan was here and came to bid him welcome.' She hoped she didn't sound too feeble. 'To ask him to take tea with Lady Albright and me in the drawing room.'

Dunstan's face lit up. 'Very kind of you, Lady Selina, I must say. I fear I cannot take advantage on this occasion. I have urgent business in the neighbourhood and came to discuss it with your father as local magistrate.'

'Trouble?' she asked.

'Selina,' her father said in a warning tone.

'Smugglers,' Dunstan said at exactly the same moment.

'Oh, my goodness, are there really such villains abroad around here?' she said with a hand to her throat and a gasp. She gave him a glance that said in her mind he was a hero.

'Don't worry, Lady Selina, my regiment won't let them escape us, I can assure you. You have nothing to fear.' The paternalistic tone made her grit her teeth. But he was only trying to soothe the feminine nerves she had put on display and there was nothing in his manner she should resent.

She fluttered her lashes. 'I am so glad you are in charge, then.'

He bowed, took her hand and kissed it. 'Until we meet again.'

His touch left her cold, calm, uninvolved. No wild flutters invading her body—just as she preferred.

'Lieutenant Dunstan is engaged to us for dinner next week, Selina,' her father said. 'There will be lots of time for chatter then.'

Next week. Her future would be settled next week. The delay felt like a reprieve from the hangman's noose, when she should be impatient for it to start.

'I will look forward to it,' she said, giving him her most brilliant of smiles and watching him blush with a sense of foreboding. Had she made a mistake in this man? Was he weaker than she had thought? She wanted him malleable, it was true, but not spineless.

It was too late for second thoughts. Too late to change her mind. She had made her choice and must abide by it, or be deemed beyond the pale.

Dunstan turned back to Father. 'This will be the end

of them, I promise you. I bid you good afternoon, Lord Albright.'

With a sharp bow, he strode from the room, his spurs jingling with each booted step on the stone stairs leading down to the hall below.

'The end of whom?' Selina asked.

Her father waved her question aside. 'You sounded over-anxious. You have done well to catch a man from such an important family. We don't want to scare him off.'

'Scare him off? I hardly think so,' she drawled, hiding her hurt.

'Two jilted suitors are enough to make any man think twice.'

It seemed the *ton* had a long memory. 'I will be more circumspect next time he calls, Papa,' she said, dipping a curtsy.

'Good.' He rubbed his hands together. 'If this thing goes well tonight, I believe I will have a buyer for Dunross, too.'

She gasped. 'You are going to sell Dunross?'

'Dunstan has no need of a keep in the wilds of Scotland. You don't want to live here. With the proceeds, he can buy a country house close to his parents in Sussex and a house in town, just as you wanted.'

For some reason, she never thought Dunross would be sold. It was her dowry. She thought it would be settled on one of their children.

She frowned. 'What does success catching the smugglers have to do with selling Dunross Keep?'

'Ian Gilvry has been nothing but a thorn in my side and a deterrent to any serious purchaser. With him gone, we should get a good price.'

Her blood ran cold. All she could do was stare.

'Well?' her father said.

'I… Nothing. I really should go back to Chrissie and tell her we are not expecting the lieutenant for tea.'

'Never mind. I will join you instead.'

Blast. Now she needed to let the housekeeper know to deliver a tray to the drawing room, when what she wanted to do was be alone to think.

Chapter Four

Selina thumped at her pillow, sure someone had put rocks in it instead of feathers. She tossed onto her back. If Dunstan's plans came to fruition, Ian would find himself behind bars, or worse. The fool. How could he risk his life with so many relying on him?

The cottages in the village were in terrible shape—certainly much worse than when she'd left seven years ago. The children playing in the street hadn't just been ragged and dirty, they'd been painfully thin. The people were slowly starving. He should be helping them sell their crops, not seeking wealth from criminal activities.

Potatoes and barley were the only crops suited to the poor soil in the Highlands. And they used the barley to make whisky instead of bread. It was one of the reasons her father despised them so—their preference for hard spirits over food.

The Highlanders swore by their whisky, attributing healing properties to the malted liquor. They even gave it to babies.

And it wasn't only illiterate crofters who held fast to the old ideas. The nobles did it, too. A school, education, would bring them into the nineteenth century, but it wouldn't get off the ground if Ian ended up deported or worse. Didn't he realise that, by taking risks with his own life for a few barrels of brandy, he was risking their futures?

Or was he smuggling in order to put food in their bellies? Because her father cared not one whit for the people on this land.

Her blood ran cold. She didn't want to believe it, but her father was completely ruthless when it came to money and power. It was what had made him so successful.

He'd be delighted to see the Gilvrys out of his way.

The memory of Ian's strong arms around her shoulders, beneath her thighs, haunted her as if she was still some besotted schoolgirl. Only worse, because other sensations tormented her too, little pulses of desire she couldn't seem to control.

And the way he had looked at her in the tithe barn had only made them worse.

Hot and bothered, she slid out of the bed and walked to the mullioned window. Clear. The rain clouds gone. Stars twinkled teasingly.

The perfect night for smuggling.

The perfect night for a trap.

She gazed in the direction of the village. Was it her imagination, or could she see men leading strings of ponies across the heather between here and the village?

Imagination. It was too dark to make out anything except the dark shape of the distant hills against the sky.

Was Ian out there? About to be caught in the hated Revenue men's net? She should have gone to warn him this afternoon, instead of telling herself it was none of her business. She owed him more than a thank you for helping Alice. And even if Dunross's people hated her, she had this strange feeling of responsibility. Dunross Keep might be her dowry, but Ian Gilvry was their laird. She would never be able to live with herself if she didn't at least try to warn him.

A clock struck eleven. What had felt like hours was only a single turn of the hour hand. It might not be too late to tell them. It wasn't as if everyone didn't turn a blind eye to smuggling.

Good Lord, her own father had a cellar full of smuggled wines in London. As long as those responsible didn't hurt anyone along the way, smuggling, while a crime in the eyes of the law, was seen as more of a game.

A game Ian should have avoided with her father in residence at the keep.

Hands shaking with the need for haste, she sorted through the clothes in her press. Stays. How would she lace her stays without her maid? She lifted up a gaudy skirt she'd worn to a masquerade in Lisbon. She'd played the part of a Portuguese dancer. Somewhere she had a peasant blouse and an overbodice, which laced up the front.

But if she wanted to ride Topaz, she would need breeches, because she'd have to ride astride. She dug out a pair she'd worn on her childhood adventures when Father had left her with servants and hadn't cared what she did most of the time. Tonight she would wear them under her petticoats.

Anyone seeing her, such as the Revenue men for example, would take her for one of the village girls in such attire.

As long as she didn't run into Dunstan.

Her stomach rolled in a most unpleasant way. If she was caught, it would be the end of all her hopes for a good marriage.

She would just have to make sure he didn't see her. She was only going to the village and back. He would be waiting on the shore for the smugglers. Hopefully in vain.

She finished dressing swiftly, throwing an old woollen cloak around her shoulders and hurrying downstairs in bare feet, carrying her shoes. She put them on at the side door and went out to the stables.

Blast. A light shone from a window above the stalls where Angus lived. He'd hear her and stop her if she tried to take Topaz.

Then she'd walk. The gate, of course, was locked and barred. Anyone would think they were at war, the way they locked up the keep at night.

There was another way out. The old sally port—an escape route for if the keep was ever besieged. Long ago it had been her route to freedom and a few secret meetings with Ian.

Hopefully no one had blocked it up in the meantime. She took the stairs down to the ancient undercroft. In medieval times the kitchen was located here; nowadays the space was used for storage.

The next flight of stairs was barely wide enough for her feet and twisted in tight circles. She wished she'd thought to bring a lantern. Damp and musty-smelling air filled her lungs and tainted her tongue as she felt her way down in the dark until she reached the door at the bottom.

The last time she'd been down here she'd hidden the key up on the lintel. She groped around and shuddered at the clingy touch of spider webs. Her fingers touched a metal object. She grinned. It seemed her old way out remained undiscovered.

The key turned easily in the lock and she slipped it in

her pocket and entered the tunnel, a dank place, smelling of earth, dug into the hillside. It came out among a pile of rocks some distance from the keep.

Once outside, the air was fresh and even felt warm compared to the dank chill below ground. As she hurried down the hill to the village, the stars gave her just enough light to avoid the worst of the ruts and it wasn't many minutes before she was standing outside Ian's house.

A light in both ground-floor windows gave her hope she was in time. She banged on the door.

From inside she heard the sound of coughing, but no one came to the door.

She banged again.

'Come in,' a woman's voice called out and the coughing started again. Mrs Gilvry. Did that mean Ian had left already?

What should she say? Accuse this woman's son of being a criminal? No doubt that would be well received. Perhaps she should just leave.

'Come in,' the voice called again, stronger this time.

She could hardly leave the woman wondering who had knocked on her door and fearing for her safety. She pressed the latch and the door swung open.

'In here,' the voice said through an open door on her right.

Selina entered the chamber, expecting a drawing room, and instead found a large four-poster bed containing a pallid-faced woman with greying hair tucked beneath a plain cap propped up against a pile of pillows.

'Mrs Gilvry?'

'Aye.' Pale fingers tightened on the sheets under her chin. A pair of eyes the colour of spring grass regarded her gravely. Andrew and Logan had inherited those eyes.

Ian must take after his father. 'And who is it who comes calling in the dead of night?' Her voice was wheezy, breathless.

'Selina Albright. I am looking for your son, Ian. Is he home?'

The woman's eyes widened. 'Ian, is it? And what would Albright's daughter be doing looking for him at this time of night? Hasn't your family done enough to our people?'

The sins of the fathers were still being visited upon the children. 'I need to give him a message.'

The green eyes sharpened. 'Is there trouble?'

Selina nodded. 'The Revenue men are out tonight.'

The woman in the bed twisted her thin hands together. 'I told him not to go.'

'Ian?'

'No, Logan. My youngest. He was supposed to stay with me, but he couldna' resist. He followed his brothers not more than a half-hour ago. He'll no listen to me any more. Am I to lose all of my sons?'

Selina's heart ached for the torture she heard in the woman's voice. 'Do you know where they went? I...I could warn them.'

The woman looked at her with suspicion in her gaze. 'Why would you do that?'

She shrugged. 'Ian is a friend.' It was true, if not quite reflecting the nuance of their relationship. An uneasy friendship.

The woman turned her head upon the pillow, staring at the fire, her mouth a thin straight line. Then she turned back to Selina. 'It goes against the grain to trust an Albright. If you play me false, I will curse you for all of my days, however few they are.'

Selina recoiled at the bitterness in the woman's eyes. 'Tell me where they are.'

'Balnaen Cove.'

The name tore at a scar she thought long ago healed, yet was now raw and fresh. Ian had taken her there once, the last time they'd met. They'd shared a kiss, a moment full of magic and dizzying sensations and walked the sand hand in hand, until his brothers had come across them. Then he'd heaped scorn on her head.

She forced herself not to think of that day, but the task at hand. The cove was at least three miles from the village. She would not reach it by midnight. 'Do you have a horse?'

'There's one in the stables. Take it if you must,' Mrs Gilvry croaked. 'But 'tis no a friendly horse and there's no one to help.'

Of course it wasn't. Nothing about the Gilvrys was friendly or helpful.

'I'll manage.'

'Go through the kitchen and out of the back door.'

The directions took her straight to the stable where a lantern flickered above the door. She took it inside with her and found three empty stalls and one full of a large black stallion. It shifted uneasily as she entered.

A small shadow came out of the gloom, wagging its plumed tail. 'You,' she said, staring at her nemesis of a dog. 'I might have guessed you'd be along to cause trouble.'

She hung the lantern on a beam, found a bridle and bit and took them into the stall. The horse showed her the whites of its eyes. Not a good sign. Nor were the bared teeth.

'Easy,' she said softly. 'I'm not here to hurt you.' She patted its cheek and ran a hand down its wither. The blasted dog came wandering in. Troublesome creature. The dog sat at her feet and leant up against her leg.

The stallion eyed it, then lowered its head. Nose to nose, the creatures greeted each other.

The stallion calmed.

She patted the dog's head. 'Well, now, is this some sort of formal introduction to your friend?' It seemed so, for while the dog sat grinning, the great black horse allowed her to put on a bridle. But would he accept her on his back? Or was she just wasting time here? She might have walked a good way along the road by now.

No time for a saddle. Nor could she do it by herself. A blanket she found over a rail would have to do. Riding a horse bareback? She wasn't even sure she could. But she had to try. She led the stallion out to the mounting block in the yard and lunged onto its back, one hand gripping the reins, the other grasping the long black mane before it could object. It shifted, but didn't bolt.

The dog barked encouragement and shot out of the courtyard and into the lane. The horse followed.

She kept the stallion at a trot. She daren't go any faster through the village in case she attracted unwanted attention. The dog ran alongside.

The bouncing made her teeth clack together and jarred her spine. As they passed the last cottage, she urged the horse into a gentle canter. Its long stride smoothed out and she felt a lot less like a sack of potatoes. Perhaps she really could make three miles without falling off.

At the crossroads she hesitated. The right fork led to the path along the cliffs and a long gentle slope down to the cove. Straight ahead and she'd have to cut across country. The way down to the beach there was difficult and steep. It was quicker.

Nose to the ground, the dog dashed straight ahead.

The horse followed. It seemed as though her decision was made. Shorter and quicker was better.

She let the stallion have his head and concentrated on retaining her balance and watching out for danger. After ten minutes or so, the dog veered off towards the sea. If there was a path, she couldn't see it, but she urged the horse to follow and in no time at all, she could hear the steady roar and crash of surf. Salt coated her lips and she licked it away, inhaling the tang of seaweed. 'Tangle', the locals called that smell.

If she remembered correctly, the rest of the way was rocky. Dangerous to a horse. She brought the animal to a halt and slid down. Her bottom was sore, but her injured leg easily held her weight. Riding astride, even bareback, was apparently easier on her leg than a ladies' saddle.

'Where are they, boy?' she asked the dog, looking around warily. One thing she did not want to do was run into the Revenue men or, worse yet, Dunstan's company of militia.

The dog set off at a trot. She followed, leading the horse. Would she be in time?

The dog circled her as if to assure her everything was all right. Or was he, in the nature of his breed, trying to herd her in the direction he wanted her to go?

Stumbling on the rough ground, Selina followed Gilly, hoping he would lead her to his master and not on a rabbit hunt.

A dark rift in the rocks where a small burn ran in a gully down to the sea told her she had remembered correctly. She'd climbed down beside the stream to the beach on one of her forbidden explorations.

A sound behind her. Cracking of twigs. She whirled around, hand to her heart.

A large figure loomed out of the low brush off to her

left, an outline against the empty sea and starry sky. It lumbered towards her.

'Hold,' a male voice whispered loudly.

Why hadn't the dog warned her? Friend or foe? Could she take a chance?

She turned to flee.

The man threw himself at her legs and flung her down.

Pain. Her shoulder wrenched. Her cheek scratched by heather. She cried out.

He cursed.

A hand came over her mouth. Heart racing wildly, she kicked out. Missed. Kicked again.

A brawny arm lifted and set her squarely on her feet. 'Hist, now,' he said in a low murmur. Scottish, she thought.

'Silence, man,' someone whispered from not far away. 'What the hell are you doing?'

'Ah,' her captor said. 'It seems I have caught myself a spy.'

Chapter Five

The taste of salt was strong in the back of Ian's throat. He stared into the dark, catching the occasional glimmer of foam-crested waves. The steady crash and hiss of waves breaking on sand and the louder roar of water pounding the rocks filled his ears.

But his mind kept wandering. Hell. He had almost kissed Selina back in the tithe barn. The urge to taste her full lips, to feel her body pressed against his, to explore her soft curves with his hands had run hot in his blood. And if he wasn't mistaken in the way those lips parted and her gaze had softened, she would have let him, too.

The attraction between them had not diminished over time. Indeed, if he wasn't badly mistaken, it had increased exponentially. Damn it all, he had betrayed his family for her once. He would not do it again.

To be so distracted at such a time as this was insane. He forced his mind back to the job at hand. This last run of brandy would give him the money he needed to buy all the copper required for the still.

Everything was ready for the boat. Nothing could possibly go wrong.

He glanced at the man standing at the very edge of

the promontory with a lantern at the ready. 'Any sign of her?'

Gordy, the signalman, shook his head. 'Nought.'

Ian grimaced. Time was wasting. He narrowed his eyes to look back across the rocks and the strip of beach into the gully where the men and ponies awaited the signal. They would come out on to the open beach only when the boat was almost aground. Well versed in their respective tasks, they would unload a boat and have the goods travelling back up on to the cliffs in less than ten minutes.

He scanned the cliff tops. No sign of his guards. And nor should there be. But they were there, ready to warn of intruders. He smiled grimly. As usual they'd outwitted the gaugers. Everything was going according to plan. Except the damned boat was late.

Hairs stirred on the back of his neck. The sensation had nothing to do with the stiff breeze hurling itself off the waves. He tried to shake off the feeling all was not well. Over the years, he'd learned to trust his instincts. Why would he ignore them now?

He glanced out to sea. Still no light from the ship. 'I'm going up top to take a look around.'

Gordy nodded without turning, then stiffened, pointing. 'There!' he whispered. He fumbled with the lantern cover. 'The light dipped beneath the waves, but... yes, there she is.' Ian, too, could see the faint twinkle far out on the water.

Gordy flashed four times. Two flashes came back.

'That's them,' Ian said. 'Guide them in, lad. Any trouble, flash two long and two short, out there and up towards the cliffs, as well.'

'I ken my job, Laird.'

Ian slapped him on the shoulder. 'That you do, lad.

Just reminding myself. I'll let the men know we've sighted the ship.' Then he'd climb the cliff to check on his guards.

He clambered across the rocks guarding each side of the small bay, keeping to the shadow. Once in the gully, out of the light of the stars and sheltered from the offshore breeze, he smelled the ponies. Manure and the smell of hardworking horse. And hardworking men. A familiar pungent smell. It had surrounded him most of his life. That and the danger. But the joy had gone out of it since Andrew had gone. His brother had loved the adventure of it.

This would be the last run. There was enough money in the coffers to buy the new still. A still that would be legal anywhere else in Britain but here in the Highlands.

'Tammy,' he called in a low voice. The man rose up from a rock. 'She's coming in.'

'Aye,' Tammy said. He nudged the man beside him. 'Pass the word.'

'I'll be back down before she lands.' Ian walked past the line of horses and men. Men he had trusted with his life more than once. Good men, who trusted him and who'd lose their homes if they didn't bring this off safely. One or two of them muttered greetings as he passed.

At the end of the line, he passed a slight figure holding the bridle of an ass. Ian frowned. That made nine men. He'd thought there were eight. Was this the source of the troubled feeling he'd had out on the point? The man had a cap pulled down over his eyes and was trying to hide on the other side of his wee beast. Another thing that wasn't right. They used ponies because they were more docile.

Ian reached over the animal and grabbed the man by the collar. A familiar face grinned up at him.

'What the hell? Damn it, Logan, you are supposed to be caring for our mother.'

His brother shrugged him off. 'It is a woman's job,' he said sullenly.

Ian closed his eyes in silent prayer for patience. 'You know what Mother will do if anything happens to you. Make sure you stay out of trouble.'

'She knows where I am. I'm no child to be left at home. You were out here at eighteen and I'm near twenty.'

'That was different.' In those days there hadn't been anyone else to go. The clan had relied on him and Andrew to help them get through the winter. But for all his slight stature, Logan was right, he was old enough. And another pair of hands wouldn't hurt.

'Fine,' he said. 'But if the gaugers come, you are to run. I'm relying on you not to get caught. You'll need to warn the village.'

Logan grinned, his teeth a quick white flash in the dark. 'Aye. I'll run like the wind. You can count on me.'

Ian knew he could. And if he tried to protect him, Logan would rebel and go his own way as Andrew had. 'See you keep that damned beastie quiet.'

A dog whined. It jumped up at Logan, who pushed him down.

'What in the devil's name is Gilly doing here?' Ian asked.

'I dinna ken. I locked him in with Beau. He must have escaped.'

'Carelessness,' Ian said. 'Keep the damn animal quiet.'

Logan glowered and made a grab for the dog. It darted out of reach.

The man next in line chuckled.

Ian smothered a cursed and left his brother to it.

The prickles on his neck had not subsided. If anything, they were worse. He climbed the steep path up the wall of the gully instead of following the track beside the burn tumbling down to the sea.

As he raised his head over the brow, a whiff of pipe smoke tickled his nostrils. 'Damn it, man. Put that out. It can be seen for miles.'

Davey had brawn, but no brain. He knocked the bowl on his heel and stamped on the embers. ''Tis all right for them down in the gully. The wind's damn cold up here, Laird.'

'It'll be hot in hell if you get yourself shot.' Ian swept his gaze around the surrounding countryside. 'Hear anything?'

Davey gave a smug laugh. 'Aye, I heard something, all right. At first I thought it was a rabbit. I walked back along the path a ways.'

'And?'

'I caught a lass creeping up on us. Ranald has her.'

What had been a faint unease across his skin was now a full-fledged alert in his gut. 'A woman?'

'A *Sassenach* by her voice.'

This really wasn't good. 'Stay here and keep a sharp look-out.'

'Aye, Laird.'

Ian strode along the stream bank, until he came to the place where it disappeared underground. 'Ranald?'

The burly innkeeper rose up out of the heather. 'Here.'

'Davey said you caught a wench spying.'

'Aye, Laird, I have her tied up over there beside the horse.'

Definitely not good. And yet something lightened inside him. It was the oddest sensation. Shoving it aside, he strode to the cluster of rocks indicated by Ranald. He held up his lamp and looked into a pair of very angry brown eyes.

'Lady Selina. I might have known.' He knelt beside her and undid her gag.

'Your man is an idiot,' she hissed. 'I told them I had a message for you. I told them to fetch you, but they wouldn't listen.'

He pulled out his knife and sawed at the ropes around her wrists. 'What message?' He started on her ankles, keeping his gaze fixed on the job and not letting them stray to her shapely calf. Or at least, not much.

'The Revenue men know about tonight. They have set a trap. You have to leave here right away.'

So, his instincts had not played him false, curse it. If they left without the goods, it would be another year before he could set his plans in motion. And Lord Carrick would not be best pleased. 'How do you know this?' He cut through the last of the rope and helped her to her feet. God, she was small. The top of her head barely came to his shoulder.

She rubbed at her wrists. 'Never mind that. You have to go. Now.'

'Where are they waiting for us?'

'Surprisingly enough, they didn't give me any details.'

The sarcasm in her voice made him want to laugh. 'How did you get here?' And then he saw for himself. Beau. And no saddle in sight. 'You rode bareback?'

'I couldn't saddle him myself.'

He shook his head. It seemed there was still something of the spirited girl inside the sophisticated woman.

She pulled her cloak around her. 'I'll go now.'

'No.'

'Why not?'

'Because I said not.' Gaugers weren't above firing their muskets at shadows, let alone at a fleeing horse. 'Ranald,' he called softly.

The innkeeper appeared like magic. Obviously, he'd been standing close by, listening. 'Keep her here. I'll go warn the men on the beach and return to take her home. And, Ranald, not a word of this to anyone, understand?' Ranald nodded.

Ian glanced at the stubborn set of Lady Selina's jaw. 'Whatever you do, keep her here.'

What they needed now was some sort of diversion.

Selina glared at Ranald. 'I told you he would want to hear my message.'

The man mumbled something under his breath, then covered his lantern. Selina blinked furiously to adjust her vision to the gloom. She should leave. She could be home in bed before anyone noticed her departure, her conscience clear.

What Ian did on his own account was his concern. But if she was caught aiding them Father would be mortified. And furious. If Dunstan discovered she'd warned the smugglers, after he'd let fall information about his mission in her presence, he'd call off their betrothal. If nothing else, a man expected loyalty from his wife. And that meant she'd have to start looking for a suitable husband all over again. Unless the scandal ruined her completely. It probably would.

But she'd known the risks when she set out. And she would do it all over again if required, because she was honour bound to help him as he had helped her when she'd asked. Not to mention that she did not like the thought of him being sent to prison.

Only now she needed to go home. She rubbed her

cold hands together and looked at the horse and then at Ranald. 'Let me go. I'll return the horse in the morning.'

'Ye'll stay put,' the burly man said. 'The Laird said so.'

'The Laird is an idiot.'

'Take one step and I'll tie you up again.' The tone of voice made it clear he meant it. She huffed out a breath. Men. They always wanted to rule the roost.

The minutes lengthened. She watched Ranald, waiting for him to lose interest, to give her a chance to slip away. At any moment the Revenue men could be upon them, or, worse yet, Dunstan and his militia.

That really would be her undoing.

The sound of booted feet on rocks brought her head around. Men. Coming up from the shore at a run, leading a couple of ponies with muffled hooves and ladderlike carriers on their backs. Empty carriers. They guided the beasts to the path along the cliff top towards the village. What on earth were they doing?

Another pony emerged from the gully. This one was laden with tuns and turned away from the village and disappeared into the dark. Blast the man. He had taken absolutely no notice of her warning and was continuing as if nothing was wrong. She was a fool to have thought she could help.

A shout rang out on the headland in the direction the first two ponies had gone. A flash. A loud bang. Clearly a shot. Then more flashes and bangs, getting closer.

They were shooting at the men he'd sent along the headland. Someone was going to get killed. Was Ian mad?

The train of loaded ponies continued on, one after another, while she bit her knuckles to stop from giving voice to her fears. The men leading the ponies passed by at a run, heads down and faces covered with mufflers. Then there were no more. Like ghosts, they had disappeared.

Where was Ian? She peered into the gloom, moving closer to the rocky path.

Shouts came from farther along the cliffs. The sound of men fighting hand to hand. Ranald muttered a curse, clearly impatient to be gone. Could Ian have somehow slipped past her to join in the fray now that the smugglers had departed with their booty?

Another figure emerged from the path up from the beach, cursing and swearing as he pulled on the leading rein of a resisting animal. It squealed indignantly. Its handler threw an arm over its nose to muffle the sound. The ass snorted a protest.

Selina understood just how it felt.

Then the damn thing surged forwards as if terrified. The man holding it cursed again. A flash of white at the animal's heels told Selina all she needed to know. 'Gilly,' she whispered.

The handler halted the ass and stared at her. 'Lady Selina?'

'Logan Gilvry. Another idiot. Where is Ian?'

He shook his head. 'He'll be up shortly. He's helping the boat to shove off. Giving us a chance to get clear.'

'Then go,' she said.

'Aye. Gilly, set him on.'

The dog nipped at the ass's back hoof. It jerked forwards and set off at an awkward run with Logan at its head and Gilly close behind.

The sounds along the cliff had ceased. The smugglers—a decoy, she guessed—must have run for it. No doubt the Revenue men and the militia would soon realise they'd been tricked and make their way along here.

She had to leave before they caught her.

Ranald also hopped from one foot to the other, looking worried.

'Go,' she said.

'The Laird said I was to watch you. Here.'

'The soldiers could arrive at any moment. I'll ride and warn Laird Gilvry, while you follow your men. Help me up on the horse and then you can leave.'

Ranald scratched his head. 'You'll go to him?'

She nodded.

'All reet, my lady, but I am trusting you to keep your word.' He tossed her up on the big stallion's back and led the horse to the top of the pathway. 'Watch your step. It is verra steep.' He touched his forelock and took off after the others.

She urged the stallion down the rugged slope and hoped to goodness the animal wouldn't stumble as she let him have his head. Miracle of miracles, the horse seemed to know his way down the rock-strewn path. Ian must have ridden him down this way in the past.

It was a small lonely patch of beach along a rocky shore, known to few but the locals. Or that's how Ian had described it that long-ago day. A place where they could be alone. She realised now that he had been ashamed to be seen with her.

At the bottom of the incline she found Ian walking up the beach towards her; behind him a rowboat was steadily pulling out to sea. He glared at her as she drew up beside him.

'What the hell are you doing here? I'll have Ranald's—'

'Hush. The Revenue men are close behind me.'

He frowned. 'They followed you? Damn it. What game are you playing?'

'They didn't follow me. They know exactly where

they are going and they will be here any moment. While they come down this way, we can ride up the path on the other side.'

He pressed his lips together. 'Aye. Hang on tight, then.'

She grasped the stallion's mane. Ian took a few steps at a run, then leapt up behind her. Impressive.

The sound of men in heavy boots echoed off the gully walls along with curses as they slipped and slid on the tricky path.

'Time we were gone.' He leaned forwards and they were off.

The feel of his hard thighs cradling her buttocks was positively indecent. So was his arm around her waist. But locked in that strong embrace, she felt perfectly safe, when she should be feeling terrified.

A cry went up behind them. The Revenue men must have heard the beat of the horse's hooves on the sand. It also meant they weren't far behind, but a man on foot was no match for this horse, even carrying two riders.

She set the horse's head towards the zigzagging path at the other end of the cove. A gentler climb up to the headland. They were halfway there, when a stream of men poured onto the beach from that direction.

'A pincer movement,' Ian yelled. 'That's how they meant to catch us.' He yanked the horse's head around. The beast turned in a circle while Ian scanned the cliffs and the men coming at them at a run from both sides at once.

'Look's like we've only one option,' he yelled. 'Keep your head down.' He set the horse running at the sea.

Her mouth dried. Her heart thundered. What could he be thinking? They'd drown. From horseback, the sand looked very far away. Too far to jump off. At this speed there was nothing she could do but hang on.

The wind whipped her hair out of its pins and it flew wild in her eyes. She leaned low over the horse's neck so Ian could see where they were going.

Where were they going?

Surf splashed up around them. Ian didn't slow the horse's pace. The water hit her face like icy needles and soaked her legs through the clinging fabric of her skirts and then the wool fabric of her knee breeches all the way to her waist. She gasped.

A howl of dismay went up from the men running after them.

'Load.' The terrifying shout came from the behind them. They were going to shoot!

The horse tried to turn back as its feet lost contact with solid ground.

Ian slid from its back into the water. 'Come on, Beau,' Ian yelled. 'It's all right, lad.' The horse's ears pointed forwards, its body low in the water, its breathing fast and laboured.

A volley from the beach kicked up spurts of water all around them. Selina closed her eyes, waiting for the pain. Nothing.

'Hang on,' Ian shouted. 'We are nigh out of range.' He struck out strongly, with the horse trailing behind. Laying along the stallion's back, her skirts a tangle around her legs, Selina clung to the horse's neck for dear life. Waves hit her in the face with a salt-laden slap, making her gasp and blink to clear her stinging eyes. It was impossible that this horse could swim very far.

Another volley. Selina glanced over her shoulder to see the waterspouts a few feet behind and, if her eyes weren't deceiving her, the men were already waist-deep in the sea. Surely they didn't stand a chance of hitting them now. She prayed she was right and concentrated on holding on to the pitching beast.

Ian slowed and swam alongside. 'Come on, old fellow, you can do it.' He directed the horse to swim parallel to the shore, heading south.

How Ian kept swimming in such chilly water she didn't know. Her hands and legs were numb, her teeth chattering. She tried to remember how far it was to the next beach and wondered if they would get there before they drowned. Or perished from cold.

It might be better to drown than be caught with a known smuggler. Father would never forgive her and even the placid Dunstan would never marry her.

When she'd finally found the perfect man and plucked up the courage to take the matrimonial plunge, she'd ended up up to her neck in the sea instead.

She just had to make it home without anyone finding out.

Chapter Six

The cold seeped into Ian's bones. He wanted to turn over on his back and float as what little heat he generated from motion was leached away by the chill of the sea. With an effort he glanced over at Beau and his passenger. The lass had heart and no mistake, but it was clear she'd not last long. And the horse was snorting and blowing hard, starting to tire.

He peered through the spray at the top of each wave, searching the shore, seeing only the faint phosphorous glow of sea breaking on rocks. There. A dark patch. He veered towards it, praying there were no watching eyes up on the cliff.

Unlikely. It would take those on the beach too long to make the climb, and surely they'd be more interested in chasing the contraband.

It had seemed like eons before he felt sand under his feet and heard the gentle hush of surf on sand. Not that there was much of a beach. A sliver, only revealed at low tide. But it was enough. The horse passed him, eager to be clear of the water, and pranced up onto the dry ground like a colt, while Lady Selina clung on for dear life.

Ian dragged his weary legs through the surf, weighed down by his kilt and grabbed at the bridle. 'All right,' he soothed, patting the sodden neck. 'You did it, old fellow.'

He reached up for the girl. She fell into his arms a dead weight. Dear God, don't say she was hit. He didn't think the shots came anywhere close. 'Selina. Are you injured?'

'J-just c-c-cold.' Her teeth clattered together.

He had the answer for that, if she could hold on long enough. 'Can you walk?'

'C-c-can't feel my legs.'

Oh, hell, what had he been thinking? It was all right for him to swim in the ocean, he'd been brought up on it, swimming in the cold lochs in the hills when there was nowhere to bathe, but this delicate creature wasn't used to such hardship.

He swept her up in his arms.

'No. You must be tired.'

'Aye.' He was. But he was used to battling on, no matter how exhausted. Hardship was a fact of life in the Highlands.

He staggered up the narrow beach, clicking his tongue for the horse to follow. Rocks jutted out from the cliffs, forming a natural inlet invisible from the overhanging cliff top. From the sea at high tide, one needed a boat, but right now, the entrance to the cave was a gentle slope into the dark. A cave wrought by seawater and an ancient underground river.

He ducked inside.

The sound of the waves became a muffled roar—a bit like listening to a shell up against your ear.

The fragile body in his arms vibrated. Shivers. He was feeling chilled himself, but out of the wind it wasn't so bad.

Beau shook himself, water drops flying. He obviously approved of the dry and followed Ian willingly.

The incline got steeper, rockier. The horse's hooves slipped here and there, but the animal kept close behind, trusting. God, the whole clan had trusted him to bring this off tonight. And now he was stuck here with no idea what was happening.

If not for the girl, he'd probably be dead. And now she lay lifeless in his arms, her dark hair hanging like seaweed over his arms, her body cold and suddenly still. He should have called the whole thing off the moment he saw her. Got the men away. Ignored the boat.

Either that or given himself up instead of plunging into the sea. Please God, he could get her warm and dry before she succumbed to the cold.

The cave was black as pitch and freezing, but he knew it as well as he knew his own bedchamber in the dark. His senses told him when the passage opened into the cave proper. That and the light touch of air rushing by his cheek. He set the fragile female in his arms down on the sand. She struggled to a sitting position and he felt relief flood through him at the sound of another round of clattering teeth.

'Wait there,' he said and felt his way to the corner where he found several oilcloth-wrapped parcels.

It wasn't long before he had candles lit, tinder and peat laid out for a fire and blankets spread on the floor. He lit the kindling from a candle and nursed the fire to life, gently blowing on the embers until flames flared up and beat back some of the darkness.

'W-w-what is this p-p-place?' Her voice was an echoing whisper.

Thank God, she was alert enough to talk. ''Tis an old cave used by fisherman.' He kept his voice matter of fact.

No point in letting her know how much he had feared for her. He strode to her side. 'Sit by the fire. There are more blankets. We'll get you out of these wet clothes.'

He helped her to her feet. Made to pick her up.

'I can walk,' she said. She staggered a few steps, but, unable to stand the sight of her weakness, he picked her up and carried her to the warmth of the fire.

'I'm cold too, lass. I've no wish to be waiting a week for you to get yourself by the warmth.'

He put her down on the blankets and handed her another. 'Put that around you and take off your wet things.'

He turned his back, more and more aware of the sodden cloth clinging to his legs and dripping onto the floor. He grabbed Beau by the bridle and led him to an iron manger some enterprising ancestor had attached to the rock wall. There were oats and hay in a sack, waiting for just such an occasion as this: a need to hide from the authorities or to save a fisherman caught out in a storm.

It hadn't been used for a good long while, as far as he knew, but one of the local fishermen had the job of keeping it stocked in case of a wreck.

After emptying the hay into the manger, he used the sack to rub the horse down, then went farther up the tunnel on the landward side, to the rain barrel. The water was peaty-tasting, but clean and fresh. He filled a small pan for the horse and a couple of leather flasks.

Busy work, because all he could think of was her slipping out of her clothes, baring her lush body. He gritted his teeth. He was not the adolescent he'd been that long-ago summer, fancying himself in love with a girl he should have nothing to do with. None the less, the images were certainly warming his blood. And that wasn't such a bad thing.

By the time he got back, Lady Selina's clothes lay

near the fire and the blanket was wrapped tightly around her delicious curves. She looked beautiful. Pale, her lips a little blue, strands of damp hair curling around her face, sticking to her skin. A legend come to life.

He grinned. 'You look like a selkie.'

'A sea witch? I feel more like a bit of jetsam washed up on the shore.' The brave smile on her lips as she dragged her fingers through her hair caught at his heart.

'Are you warmer?' he asked.

She nodded. 'What about you? Shouldn't you…?' Her words trailed off and she looked away, embarrassed.

Noble lasses like her didn't think about men taking their clothes off. Indeed, they probably didn't think a man had anything beneath his clothes. Clothes made the man, if the strutting peacocks in Edinburgh were to be believed.

Well, he wasn't going to stand here and drip to save her sensibilities. 'Aye. There's a spare kilt here, but nothing fit for a lady to wear. You'll have to dry your clothes before we leave.'

He grabbed the supplies put there for men prevented from landing their fishing boats at the quay during a storm. Or smugglers forced to flee the long arm of the gaugers.

He moved out of the light of the fire, wrapped a blanket around him and stripped off to his coat and shirt, using another blanket as a towel.

When he turned back she was eyeing him from beneath lowered lashes. She probably didn't realise the light from the fire, while distorting her features with flickering shadows, did not hide her expression of interest.

Heat travelled up his neck to his face.

Blushing like a lad. Surely not?

'What the hell did you think you were doing, coming down to the beach?' he said, his voice gruffer than he intended. 'What you did was brave, but foolhardy.' There, that was less ungrateful if still grudging.

'You are a fool, Ian Gilvry,' she said scornfully. 'All that danger for brandy.'

Stung, he glared at her. 'The brandy pays for other things.'

She gazed at him blankly.

He shrugged. What would a privileged lass like her know or care about the hardships his people faced? All her father cared about was the hunting and the grouse. 'As soon as your clothes are dry I'll get you home.'

Her gaze wandered to his horse. 'I have never seen a horse swim that way.'

'I lost a horse in a river once. He went in at a ford and got confused. I swore I would never lose another horse to the water.'

She rested her chin on her knees. 'I can see why. They become like friends…' She hesitated. 'Your mother gave me permission to ride him.'

'Did she know who you were?' He sat down beside her on the blanket. The fire's warmth was painful to his icy skin.

'Yes.'

That did surprise him. His mother had always been opposed to everything English—it was a point of honour. If she ever learned Ian had sent Drew off to America at the behest of Albright's daughter, she would never forgive him.

He'd done it for the memories of a short time when he'd felt happy and carefree, when he'd forgotten his duties and responsibilities. Very selfish reasons wrapped around youthful dreams and wishes. Reality in the shape of his brothers' shock at seeing them together had brought him back to earth, but he'd never stopped feeling guilty for the hurt look on her face at his rejection and cruel words spoken in parting. That guilt had sent Drew to his death. He would not let her influence him against his family again. But she had made up for it in part, at least, with tonight's warning.

'Thank you for coming tonight. Without your warning we would have been caught. I wish you had not come down to the beach, though. I would have handled it.'

She sighed. 'I thought the Revenue men would follow the goods and we could ride up the path on the other side.'

He was surprised by the resignation in her voice. 'How did you know of their plans?'

'Through my father. I should have sought you out earlier in the day.' She sighed. 'I was almost too late.' She shook her head. 'Why risk lives for a few tuns of brandy? How will the women and children survive without their men?'

She was lecturing him? After all her father had done to destroy their way of life? 'They can't live on fresh air.'

'Well, they can't live on brandy.'

'You are a *Sassenach*. What do you know about what my people need?'

She flinched and he felt like a brute. His rough direct ways did not suit a drawing-room miss. Not that she'd seemed much like a lady riding bareback to his rescue.

'It brings money to purchase what they can live on,' he explained. More than that, though—it was an investment in the future.

After a few moments' silence, she turned to face him. 'Do you think we were recognised?'

He shook his head. 'They were too far away.'

She breathed a sigh of relief. That small little breath, that mark of gladness, sparked warmth in his chest. Foolish warmth. She was the daughter of his clan's worst enemy. He'd do well to keep that in mind.

But she had risked a great deal tonight and he would not have her suffering for it. 'The sooner we get you back to the keep, the better,' he said, 'before you are missed. Hold up your clothes to the fire so they will dry.'

She did as he bid and they both sat toasting her clothes, watching the steam rise from them to mingle with the smoke from the fire.

'Why do your people try to turn back the clocks? Bonnie Prince Charlie is never returning.'

She understood nothing. 'My people were here long before the English. Yes, they need to move with the times, but not give up who they are, their traditions or their homeland. All the great landowners are turning their land over to sheep. Or using it for sport. They are leaving nothing for the clan members. If you take away their livelihood, then they need other work to replace it. Instead of that, they are being left destitute, labouring in the kelp fields or smuggling whisky. Hundreds of them have shipped off to America. Soon there will be no Highlanders left.'

She frowned. 'Don't the crofters earn enough to pay their rents?'

'The rents keep going up.' He combed his fingers through his almost-dry hair as he sought for a way to explain without giving away his plans. 'The old ways, such as crofting, are no longer viable, but I believe other ways can be found to keep the people here. In Scotland. But the English, men like your father, pass laws that make it impossible for us to earn a living. Those are what need to be changed.'

Her silence said she wasn't convinced. Hell, he was barely convinced himself that changing the law would make a difference. Yet some men were making a go of it, but they were men who owned their estates, who had the power to decide the best way to proceed. If Albright decided to clear his lands, in the end there was little Ian could do about it.

'Must we swim back?' she asked.

At last a question he could answer with confidence. 'No. The cave has a back door. Or a front door, depending on your point of view.'

'Then we should go. I cannot be found missing from my bed when the maid comes to light the fire.' She shivered.

Instinctively, his arm went around her. He touched her cheek. The skin was warm and alive beneath his fingers, her mouth so deliciously inviting. Her back was frigid beneath his arm. No wonder she had shivered.

'We have to get you fully dry first.'

'I am much warmer than I was.'

'Aye, but not warm enough.' He lifted her easily and set her between his legs, so her back was against the warmth of his body, her round little bottom nestled between his thighs. He almost groaned with the pleasure as his body hardened and he prayed she could not feel it through the blanket. He forced himself to ignore the delightful sensation and instead focused on the feel of her cold back permeating through her blanket and his. He pulled her close up against his chest.

'What are you doing?' she asked breathlessly.

'Body heat. The closer we sit together, the warmer we will both be. Something I learned on cold nights when out on the hunt with the men of the clan.'

She leaned back and hummed her approval. The

sound struck low in his gut. His arousal swelled painfully. He forced himself to breathe and to think. This woman was not for him.

She laughed a little.

'What?' he said through gritted teeth.

'I'm thinking about a bunch of men snuggled together.'

'Not pleasant, believe me. Men stink after days in the hills. But it saved us from freezing to death or returning empty-handed.'

'The clan always protects its members.'

'Aye.'

'One of them gave you away tonight.'

'Possibly.' A traitor in their midst. The thought gave him a cold feeling in his gut. It would have to be addressed, though. As soon as the hue and cry died down. 'You didn't hear who spilled the beans?'

'No.'

Of course, it wouldn't be that easy, would it?

He rubbed her finely boned arms with his hands, taking care not to hurt her. Heat blossomed beneath his palms.

'That feels good.' She sighed.

He wanted to do more than warm her arms. He wanted to take her with him to the stars and back. A boy's long-ago dream. It was no more right today than it had been then.

The sooner he got her home, the sooner he could be rid of temptation. It would lead to nothing but trouble for all of them.

The thought of her leaving made the fire seem to blaze less brightly and the cave seem more cavernous and empty. Not since Drew's departure had he enjoyed one of these night-time adventures, he realised, or shared his worries about the future.

How much more disloyal could he be to his brother's memory? Probably a whole lot more when it came to this woman, unless he was careful.

He was always careful. Always in control. Tonight was no different.

Chapter Seven

Selina let the blessed warmth of Ian's body at her back and the heat of the fire in front gather her up and set her adrift. The feel of his arms around her made her feel safe, protected from the world beyond their cave.

Men usually made her nervous. They had to be watched and judged and kept at a distance. If you let them get too close, they found a way to hurt you.

Ian had taught her that lesson when she was an impressionable schoolgirl. How could she forget that about him now?

Or was it the schoolgirl who had once more taken over her mind and her body reminding her of those old foolish longings?

Certainly not. She knew what this was, what it had always been: forbidden desire. A fragile woman always brought out a male's urge to protect. And thus she held the upper hand, as long as she didn't allow herself to be drawn under its spell. Under those conditions, there was nothing wrong with a little bit of mutual lust. Provided it didn't go too far.

A lady had to be careful of her reputation, especially if she hoped to marry.

Then why this pervasive sense of well-being wrapped in his arms when tonight she had risked everything?

She turned her face up, looking at his hard square jaw covered in stubble. Her gaze traced the shadow of his cheek and the carved cheekbone. And the longing inside her seemed to increase with the expansion and contraction of his ribs at her back. A silent sigh, yet she felt it with every bone in her body.

'I never forgave myself for what I said to you, that day at the beach,' he murmured low in her ear. 'Children are cruel, but I was old enough to know better. I had an overabundance of pride in those days.'

Surprised, she twisted in his arms to better see his expression, to assure herself he wasn't mocking.

Indeed, his lips did smile, but it was a lovely generous smile, youthful, touched by regret, his eyes gleaming with firelight.

Her insides drew tight, pulsed with a sensation that made her eyelids droop and her body soften.

Looking down at her, he inhaled a swift breath. The glimmer in his eyes burst into searing flames.

The air crackled and warmed. All around them heat conspired to make them short of breath and wordless. His arms tightened around her body, his head dipped until his mouth was close enough to brush her lips. The soft caress of each exhale tickled her lips, the scent of him, salt and sea air, and something very male filled her senses.

'It seems we are destined to rescue each other from time to time,' she said on a breathless laugh. 'Though it must never happen again.'

Without thought, she put her arms around his neck, tipped her head and kissed his cheek, much as she had as a girl. 'I'm glad I reached you in time.'

A groan broke in his throat. 'Me, too.' His hand came to her jaw, cradling her chin, angling her head the better to kiss her back.

His lips firmed over hers, testing and teasing. His lips parted and his tongue licked her bottom lip. Thrills ran amok in her body, making her gasp with shock at the pleasure of such an intimate touch.

Heavenly sensations coursed through her veins and turned her bones liquid.

His parted lips matched hers and, open-mouthed, their lips melded and moved in a harmony she hadn't expected. Tentatively, she tried a taste of her own. Their tongues met and danced and played, at first gently, carefully, and then with wild fervour.

Dizzy, breathing hard, she lay in his arms. The magic of his kiss took her out of her body. Whereas she'd been floating before, now she was flying, soaring, released from the chains of the world.

Inside she trembled.

Never in her adult life had she lost her sense of self so utterly as now, as if some part of them had fused and become something different altogether. It exhilarated. And terrified.

Fear made her struggle.

He drew back, breathing hard, looking into her face with a jaw of granite, with eyes the colour of midnight, hot and demanding.

'We must not,' he said, gravel-voiced.

'No,' she agreed, gazing up at his hard expression. Yet longing was there, in the way his gaze devoured her face, in the way his hands trembled where they touched her cheek, light and gentle as a butterfly. Forbidden wanting. Or was it only her fevered blood making her wish it?

She closed her eyes against such traitorous thoughts. She'd made her choice.

When she opened her eyes she saw anger in his. Perhaps even revulsion. Yet it did not seem so much directed at her as directed at himself as he stood up, leaving her cold and bereft.

'You must be warm by now,' Ian said, matter of factly.

Warm? She was burning. 'Yes. Thank you.' There, didn't she sound equally calm? Equally unaffected?

'Here.' He handed over her skirts and her bodice. 'These are dry.' He frowned when her breeches fell to the floor.

'For riding,' she said defensively. 'What about you?' She glanced at the blanket he had wrapped around his waist and then at the still-steaming mass of his kilt. It would take hours to dry. A small shiver ran down her back at the thought of hours of temptation in this cave.

'There are spare clothes here.' He picked up one of the packages and unwrapped it.

Fascinated, she watched him. 'You would spare your maidenly blushes if you will look away now, Lady Selina.' The mockery was back in his voice. Maidenly blushes. After that kiss he no doubt suspected they were nothing more than a front.

Her cheeks hotter than the fires of hell, she whipped her face away and fluffed the billowing fabric of her skirts. Yet for all her good intentions, she could not help but cast a glance from the corner of her eye as he let the blanket fall silently to the floor.

At the edge of the firelight the gleam of his skin was like marble. The image of wide sculpted shoulders tapering to lean waist and firm flanks, the swell of firm lean buttocks and strong thighs seared her vision. Her body clenched at his sheer beauty.

So large and so male. Lithe and perfectly formed. Athletic and sure in his movements as he bent to adjust the cloth. So opposite to her small stature and rounded curves and the awkwardness of her halting gait.

The silhouette of his erection made her gasp. Had he heard and guessed she was watching? If so, he gave no sign. She ducked her head and busied herself with her clothes. Swallowing against the dryness in her mouth, she kept her gaze fixed on her task.

The fire was hot and the light cotton fabric dried quickly. She concentrated on holding her breeches out to the flames. She glanced up when he returned bare-chested. Another delicious clench of her insides. He picked up his shirt and held it to the warmth. The trousers were on the tight side and too short and made his thighs look huge. Not that she was measuring. She wasn't. But a woman would have to be blind not to notice how strong his legs were and that his feet were large, just like his… She forced the thought to be gone.

But never would she forget the image of his body, the way he looked in profile. Different. Glorious.

'Time for you to dress now,' he said, 'if we are to get you home before dawn.'

She jumped at the sound of his voice. He was right. They really should not linger. 'Turn your back while I dress.'

An eyebrow flickered up—no doubt she had sounded too harsh, but he walked away, went to his horse with clearly no interest in spying on her.

So they'd kissed. A moment of passion after a wild escape. Whatever had happened between them had been the result of shock. Mutual comfort. Nothing more.

She pulled her hair back from her face; it felt matted and still damp, but she didn't care. She made a rough plait to hold it, then dressed beneath her blanket, not because she feared he would look, but to ward off some of the chill of the cave. Dressed, she turned back to find him rubbing the horse down with the blanket he had discarded earlier.

She picked up her shawl, still saturated from the sea, and folded it up. A blanket would make a better cloak and be warmer, though heaven knew what her maid was going to say. She wrapped it around her shoulders and tied it behind her waist as peasant girls did, then gathered up his kilt, folding it to give her hands something to do while she waited for him.

'Are you ready?' he asked, leading the horse towards her.

She nodded. It was a lie. A knot formed in her stomach. The thought of returning home made her feel the way an escaped prisoner must feel about the return to prison. A prison of her own making. Which didn't make a bit of sense, not when she was about to marry the man she had chosen for herself. She held out his kilt. 'You will want this.'

He used one of the ropes to tie it, then rested it across the horse's withers. 'We'll mount up outside.' He picked up a bucket and emptied it on the fire. Choking smoke filled the cave.

Selina coughed and rubbed at her streaming eyes. 'You idiot. Couldn't you wait until we had left?'

He chuckled. The next moment, he was behind her, lifting her onto the horse. 'We need to make haste, now.' He jerked on the bridle and led the big black into the tunnel, holding a torch up so they could see ahead of them. They climbed upwards through the narrow space. Sometimes, when the surf was quiet, she could hear running water—what was left of the stream that had carved its way through the rock and out to the sea, no doubt. And then they were out in the cold night air.

He doused the torch, tossed it over the cliff and continued leading the horse, back towards the road.

She clung on to the stallion's mane and prayed they would make it home in time.

A good few yards from the keep's entrance, Selina directed him across country. 'There is an outcropping of rock on the back side of the hill,' she murmured quietly.

'I know it.' Why had he never suspected it might hide an entrance? As lads, his brothers would have been delighted. The thought of the trouble they might have caused made him shudder.

They needed to hurry. Dawn was already changing the eastern sky from black to grey. Beau shied as a figure rose out of the heather. Ian jerked the horse to a stand.

'Angus,' Selina cried.

'Shh,' Angus hissed. 'What by all that is holy are you thinking, Ian Gilvry?'

'What are you doing here?' she asked.

Ian had a sinking feeling in his gut. Who else knew to expect Lady Selina?

Angus shot a glance up at the keep. 'Do you think I don't know every nook and cranny of my master's house, my lady? So it is true.'

'What are you insinuating, Mr McIver?'

Never had Ian heard her sound so haughty. So much like the stuck-up noblewoman Andrew had described on his return from London.

'What is happening, Angus?' Ian asked, jumping clear of Beau.

'That young lady has been missed from her bed and her fiancé is crying foul, that is what is happening.'

'Fiancé?' His gut slipped sideways. He glared up at Lady Selina. Had she been playing some sort of game with him back there in the cave, the sort of flirtation engaged in by ladies of the *ton*, according to what Andrew had told him?

'Nothing has been formally announced,' she said, sounding defensive. She slipped down off the horse and stood at his side.

'It may not be official,' Angus said, 'but he is verra angry. Threatening to ruin your reputation and that of your father. Interfering in official business makes you an accomplice under the law.'

'He can't know for certain,' she said heatedly. 'No one saw me.'

Ian had the feeling she had her fingers crossed when she said the last. 'Did someone see her?'

'I'm no privy to that information. I do know that young Dunstan is beside himself with anger. No doubt he expected a bit of glory out of tonight's affair. Instead...'

She winced. 'Father knows I knew what was planned for tonight and he thinks I betrayed him.'

'Well, you did, didn't you?' Angus muttered, his deep voice turning into a low growl of frustration. 'Lady Albright is in tears, speaking of ruin and disgrace. Your father...' He shook his head.

Ian stiffened, but for all the anger he felt, he had to acknowledge that if word of her escapade got out Lady Selina would be ruined. Helping a Gilvry escape the gaugers would not be seen as heroic by her people. They also might ponder why she had helped him, and not to her credit.

'I'll just have to face the music,' Lady Selina said in a small breathless voice. 'It is no one's business what I was doing tonight and so I will tell him. Father will forgive me, eventually.'

'I advise against such a step,' Angus said, his voice as dry as dust. 'That young man won't be satisfied until you admit where you were tonight and give evidence against the Laird. If he persuades your father he is right, you'll have a hard task standing up to them.'

Ian's fists clenched at the thought of her being bullied.

'And once they have what they want,' McIver continued, 'the Laird will be convicted.'

'But what else can I do?' she said.

He gave her a sharp look. 'According to that maid of yours, it wouldn't be the first time you'd gone off on a whim in the middle of the night. All you have to do is disappear for a while and turn up somewhere else safe and sound.'

'So Mary has been gossiping, has she?' she said icily.

'Mary is worried out of her wits that she will get the blame.'

Lady Selina's shoulders sagged. She shook her head. 'Surely, Father would not blame a servant for my actions? Besides, he knows I don't do that sort of thing any more.'

'Who's to say what maggot gets into a woman's head?' Angus said. 'There has to be somewhere you could go, some friend you could visit who could vouch for your whereabouts?'

She turned to Ian, her face full of worry. 'There is Alice. Lady Hawkhurst as she is now. Hawkhurst is a formidable man. He might be able to convince them I left before all this occurred. Father would listen to him.'

'You'll have to be careful,' McIver warned. 'They'll be searching the glens for you both by morning.'

Ian stared at McIver. 'Are you proposing I escort her there?'

'Aye. Unless you have a better idea.'

A curse sprang to his lips; he swallowed it. 'Perhaps if you bat your beautiful eyes at them, Lady Selina, and tell them you were out for a walk, they'll believe you.'

'I'm willing to give it a try,' she said with a defiant little toss of her head.

'Laird, if I might have a word with you in private?' Angus said. He looked up at Lady Selina. 'Clan business, you ken, my lady.'

'I suppose you are afraid I will tell them your secrets,' she said. 'Well, I'm not so poor spirited. However, speak privately if you must.' She walked a few steps away.

Ian drew closer to Angus. 'What is it, man? More bad news?'

'It depends on your point of view.' Angus gripped his arm hard. 'I ought to beat you to within an inch of your life for involving her in your doings.'

Anger rising in his craw, Ian stepped toe to toe with the man. McIver was big, but Ian was taller and fitter. He clenched his fists and pitched his voice low. 'Speak your piece, man.'

'Marry the lass.'

The words hit him like a punch to the jaw. Words would not form for a moment or two. More shocking yet was the deep sense of longing filling his chest, as if some hitherto-unrecognised hope had been forced to the surface. No doubt the wrong part of his anatomy doing the thinking. 'Are you mad? She's Albright's daughter.'

The child of his family's enemy. That was why he'd driven her off all those years ago, when he realised he was in danger of losing himself in her velvet-brown eyes. When he'd felt the stirrings in his blood and in his heart—and seen his brothers' horror.

Albright would never have countenanced their friendship, let alone anything closer.

And Andrew. Andrew would haunt his every moment if he did such a thing. If not for Selina's request, and his lingering guilt at the way he had treated her, Drew would still be alive. Instead, he'd forced his brother to leave London and his pursuit of the heiress, his answer to the clan's financial troubles, who just happened to be Selina's good friend. Not only that, Ian had shipped the furious Andrew off to America, where he'd been killed. How could he marry a woman who had twisted him around her little finger to the detriment of his brother? He certainly didn't deserve the surge of happiness the thought of it brought him. 'You are out of your mind.'

'I'm being practical, laddie. Marry her and even if they badger her until kingdom come, her word is no good in a court of law.'

'I don't believe Lady Selina would give evidence against me.'

'She might do her best to hold out, but she's made a complete fool of that young *Sassenach*. Let her go in there now and you might as well go in, too, with a noose draped around your neck. It'll be the end for the folks around here. With you gone there will be nothing to stop them from clearing the land. As I said, Dunstan is threatening retribution against her and against her father. Who do you think she will choose, once you are hiding out in the hills?' His grey brows drew together. 'Think about it, Gilvry. No matter what happens, she is ruined. I just can't see her letting her father be implicated, too.'

Damn it to hell. It was too hard a choice for any

daughter to make. She owed Ian nothing and her father everything. But marriage? 'There must be another way.'

Angus looked grim. 'Your brother Andrew cut a swathe through the lasses in every glen from here to Edinburgh, but you are the Laird and she is a lady. Have you no honour?'

Resentment at the distaste in the other man's tone fired his temper. 'I haven't touched the lass.' He flushed red as he recalled their kiss and was glad of the poor light. But it was only a kiss. 'I didn't ask her to follow me tonight.'

McIver sighed. 'But she did. Will you let her suffer for trying to help? You are not the man I thought, if you do not do the right thing.'

He squeezed his eyes shut, trying to focus, to see his way clear. He needed time to think. Time to plan. 'I will take her to her friend, but that is all I will do.'

McIver shook his head as if disappointed. 'Think on what I have said, lad. In the meantime, travel as far as you can from here before it is light. You'll find a welcome in the glens until you get far enough south. Do not dally. There will be a price on your head by morning.'

Reeling with the conflicting thoughts in his head, Ian returned to Selina with McIver on his heels.

'Well?' she said.

Ian gave her a rueful grin. 'I will take you to your friend.'

She turned to McIver. 'Are you sure this is the only way?'

Angus nodded. 'Go with Gilvry or your help will have been for nothing.' He plucked a saddlebag off the rocks where they'd first seen him. 'There's water in here, oats and supplies, some coin. Enough to see you on your way. Get a message to your brother, Laird, when you have things in hand.' He emphasised the last word with a hard look.

Ian didn't like McIver's glibness. He seemed to have thought everything out, as if he had some purpose of his own. But he couldn't see any alternative.

Certainly not marriage.

He looked up. Dawn was reaching into the sky and he could see Selina's features more clearly and the anxiety in her eyes.

'We need to go. Now,' he said.

Wearily, she nodded her agreement and let him throw her up on Beau. She clung there looking down at him with worry and trust.

If anything, it made him feel worse. Somehow he had to find a way out of this mess. For them both. He mounted before her and looked down at Angus. 'Tell Niall I will send word.'

He turned Beau around and dug in his heels.

Chapter Eight

Selina had no choice but to cling to the firm waist of the man before her as he turned across country. A dull ache filled her chest. In trying to help Ian, she'd ruined her own future. If only she'd stayed in London, none of this would have happened.

And Ian would have been caught.

It was all the fault of that stupid man Ranald. If he would have just taken her warning to Ian, she could have gone home and no one would have been the wiser.

She looked back over her shoulder at the keep, its outline already distinguishable against the sky. Was she now doing the right thing in going with Ian?

While her heart had said 'yes', which was why she hadn't given them too much of an argument, her head thought it a huge mistake. She had learned a long time ago not to listen to her heart. A cold feeling sank into the pit of her stomach as she realised she was putting her faith in a man she barely knew and had absolutely no reason to trust.

But if Dunstan was threatening to charge her with complicity in smuggling, she needed an alibi. Someone who could vouch for her presence elsewhere.

Alice had been the only person she could think of. But her husband, Hawkhurst, might well not approve. Selina had always had the feeling he didn't like her very much.

They travelled west, away from the sea and the keep. After an hour or so, Ian slowed the horse to a walk. The beast's head hung low, foam white around the bit.

He threw one leg over the horse's withers and jumped down. He lifted her off. 'We'll walk for a while.'

She rubbed at her thigh, easing the stiffness that always beset her after sitting for too long. It felt good to be off the horse and on her feet. The doctors had advised lots of walking to strengthen the muscles in her leg, though nothing would cure the hesitation in her step. She was lucky Dunstan hadn't cared that she was no longer a diamond of the first water, no longer the perfect pocket Venus, but then money solved many problems.

'Where are we headed first?' she asked.

He grinned and grabbed the bridle. 'Into the glens. Where the Scots always go when plagued by the English.'

She matched his pace. 'That I know. But where?'

'There is a place I know where we can spend the night, if we can reach it before nightfall. It is a long hard walk, so save what you can of your breath.'

She stumbled on a rock hidden in the heather.

He caught her arm before she fell. 'Be careful. I always forget what a little bit of a thing you are.'

'I'll try to be taller.' She took bigger steps.

He laughed. 'You are a surprising woman, Lady Selina. Any other lady of my acquaintance would be twisting her hands together and bemoaning her fate.'

'If hand-wringing would do me any good, be assured I would put it to good use.'

He glanced over his shoulder. 'We are far enough from Dunross that we can slow our pace, I think.'

'I'm not an invalid. I am perfectly capable of walking.'

'I see that.'

Still she couldn't help but be aware that he had adjusted his stride to match hers. She decided there was no point in saying anything. It clearly wouldn't do any good. He saw her as crippled, no matter what she said.

After what felt like hours, with the sound of the curlews and the wind the only noises, he stopped by a stream. 'We will let the horse drink and then ride for a while.'

She tried not to sigh with relief at not having to walk as she sank down and she scooped up water in her hands and enjoyed the cold trickle down her parched throat.

He drank, too, once he had seen to the horse, then crouched down beside her. 'It would be better, if we meet anyone, if you do not give your real name.'

A pang tightened her chest. Of course he would not want it known he was in her company. She smiled brightly. 'Who shall I be? Mary Queen of Scots?'

He frowned. 'The cousin of a friend, on her way to her family. I don't suppose you speak any Gaelic.'

'A word or two, but I can speak with a Scottish burr,' she said in broadest Scots.

He nodded. 'Och, I remember you doing that before. It was days before I realised you were English.'

'I'm like a chameleon,' she said with a laugh that was a little more brittle than she intended. 'I fit in with my surroundings.'

It wasn't true. She fit in London. Not here.

'We can say you have been away to school in England and lost the Gaelic. Come, we must keep moving.'

'How long do you think it will be before they give up looking for us?'

He shrugged. 'For you? Until you send them word you are safe, I assume.' He bent and laced his fingers together beside Beau.

'And you?' she asked as he tossed her up.

'With no evidence, there will be no point in them looking.'

Once more she found herself clinging to Ian's waist, thoughts churning around in her head.

She just wished she could be sure she was doing the right thing running away with Ian instead of seeking out her father and denying it all. Unfortunately, that kind of blatant lying was not her forte.

If only she could think of a logical explanation for being gone in the middle of the night. Something that would not leave them suspecting her of betraying what should have been a confidence, though no one had specifically asked her not to speak of it.

Unfortunately McIver was right—the smugglers' escape and her disappearance were just too much of a coincidence. She wasn't even sure that Hawkhurst could, if he even would, give her the alibi she needed.

On the other hand, no one but the smugglers had seen her.

She stared at Ian's back. One of his own men had betrayed him; if that person had seen her, it wouldn't matter what kind of alibi she had, there would be a witness against her.

Was that why McIver had drawn Ian aside? Did he know who had betrayed them to the Revenue men?

She bit her lip. Perhaps it was better not to know. The

thought gave her a horrid churning feeling in her stomach. Surely Ian wouldn't… Smugglers were known to be exceedingly dangerous if crossed.

Oh, dear. Had she gone from the frying pan into the fire? She could not, would not, believe Ian would do her any harm. He was simply trying to help her escape the consequences of her folly, because she had helped him. Nothing more.

'Do you have any idea who gave you away?'

His back stiffened. 'I have been thinking about it, to no avail.' He gave a short laugh. 'No doubt he was forced to it by circumstance.'

'What do you mean?'

His shoulders rose and fell. 'Who knows what people keep hidden? It could be debt. Or illness. Or fear of being turned out. There are many ways to make a man betray his loyalty.'

And it depended on where you stood as to what was or was not deemed loyal. 'Which means we can't trust anyone in your clan.'

He didn't answer for a long while. 'Let us put it this way. There are people I know I can trust and people I am not sure of.'

'What about me?' She winced. Did she have to ask? How could he possibly trust an Albright. A *Sassenach*.

'I trust you.' He sounded almost surprised. 'But I have to be honest, I also believe your first loyalty is to your father.'

She could not deny it, though Father might not exactly see it that way at this moment.

They kept moving all day, sometimes riding, sometimes walking, the hills becoming higher and steeper with every passing hour. They travelled in silence, saving their breath for travelling. And always she felt his urgency, though he never gave a sign he thought she was holding him back. He didn't have to—she knew she was. Often she had the feeling he only stopped because she needed to rest.

The farther away from Dunross they got, the more she began to fear that her running away was not the right answer. Surely she could have bluffed her way out of the mess. Batting her beautiful eyes, as Ian had said.

He thought her eyes beautiful. When he had said it, she had been too worried to let the words sink in. Now strangely, they made her feel warm inside.

On foot once more, she lifted her gaze and became aware of her surroundings. It was all so wild and beautiful. Misty hills stretched in every direction, their outlines softened by heather and scarred by the odd outcrop of ancient granite. She'd been enchanted by it all that long-ago summer when her father had brought her here after her mother had died. He'd been desolate and had wanted to return to the place where he had spent his honeymoon. Then he'd run off to Inverness—for business reasons, he'd said—leaving her to mourn alone.

Later, he'd admitted that she reminded him too much of her mother and he just couldn't bear it, but at the time she'd felt abandoned. By them both.

Sixteen and utterly lonely, she'd been ripe to fall in love with the first handsome young man who came her way. Naturally it had to be the worst possible person. Had Ian actually suggested she run away with him then, she would have said 'yes' in a heartbeat.

He'd been a knight in shining armour the day he carried her back to the keep in his arms. He'd made her feel soft and feminine. A rush of longing for that feeling filled the empty place in her heart she'd refused to acknowledge.

She shouldn't be noticing now when they had so many more important things to think about.

'Do you think we will make it to this place you know of by nightfall?'

He glanced up at the sky. 'Yes. It is not more than a mile or two now. You've done very well for a *Sassenach* lass. Far better than I expected.'

Praise indeed, though she could have done without the reminder that she was English. Even so, she found herself smiling. He grinned back. How odd to feel happy in such peculiar circumstances.

'How long do you think it will take to reach Hawkhurst from there?'

'Once we cross the border and pick up a stagecoach, it shouldn't take more than a couple of days.'

They crested the rise of a hill and, as nothing but hills stretched before them, the enormity of the distance they would have to travel became real.

'What will you do, after?'

He shrugged. 'Come back and continue on as before.'

'More smuggling, I suppose. Until they finally catch you.'

He shot her a look that was both devil-may-care and world weary. 'They won't. And what else can we do until the law punishing us for supporting the true king is changed—the one separating the Highlands from the rest of Scotland and making it impossible to survive?'

Such bitterness. 'Can the law be changed?'

'Who will take our part in Westminster?'

Not her father. He had no interest in his Scottish estate, except for sport and a means to political advantage. 'Lord Carrick?'

'He does what he can, but Carrick is one voice among many. Highlanders are not popular with the English aristocracy.'

'It shouldn't be a matter of what is popular. The laws should be fair.'

He grinned at her. 'So they should. But since they are not, then we deal with them our own way.'

There was more than a smidgeon of pride in the way he spoke. Clearly it would irk a man like Ian to be begging for help. But if he had brought his case to her father, might he not have tried to assist?

She stopped and looked at him. 'Did you ask my father?'

'Albright? Ye jest.'

The bitterness and scorn in his voice cut like a knife.

A shot rang out, the sound bouncing off the hills.

Ian jerked and clutched his arm with a cry, then spun around. He grabbed her arm and drew her down to the ground. 'Keep your head low.'

'They were shooting at us.' The shock of it left her dizzy.

'Aye.' He got up on his knees and looked down the hill they'd so recently walked up. He cursed. 'Soldiers. It won't be long before they are upon us.'

Crouched low, he ran the few steps to the stallion, whipped the blanket from the animal's back, rolled it up and tied it lengthways along the horse's back.

'What are you doing?'

He shot her an impatient glance, then began talking in a low voice into Beau's flickering ear. To her shock, he whacked the horse hard on its rump. It took off at a gallop.

Lying flat in the heather, she stared after the horse in dismay. 'Why did you do that?'

Crouching low, he picked up the saddlebag and reached out to take her hand. 'Buying time. Keep your head down until we get over the brow of the hill.'

And then they were running, at first at a crouch, then, once they had crested the rise and were going downhill, at full tilt.

Her heart thumped against her ribs. Her breath came in short little gasps. She skittered along after him, trying to keep her head down, imagining at any moment a bullet slamming into her back, all the while wanting to lie flat on the ground and put her hands over her head. She sensed she wasn't going fast enough for Ian. Breath rattled in and out of her lungs. Her legs, already tired, felt as heavy as lead. She really could not go any farther.

She let go of his hand and sank into the heather, gasping for breath. 'Go. Leave me here.'

The look he gave her from beneath his brows was fierce and uncompromising. Before she realised what he was about he swept her up in his arms and tossed her over his shoulder. He took off, in an awkward jolting run.

With each step his shoulder dug into her belly and pushed the air out of her chest. The blood rushed to her head where she hung over his back.

She didn't know which was worse, the pain under her ribs, or her difficult breathing, but she bore it in silence, glad he hadn't abandoned her to save his own skin. He didn't seem to even notice her weight. He was as lithe and sure-footed as one of the deer that roamed these hills, but after a while even his breathing became harsh and laboured.

They crested two more hills and then he stopped. 'Get your head down.' He threw himself flat and she did the same, lying on her back, trying to catch her breath.

'If I tell you to run, head for the burn at the bottom,'

he instructed, his voice a rough rasp. In a crablike crawl, he went to the top of the rise behind them and once more lay flat, looking out. She tried to listen, but all she could hear was the blood rushing in her ears. She kept her gaze fixed on Ian, ready to run should he give her the signal. Or at least try to run. She wasn't sure she could take another step.

He sauntered back to her with a grin on his face. He actually looked as if he was enjoying himself. She wanted to shake him. She pushed to her feet. 'I assume they took the bait?'

'They did that.' His grin widened. 'If we are lucky, Beau will beat them back to Dunross.'

She couldn't help an answering grin.

His expression turned serious. 'We are not out of the woods yet. They no doubt have a glass and, if they realise there is no rider, then they will circle back. We must hurry.'

'Hurry where?'

He grinned. His blue eyes danced. 'Over there.'

This time he directed her across the hillside, rather than down. He seemed to be searching the ground, for what she couldn't imagine. There was nothing here.

He dropped to his knees and parted the heather around a large boulder. 'Ah, here it is.' He pulled aside what had looked like twisted clumps of dead heather on solid ground, but was really more like a thatch covering a deep scoop in the side of the hill.

'In you go.'

A quick breath of fresh air and she crawled in. A strange smell filled her nostrils. Peat smoke and something else. Trusting he knew what he was about, she turned around and waited.

He followed, pulling the undergrowth back in place. It

wasn't completely dark inside. As her eyes adjusted, she realised they were in some sort of earthen room and that daylight came in through chinks in a roof made of brush.

The space, a sort of earthen cave, contained a couple of stools, a rotten straw pallet in one corner and a rusted metal object standing on the remains of a fire. A twisted piece of metal hung down beside its chimney. 'What is this place?'

He drew her close and placed a finger to her lips. 'Listen.'

Over the thud of her heart, she heard a different kind of thud. Horses. The sound vibrated up through her feet. They sounded very close. Would they trample over what was a very flimsy roof and end up falling in on top of them? The sound of her breathing and her heartbeat filled her ears.

She could only imagine what was happening outside. Without thinking, she drew close to his large protective form. Strong arms went around her, holding her firmly. She snuggled closer, listening to the strong steady beat of his heart instead of the sound of nearby horses, drawing strength and courage from his warmth and his closeness, wanting to burrow deeper every time they came so close she could hear the laboured breathing of the horses.

Slowly the sounds receded.

'Whoever is in charge has a brain,' Ian murmured into her hair. 'I'm thinking the rest of the group followed Beau, but he sent a couple this way just to be sure. No doubt they will be back the moment they discover they were tricked.'

'How comforting,' she said, easing away from him. It seemed to her that he was reluctant to let her go, as if he had drawn some comfort from having her in his arms.

What an imagination she had. The sooner they left here the better.

She patted her hair, smoothing her skirts, hoping she did not look as if she had just huddled against him like a frightened child.

He hissed in a sharp breath. One of pain.

She recalled his jerk and the cry right after the shot. 'Did they hit you?'

She felt sick. Nauseous. Her father wouldn't have ordered him shot. He wouldn't.

'A scratch. The ball was spent.'

Her knees went weak. 'I should look at it.'

'It is fine.'

She wanted to believe him. 'Perhaps I should look at it just to be sure? It's too dark in here to see anything. We should go outside.'

'Not yet. Not until we are sure they are not coming back. It will be hard for them to return to this exact spot. Since they will expect us to run, we will stay put. We'll move on in the morning. More carefully.'

'What of Beau?'

'He's used to these hills. He'll go home.'

'And if they catch him?'

He shrugged. 'They will eventually. Either on the hoof or at my house. He was an army horse before I bought him. He'll probably be happy to rejoin.'

But Ian wasn't happy. She could hear it in his voice.

She once more looked around the cave. The smell had an underlying musty scent. 'What is this place?'

His mouth tightened as if he preferred not to say. She stiffened her spine against the hurt of his distrust. 'It was an illegal whisky still.'

He had trusted her after all. Something inside her

softened. She sat down on the stool, looking up at him. 'How did you know it was here?'

He grinned, his teeth flashing white in the gloom. 'Just brimming with questions, aren't you, Lady Selina?'

'How do you know the soldiers don't know about this place?'

'No one does.' He crouched down and poked around in the fire. 'It hasn't been used in years. It was my father's.'

No wonder he hadn't wanted to say where they were headed. In a strange way she felt honoured.

'Is your arm really all right?'

'It stings like the blazes.'

She winced. 'You could have been killed.' Or she might.

'Aye.' He picked up the saddlebag and sorted through it, setting out its contents on the floor. 'Flint. A couple of candles. Oats. Bannocks wrapped in cloth. A flask.' He shook it and something gurgled inside it.

'What is it, water?'

He opened the stopper and sniffed. 'Something better. Whisky.'

She huffed out a breath. 'Water would be better.'

He chuckled and the sound was warm and low and easy. 'There's clean water in the burn, lass.'

'So now we just sit here and wait for morning,' she said with a sigh. 'Do you have somewhere we can go next?'

'I've a friend to the south and east of here. Captain Hugh Monro. He has contacts. He might lend us a horse. Or even a cart.' He looked at her. 'The thing is, I am just not sure he would see my side of it. He's a law-abiding man. I doubt he'd approve of smuggling, no matter the reason behind it. And he is more than a day's walk away.'

More walking. And worrying about being shot at.

'We'll make ourselves as comfortable as we can to-night,' he said. 'When it gets dark, I'll fetch water from the stream. We will eat the bannock and we will soak the oats for the morning.'

'It sounds most appetising,' she murmured.

He cracked a laugh. 'A banquet.'

She rubbed her arms. The warmth she'd gained from walking and running had faded. Chill now seeped into her from the surrounding damp earth. In a while, it would be dark and much colder. 'Do you think we can light a fire?'

'If we hadn't been seen, I'd risk it, but they might come back once they catch Beau.'

They would have to make do without heat, then. They had one blanket between them. Sadly, the other had gone with the horse. Although he did have his kilt, which had dried over the course of the day.

'Why did your family abandon the still?'

He grimaced. 'The gaugers get wind of them and de-stroy them. See, the kettle's been split with a hammer.'

She stared at the odd-shaped stove. 'How does it work?'

'This metal kettle here is a wash still, and when it is heated up over the peat fire, the steam containing the alcohol passes up the chimney and then down the worm, the coiled pipe there, and into a spirit still. All that's left here is the first part of the process. Father used to pre-pare the mash in a local farmer's barn and then bring it up here to turn it into whisky. Good whisky, too. We've a dram or two left in our cellars.'

There was pride in his voice. Over illegal whisky. It was a world in which she was a foreigner. The thought made her feel rather dismal.

'We should eat now, while we can still see.' He glanced upwards and she became aware of just how much the light had faded.

He unwrapped the bannocks and handed her one. They were surprisingly tasty. Or was she so hungry that anything would have tasted good? There were six altogether. She ate two. When he had wolfed down three of them he eyed the one remaining. 'Do you want it?'

'Oh, no,' she said lightly. 'I couldn't eat another bite. You finish it.'

He didn't speak.

She looked up to see him watching her. It was hard to fathom his expression, his eyes looked so dark. 'Is something wrong?'

'Why do you do that?'

'Do what?'

'Lie to me in that stupid little voice. Eat the bannock.'

She flashed hot. 'You need it more than I do.'

'Right, and I am the kind of man who takes the food out of the mouths of women and children.' He stood up and bent to rake around in the rubbish in the corner. A grunt of satisfaction told her he'd found what he was looking for. When he stood up, she saw he had an old and bent metal pot in his hand. She couldn't understand why he looked so pleased.

He must have sensed her puzzlement. 'I recall using it the last time I was here. If it had been gone, we would have had to use the flask for water.'

'And thrown out the whisky,' she said.

'Never.'

'You'd rather do without water, than waste the whisky. I should have guessed.'

'*Uisge-beatha*, lass. The water of life.'

She watched him leave, a smile on her lips, then tackled the last of the bannocks.

Chapter Nine

By the time he returned with water, their dwelling was pitch black and a chill permeated the air. Perched on the stool, wrapped in her blanket, she really wished they could light a fire. She forced her teeth not to chatter, though stilling her shivers was harder.

The sound of Ian's breathing filled the small space. She sensed him fumble around, heard the clang of metal on rock and guessed he'd set down the pan of water. 'I'd forgotten how dark the night can be out here,' he muttered.

And how cold, she wanted to add. She shivered. 'Are you sure we can't light a fire?'

He hesitated, then sighed. 'It would be a mistake. I think we can light one of the candles, though. Its flame is too small to be seen at any great distance.'

The sound of steel striking against flint only made her think more of warm fires. Yet when the wick caught and the small light flared, putting shadows in the corners of their small den, it did seem a bit warmer.

Then she noticed his grimace and the way he flexed his left hand.

She got up from the stool. It was a rickety old thing

and did not sit flat on the ground, but it was all they had. 'Sit down and let me look at your arm.'

'Getting a little bossy, aren't you?'

'Sit.'

He sat.

She took a deep breath. 'Perhaps you should take off your jacket, so we can see how bad the wound really is. It won't help us if you become ill.'

'Aye, I suppose you are right.'

'I wish we had some basilica powders.'

Looking surprised, he eased first one arm out of his coat and then, wincing, drew it slowly off the other arm. The fabric was dark with blood.

She gasped. Her stomach rolled. The blood seemed to drain from her head and the small space spun around. His coat had hidden the extent of the wound.

'Oh, Ian,' she whispered, 'you need a doctor.'

'It is not as bad as it looks,' he said through gritted teeth as he pulled the fabric away from the wound. He cursed softly.

Throat dry, she swallowed. 'We should clean it.'

Looking up, he raised a brow. His eyes gleamed with amusement. 'We?'

She took a deep steadying breath. 'Me, then. Look, it is bleeding again. Take off your shirt.'

Now he really looked surprised. 'All right.' He fumbled at his collar with his good hand.

She brushed his hand away. 'Let me.' Standing this close to him, with the light coming down from above making every sinew and bone as sharp and clear as a portrait as each breath expanded and contracted his chest, she could feel his warmth against her skin. Unnerved, she felt her hands tremble. Indeed, her very bones shook with a force she couldn't quite grasp. When she breathed in to steady herself, it was like breathing in his air, his essence.

A shock jolted through her. How could that be?

It couldn't. She was being stupid, just as she had been as a girl. In real life, they stood on the opposite sides of a line drawn on a map.

She forced the inappropriate sensations aside. The man was hurt and patiently waiting without complaint with his chin raised for her to undo the darned knot.

It came free and she cast the cloth aside and went to work on the buttons. Undressing a man—never in her life had she done anything so daring.

The collar fell open with each button she freed from its mooring, slowly revealing the hollow of his strong throat, his collar bones, a wedge of chest lightly furred with dark crisp curls that brushed against her knuckles as she released the final fastening, enticing to her fingertips and her gaze.

Such feelings led in only one direction. Down a path that would do her no good.

She let her hands fall to her side and stepped back. She glanced up to find his gaze fixed on her face. Intense. Heated. He was breathing faster than before.

He also felt desire.

It hung between them, hot and heavy. Terrifying. With effort she made a small gesture with her hand. 'You should be able to take your shirt off now.'

The fire deep in the blue of his eyes flared, then died.

'Aye. I can do that.' He pulled the shirttails free and with his good arm pulled the shirt off over his head, unveiling the body of a Norse god she'd only dared to peek at in the sea cave.

The muscles of his arms were carved and hard, his chest vast and sculpted beneath its smattering of hair.

In the face of such magnificence, breathing was nearly out of the question.

But breathe she must. 'Hold out your arm.'

She knelt close to his knee. He held his arm steady with his other hand, bending his head to look at the wound.

Their foreheads collided.

A nervous giggle escaped her lips. Heat fired her face. The schoolgirl was back. She felt giddy, and not from the sight of his blood.

He grunted. 'It doesn't look too bad.'

'I can't see.'

He leaned sideways.

A nasty gash scored his arm. Bile rose in her throat. She swallowed it down. 'You are right, it seems to be nothing more than a flesh wound.' She controlled a shudder. 'I will clean it and bind it.'

Blood from where he'd pulled the shirt free of his skin trickled down to his elbow. She grabbed up the flask. 'If I recall correctly, this is better than water for a wound.'

'A terrible waste, lass.'

'I'll save you a drop. Give me your knife.'

He eyed her aslant. 'Why?'

'Unless you have a nice clean handkerchief, I need some cloth to pad the wound. We will use your stock to hold it in place.' She looked at his shirt. He'd need to put that on again, bloody sleeve or no. She lifted up her skirt and looked at the hem of her petticoats. The lace of the top one was in tatters after being soaked in sea-water, straddling a horse and dragging through heather. Now it would serve to staunch the blood.

He pulled his dirk from his sock and handed it to her, hilt first.

She shook her head. 'I'll hold the fabric taut while you cut. I am sure you will do a better job than I.'

An eyebrow shot up and he looked at her rather oddly, but he bent to the task. It felt a little strange with his face so close to her legs, even though he must be able to see little more than her shoes, since there were two more layers of cloth beneath the first petticoat. Portuguese women adored petticoats.

He soon had a long strip cut from around the bottom.

'Cut it in two,' she said, 'and I'll use one piece as a rag for washing.'

A frown creased his forehead. 'Where did you learn such skill?'

'I wouldn't call it skill. I hate the sight of blood. But my friend, Lady Hawkhurst, convinced me to volunteer at the hospital she funds for injured seamen. I read to them and roll bandages.' She soaked one of the rags with whisky.

'So you have no experience in binding wounds and such like?'

'None at all,' she said cheerfully, 'but I have seen it done.' No point in telling him she'd thrown up in the nearest chamberpot when she'd looked at the wrong moment. Instead, she gritted her teeth and dabbed the cloth at the ragged cut.

He hissed in a breath and she waited for a spewing of swear words.

He remained utterly silent.

Impressed, she continued dabbing. If he could put up with the pain, she could put up with the sight. Although if anything the dizziness of earlier was growing worse. She continued dabbing and wiping until all the dried blood was gone.

The wound looked nasty—ragged edges and fresh welling blood.

Black edged her vision. She felt herself sway. She squeezed her eyes shut, regaining her balance and fighting the sickness.

This wound was nowhere near as bad as the one to her own leg. One brief glimpse of that and she had passed out cold.

Jaw clenched, she tried to remember what Alice had said about the symptoms of spreading infection. Redness? Yellow pus? No sign of anything like that. Yet.

She looked away and drew a deep breath in through her nose. 'There is not much more I can do, except bind it.'

'I am glad to hear it,' he said wryly.

Her gaze flew to his face. His mouth was set in lines of pain. She'd been so busy trying not to pass out that she hadn't thought about how much she must be hurting him, because he hadn't made a sound.

Because he was strong and she was weak.

'Hold still,' she said gruffly. She placed the pad over the wound, then wrapped his neckcloth around it, tying it off with a knot.

He flexed his hand and she watched, fascinated by the way the muscle in his upper arm bulged against the bandage. He did it again. This time something happened to his chest; it seemed to grow firmer and develop more definition. It almost made her forget just how ill she felt, until her gaze fell on his torn and bloody shirt.

The room wavered in and out of focus. Her knees buckled and the shadows leaped out from the corners to take over the room. And she was falling.

'Selina?' he asked as though from a great way off.

A strong arm banded around her waist. It pulled her

against something warm and hard. She collapsed against it, her stomach heaving as the candle refused to remain in one place.

'Selina.'

Ian. Ian had hold of her. She closed her eyes and waited for the horrible sensations to pass. Slowly she became aware that she was sitting on his knee, cradled within his arms. He was stroking her back. She opened her eyes and was glad to see that nothing was spinning.

'Feeling better?' he murmured, his voice low in her ear, the roll of his 'r' a sweet comforting sensation in the pit of her stomach. She always seemed to feel better when he had his arms around her. Too bad he couldn't keep them there.

'I'm such a coward,' she said, trying to sit up, but he held her against his chest and she realised he was rocking gently back and forth.

'No, you are not. You have been very brave. I promise everything will be all right,' he whispered. 'I'll get you safely to your friend and we will sort it all out.'

She half groaned, half laughed. 'I'm not worried about that. The sight of blood always makes me feel ill.'

His rocking ceased briefly, then continued. 'Then I am all the more grateful, lass.'

Oh, that wonderful deep velvety voice, so close to her ear. She was melting, burning up with a fever of longing and desire.

'You must think me completely useless.'

'You are braver than anyone I know, because you knew how it would affect you.'

But she hadn't been thinking. She'd acted on instinct. She never seemed to think straight around him.

A prickle of awareness made her look up at his face.

A slight curve to his mouth and the twinkle in his eye caused her heart to clench.

She couldn't resist the temptation. She reached up and put her hands on his nape and kissed him full on the lips.

He groaned softly.

His lips parted against hers. His tongue traced the seam of her lips. It felt delicious. Her spine tingled, her hands cradled his head, feeling the soft curl of his hair between her fingers.

His hand came to her cheek, his fingers shaking with the power of this moment between them. Never had her heart raced so fast or her body grown so warm with such a whisper of touch.

He was a big man, huge in comparison to her, and for him to tremble at the mere touch of her lips was heady indeed.

Many men had desired her over the years, lusted for her and declared their love, but they'd only ever seen what she wanted them to see. The perfect nobleman's daughter. The diamond of the first water. The impeccable manners. The flirtatious wit. This man knew her weaknesses, and yet he trembled.

The knowledge melted her bones.

She parted her lips and let him into her soul. The kiss wasn't all one-sided. Oh, no. Her tongue slid wantonly along his, tasting whisky and earthy man, while she inhaled the scent of horse and leather and fresh air tinged with peat smoke. Sensual sensations rippled through her body with every beat of her heart.

She arched against him, pressing her breasts against his hard wall of a chest, wound her arms around his neck and submitted to her hunger.

He growled deep in his throat, shifting beneath her,

making her aware of the male part of him that pressed against her thigh through her layers of clothing.

She breathed his scent, revelled in his heat and the feel of hard muscle and sinew beneath her exploring hands.

Breathing hard, he slowly pulled away, looking into her face. Could he see in her face the awe and wonder rioting through her body? Could he feel the heat burning in her belly, in her breasts, flowing through her veins?

Helpless with need, she gazed up, waiting.

'You'd tempt the devil himself, Lady Selina.'

She didn't want the devil. She wanted him. She gazed back at him with longing and desire and a sweet softness that made her insides feel open and yearning.

He reached around to catch her hands clinging around his neck and tore them free, holding them fast in his. 'This must stop,' he said harshly. He disengaged his hands from hers.

'Don't you want me?' she asked, feeling suddenly bereft, even knowing the question was unfair. She felt his desire, insistent, rampant against her bottom.

'Not want you?' he growled. His mouth descended in a punishing kiss, full of ardour and passion and heat. Her mind refused to form a single thought. Her hands, freed from his grip, wandered his broad sculpted chest and floated over his back, measuring the width and strength of him.

Lacking air, they slowly parted, their chests rising and falling in perfect harmony as he nibbled and licked at her lips, her chin, her jaw. He teased the tender place beneath her ear, breathing against her neck. 'I want you. But if we do this now there will be no going back. We will have to be married.'

The words were like a splash of cold water. Have to

be married? Clearly it was not something he wanted, any more than she did. Did she?

He groaned and rose to his feet with her still in his arms. He set her back on the stool, wrapped the blanket around her and cleared the opening to the outside.

'Where are you going?' To her chagrin, panic edged her voice.

'I'll be right back.'

'That wasn't an answer,' she said. Too late. He was gone.

Shame at her cowardice roiled in her stomach. Why would he abandon her here? It didn't make any sense, but the fear was real enough. The fear of being left as her father had abandoned her the year he'd brought her to Dunross. For years, she'd worried that he would forget about her again, when she was at school, when he was away on business. Even now, when she knew the reason why, she hated knowing that people important to you could just walk away. It was better if you did not allow them to become important, then you didn't have to worry.

And Ian hadn't left. He sounded as if he was searching through the heather. Hunting?

Then he was back, pushing something ahead of him. The smell of fresh-cut vegetation filled the cave. Fuel for a fire?

But, no, he didn't go to the hearth. He spread it out in the corner. 'Give me your blanket,' he said.

'Why?' The thought of losing even the little amount of warmth it provided was unwelcome.

'We need it to make a bed.'

'A bed?'

'Aye. We can't sleep sitting up. The heather is springy enough that it will do us for one night. With a blanket beneath us and my kilt for a quilt, we'll be warmer than toast. Drew and I did it all the time as lads.'

A bed. With him, and after her wanton behaviour? She blushed from head to toe. Now was really the time she should object. Somehow the words wouldn't form. She stood up and handed him the blanket. He laid it across the shrubbery.

'Lay yourself down,' he said. His voice was grim and when she peeped at his face, she saw his mouth was set in a stern line.

What was the matter with him? She settled herself down on one side of the makeshift bed, looking up at him.

His hands went to his belt, then glanced at her. He picked up his shirt and drew it over his head. 'Close your eyes.'

'A bit late for modesty, isn't it?' she asked, stifling the urge to giggle.

He turned away, uttering a sound between a curse and a laugh of his own.

A huff of his breath blew out the candle and a moment or two later came the sound of him unfastening his belt. Her unruly mind travelled right back to the scene in the cave, him standing there dressing. Now he was undressing. She didn't need a candle to see.

Cursing silently, she tried not to envisage what was taking place.

A moment later, she felt his warmth along her side and the weight of the thick wool of his kilt settle onto her body. It retained some of his warmth.

She'd slept on softer mattresses, been covered by finer linens, but given her state of exhaustion she could not say that any had felt better than this bed of heather.

'Thank you,' she said.

'You are welcome.'

She shivered.

Ian's arm came around her shoulders and he pulled her towards him, tucking her against him so her head rested on his chest. Instantly, she felt warmed by his heat, by the feel of his hand on her waist. But more than that, she felt safe. Protected.

It felt wonderful.

She snuggled closer. 'Body heat,' she said, laughing softly, feeling wicked and a little giddy suddenly from lack of breath. 'Goodnight,' she breathed and tipped her face up to kiss his cheek. At least she was sure that was what she had intended, but she found his mouth instead.

He kissed her back, long and deep until her senses swam. He rolled her on her back, plundering her mouth with his tongue, gently cupping her breast, tenderly pressing her legs open with his firm thigh.

She moaned as her feminine centre responded to the pressure. Her hips arched upwards as she accepted Ian's deepening kiss.

Suddenly, he jerked away as if stung and uttered a curse. He rolled away from her and she could hear the sound of his ragged breathing in the dark.

'Ian,' she said tentatively.

'Go to sleep, little *Sassenach*. I'll no be touching you and you'll no be touching me. Are we agreed?' It seemed that what to her had been a moment of bliss to him had been…well, something inconvenient.

He lay perfectly still beside her, slowing his breathing, pretending to be asleep, no doubt. Unbelievable. She was lying next to a nearly naked man, out in the wilds of Scotland, a man she found hugely attractive and who had just kissed her senseless, and he was acting as if he was her brother.

Perhaps the idea of making love to a cripple was more than he could stand. It was hard to blame him if that was the case. She had to admit the scars were pretty ugly and the limp was far from alluring. She was lucky Dunstan had been willing to overlook her flaws. Her stomach sank. Dunstan had done it for the money. He was also a nice man. Kind. Sweet.

A thought, crystal clear and dreadful, came out of nowhere. For the first time since they'd left the keep, her mind seemed sharp.

She shoved at his shoulder.

'What now, lass?' he mumbled as if he was really asleep.

'My father will guess I have gone to Alice. I always do.'

'So?' Ah, now he sounded more awake.

'What if he gets to her first?'

'What if he does?'

'Then the alibi won't work.'

Chapter Ten

The next morning, they turned south. As she strode along beside him, she noticed that her leg barely ached at all. The doctors were right—walking was good for her, though they had not envisaged her tramping through the heather for days. Even so, she needed all her concentration not to trip over the clumps of heather and rocky outcroppings.

While they walked, Ian continually scanned the hills, ahead and behind, especially before they crested each hill. Each time he signalled for her to duck down, her heart rose in her throat. He was clearly intending not to be surprised as they had been the day before.

The next hill they crossed brought them to a valley so small it was more like a crevasse. A cottage snuggled against its craggy cliff. A tiny croft with a peat-covered roof neatly held down with a spiderweb of ropes weighted with boulders. Two people conversed outside the front door, an old crone and a ragged child with a basket over her arm. Rust-coloured chickens were picking about in the dirt at their feet.

'Let's hope Grannie has a stew pot over the fire,' Ian said. 'And whisky on her table.'

Selina's stomach growled at the thought of hot food. She quickened her pace.

Ian stayed her with a touch to her arm. 'Wait here. I'll make sure things are what they seem.'

Whereas she would have charged in and devil take the hindmost. It was a good thing one of them had some sense. Sighing with relief at the chance to rest, she sank down on a rock and watched him stride down the hill.

Such a braw laddie he looked in the sunlight. Her heart lifted at the sight of his broad shoulders and the way his kilt revealed his strong calves and manly knees. He looked at home and very much in command.

The chickens scattered with clucks and squawks at his arrival. The old lady shielded her eyes from the sun. The girl stared up at him with awe.

The old woman beamed, obviously recognising him. She might have been welcoming the Prince Regent, so effusive was she as she gestured for him to enter, bridling like a girl in her eagerness.

The child curtsied.

The charming smile on Ian's face would make any female bridle. He looked so handsome when he smiled. He glanced in her direction, indicating he had a companion. Once more the woman put a hand up to shield her face. In an instant, her demeanour changed. She waved her arm first in one direction, then in another. An argument seemed to ensue. Selina could hear the old woman's raised voice, but not the words. She ended her diatribe, waving an admonishing finger in his face.

The child fled.

How very odd. Highlanders were known for their courtesy, especially to travellers, even if it was only a dram of whisky and an oatcake to see them on their way.

To her surprise, the woman disappeared inside the

croft and slammed the door. The sound reverberated off the rocks and crags and faded in ever-quieter echoes.

Ian stomped back towards her. As he drew closer, she could see the glower of anger on his face and behind it worry.

She pushed herself to her feet. 'What happened?'

His mouth flattened to a thin line. 'The soldiers were here.'

Her heart picked up speed. 'Looking for us?'

'Aye. She sent them off with a flea in their ear.'

'I thought she was going to let you in.'

'Aye.'

'Then she realised I was with you.' The rejection stung.

'I told her you were my cousin, but, given what the soldiers told her, she refused to believe it.'

'And because I am an Albright she doesn't feel the need to offer hospitality.'

'Her son was transported for poaching on your father's land.'

'Oh, dear.'

'Her son was one of the lucky ones. Tearny shoots first usually.'

Tearny was the land agent. 'Not on my father's orders, I can assure you.'

He shrugged. 'Be that as it may, we have no choice but to go on.'

She glared at him. 'If Mr Tearny is shooting people on Albright land, he will be punished.'

He cocked his head on one side. 'All right. You will speak to your father. Let us leave it at that. We will walk many a mile before we find another house where we can request food.'

'And no doubt they will turn us away, too.'

'Not everyone is as bitter as Grannie.'

Hopefully not, or it would be a long hungry walk to the mail coach.

He looked off into the distance. 'I think I will speak to Niall before we go too much farther. Find out what the soldiers are doing. I may have to go to Dunross myself.'

A feeling of panic ran down her spine. 'You can't leave me out here.'

'Laird.' The high-pitched voice came from behind them. 'Laird.'

Ian glanced back.

Selina turned right around. It was the girl who'd been at the old lady's door, hurrying after them, her basket held out to the side as if she feared whatever was in it would break.

'Wait,' Selina said to Ian, who seemed inclined to keep walking. 'Don't make her run.'

The girl arrived, bright-eyed and panting. Russet curls escaped from beneath the ragged shawl she had pulled over her head and her dark green eyes darted over Ian and Selina in several wide-eyed passes. Her cheeks flushed scarlet.

'Well,' Ian said when she didn't speak, 'what do you want, Marie Flora McKinly?'

'Ian, you will scare her. Give her a chance to catch her breath.'

Still the girl didn't speak. She curled her toes around a stem of heather, watching her foot, peeping up at Ian as if he was some sort of ogre.

Ian said something in Gaelic in a gentler tone.

The child took a deep breath and gabbled away for a minute or two.

He shook his head at the child and again spoke in Gaelic.

The child's chin went up. Her eyes flashed.

'What have you said?' Selina said. 'Why is she angry?'

Ian muttered a curse. 'She's offering us food at her father's house a couple of miles from here. I don't want to put them in danger.'

'There's only Da, miss,' the child said in a lovely Scottish brogue. 'And me and my two brothers. My Da would never forgive me if you didna' take a dram with him, Laird. He's been dying for some company and news for weeks. We've food in the larder.'

Selina looked at Ian. The child looked at Ian. The frustration on his face was evident. Not only did his people have a duty to him, not to accept an offer of hospitality would be an insult.

'Very well. We'll visit with your Da for an hour or two and then be on our way.'

Marie Flora gave a pleased little hop and a skip. 'This way.'

She started up a hill that seemed steeper than all of the others they'd come across. Instead of heading south, she was going west.

Selina took one look at the miniature mountain and groaned.

'Do you think you can make it?' Ian murmured and took her arm to help her. 'It might be better if we didn't use your last name with these folks.'

'Doesn't she know it?' She indicated the child.

'Grannie McLeod guessed immediately, but didn't speak your name. And nor did I.'

'McLeod. I remember her, now. She used to live in the village.'

'Aye, until a year ago when she didna' pay her rent and was evicted. That was her son's place. When her son was shipped off, she cursed the Albright name all seven ways to Inverness.'

She flinched. 'I'm not surprised she was angry.'

'She's an evil auld woman. She cursed the factor, too,' Ian said. 'He came down with an enormous boil on the end of his nose the day after he barred her door.'

He was teasing her. Had to be. 'Served him right.'

''Tis no laughing matter. She cursed auld Willie McLaughlin and he died within the week.'

A year ago was when she had had her accident. The thought of the old crone's curse being responsible sent prickles racing across her shoulders. 'Superstitious nonsense.' Yet she shivered.

'Believe what you will, my lady.'

She huffed out a breath. Now he'd gone all stiff and starchy again. She glanced up ahead and saw they'd reached the top of the rise. Her aching calves and thighs were looking forward to a downhill incline.

In the valley below them, a croft sat beside a small burn, longer and lower than the one they'd just left and as small as a doll's house. They had a good distance yet to go and Marie Flora was waving at them impatiently.

Worry consumed Ian. Its cold breath licked at his brain, at his gut, deep in his chest.

You abducted Albright's daughter, Grannie had said, repeating what the soldiers had said. *Are you mad? He'll hang ye and anyone helping you.* The old witch had shut the door in his face. A face that probably looked guilty, because while he hadn't abducted her, he had spent the night with her in his arms. And he would have liked to do a hell of a lot more than that, after their kiss.

The force of what he had felt for this *Sassenach* girl was quite different to anything he'd ever experienced in his life—and he and Drew had sampled their share of females in their wild youth. Women far more experienced in tempting a man than Lady Selina. Hell, he'd even considered marriage to a warm comfortable widow he'd been seeing for years, until Selina's letter had arrived and turned his life upside down.

Thank God, he'd had enough control not to ruin her last night.

But she was ruined. Somehow the soldiers knew Lady Selina was with him. Or they suspected it, anyway.

The only way to avoid it was to marry her. Acknowledging the truth was like taking a fist to the gut. He didn't want to think about it.

The very idea left his head spinning. He couldn't afford a wife, certainly not one of her calibre, a woman used to nothing but the best. And Albright's daughter, to boot. But he was beginning to feel as if there might be no other option, just as Angus had suggested.

The cottage at the bottom of the glen drew ever closer. William McKinly was a proud, stiff-necked man. If he would take payment for their lodging instead of seeing it as charity, Ian wouldn't feel so bad about accepting food and drink. But he wouldn't and that was that.

Before he realised what she was about, Selina left his side and cut across the side of the hill, heading for a burn. Cursing, he followed, watching as she stood on the bank, looking down at the water. What the hell was she about now?

Did she have any idea how delicious she looked in her wild gypsy skirts, with her dark hair hanging in a tangled mane down her back? She looked like a lass well bedded, that's what she looked like. Even if she wasn't.

The constant arousal that he'd been dealing with since she'd kissed him of her own free will and a night spent curled around the softness of her curves, her scent filling his nostrils, hardened to rock.

He wanted to reach out and pull her into his arms, kiss those lovely lips and plunge into her heat. Know her, the way a man wants to really know a woman. And if he was honest, it seemed it might be only a matter of time before he gave in to the torment of lust.

Well—apparently he'd made the decision. He could only imagine what she was going to say.

'Don't fall in,' he said, reaching her side.

She gave him a mock glare. 'I'm not that clumsy.'

She wasn't clumsy at all. She was graceful, even with the small hesitation in her step that appeared when she was tired. Small and delicate like a wee faery. And all he could think about was getting her in his bed. And there was only one way to accomplish it. Marriage.

It seemed that the seed planted by McIver had taken root.

He watched her balance on a rock, crouch and scoop the water in her cupped palms, sipping delicately as water trickled through her fingers. A sylph who had used her magic to capture him. She shook her hands, wiped them on her skirts before jumping clear.

This was the way he'd remembered her as a girl. A free spirit wandering the hills. Sneaking out of the keep to meet him day after day until he'd been thoroughly enchanted. But she wasn't a sprite. She was the daughter of a powerful man. His enemy. And if the man had hated his family before, this was going to make things worse.

She looked over. Caught his gaze and smiled. 'It tastes lovely.'

Hellfire and brimstone, he'd been staring like some besotted calfling. 'If you are done, we'll get along or McKinly will think we are no coming at all.'

He hadn't meant to growl, but it was better than grinning at her like an idiot.

The smile left her lips. She climbed up the shallow bank. He turned and walked down the hill, leaving her to make her way as best as she could. It was either that or take her in his arms and kiss her senseless.

Tonight. He'd reveal her fate tonight, after dinner.

Marriage to a *Sassenach*. And an Albright to boot. What the devil would his mother say? And the clan? Damn them all, if they didn't like it, they would have to put up with it. He was their Laird. They would abide by his decision.

Marie Flora and her father were waiting at the croft door, where the heather had been beaten back by soft springy grass. A small vegetable patch behind the cottage was bare of all but a few turnips.

'McKinly,' he said, holding out his hand as he neared the man's threshold. For once, Selina hung back. Afraid of her reception, no doubt.

'Laird,' McKinly said. His hair was copper-coloured. Darker than his daughter's and shot through with silver. The man was stooped and weathered and could have been anywhere from forty to sixty years old, but Ian knew him to be in his late thirties. Crofting in the Highlands aged a man early.

'Are you well?' he asked.

'Aye. Come in. Come in. Take a dram with me. The lass says you're in need of sustenance.' His gaze went to Selina, curiosity shining in his blue eyes.

'Aye, if you can spare it. My wife here is bone weary.'

Wife. The moment he saw McKinly's measuring stare he realised there was no honourable alternative. Having said it, he had a sense of accomplishment. She'd got herself into this mess trying to help him for friendship's sake, or out of some misguided sense of obligation, and a Gilvry always paid his debts. They didn't ruin innocent females, either.

He'd bring the clan round to his way of thinking. Indeed, it was none of their business whom he took to wife. They'd accepted his decisions up to now and they would damned well accept this one. His mother and brothers would be a different matter and so would her father. It was customary to ask a father for his daughter's hand, but it wasn't as if Albright could refuse. Not under the circumstances.

Marriage to Selina wouldn't be such a bad thing. He definitely wanted her in his bed more than any other woman he'd ever met. He'd been aching from the denial all night. And he had no doubt that she wanted him, too. It was a starting place and surely not such a bad one.

Aware of Selina's sharp stare and her prodding finger in his ribs, he glanced down into her upturned face. 'Isn't that right, my sweet?' The thought she might deny his words burned a path through his gut.

'So you are married, then?' McKinly said.

Ian looked at Selina, warning her with his gaze.

'Yes,' she said finally. 'We are married.'

And that was that. Guilt churned in his gut that he'd not discussed this with her, but there would be time enough later.

She smiled at their host. 'I am sorry to be such an imposition, Mr McKinly. We appreciate that you were not expecting us and would not wish to put you to any trouble.'

Politeness itself and no brittle society manners, no breathy little-girl voice, just a calm friendly manner with a touch of a lilt to her voice. He let go a sigh of relief.

McKinly grinned. 'Welcome, lady.'

His last-minute instinct had been right. As his wife, she lost her status as *Sassenach*. Stranger. As his wife, any discourtesy to her was discourtesy to him.

A boy of about six wiggled his head between his father's legs. 'Is that the Laird, Da?' He turned his face upwards to look at Ian. 'Is it?' The child spoke the Gaelic.

'Oh,' Selina said. 'And who are you?'

'My youngest son, Tommy,' his father said, shaking his head at the impish face. 'Come away, lad. Let me pass. How is the Laird to get through the door with your head blocking my way?'

The head disappeared.

McKinly stepped aside and gestured for them to enter. Ian bowed to Selina and waved her forwards.

'Thank you, Mr McKinly,' she said as she passed the man and stepped inside. 'I am honoured by your hospitality.'

He felt as proud as a barnyard cock as he followed her in. A peat fire smoked in a low stone hearth with a stew pot hung over it. The dwelling was poor, but it was clean. The small boy retreated to settle beside the fire and pulled a whittling knife from his pocket and a small piece of wood.

Ian watched the way Selina looked around the croft, her face carefully blank, but he could imagine what she was thinking.

A pang of guilt twisted in his chest. This was not the kind of dwelling for a woman used to the luxuries of life, a woman brought up to live in the society of London. Married to him, her lot would be little better.

He would make it better.

'I am glad to see you well, McKinly,' he said in tones a little too hearty, but apparently McKinly noticed nothing wrong.

'You were lucky to catch me at home,' McKinly said as he poured drams into clay drinking cups. 'I was off to make hay in the next valley this afternoon.' He offered one to Selina. She smiled and shook her head. McKinly's eyebrow shot up, but he made no demur.

McKinly did not deserve to have his hospitality thrown back in his face. Ian's voice was harsh when he spoke. 'Take a dram with us, lady wife.'

Eyes wide, Selina looked ready to argue, then pressed her lips together as McKinly handed her the rejected cup and poured another for himself.

Selina shot Ian a look while the man's back was turned. No doubt he'd hear some words from her, but he was glad she decided to wait to get him alone before speaking her piece. She was a smart woman, no doubt about it.

'I'd no heard you were getting married, Laird?' McKinly said, his face full of curiosity. He shook his head. 'Though there's no reason why I should, I've seen no one for weeks. My congratulations to you.' He smiled albeit a little grimly. 'And to you, lady. Please be seated.'

Selina's smile as she took the wooden chair he offered was stiff. 'You are very kind, Mr McKinly.'

Marie Flora stood beside her, staring at her adoringly. Ian knew the feeling. Even here in these dreadful surroundings, and after a night spent in the worst of circumstances, she was lovely.

'To you and your bride,' McKinly toasted.

Ian tossed off his dram. Selina wet her lips and her eyes watered. At least she didn't cough and choke.

While McKinly turned to refill his and Ian's cups, Ian took hers and swallowed down the contents. She gave him a smile of gratitude and refused the refill offered by McKinly.

The man gestured for him to sit on the trestle at the table, his eyes sharp and bright. 'What brings our Laird wandering the hills on foot?'

'Gaugers,' Ian replied, seeing no reason to lie. All Highlanders despised the King's Revenue men.

McKinly frowned. 'You're a fool to be running afoul of them and you just married.'

'Aye.' Ian grinned. 'Needs must.'

'You'll be wanting a room for a night or two, perhaps?' McKinly said.

'At least one night, if you can spare it. A corner by the fire or in the byre.'

McKinly looked shocked. 'Certainly not.'

Selina looked doubtful. 'We should really be moving on.'

Ian shook his head. 'Not until we know how things stand at Dunross.'

She looked ready to argue, then shrugged. 'Then thank you, Mr McKinly.

'Not at all,' the Scotsman said. He glanced at his daughter. 'Marie Flora, put fresh linens on the bed.

The child beamed. 'Yes, Da.'

Selina smiled at the child. 'Show me where it is and I will help you.'

The lass was doing her best not to shame him. Somehow she knew this was important. His heart seemed to grow too large for his chest, as if he really was a proud bridegroom. Well, he was, really, wasn't he?

He gave her a grin of approval. She raised a brow in reply and rose to follow the child.

'I'll see you at supper,' McKinly said, rising to his feet. 'My older lad has already left for the fields. I was waiting for the girl to return with the eggs before joining him.'

'About that older boy of yours—I've an errand for him.'

'Oh, aye.'

'I need him to take a message to Niall.'

McKinly looked grim, but nodded his agreement.

Ian had a pretty good idea of the source of his worry. 'I'll take up his scythe while he's gone. It will do me good to get some exercise.'

McKinly's face split in a grin, clearly relieved. 'Well, now, there's always plenty to do around here.'

'Can I come, Da?' the boy sitting in the corner asked.

'No, Thomas,' his father replied. 'You have your own work to do. And I need you here to take care of the womenfolk.'

The boy's scrawny chest puffed up and then he returned to his work with the knife. Ian moved closer to see what he was working on, but the lad hunched over it. 'It's not finished.'

'Leave him, Laird. The lad is a mite odd about his carvings. Doesn't let anyone see them until they are done.' He raised his voice. 'Marie Flora?' The girl popped her head out of the adjoining room. 'We'll see you at suppertime. Be sure you have a good meal waiting.'

'Yes, Da.'

Selina appeared beside the child. Ian leaned in and kissed her lips and almost chuckled at her gasp of surprise. 'We'll talk later,' he murmured against her mouth. When he pulled away he saw a blush creep up her snowy cheeks.

Because he'd kissed her in public. He wanted to do it again.

'Yes,' she said, with a tight little smile. 'We will talk later.' That sounded like a threat.

She ducked back into the chamber.

Ian shrugged and followed McKinly outside. He would just have to find a way to make her see he was right.

What a wretch, Selina thought, staring at the four-poster bed crowding the small sleeping chamber off the kitchen. Beside the bed there was a chest in one corner and a faded and patched runner on the floor.

Lies had tripped off Ian's tongue as if he was the devil himself. She should have denied it all. But she couldn't. Not without shaming him in front of his people.

'Whose room is this?' she asked Marie Flora as the girl expertly twitched the blankets off the bed and piled them on the rug.

'It used to be Ma and Pa's room,' the girl said. 'Now I sleep here and he sleeps in the loft with the boys.'

'Oh, dear. We don't want to put you out of your bed.'

''Tis a privilege and an honour to serve the Laird.' The girl smiled shyly at Selina. 'And his new wife.'

Guilt twisted in her stomach. These people would be so angry if they knew who she was. Selina took the end of the sheet at the foot of the bed and Marie Flora took the end nearest the head and they pulled it free. The mattress had seen better days, but it was clearly the best they had and Selina was certainly not going to complain.

The child pulled out linen sheets from the chest, thin and patched here and there, but spotlessly clean. Together they made up the bed. When they were done, Marie Flora patted the blanket with a smile. ''Tis a comfortable bed. Not many has one like it. Father built it when he was first married. Ma died when Thomas was born.'

'I'm sorry,' Selina said.

The girl shrugged. 'We buried her up on the top of the hill. She liked to go up there and look at the mountains.'

There was a little sorrow in the girl's voice, but mostly acceptance.

'How many children are you altogether?'

'Four. My older brother is away south to the mines, he sends money when he can.' Marie Flora headed back into the main room and Selina followed her.

'What else can I do to help?' Selina asked.

'Can you peel tatties? We've to make the stew go further.'

'Tatties? Oh, you mean potatoes.' It was a long time since she'd heard that word used. Not since she used to hang around the kitchen at Dunross, getting under Cook's feet. 'Yes, I am sure I can.' How hard could it be?

Chapter Eleven

Marie Flora stumped in with a bucket of water and a frown on her face. 'Thomas, are you still here? Did Father not ask you to move the cow to the other pasture?'

The boy shoved his whittling in his pocket and left without a word.

'He's such a dreamer,' Marie Flora said. She put the bucket between them and went to a bin in the corner where she gathered an apron full of potatoes and put them beside the bucket. She handed Selina a knife. ''Tis sharp. Mind you do not cut yourself.'

Quite the little mother and not at all shy any more. Selina couldn't help but smile. She watched the child peel her first tatty and then began to work on her own.

'Not sae deep,' the girl said sharply.

Selina looked up.

'You are cutting too much of the flesh,' Marie Flora said. 'There'll be nothing left. Watch.'

Clearly if she didn't get this right her worth was going to go down in this young lady's eyes. She watched closely, saw how she rested her thumb against the vegetable and skimmed the skin away.

She tried again. This time she did better and the child

nodded her satisfaction. She grinned to herself. This was nice, sitting here working on something useful with a companion, instead of setting fine stitches within an embroidery hoop on a piece of cloth only fit to adorn something that was already beautiful enough.

'Dig the eyes out like this,' Marie Flora said, showing her how she twirled the point of the knife in the little brown indentations. She put her finished potato in the bowl and washed another one before starting in on it with her knife.

Selina finished her first one by the time Marie Flora had done three, but she elicited no more criticism so she assumed she was doing it right, if slowly.

Thomas wandered in with a wooden bucket full of creamy milk. It sloshed over the side when he closed the door. His sister muttered something in Gaelic and leapt to her feet. The boy went bright red. She snatched the bucket from his hand, all the while scolding. The boy shot Selina a considering glance.

'Don't you have any Gaelic at all?' he asked.

'Not really.' She knew a few curse words, but it would be better not to say those. She would save them for Ian when he returned.

Married, indeed. At least he could have warned her. And now they were to share that bed in there. Her traitorous body tightened at the thought and she flushed warm all over. But it would be just like last night, she reminded herself. They would sleep. Nothing more.

The potatoes were finished and her hands were red, raw and numb from the cold water. This would be the kind of thing she would have to learn if they really were married. It would be a very different life. And fraught with danger, no doubt. A trickle of excitement flowed through her.

Marie Flora handed her a towel and turned to her brother. 'Thomas, take these peels outside, then take yourself off and cut some peat for the fire.'

Thomas picked up the bucket and heaved it out of the door. 'I'll add just these tatties to the stew and then we'll make bannocks,' Marie Flora said.

'You'll have to teach me that, too.'

'The Laird's wife doesn't know how to make bannocks?'

She winced. 'I'm afraid not.'

'Oh, aye, you'll be living in that grand house in the village. Da took me there once to sell—' She clapped a hand to her mouth.

She rushed off and busied herself at the table, cutting up the potatoes and adding them to the pot over the fire, which was already giving off a delicious aroma.

First Marie Flora put a large flat rock on top of the fire. 'The bannock stane,' she said at Selina's surprised expression. 'We don't have a *girdle*.' She meant a griddle, Selina guessed. The girl then put out flour in a bowl and mixed it with water. After turning it into a flat round bread, she carefully put it on the hot stone. 'It won't take long.'

Selina's stomach grumbled loudly.

The girl looked at her in astonishment. 'Are you hungry?'

It was then that Selina realised that she had eaten nothing since dinner time the night before, apart from a handful of oats this morning. How could she ask for food when these people had so little?

'A glass of water is all I need,' she said, taking a mug from the shelf on the wall and pouring a glass from the pitcher on the table. It would hold her until supper. Unless by some wonderful chance of fortune they ate at midday.

Marie Flora finished cleaning up from her baking and Selina smiled at her. 'What next?'

'I have some darning if you've a mind to help me. With Da and two boys there's always a muckle of mending to be done.'

Selina laughed. 'Well, that is one thing I know I can do.'

Marie Flora pulled out a basket full of what looked like rags, but as she held them up Selina saw they were rough homespun shirts and hose that had been patched and darned more than once. Immediately, she settled herself down to make the necessary repairs and while she worked she asked Marie Flora to teach her the Gaelic words for the things around them. The time flew by.

Selina didn't remember a time when she had felt more at ease within herself or had spent so pleasant an afternoon. She was still wondering at the strange feeling of contentment when a noise outside had Marie Flora leaping to her feet. ''Tis Father home for his dinner.'

She packed her sewing in the basket and took the shirt from Selina, who had just finished turning the cuff, and began setting the table.

Selina went to the window and saw a man dismounting from a horse.

Not in uniform, but still her heart began to race. Was it someone looking for her and Ian? What should she do?

'Marie Flora, it is not your father.'

The child left what she was doing and came to the window. She frowned. 'Why, it is Mr Tearny, the rent man. It is not his day to come.'

Tearny. An employee of her father's. Was it coincidence he was here?

'The Laird and I do not want anyone to know where we are,' she said quickly.

The girl's face asked why.

'Please, Marie Flora, do not mention you have seen us.' She slipped into the bedroom listening as the girl answered the knock on the door, hearing the rumble of the man's voice, but not clearly enough to make out the words.

Her heart banged against her ribs. Her body vibrated with the force of its beating and all the while she was torn as to whether she should simply go out there and ask him to take her home.

Leave Ian without a word of farewell?

She couldn't. It would be wrong. Besides, she had no idea what sort of welcome awaited her there. She might be thrown in prison as a smuggler.

The moment Marie Flora closed the outside door Selina stepped out of the bedroom. The child's face was white; she looked ready to faint. She held a paper in her hand as if she feared it would bite.

'What is it?'

She raised her gaze and Selina saw tears standing in her moss-green eyes. 'I have not opened it. It is addressed to Pa, but Tearny said it is a notice to leave.' She held the paper out and Selina saw the Albright seal.

'Why?'

'We havena' paid our rent this quarter. Da needed a bit more time.'

Her stomach sank. What was Father about? It was wrong to throw families out of their homes. He might be ambitious, but she had never thought him cruel.

Sounds of voices outside sent Selina skipping back into the bedroom and Marie Flora running to the window.

'It is all right,' Marie Flora called out. ''Tis Father and the Laird washing up for dinner at the stream.'

Selina closed her eyes with relief, but the heartache remained. It was wrong to turn out this family.

His hair damp, his shirt wet and clinging to his broad shoulders from where he had bathed, Ian looked weary, but also mouth-wateringly attractive. Selina had trouble forcing herself not to stare.

She'd been running into this problem from the moment she had seen him at Lord Carrick's drum. It was pathetic. Where Ian Gilvry was concerned, she was pathetic.

And now she had all her hopes pinned on him being able to help this small family.

''Tis a good day's work we did today, lass,' McKinly said, his weary face wreathed in a smile as his gaze rested on his daughter. 'The Laird did young Willy's share as well as his own.'

'That's good news, Father,' Marie Flora said. Her gaze dropped to the letter on the table.

'What's this, then?' he asked.

'Mr Tearny left it but a few moments ago. I am surprised you didn't see him.'

All the joy went out of the room and the shadows in the corner seemed to encroach as McKinly picked up the paper. His gaze went to Ian, who gave a single regretful shake of his head.

Young Thomas barrelled in. 'Pa,' he yelled, 'there are soldiers riding in the glen.'

'Ah, saints give me strength. Not so soon.' He ripped

open the paper. He stared at it, his lips moving as he read the words.

Ian's shoulders tensed. He looked as if he wanted to snatch the paper and read it for himself. Instead he went to the window and looked out. 'How far away are these men?' he asked Thomas.

'They were at Grannie's house.'

His father looked up sharply. 'You ijit, boy, I thought you meant they were coming here.'

The boy looked offended. 'They might come here next. They were asking Grannie if she'd seen any travellers in the past two days.'

Ian stiffened. 'What did she say?'

The lad gave a sly smile. 'She said the only thing strange within twenty miles was the boggert she'd seen last night wandering the hills to the north. They rode off in that direction.'

Ian relaxed. 'She's an evil old woman, but she's not a traitor.'

McKinly glanced down at the paper in his hand and then handed it to Ian. 'We have a week to come up with the back rent or we must pack up and go.' Hands flat on the table, he bowed his head, his eyes closed.

'I could—' Selina started.

Ian cut her off with a sharp chop of his hand and a glare.

'We will sell the cow and the calf,' McKinly said. 'I'll take it to market.'

'But, Father,' Marie Flora said, 'we need the milk.'

Her father let go a long breath. 'You are right, lass.' He looked at Ian. 'Will you buy my barley? It will soon be ready for harvest.'

Ian's jaw flickered. 'What about bread for your children.'

What on earth did he mean?

'Happen there'll be enough coppers left after Albright is paid off to buy bread.' He looked hopeful.

Selina felt sick. How could Father do this?

Young Thomas crouched beside the hearth, his face pale, his eyes scared. A weight descended on Selina's chest. She longed to offer comfort, to reassure this small family that everything would be all right, but she couldn't. She had given up any hope of influencing her father by warning the smugglers and then riding off with Ian. And if she hadn't, she would not have known any of this. But there must be something she could do.

McKinly glowered down at the paper. 'These notices have been going out for weeks to anyone behind in their rent. Will you buy my barley before I bring it in? Will you risk it?'

'Aye,' Ian said, nodding. 'It looks like a good crop. Too bad we didn't know about this before your boy left, he could have brought the money back with him.'

'We have a week,' McKinly said. 'I look forward to seeing Tearny's face when I hand him the money.'

Ian held out his hand with a grin. 'It is a bargain. Tomorrow we'll work on clearing the other field of rocks, so you can plant more barley next year.'

McKinly turned to his daughter. 'See what it is to have a Laird who cares about his people, lass? Now, where is that dinner I am smelling? My guts are kissing my backbone, I'm that hungry.'

The sight of McKinly acting cheerful, when he must be feeling desperate, made Selina feel worse than ever. She could only be thankful he didn't know who she was. He would surely not be inviting the daughter of his landlord to sit down at his table.

The sense of being watched made her glance at Ian

and she found his eyes fixed on her, his eyes narrow, his lips pressed together, as if he was holding back words, yet his gaze when it rested on her was hot.

An answering heat flared in her body.

'After dinner, we'll talk.' His deep voice held a promise.

Supper over and the children put to bed, Selina sat beside Ian on the settle with the obligatory dram of whisky in her hand. She took a cautious sip. This time it did not burn so much. Holding the cup between both hands in her lap, listening to the men chatting idly about the weather and crops, she could almost imagine living this way for ever. Preparing food for a husband and children and then sitting companionably in the evening talking about the day. It wouldn't be an easy life, but it would have purpose.

For the first time in a very long time she felt a sense of belonging. She sighed.

Ian's hand closed around hers. Startled, she glanced up at him.

'The glass was about to fall,' he said with a smile. 'You must be exhausted.'

It was a pleasant kind of exhaustion. Not the kind one experienced after a ball, when one's head pounded and one's feet ached from being trodden upon. It felt good. She nodded. 'I should go to bed.'

'A toast before you go,' McKinly said, filling his and Ian's glass. 'To the Laird and his bride. May you be blessed with many sons. *Slàinte!*'

The two men downed their drinks in one swallow. Selina took another sip.

McKinly refilled his and Ian's glasses. Selina held her hand over the top of hers. 'No more for me, thank you.'

Ian raised his glass. 'To my host. May your sons and daughter grow straight and true.'

McKinly looked pleased and the two men downed their whisky in unison.

Ian looked pointedly at her glass.

Oh, dash it. She tipped her glass and swallowed it down, sitting utterly still as the heat travelled down her throat into her belly and she tried not to gasp.

Both men laughed, but there was a pleased look in Ian's eyes, a warmth that heated far deeper than the spirit.

'It will help you sleep,' he said.

'Aye, and keep out the chill,' McKinly said. 'There's no fire in yon room, but there's privacy.'

'Go to bed, wife,' Ian said gently enough, but there was no mistaking the command.

She bristled.

He must have seen because he raised a dark brow. 'I've a few matters to discuss with McKinly, but I'll be there shortly. You will not be lonely for long, that I promise.'

Heat rushed to her face. He was making it sound as if, as if… Well, as if they really were man and wife.

She got up with a smile and sent a narrowed-eyed glance his way so he would be under no misapprehension that they would indeed talk. The grin he sent back was deliciously cheeky.

The man was impossible. And incredibly handsome.

Still, he was only playing his part—besotted bridegroom—when the truth couldn't be more different.

Ian handed her a candlestick and escorted her to the bedroom door where he raised her hand to his lips.

'I'll be along soon,' he murmured, his voice offering a sensual promise. She didn't know if she wanted to slap him, or rise up on her toes and press a kiss to his smiling mouth. She whisked into the room before she did either and shut the door behind her, leaning against it.

She heard his deep chuckle before he moved away. The sound drifted around her like smoke, weakening her limbs, making her heart open with tendrils of hope.

No.

The world had turned upside down. Her heart was lying to her. Ian was a dangerous man. He thrived on adversity. All she wanted was a pleasant husband, a house in a good part of town and a comfortable life with the people she knew in the society where she belonged.

This tramping around Scotland was like Marie Antoinette pretending to be a milkmaid in the gardens of Versailles. It wasn't real. It wasn't her life as she had planned it.

The sooner they parted, the better it would be for her peace of mind.

Running from the keep had been madness. She could have handled her father's anger. And she would not have buckled under any amount of badgering. After all, who could possibly believe a feather-headed society miss would ever step out of the bounds of propriety to aid smugglers?

Father might suspect the worst after Lisbon, when she ran off without her chaperon, but suspicion wasn't proof. Clearly in hindsight, running away with Ian had been a mistake of monumental proportions.

Her only hope was to get to Alice before Father did. Hang waiting for word from Ian's brother Niall. They had to go and go quickly, first thing in the morning. They'd wasted too much time here already.

'That's a right pretty bride you've found yourself, Laird,' McKinly said, his deep voice carrying through the door. 'And a good lass from what I see, but delicate. 'Tis a shame about the limp. The Highlands is no place for the weak. You'll need to guard her well.'

'Aye,' Ian said, non-committally.

A burst of anger filled her veins. Whether it was because he made no attempt to deny her weakness, or because of the lies they were telling a man who had shown them nothing but respect, she wasn't quite sure. Either way it was only by clenching her fists that she managed not to open the door and tell them she could hear every word, thank you very much.

The voices reduced to a low rumble, probably moving on to other topics. There was no point in airing her grievances with Ian in front of one of his clan. She'd save her words for when they could be private.

She placed the candlestick on the table holding a ewer of water and a bowl and stripped out of her bodice, skirts and the breeches beneath, leaving on only her shift, washing herself quickly with the rag provided and clenching her jaw to stop her teeth from chattering as the cold water hit her skin. If Ian could wash in a cold stream out of doors, she could surely manage this, even if she was sure she could see her breath rise in front of her face.

She stripped the blanket off the bed and dumped it on the small rug, then spread her cloak over the rough linen sheet before climbing in. Shivering beneath the thin covering, a sense of disappointment filled her. McKinly was right after all. She was not hardy enough for this life.

She watched the shadows from the candle dance on the rough ceiling and tried to stop the spasms of shivers by rubbing at her arms and legs to generate warmth.

Would her life ever return to normal? There would be no marriage, of course, no home or little Dunstan children, even if her visit to Alice was taken at face value. They'd all assume she'd jilted the young lieutenant. It would be the *on dit* in town for weeks. A man didn't suffer that kind of embarrassment lightly.

She'd have to start all over again, looking for the right kind of man for a husband. Strangely, the loss of Dunstan didn't bother her as much as she might have expected. Indeed, it was as if she'd been carrying an enormous weight and someone had lifted it from her shoulders.

Perhaps Dunstan hadn't been such a good choice after all. Perhaps she wouldn't marry anyone. The little bit of money left to her by her mother would allow her to live in independence, if not luxury.

She'd be an outcast. Considered odd. After she'd spent all her time these past many years trying to fit in with society's expectations, too. All her hard work destroyed in a moment of madness. A moment of fear for a man she should have ignored altogether.

The voices on the other side of the door fell silent.

The door opened, the draught making the candle gutter. She sat up.

His gaze flicked down to her chest and back up to her face, his brows climbing.

Oh, right. She was wearing nothing but her shift. Heat flooded her face. She pulled the hem of her cloak up to her chin and opened her mouth to speak.

He pressed a finger to his lips and jerked his head towards the door, obviously not wanting McKinly to overhear their words. He closed the door and stared down at the blanket on the floor and then over at her.

She could not read his expression. 'We must talk,' she whispered.

He strode to the bed. He looked big in the dim light. Huge. In some way, he reminded her of a predator stalking its prey. In another, of a male standing guard over his female. In either case, it was imagination playing tricks. He no doubt regretted their wild flight as much as she did.

The thought made her feel hollow.

Ian sat on the edge of the bed. The ropes creaked and her body tilted towards him as if it sought the comfort of his heat and his strength. She resisted the pull, leaning away, gripping the fabric in her hands more tightly.

'I thought you'd be asleep by now,' he said softly. 'But here you are, waiting up for me.'

She gasped at the audacity of his words even as her insides melted.

He looked so beautiful, rugged, the haze of stubble darkening his jaw, his full lips curling in a half-smile that teased.

She drew in a quick steadying breath, determined to resist his allure. 'Why on earth did you tell McKinly we were married? I thought we were going to give a false name. Tell him I was your cousin.'

'He knows all my cousins. It was better than telling him you were my—' He shut his mouth with a snap.

'Your mistress?'

'That is one word for it.'

'He won't be pleased when he learns who I am and that we are not married. I feel bad about lying.'

His mouth tightened. 'We do have to talk about that.'

'We can't stay here. We must leave first thing in the morning. We have to reach Hawkhurst as quickly as possible.'

'We will wait to hear from Niall.' He touched a finger to her cheek. 'I was proud of the way ye helped the young lass there with the meal.'

A warm glow suffused her skin. Furious at herself,

at the way she responded to this man, she jerked her head away. 'I did what anyone would do. Ian, listen, if I am to salvage anything of my reputation, I must get to Hawkhurst soon.'

His eyes turned hot. 'Your eyes are beautiful when you are passionate.' His low whisper strummed chords low in her belly.

A breath caught in her throat. Her heart stumbled. The glow turned to fire and she saw the answering blaze of heat in his face. And then his mouth was on hers and she was surrendering to the delicious sensations of the warm slide of his tongue, the feel of his large solid body under her hands.

Swept away by the passion he seemed to arouse in her so easily, she kissed him back. Whisky. She should not have had the whisky. It seemed to have muddled her head, taken away her will and left her longing for his touch, for the delectable sensations of the night before.

She dragged her lips free, felt the sting of regret. 'We must not.'

His glace flickered to the blanket on the floor. 'Ah, that is a hint, is it? It seems a little unfair when it is our wedding night.'

Blankly she stared at him, at the rueful twist to his mouth, the wariness in his eyes. And the regret.

A trick of the light? Or some sort of horrible jest? The kind his brothers had played on her that long-ago summer. Luring her on, then running away. Before he'd arrived and turned her world upside down. 'I don't think much of this joke.'

He reached out and forced her fingers free of the cloak. He frowned. 'Are you always this cold?' He enfolded her fingers in his and she felt his heat permeate through her skin. Seductive warmth.

She tugged at her hand, but he did not let go. His eyes regarded her intently. 'It is no joke. You see,' he said softly, 'under Scottish law, if a couple says they are married and act married, before witnesses, then that is what they are. We declared ourselves wed before we set foot in this house. McKinly is our witness.'

She uttered a cry of horror.

He quickly covered her mouth with his hand. 'Hush. Do you want to bring McKinly down on us?'

His hand was large and warm and gentle. She glared at him.

'Speak quietly,' he said.

She nodded and he released her.

'I am not Scottish,' she whispered. 'It was just a story, to…to protect my reputation. We can't possibly be married.' The pitch of her voice rose in panic.

An expression flashed across his face. Anger? 'The law applies to whoever is within our borders,' he spoke flatly, his face like granite. 'When McKinly questioned you, you confirmed it of your own free will. We are married.'

'Y-you tricked me,' she spluttered. 'You don't want to be married to me.'

Resignation filled his expression. 'We have no choice in the matter.'

Hurt by his obvious regret, she glowered. 'No one but McKinly knows. We can just pretend it never happened.'

His brows lowered, his expression became harsh. 'Just because I'm a Scot doesna' mean I have no honour. The law is the law.'

'What about the law banning smuggling?'

'That's different. It is an unjust law.'

'So you pick and choose the laws you follow?'

His lips pressed together. He shook his head. 'Don't

you see, we dinna have a choice? You said it yourself. Your father will reach your friend before you do.' He stared at her for a long moment as if considering what he should say next. 'I'm not unhappy about it.'

'Nothing has happened between us.'

'We kissed,' he said softly, his blue eyes dancing. 'You slept beside me.'

And there it was again. The pull inside her. The longing to melt against him. The desire to give in and enjoy.

No other man had had this kind of power over her. If only she could truly believe he wanted this marriage. That he wouldn't regret it later.

Hadn't she already seen the regret in his face? Heard him agree with McKinly that she was not the kind of lass who could live in the Highlands?

'My father will never allow it. He will have it dissolved.' Could he?

His expression darkened. He muttered something under his breath in Gaelic. 'Let him try.'

This wasn't working. He wasn't listening. She touched his arm and felt a tingle in her fingers. Saw his arm twitch in response. She forced herself to ignore the sparks dancing between them and softened her tone. 'Ian, you don't want this. Neither of us does. Just get me to Hawkhurst and I will plan some way out of this from there.'

He shook his head. 'It is done.'

Done. Why did it sound like he'd been given a prison sentence? Because this was not what he wanted. No doubt he felt as trapped as she did. 'Alice will say anything I ask her to say. Even if Father reaches her first and she says she hasn't seen me, she will recant. She could say she was afraid for me and had me tucked away in her house all the time.'

'He would believe you walked there alone, no doubt?'

Did he have to be so practical? And was that hope she heard in his voice? The hollowness in her chest grew. 'I am sure I can come up with a plausible explanation. A ride with a carter.' She gave him a sweet smile and batted her eyelashes.

His brows went up. 'Days and nights on the road alone. Your reputation will still be ruined.' He shook his head. 'You helped me, now I will help you. Our being wed is the only option.'

Chapter Twelve

Ian had never seen a more beautiful woman. Her heart-shaped face was female perfection, her creamy skin translucent in the candlelight. However, her expression was determined.

For a moment, when he'd first mentioned marriage, he'd thought she seemed pleased, but her arguments said otherwise. Disappointing, but not surprising. His only option was to make sure the bargain was properly sealed, irrefutable.

He would have to mount a seduction. His blood warmed. He caressed her small palm with his thumb and felt her tremor in response. Her ruby lips, so lush and so delicately bowed, parted in a small gasp.

She was a passionate woman and her response to him was all in his favour.

'It doesn't matter what you say, lass. In the eyes of the world, we are married.'

She bit that lovely, full bottom lip with small, even white teeth. He wanted to bite it, too. He leaned closer, watching her eyes widen and sensing the movement of her throat as she swallowed. She straightened her shoulders.

And that was what he found so damnably attractive. Yes, she was tiny and delicate, but she had an inner resilience. She met life head on. She was just the sort of woman a man would be proud to call wife and not just because of her beauty.

'Come, now,' he cajoled. 'What do you say?'

She tilted her head, looking at him sideways, smiling just a little. 'I say I don't recognise this law of yours.' The tone was teasing, as if she knew she was defeated, but was fighting a fine rearguard action he couldn't help but admire, even as it infuriated.

It was as if the wild Scottish blood of his ancestors took over his body and his mind. He wanted to roar like a berserker and swing his claymore at his enemy—only there wasn't one, not one that could be seen. The problem was their history and that he couldn't change. His best weapons were logic and soft words, but he was having trouble keeping that in mind. 'You would prefer the wedding night wait until a minister can be found?' It wasn't a fair question. She was already flushed. Already breathing fast. But he wasn't going to rush her. Tonight was too important.

She leaned back against the pillows, looking up, considering, gauging. 'Are you saying you would marry me against my will?'

'I did not take you for a fool, Lady Selina,' he growled, his voice like gravel, his body rigid with the desire he fought to contain. 'No man will have you after you ran away with me, especially since, without a word of protest, you played my wife. You have no choice but to wed me. Or I you.'

'How romantic you make it sound.'

He winced. Clearly he did not have a courtier's way with words, but the twinkle in her eye said she was playing with him. 'We are in this together whether we wish it or not.' He gazed at her lovely face, at the hint of the delectable body he'd held close and not touched. He lowered his voice, let his longing show on his face. 'Why should we not make the best of it?' He reached out and stroked his thumb across her cheekbone. 'Don't fight me on this, lass. We both know what we want.'

The shocking words tightened Selina's core.

She fought the desire inside her and gave him a soulful pout and a doe-eyed glance and let a teasing smile play about her lips. 'La, sir, you are indeed very forceful in your arguments,' she said in a whispery voice. 'but I am not so sure we will suit.'

His eyes flashed fire. 'Don't do that.'

Forcing herself not to recoil, she raised a brow. 'Do what?'

'Simper at me as if I am some Bond Street beau and we are engaged in a drawing-room flirtation.'

'Is it more than that?'

A muttered word in Gaelic ripped through the air. He rubbed the back of his neck. 'Of course it is. Your reputation is at stake.' His Scottish brogue seemed to deepen, become more darkly delicious. More him, yet the words were painful to hear. An admission that it wouldn't matter what woman had rescued him, he would feel honour bound to marry her.

So was he glad that it was she and not some other woman whom he found himself tied to?

'Our families are enemies.' She raised an arched brow as if they were discussing the latest fashion, instead of dire consequences. 'Your father would turn in his grave.'

He shook his head. 'I am not my father. Besides, a marriage between us can be a way to make peace between families. A way to move on from the past.'

Irrationally hurt by the cold of his reasoning, she closed her eyes briefly. It did make sense. As much, if not more sense, than an alliance with Dunstan's family. The Dunstans were old stock, but not particularly ambitious—one of the reasons she'd thought him such a good prospect.

Father might be brought to see the benefits of a marriage in time.

'Wouldn't a wife cramp your style? You would have to give up smuggling.'

His shoulders stiffened. 'That is my decision to make.'

Not about to be guided by a wife, then. Most men weren't, which was why she had been so careful in her choice of Dunstan.

Strangely, the thought of marriage to Ian made her heart pound hard—a much different reaction to the thought of wedding Dunstan. Dunstan was safe. Ian Gilvry represented all that was danger.

'The idea of marriage to you scares me.' The words flew out of her mouth before she could stop them.

A brow flew up. 'I see you as scared of nothing.' His voice was dark with amusement. 'You used to give my brothers as good as they gave.'

'Until you took their side.'

He inhaled a deep breath. 'And regretted it every day since.' He leaned forwards and brushed his lips across hers. 'You were such a brave little thing.' He sighed. 'And you never told your father. He would have crushed us with a word from you, yet you never complained.'

'I'm no telltale.' She frowned. 'Which is why you should have trusted me enough to let me go home.'

'That had nothing to do with trust.'

And everything to do with the safety of his clan. She sighed. It was too late to worry about what might have been. He was right. Whatever she did now, she would be ruined. She'd been discovered missing from her bed. Not even Alice could protect her from such a scandal.

'What do you say, Selina?' he murmured, eyeing her mouth like a hungry wolf. He brought her hand to his mouth and brushed his lips across her knuckles. 'Do we consummate this legal marriage tonight? Or do we wait until we find a minister and I retreat to my cold hard bed on the floor?'

So, he'd thrown down the gauntlet. Likely a foolish thing to do with a woman as strong willed as this one, but he couldn't see any other way to proceed. He just wished she'd trust him to decide what was right or wrong. She saw smuggling as criminal, instead of a way of feeding his people. She had to learn to trust his judgement, as his clan did.

He stroked the hair back from her face, willing her to understand that he had duties and responsibilities apart from pleasure.

Her skin warmed to his touch. Her eyelids fluttered, her lips were parted, ripe and ready for him, and he took them carefully. Like last night, when her response had been hungry and full of fire. Only by dint of will had he left her as he had found her. An innocent.

But not tonight. Tonight he was a married man.

A pulse of heat tightened his groin and he almost groaned aloud with the rush of pleasure. He cupped her jaw and angled her head for better access to her honeyed kiss. Her hand released its death grip on her cloak and lay flat on his chest.

For one moment he thought she would push him away, a last-ditch effort to deny him, but her small palm caressed the contours of his chest, her touch feathery light, but searing.

Then her arms crept up around his neck, pulling him closer, melding against his chest where they touched, her heart beating wildly, her breathing coming fast and furious against his cheek. The vibration of a soft moan in the back of her throat sent a jolt of lust to his belly. Beneath the heavy wool of his kilt he hardened.

Grim satisfaction filled him and he tasted her whisky-flavoured tongue and the dark recesses of her sweet mouth.

He wooed her with his lips, his teeth and the hands gently stroking her chilly shoulders and stifled a groan of frustration.

Unless she accepted they were well and truly wed, he could do nothing about the lust gripping his body.

His mouth on her lips, his large warm hands on her shoulders plied her with unexpected gentleness. Sensual. Seductive. Heat trickled along her veins, searing her skin, leaving it tingling and burning. Her breasts, pressed against his chest, felt heavy and full. Her core ached and pulsed, begging for the pleasure he'd brought her before.

Her head swam at the battery of sensations rippling through her body.

Gentleness was not what she wanted. She didn't want to be the china doll upon the shelf, the spun-glass ornament to be looked at, but not touched for fear of shattering.

His touch was delicious, achingly so, but it wasn't enough for the woman inside, the tempestuous female she had spent years battling into submission. The one who, left to herself, took risks. That woman, who wanted this big rough Scotsman who had carried her off to the hills. And that woman seemed to have taken control of her body.

Exploring his shoulders through his shirt, she was very much aware of their magnificent breadth and power as the muscles bunched and rippled beneath her hands. She raked her fingers through his silky-soft hair. Wound the strands around her fingers and tugged.

A hitch in his breathing. Surprise. A quickening of his heartbeat. More urgency in his kiss.

His tongue swept her mouth, then began to withdraw. What madness drove her, she wasn't sure, but she captured it with her teeth. He stilled.

She released him.

He drew back, breaking the contact between them, except for his hand on her upper arms and hers sunk deep in his thick dark hair. His eyes glittered and his chest rose and fell with each harsh breath.

Ah. It seemed she'd gained his full attention. Her lips were tingling, her face glowing from contact with his scruff of beard and she flashed him a saucy smile.

'So, Ian Gilvry,' she breathed in the little-girl voice that had brought the men of the *ton* to their knees, 'this is our wedding night.'

His gaze dropped to her mouth and then rose to meet her gaze. He smiled. 'It is, indeed.'

He sounded relieved, as if he really did want this marriage. She let her fears, her suspicions, slide away.

Her heart raced as if she had run a great race. His large body pressed against her chest as he leaned over her, the circling of his fingers on her shoulder, his breath against her cheek. Her chest felt so full of longing, she couldn't breathe around it.

'Well, the floor does look very hard and very cold. I could not let you spend such an uncomfortable night.'

His lips curved in a smile of pure seduction. His eyes lit up, gleaming like sapphires. Never had she seen him look so young or so boyish.

'So this surrender is all for my sake, is it?'

She grinned. 'Oh, I think it brings some benefits to me, too.'

He leaned in and bit her bottom lip. Pleasure raced through her body, settling deep in her core. She gasped at the wildness of it.

On a soft laugh, he thrust his tongue in her mouth commanding her to yield to him, pressing her down into the mattress as his body lined up with hers and his thigh pressed between hers. The weight of him melted her bones. She felt as if she could absorb him into her skin, as if they could fuse into one being. And all the while his lips teased hers and his tongue darted into her mouth, leading her on, encouraging her to follow.

Emboldened, she tried a hesitant lick. He captured her tongue with his teeth, then sucked.

Shivers of pleasure racked her from head to toe. Something deep inside her pulled tight. She gasped at the onslaught. He released her.

'You taste so good I might just swallow you whole,' he murmured and kissed the tip of her nose.

She nipped at his lower lip. 'Not if I eat you up first.' He chuckled as if she'd made a grand jest. She bit his rough chin, his cheekbone, his earlobe when he turned away. A quick hiss of his breath tightened the knot low in her belly. Interesting. It wasn't only what he did to her that felt good, but how he responded to what she did to him that made her body quicken and burn.

He captured her face in his hands, his thumbs gliding

over her cheekbones, his gaze intense. 'I swear, from this day forth, I will honour you as my wife all the days of my life, in sickness and in health until death do us part.'

A wedding vow. It made her heart clench painfully, a kind of aching joy as it seemed constricted within her chest. 'As will I,' she managed, despite the tightness in her throat.

Then he was kissing her again. Through the haze of the delicious sensations produced by his mouth on her lips, she was aware of the sharpening need between her thighs as his knee forced them wider. The pressure of his hip against her mons felt both wonderful and tantalising.

A thumb grazed the underside of her breast, leaving a searing trail of heat, but his touch was still too light, too gentle. She made a sound in her throat, half growl, half purr, that he captured in his mouth. She wasn't even sure if he heard it. He must have. His hand moved higher, covering her breast, exploring and massaging.

She writhed beneath his touch and a sound of approval rumbled up from his chest.

His thumb teased her nipple through the fine lawn of her chemise. Another zing of shocking pleasure. She gasped. Shock had no place in this congress between them. They were now man and wife and she was melting and tingling all at the same time. Beneath her palms the vast plane of his back felt hot through his shirt. Her skimming fingers felt muscle and bone; the scent of him, soap and male, filled her nostrils and her heart felt full.

She was in the arms the man she'd always…loved? She closed the door on that thought. It made her feel far too vulnerable. They were marrying for expediency, accompanied by pleasurable benefits.

He wrenched away from her, breaking the seductive

spell. Slowly her mind cleared as he gazed down at her, his eyes hot, his expression hungry.

All her life she'd been running from men who looked at her with heat. Putting up barriers. He was the only man she'd ever run towards. What was done could not be undone. The consequences would be in the future.

He knelt up, pulled his shirt free of his belt and pulled it off over his head, tossing it to the floor.

She gazed at him with awe, just as she had the first time. He was glorious. Carved beauty. A god of war complete with battle scars and a bandage around his most recent brush with danger. Rather than mar, the silvery lines of old scars accentuated the purity of his form.

Not so the ruined flesh of her thigh. Would he find it as ugly as she did? Would he regret his offer to wed once he saw the damage her foolishness had caused?

With hesitant fingertips, she traced a scar slicing across two of his ribs. He caught her hand and brought it to his lips.

He slid off the bed and unbuckled his belt. 'We'll have no secrets between us.' His voice was a low growl. And a challenge shone in his eyes. 'No uneasy coupling in the dark.' He let the kilt fall.

His phallus stood erect, dark and huge, aggressively jutting from its dark nest of curls. It was enormous. A pearl of moisture beaded on its tip.

She swallowed. Licked her lips, her mouth gone dry. Her face blazed with heat. She raised her gaze to meet his.

'Dinna be afraid, lass,' he murmured quietly. 'Not of me. I would never do aught to hurt you.'

'I'm not,' she assured herself in a whisper. Not of him physically, in truth. Mostly she feared what she might see on his face when he saw her body. Her scars. That she might see revulsion or, worse yet, pity.

'What troubles you?' he asked.

She must be wearing her fears on her face—something she never did as a rule. She took a deep breath. There was no going back. No changing the past, so she had best have it done with.

'No secrets.' She flung back the cloak, which had slipped below her waist along with the sheet. With a swift intake of breath, like the one taken before plunging into cold water, or before telling the truth when a lie would be easier, she hitched the chemise up to her waist and drew it off over her head.

Gooseflesh raced over her skin. Her nipples tightened with cold and with nerves. Determined not to flinch, she stared at his face, watching his reaction.

At first, he looked startled. He probably hadn't expected her to be quite so bold. Then, as his gaze swept downwards to her bounteous bosom, a bosom which had been the subject of more than one rake's ode, his expression softened to heavy-lidded appreciation.

He inhaled a long breath. 'Lovely,' he said.

She resisted the urge to cross her arms over her breasts. The males in London had, after all, seen all but the deep-rose peaks rising from her skimpy muslins and silks. They'd ogled her figure from the moment of her come out and must have had a pretty good sense of what lay beneath.

What she really wanted to do was turn on her side, hide her right leg with her left, but it was too late. His gaze had already reached her navel and was travelling to the nest of curls below the curve of her belly.

She knew when he took in the scars. His brows drew together and he glanced up at her face. Despite being

ready, she averted her face and reached for the sheet to
hide the ugliness, but his hand was already smoothing
first down one thigh, then the other.

She dared a peek at his expression. No pity, just raw
sensuality. Perhaps he hadn't noticed? She placed her
hand over the ruined flesh, halting the soft swoop of his
hand travelling upwards from her knee.

He glanced up as if surprised.

She felt her face heat. 'It is not a very pretty picture,
I'm afraid. I was such an idiot and lucky I didn't injure
anyone else. Hawkhurst saw the whole thing and managed to free the horses before they came to any harm.'

'Your friend's husband?'

His matter-of-fact tone made her feel a little less unsure. At least he wasn't reacting with horror. 'Yes. His
quick thinking saved my leg. The doctors didn't think I
would walk again.' She gave a casual flick of her fingers
across the ruined flesh, hoping her voice did not reveal
her embarrassment. 'If it disgusts you, we can blow out
the candle. Or we can forget all about this.'

'Oh, *leannan*, sweetheart, is that what you think?'

He picked up her hand and kissed her palm. Heat shivered through her veins. He placed it on the scar on his
chest. 'Do you find this unpleasant to look at?'

She swallowed. 'It makes you look like a warrior.'

A low chuckle vibrated beneath her palm. 'I thought
so, too. I caught myself with a scythe when I was fifteen,
but I told all the ladies it was a sabre cut.'

'Men are supposed to have scars. Women are supposed to be perfect.'

He shook his head. 'It is a part of you now. And just
as perfectly lovely as all the rest.' His hot gaze swept up
her body to her face.

He must have seen the doubt because he continued

talking, his tone low and seductive. 'There is far more to a woman than mere physical beauty. There is the spirit too, you know. But you are just as beautiful to me here...' his fingers traced the jagged criss-cross of pink lines and the misshapen muscle, his touch gentle, almost reverent in its lightness '...as you are here.' He tickled the back of her knee.

Tears welled in her eyes, even as she smiled. Too much emotion. Too much gladness.

'Don't cry, darling,' he murmured. 'I promise to be careful.' He leant down to press soft kisses along the length of the wound.

Spun glass again. 'No,' she said, grabbing his shoulders, forcing him to look into her face. 'Don't treat me like an invalid. Or a doll. I am a woman. I won't break.'

A slow smile dawned. Blue heat flared in his eyes. 'Aye.' He nodded. 'A woman you are. All spit and claws.'

He took her mouth in a punishing kiss. Hard. Demanding.

Clenching her hands on his muscular shoulders, she made demands of her own. Pulled him closer, until he tumbled down on the bed beside her, parting her thighs to accommodate his weight in the cradle of her hips.

He broke free on a muttered curse, sliding down her body, trailing searing kisses and hot caresses with his hand. He stopped at the valley between her breasts, cupping them in his hands, drawing first one nipple into his mouth, then the other.

No gentleness. No featherlight brushes. His touch ravaged, as did his mouth. The touch of a man who loved the feel of her flesh in his hands.

He laved her nipple with his tongue, swirling heat, followed by sudden chill when he paid similar attention to her other breast.

His lips and tongue teased her breast as she watched from beneath lowered lids and clutched convulsively at his hair at each liquid tug on her insides.

While his mouth brought her exquisite pain, his hands stroked and kneaded her ribs, her hip, her belly, a slow downward slide of hot rough skin on skin so alive her mind seemed ready to splinter.

Chapter Thirteen

Permission to lose control? Encouragement to let the primitive beast out of its cage? Lust gripped Ian hard.

The urge to mark her as his, to brand her with lips and teeth, to let the force of his desire take him to mindless bliss, tempted him sorely.

Beyond reason.

The bite of her nails in his back and buttocks, the way she tasted his shoulder with tongue and lips and teeth, drove him mad.

Muffling a groan, he took one deep breath after the other. She had to be ready for him. He had no choice but to hurt her, but he would give her pleasure ahead of the pain.

Arching his back, resisting her pull, he took her mouth, the faint taste of peat-smoky whisky lingering on her tongue. And as their mouths melded and toyed with darting licks and sucking, his right hand palmed her mons, the curls damp, the flesh hot.

He pressed down with the heel of his hand and she whimpered her pleasure into his mouth. Her body arched into his hand, not knowing what it needed. Not yet.

Slow and easy he parted her delicate folds by touch,

exploring her entrance, longing to see. Not this time. This was not his time. He slipped his little finger inside her, overawed at the tightness. At the barrier he could feel at her entrance.

She stilled. Her breathing hitched. He grabbed a deep but ragged breath through his nose and held still while she became accustomed to his intrusion.

He broke their kiss to look down at her face. Her eyes were hazy with passion, her lips red from his kisses, her cheeks, too, from the abrasive touch of his beard. It was a mark of sorts.

With his thumb he stroked in circles until he found that little nub that offered a pleasure all of its own. Her eyelids drooped. She looked wanton. Abandoned. His shaft pulsed its demand, dragging all thought from his head in the quest for completion.

He circled harder and faster. She gasped, her hips bucking wildly.

Her gaze flew to his face, her eyes wide with shock and hazy with pleasure. Her breathing halted. Rigid, she hung on the crest.

And tumbled over in a climax of quivers.

Now. He plunged into her. Losing himself inside her depths, still feeling her wince of pain, even as the bliss roared through her blood and claimed her.

His own climax came on him fast. Out of control, not careful as he'd intended. His hips pounded into her and she clung to him with knees and heels and hands on his shoulders. And he rode her to completion as the clenches of pleasure of her core milked him dry.

Spent, and trembling like an exhausted stallion, he kissed her shoulder. He stared at that small bone with the silken flesh stretched over its delicate contour and was horrified to see the marks of his teeth.

So much for being in control.

He stroked her glorious mane of black curls back from her sweat-damp temples and kissed the pulse beat where the skin was traced with blue, then her lips.

'You are wonderful,' he breathed. 'My wife.'

'My husband,' she whispered in return, claiming him as he had claimed her. No one could separate them now.

He rolled on his side and held her tight to his body, reaching down to cover them with the sheet and her cloak. In a moment he'd get up and get that blanket. In a moment.

He closed his eyes and savoured the warmth flowing through his body.

Fists pounded on a door.

Someone yelling. 'Open up!'

McKinly's sleepy voice cursed.

They were found. Ian sat up, his mind racing. Had McKinly's lad inadvertently given them away? He leaped from the bed and hurriedly belted on his kilt, not bothering with a shirt.

'Who is it?' Selina asked.

In the pitch black of the early-morning hours, he could hear the worry in her voice, even if he could not see her face. 'I don't know. Get dressed and wait here.'

He opened the latch on the window and pushed it slightly ajar. 'In case we need to leave in a hurry,' he explained in a whisper.

She was already fumbling around for her clothes. No words, no panic, just getting on with what needed to be done.

He slipped out of the door and closed it behind him.

'Open up,' the voice yelled again.

Niall's voice. The tension in his shoulders eased. He

nodded at McKinly to open the door and the man raised the wooden bar. The door flew back.

'Ian!' Niall said, striding into the room with Logan close on his heels. He punched Ian's shoulder. 'Thank God we heard from you in time.'

'What is it, man?'

Logan went to the fire to warm his hands, his young face troubled.

For once, Niall's expression was sharp. And worried. 'Albright has the militia crawling the countryside looking for you. For smuggling and abduction. Finally the bastard has found a way to hang you. You'll have to leave. Go to France. America.'

Like hell.

McKinly's mouth was hanging open.

'Who am I supposed to have abducted?' Ian asked.

'His daughter. Logan said she was there on the headland. Now she's missing.'

Logan's eyes widened, staring over his shoulder.

Ian spun around. The door behind him had opened and Selina stepped out. Her black hair loose about her shoulders, the bright red of her skirts swirling around her ankles, with her flushed face and rosy lips, she looked like a woman well bedded.

Niall's jaw dropped. 'God, Ian, what have you done? We'll all hang.'

McKinly looked startled.

Ian pulled her close to his side, felt the stiffness in her shoulders. Fear, when up to now she'd been fearless. He gave her an encouraging smile.

'Lady Selina has done me the honour of becoming my wife.'

'Your—' Reading Ian's glare, Niall spluttered into silence.

Logan's eyes narrowed. 'You are a disgrace to the clan, Ian Gilvry. How could you? After her family stole our birthright?' His gaze ran over her, a bitter twist to his lips. 'I can understand you wanting to bed her. But marriage? Our mother will never forgive you.'

Selina gasped, tried to twist away from him. He held her fast. 'Mother will have to accept it. As will you.'

'Albright's daughter?' McKinly echoed. 'In my house?'

Ian shot him a glare, then directed his ire at his brothers. 'The lady is my wife. You will treat her with the respect that is her due.'

Logan opened his mouth to argue and Ian thought he was going to have to take him outside and pound sense into him. One thing a Laird could not allow was his men, any of them, to disobey a command. He should have known how it would be. If this was his brothers' reaction, the other clansmen would be worse.

He glared. 'I mean it, Logan.'

The lad put his hands up. 'All right.' He bent his head a fraction. 'I apologise to your lady wife.' Disgust dripped from his tongue and Ian still wanted to hit him.

Niall's expression was simply one of confused horror.

Selina's face paled, her lips tightened, yet she remained still at his side. He should have warned her how it might be, but he thought there would be more time.

McKinly sank down on the chair and scrubbed a hand across the back of his neck. Then one corner of his mouth kicked up. 'There is no crime in wedding a willing lass. 'Tis a fine plan for revenge you are having on Albright. Running off with his daughter.'

Another gasp from Selina. She looked up at him, a question on her face. 'You planned this?'

'You know very well I did not,' he said, angered by the note of accusation in her voice.

Niall looked thoughtful. 'You sly dog,' he said suddenly, a slow smile dawning on his face. He swung a punch at Ian's gut and missed when he jumped back. 'The keep. After all these years, Dunross Keep is back in the family.'

'It is?' Logan said, raising his gaze to Ian's face. Ian stared at Niall.

'Aye,' Niall replied. He looked at Selina. 'I heard from one of the lasses at Carrick's castle that she was betrothed to a *Sassenach* and the keep was part of the settlement. It will come to you now.'

His jaw dropped.

Selina slipped out of his grip, her expression wary. 'This was your clan business with Angus, wasn't it? This is the plot the two of you were hatching out of my hearing?'

Remorse stabbed him hard. Angus had put the idea of marriage in his head, but he'd known nothing about the keep. Guilt must have showed on his face, because her expression of outrage turned to one of disgust. 'I should have known,' she said, backing away. 'You are no better than Andrew. Cheating to catch yourself an heiress.'

The words were a slap in the face. Pride rose like a beast in his blood. 'I'm proud of any comparison with my brother.'

Logan and Niall ranged on either side of him, fists clenched. They looked ready to tear her limb from limb. A week ago he would have looked the same way himself.

Instead an overwhelming urge to protect her forced him to turn and face them as he thrust her behind his back, shielding her with his body. 'Enough,' he roared.

He turned to her. She glared at him, defiant as a kitten faced with a bull mastiff, claws ready to scratch. 'We are married, that is an end to it.'

Logan spun away. 'Wait until our mother hears this news.' With that he was gone out into the night.

Ian started after him.

Niall put out a hand. 'Let him go. He'll come to his senses soon enough.' He looked at Selina. 'He'll see the sense in it when his blood cools. As will our mother. And the clan. In one blow, you've solved all our problems.'

Selina's face was as white as a ghost, her eyes dark and accusing. 'You tricked me.' She turned on McKinly, who looked as if he could catch a fly on his tongue, his jaw hung so low. 'It is not true. We are not married, Mr McKinly. There has been no ceremony. No wedding.'

The repudiation hurt deep in his chest. A visceral sensation of loss. No. It was anger. She hadn't minded the idea of marriage an hour ago and now she was shaming him before his clansmen. And herself into the bargain. He wanted to shake her. He kept his fists balled at his sides, while he fought to contain his rage.

McKinly scratched at the night growth on his chin and glanced at Ian. 'Makes no nevermind what you say now, my lady. You said you were married, then you slept in my bed as husband and wife.'

Her cheeks fired bright red. Embarrassment. Shame. Hurt. It was the last that made Ian feel sick. 'I knew nothing about the keep. It may not come to pass.'

She drew herself up to her full height, staring down her nose with an arrogance he could not help but admire, even as her resentment infuriated him. 'That was why you went apart with Angus. He told you, didn't he? That's why you looked so guilty just now. That is why you tricked me into this marriage.'

'No.'

'I don't believe you. This marriage will never stand in an English court of law.'

'It will,' he said harshly. 'It always has. Deny we are wed and what does that make you?' Ian wished he'd held his tongue as she flinched.

'Selina,' he said more gently. 'It was done of your own free will. No one forced you.'

To his sorrow, tears welled in her eyes. He reached for her hand to pull her to his side, but she dodged out of reach.

He'd been wrong about the tears. Her eyes were blazing with anger. 'I hate you.'

Damn it all, if the clan sensed he was not in control of his wife, then there would be bickering among those who thought he was right and those who thought he was wrong. It would tear them apart. 'We will discuss this later. Leave us. I have business to discuss with my clansmen.'

She curled her lip. 'More secret talks.'

'Clan business. I will join you shortly.'

She glared at him, saw he was not going to relent and tossed her head. 'If you will excuse me, gentlemen, I never stay where I am not wanted.'

That had the sound of a threat. The way her eyes flashed in temper was magnificent, and the swirl of her skirts around her legs fired his blood as she headed for the bedroom door. And his bed.

'Spoilt little *Sassenach*,' Niall said, *sotto voce*, but not so quietly that she didn't hear. Ian knew by the way her spine stiffened. But he thanked God when she said nothing and closed the door with a sharp snap.

'I'll support your choice, lad,' McKinly said. 'She's no such a bad lass. Look at the way she helped my Marie Flora.'

Niall grinned. 'I think it is a brilliant move. The answer to all our prayers, you clever dog. I'll even drink to your health, if McKinly will part with a dram of his whisky.'

Brilliant. If he could only convince Selina to feel the same way. Seduce her again? His body hardened. Again.

He hadn't had this many jolting arousals since he was a lad. But he did not want an unwilling wife. Hell, he had not wanted a wife at all until he had the Gilvrys solvent. At least, not until this woman ran across his path again.

'We need to get back to Dunross and have a word with Albright,' he said. 'Without running into the militia. They seem of a mind to shoot first and ask questions after.'

Niall eyed his bandage and whistled. 'It seems they mean business.'

'So do I. Let's have that dram, McKinly.' He needed some fortification before he faced his wife.

The sound of mugs being set out and filled percolated through the bedroom door.

The truth was a bright sharp blade to her heart. No matter what he said, it was quite clear he had used her. Tricked her. She paced away from the door, striking her fist in her palm, her anger too great for calm acceptance. Anger and mortification. She felt like a fool—worse, she felt betrayed.

If only he hadn't kissed her in the cave. Only once before had a kiss overpowered her senses. And it ended with her getting hurt. Badly.

That kiss had been Ian's, too. He'd left her to join his brothers in their teasing. He hadn't thrown any rocks, but he had said she wasn't wanted.

It seemed she had not learned her lesson. Only this time the pain in her chest felt much worse.

She drew in a steadying breath. No point in moaning about what could not be changed. At least she knew the truth. Could work out her options.

She glanced at the open window. It wouldn't be difficult to leave and disappear into the night. And go where?

To Alice. Deny the marriage had ever happened for all she was worth? Or go home, bat her eyelashes at Father and pretend she'd been lost all this while and knew nothing of smuggling or smugglers?

But as she'd realised earlier, it was too late to save her reputation. Any hope of marrying Dunstan had flown the moment she'd set out to warn Ian. Was that why she'd done it? As a means of escape? She squeezed her eyes shut. Tried to go back to the moment she had made the decision, to test her real intentions.

Had she really used it as an excuse to avoid marrying Dunstan? A form of running away. The way she'd run from Lisbon?

No matter how she looked at the situation she found herself in now, though, running was not an option. He'd taken her to bed. And she had been willing, because she thought they'd found something meaningful.

Bitterness rose in her throat. He'd tricked her into marrying him so he could regain Dunross Keep. How stupid could she be?

Tricked her with kisses and seduction.

And she'd fallen into his hands like a ripe plum. Or Dunross Keep had.

She groaned. Father was going to be so angry when he discovered she'd handed over the keep to the Gilvrys. And he must be worried. Why else would he have the militia out looking for her supposed abductor? A militia that seemed ready to shoot on sight. Her blood ran cold.

She flung open the door.

The three men around the trestle table gaped at her. Ian rose slowly to his feet, a frown on his face. 'Selina,' his said, his voice a warning.

'If we are going to Dunross, we should leave now,' she announced. 'Before it gets light and we are an easy target for some ambitious soldier.'

A smile spread across Ian's face. She glared at him. 'That doesn't mean I am happy about this situation. You've got your keep and a marriage of convenience.'

Niall gave her a narrow-eyed stare. 'You'd be a fool to trust her, Ian.'

Chapter Fourteen

To her surprise Ian had agreed they should leave right away. They'd bid McKinly goodbye and Selina left a message of farewell for Marie Flora.

She had ridden Beau, while the men had walked ahead, talking in Gaelic, excluding her from their conversation. How typical.

The sun was not very high in the sky behind a pall of grey clouds when they walked into the Barleycorn's courtyard.

Willy Gair came out of the stables and stared at them, his mouth agape. He looked at Ian, then at Selina and frowned.

Ian issued a sharp order in Gaelic.

The man seemed inclined to argue, then bowed his head and shot off.

Selina leaned over Beau's neck the better for Ian to hear her. 'I thought we were going to the keep.'

'All in good time.' Ian helped her down from the horse and guided her into the inn. 'My first loyalty is to the clan. They will have been worrying.'

And did he think her father wasn't worried? Angry, yes, but worried, too. And right now she was feeling so guilty and so stupid she wanted to see him and beg his forgiveness.

While Niall saw to the horse, Ian guided her into the inn and seated her in a corner of the taproom.

Noisy footsteps trundled down a set of narrow stairs hidden behind a curtain at one end of the room. The curtain swept aside. A man peered into the gloom. 'We're closed.'

'There's a nice welcome, Ranald,' Ian said with the ghost of a smile. 'And here was me thinking you would like to offer me dram on the event of my bridals.' He spoke in English, no doubt for her benefit.

'Laird?' The innkeeper rubbed his eyes and looked again as if to ensure he wasn't seeing things. 'Are you mad? There are soldiers everywhere seeking you.' He peered over Ian's shoulder. 'And the lass is still with you? You'll hang for sure.'

'I don't think you heard what I said. Lady Selina has done me the honour of becoming my wife.'

Shock, followed swiftly by horror, chased across his face. His mouth opened and closed.

'Would you like some coffee, my dear?' Ian said, giving Ranald time to recover. 'If mine host can remember his manners, that is.'

'Tea, please.'

The man choked. 'Tea. Right.' He picked up a bottle, uncorked it with his teeth and took a deep swallow. He clung on to the bottle like a lifeline, staring at Ian.

'Tea,' Ian said.

'I'll have Bridie put the kettle on.' He put the bottle down and scurried behind the curtain. Ian went behind the bar and pulled a fresh bottle from the shelf. He poured a dram into the glass and looked at her with a wry twist to his lips. 'That went well, don't you think?'

'No.'

'It will get better, I promise.' He swallowed the whisky down and poured another glass. Then poured one for Niall when he came in the door.

Bridie, a plump, rosy-cheeked woman of about forty, brought a tray with a tea pot and milk. She gave Selina a hard look, but said not a word. She gave the same look to Ian and hissed something in Gaelic before disappearing behind the curtain.

'What did she say?'

He hesitated.

'I can go and ask her to repeat it in English.'

'She said he ought to be ashamed of himself,' Niall said. 'The words were different, but that's what she meant.'

Selina felt her cheeks go hot. 'I really think—'

Two men entered the taproom—Tammy and Colin Gilvry, the blacksmith, Ian's cousin. Both men were staring at her as if she was a nasty insect they would like to squash. A shudder passed through her body. She thought she had her dismay well hidden until Ian moved closer to her side.

She couldn't help but feel comfort at his closeness. She drew a deep breath and gave the men look for look. After all, having brought this on herself, she wasn't going to cower, now, was she?

After those two, other men arrived and soon the small parlour was filled to bursting with large vengeful Scots. She really wished he'd taken her up to the keep and met with his clan on his own.

Coward.

These were his people. His clan. If her husband wanted her here, then she didn't have a choice. She'd given up all her rights with this marriage. Her blood ran cold at the thought, but she met their dark glances with as much calm indifference as she could muster. And she could muster quite a lot, given her training in the ballrooms of London.

Most of them let their gazes fall away. Except Willy Gair. He had a very strange expression on his face. Not horror, thought there was some of that, too—something more akin to fear.

Douglas McTavish grinned. 'I see you've dodged the soldiers, Ian Gilvry. Ye hae the luck of the devil himself.' His gaze slid to Selina and back, clearly demanding an explanation.

'A pox on the gaugers,' a man at the back cried.

Ian grinned. 'I'm glad to hear you all made it home safe and my thanks for ensuring the goods arrived safely at their destination. It will put coin in your pockets and enough food on the table to last the winter, too.'

'Good health to the Laird.'

'Aye, a toast,' someone yelled.

Ian put up a hand. 'There is another cause for celebration this day. Ranald, a dram all around,' Ian said. 'Then I'll offer you a toast.'

Niall looked up from the book he had pulled from his pocket when they entered. 'Are you sure you want to do this here and now?' he muttered in Ian's ear.

It seemed that for all his bookish ways, Niall took in more than one might guess.

He stood at Ian's shoulder as Ranald handed them both a glass.

'Lads,' Ian said, his face as hard as granite, 'let me introduce my wife, Lady Selina. A toast to my bride.'

No one moved.

'Sold your soul to Albright, did you?' someone said. The eyes around the room glared at her. Hatred made the air in the room thick and acrid. Selina kept her chin high, but couldn't stop leaning closer to Ian's broad form. He put a protective hand on her shoulder.

'There's no need for insult,' he said. 'Lady Selina risked her reputation to help us all. Without her warning, there'd be no profit and most of us would be in prison.'

'Aye, well, grateful as we are, Laird, no one here wants an Albright spy in our midst.'

Willy Gair looked almost green. He turned and pushed through the crowd and disappeared through the door.

'Aye, and what would your grandfather have said?' another added.

She felt his sigh of disappointment. 'Accept her or find another Laird,' Ian said coldly.

The men's faces looked grim, unhappy, but not one of them flinched from Ian's steady perusal.

For some reason, he had not told them what the marriage meant with respect to the keep. Why was that?

Niall let his gaze wander the room. There was no mistaking his anger. 'Don't look to me. I'll not usurp title of Laird from my brother. Not now, not ever.'

Selina glance up at Ian, whose eyes were full of shadows, but also resolve. He'd known how it would be, yet he was not using his most persuasive argument.

The innkeeper looked at Ian; of all the men present, his gaze wasn't quite so unfriendly. 'What about the plans you had, Ian Gilvry? The promises. The mill. The...' He glanced at Selina and away. 'You know. The plan.'

'Aye, what about the plan?' Several voices joined the chorus.

They clearly didn't trust her enough to reveal what the nature of this plan was. And she couldn't blame them.

She was an Albright and probably always would be in their eyes. Oh, why didn't he tell them about the keep? Surely it would make things better.

Ian gave the man who had called out a considering look. 'The plans haven't changed.'

The men looked uncertain. 'Your father-in-law is the magistrate. Don't tell me you have him in your pocket. I'll no believe it.'

'Her father does not yet know of our marriage. I came here first. My loyalty is to the clan. Without your support, there can be no plan. No future.' He shook his head. 'You might convince Logan to stand in my place.'

'No. You won't.' Logan must have slipped through the door left open by Willy Gair. He pushed through the crowd to stand next to Niall. 'I'm not saying I'm happy about this marriage,' he continued, flushing red to the roots of his fair hair, 'but I'll respect his choice until it is proved bad for the clan.'

Some of the men nodded. Others shuffled their feet. A greybeard in the corner eyed the glass in his hand with longing. 'So the Laird married a *Sassenach*. Surely any man with a brain can see she's a right comely lass. The fact she's the landlord's daughter can't be all bad. Can we no get to the toast? This whisky is evaporating before my very eyes.'

Chuckles rippled around the room.

'Any man who will not drink health to my bride, will put down his glass and leave now.' The command in Ian's voice was a force in the room.

No one moved.

'To Ian and his bride, Lady Selina,' Niall said.

'The Laird. Lady Selina. *Slàinte!*' The male voices were a deep rumble.

By sheer force of will, and their trust in his leadership, they had accepted his marriage. Her admiration knew no bounds.

Though nothing showed on his face, she sensed his relief. Niall, on the other hand, was grinning. 'That was a close-run thing, brother,' he murmured.

'I still had my ace in the hole,' Ian said.

'The keep,' Logan said, turning his back to the room. 'When will you tell them?'

Ian scanned the room. 'When it is settled. Who knows, my new father-in-law may try to wriggle out of the bargain.'

He couldn't. It was part of her mother's wedding settlements. The keep came to Selina on her marriage. Still, there was no reason to set his mind at rest—he'd find out soon enough.

'Well, I can tell you our mother is none too pleased,' Logan said.

'She'll see it differently when I have spoken to her,' Ian said.

'She won't have an Albright in the house, I'm afraid.' He nodded at Selina.

Ian saw Selina's face pale and her back stiffen.

'Right now it is her father I need to face. One battle at a time.' He raised his voice. 'Another round on me, Ranald. I'll settle with you later. Only one round, mind, and then send them home or they'll be getting no work done tomorrow.'

The innkeeper nodded. 'Don't worry, I'll see them away.'

'I'll borrow your gig, if I may.'

Ranald grinned. 'You'll want to make a good impression on your future father-in-law.' His face sobered. 'Do you have any idea who gave us to the gaugers?'

'None. But I will find out.'

'Aye. Let us hope so. We can't risk being caught again.'

Selina's eyes had narrowed in disapproval. Dear God, woman—not now, when the clan had barely accepted the fact of their marriage. They could make life very difficult if they thought she was trying to interfere in their business. He wanted them to get to know her and see her worth.

He hurried her outside before she could say anything, followed closely by his brothers. They watched Logan hitch a small brown mare to the gig.

'I hope I can manage my father as well as you managed your men,' Selina said.

He frowned. 'It is for me to manage your father.'

'I think not. I owe him an apology as well as an explanation.'

He looked at her for a long moment. 'Very well. I will let you speak first, but let it be clear between us that you are now my responsibility, not his.'

No doubt he thought of her like a chattel or a burden. 'He is my father.'

He closed his eyes, briefly, as if he regretted his harsh words. 'I just want you to remember you are my wife. It is my duty to keep you safe.'

Her insides softened at the protective note in his voice. The back of her neck prickled. Then she let go a breath. He had married her to get back by stealth what his family had been unable to reclaim by force. How else would he sound? He wanted to protect what he had won.

No doubt he thought she should be grateful he would let her speak to her father at all.

'Ready to go,' Logan said.

Ian turned to Niall. 'You two stay here and make sure things stay calm and reasonable.'

'You aren't going up to the keep by yourself,' Logan said, his face shocked.

'I am.'

'What if he strings you up out of hand?'

'This is the nineteenth century,' Selina said crossly. 'Not seventeen hundred. My father would never do such a thing. And without evidence, there can be no trial.'

Logan didn't look convinced, but shrugged and stepped back beside Niall. 'You're a fool to trust an Albright. It wouldn't surprise me if he wasn't involved in what happened to Drew.'

Ian's expression darkened. His lips narrowed. 'Don't you be a fool. His death is no one's fault but mine.' Pain filled his voice and his expression. Guilt, too. And deep sadness. He set the horse in motion, leaving his brothers to turn back and enter the inn.

Selina gazed at him curiously. 'What did you do to Andrew?'

He inhaled a deep breath and let it go slowly, as if planning what he would say. 'I made him board a ship for the New World. I sent him to see if there was somewhere the clan could settle should we be forced off this land.'

'Because of my letter?'

'I would not have known, if you hadn't written, to be sure.' He clicked his tongue at the horse to encourage it up the hill. 'But what he did to that young woman was wrong. It brought dishonour to our name and so I told him.'

She winced. Hadn't he just done the same thing with her? Perhaps it wasn't as dishonourable to trick an Albright as it was to trick a perfect stranger. Drew had been awful to Alice, pretending to love her when all he really wanted was her money. He'd pretended he was wealthy and seduced her to ensure she could not refuse to marry him. Worst of all, he'd circulated gossip about it as a sort of insurance.

Alice had refused to be blackmailed, and when Selina realised just who it was who was breaking her best friend's heart, she'd written to Ian and asked him to intercede with his brother. Drew had left town within the week.

'He didn't want to go. I had Carrick force him onto that ship. When months passed with no word, I assumed he was still angry. Then we got a letter. He had joined a group exploring new lands. They never returned. Drew always was reckless. He couldn't resist the adventure, I suppose. He went off to see more of the country instead of undertaking my commission. An acquaintance wrote and told us how it was. My mother blames me for his death.'

'That is hardly fair.'

'I should not have sent him away. He was my younger brother.'

'What he did was heartless.'

'Aye, but with the best of intentions. But I never told anyone it was you who let me know what he was up to.'

'Oh.'

'And nor should you.' His expression was fierce. 'They will never forgive you.'

Chapter Fifteen

The sound of galloping hooves behind them had Ian turning in his seat.

He cursed.

Selina turned to look and her heart sank at the sight of red uniforms and glittering accoutrements, the jingle of which drew ever closer.

Ian stopped the horse. 'We don't want to give them the idea we are running away,' he said wryly. 'One bullet wound in a week is enough for any man.'

More than enough. She steeled herself for the coming meeting.

The horses passed them and then circled around. Their leader broke rank and brought his horse close to the carriage. Lieutenant Dunstan, of course.

Dunstan's blue eyes had dark circles beneath them and his face looked weary. The pistol in his hand pointed at Ian's head. He bowed. 'Lady Selina. Ian Gilvry, in the name of the king, I arrest you for the crime of abduction. You will come with me quietly or risk further charges.'

'And just who am I supposed to have abducted?' Ian asked.

Dunstan glanced her way. 'This lady.'

'This lady is my wife.'

Dunstan frowned. His cheekbones flushed pink. The pistol lowered. He looked at Selina again. 'Is this true? Are you married?'

'Yes.'

The pink turned to red, the pistol coming up again. 'Under duress?'

This was her chance to be rid of a husband who had tricked her into marriage. Ian was looking at her, waiting for her to deny him, but it was too late for that. No doubt he'd haul witnesses in who would say exactly what she'd done. She shook her head. 'Not under duress.'

Beside her Ian relaxed. Good Lord, had the man planned to make a fight of it?

The expression of anger on Dunstan's face dissolved into one of disappointment. He returned the pistol to its holster. 'I see.'

She felt terrible. 'I'm sorry.'

For a long moment he just looked at her and then he bowed. 'I, too, am sorry.'

Sorry he'd lost her dowry, no doubt. There wasn't a pin to choose between him and Ian. She felt a bit like a bone between two dogs. One a foxhound and the other a wolfhound. She had no doubts about which one would win.

Ian shifted in the seat beside her and she glanced at him. He was glaring at Dunstan. A bone indeed.

'We were just on our way up to the keep to see my father,' she said.

'My men and I will accompany you,' he said. 'To ensure you arrive safely.'

'I am quite capable of driving half a mile to the keep,' Ian said grimly.

'And a great deal farther, I am sure,' Dunstan said in

arctic tones. He gave a brief order to his sergeant and the men fell in behind the carriage. Dunstan walked his horse alongside Selina.

'I gather your courtship was of the whirlwind variety,' Dunstan said after a few moments.

Ian made a sound like a growl low in his throat. A warning.

Selina nudged him with her elbow. The lieutenant could easily take it into his head to arrest him for some trifling offence, given the opportunity. 'Indeed, lieutenant,' she said, batting her lashes. 'A positive tornado. Although Mr Gilvry and I have known each other for a very long time. It wasn't until we met again that we realised our affections were still engaged.'

Not a bad story. Romantic. The kind of thing the *ton* might forgive after they recovered from the scandal.

Not that the *ton*'s opinion would matter, living here in the wilds of Scotland. But they did matter to her papa and Dunstan made a good sounding board for its effect.

He seemed to take it in stride, because he continued to smile even if his usually warm blue eyes seemed more like a wintery grey.

She slanted a glance at Ian. His expression was thunderous.

He probably preferred her to remain silent. She leaned a little closer to Dunstan. 'Were you able to catch the smugglers?'

The soldier flushed. 'You know I did not. I did hear there was a woman involved. Quite the adventuress, some are saying. I doubt it myself.' He raised a brow.

Was he trying to trick her into saying it was her?

Ian shot her a look that would make a lesser woman quake, but not one who had learned how to deal with the barbs issued by the ladies of the *ton*.

She shuddered. 'I can't imagine any lady doing such a thing.' She smiled up at the lieutenant. 'It is very kind of you to take the time to escort us when these criminals are still on the loose.'

Ian snorted what sounded like a muffled laugh.

Dunstan glared at him and let his horse fall back.

'You will get burned if you play with fire,' Ian muttered.

'He tried to trip me up.'

They passed through the heavy wooden gate into the keep and Ian drew the horse to a halt on the cobbles. The soldiers halted behind them in a clatter of hooves.

What had Ian said the day he brought her home last time? Oh, yes. He would not enter the gates while the keep was owned by another. Well, soon it would be his.

Dunstan once more brought his horse alongside. 'One question for you, Gilvry.' His voice was sharp, his hand on his pistol. 'How did you manage a wedding in less than two days?'

Ian looked over his shoulder. His eyes narrowed. She turned to look at the soldiers guarding the gate behind them. There was no way out. Oh, dear, they were effectively trapped. She glanced at Ian in consternation.

He raised an arrogant brow and looked at the other man. Was he planning on fighting for her, after all? If Ian was him, he would have. He held the other man's gaze. 'Scottish law doesn't require banns or a licence.'

Dunstan frowned. 'There are some formalities, though, surely?'

'All addressed and very nicely, too.' Ian's smile widened and his eyes showed a knowledge the other man would instantly understand.

Selina blushed.

The horse beneath Dunstan pranced sideways at a sudden tightening of the reins.

A palpable hit, Ian thought. Not quite a bullet to the arm, but close enough. Ian turned his attention to the portly gentleman coming down the steps into the courtyard. Albright. His father-in-law.

His colour was an unhealthy red. He rushed to the gig and helped Selina down, holding her in a tight embrace.

Something rushed through Ian's veins in a hot tide. He forced himself to step down slowly and walk around the front of the horse and stand behind his wife.

Albright held her away from him, his gaze travelling over her. 'Thank God you are safe. You gave me such a scare.'

Tears brightened Selina's eyes. 'I'm sorry, Father.' Scarlet rose in her cheeks.

Ian waited for her introduction.

Was she ashamed to admit her newly married state? He would not be surprised if she was. A little disappointed, perhaps even a trifle pained, but not surprised.

Albright became aware of his presence. His frantic gaze went to Dunstan, who hung back with his men. 'Arrest this man. He is a smuggler. He abducted my daughter.'

The blond soldier curled his lip. 'There has been no abduction, I am sorry to say, my lord. He has cleverly ensured your daughter cannot give evidence with regard to the charge of smuggling.' The starchy prig gave a stiff nod. 'If you will excuse me, my lord, I will be about the king's business.' He brought his horse's head around and moved off.

Selina frowned.

Ian held his breath, waiting for her to realise what

Dunstan meant. For her to realise his real purpose for the marriage. The one thing he could not deny.

Her puzzled gaze followed the soldier, then comprehension filled her eyes, followed swiftly by fury as she turned on him. 'So that was part of your game, too. You really are despicable.'

His anger flared. 'Tell your father our news, Selina,' he said harshly, 'or I will.'

Her shoulders sagged as she turned back to the old man also watching the soldiers leave, his jaw slack with astonishment.

She took a deep breath. 'Father, I would like you to welcome my husband, Ian Gilvry.'

'What?' he said, his mouth opening and closing, his jowls wobbling. 'What?'

Ian thought the old man would drop dead on the spot of apoplexy.

'I married Mr Gilvry.'

'No.' His gaze shot to Ian. 'It is not possible. There hasn't been enough time.'

'Under Scottish law it is quite possible,' Ian said. He was getting quite weary of explaining his country's laws.

Albright's wife came running down the steps, her face full of happiness. 'Selina, dear. You are safe.'

'Apparently not,' her father said. 'She has married this fellow.'

He didn't like being called a fellow, either.

'My ancestry in the Scottish nobility goes back far longer than yours does in the ranks of the English,' he said. 'You can address me as Gilvry, or Laird. But I do not answer to fellow or you or lad.'

Albright reared back. 'You are insolent, sir.'

'Sir is all right, too.'

'Father, Papa,' Selina said in soothing tones, her voice

light and breathy. 'I am married to Ian Gilvry. There is nothing anyone can do to change it.'

There went the twang of his conscience again. It wasn't as if she'd been asked for her hand and had accepted. Not in the sense a young woman of her rank would expect to be asked. He'd tricked her, just as she'd said. Not that she hadn't been a willing participant in the resulting seduction, he thought darkly.

'May I say how pleased I am that Lady Selina accepted my suit,' he said politely.

The old man looked ready to explode. He kept his face fixed on Selina. 'Why? When you could have had so much more?'

'It is too late for regrets,' she said, but regret showed on her face.

Ian wanted to hit something.

'You could have had a duke or an earl.'

'Before the accident, Father.'

'I would have settled enough on you to make it happen. I told you that. But you said you wanted Dunstan. And now this? A criminal. And Scottish to boot.' He glared at Ian. 'What have you done to my daughter?'

'Melville,' his pretty wife whispered, putting a hand on his sleeve. He looked at it and seemed to gather himself. It stopped his tirade at any rate.

Selina's eyes filled with tears. 'I'm sorry, Father. It was all my own doing. There was really no other option.'

So she wasn't going to tell her father how he'd tricked her.

Albright's face reddened further. 'You should be ashamed.'

He'd had enough of listening to the father castigate his wife. 'Whatever your opinion of me, my lord,' he said stiffly, 'your daughter is now legally my wife. As is usual under these circumstances, I believe there are certain settlements to be made.'

The colour drained from the old man's face. And from Selina's too, he saw. What? Did she think he wouldn't insist she receive her dowry? Did she think he would allow her to live in poverty?

'Very well,' Albright said. 'Come to my study, Gilvry. Take your spoils.' He glared at his wife. 'Lady Albright, be ready to leave in an hour. As for you, daughter, I would prefer not to look on your face before I depart.'

She reached out a hand. 'Papa, can you not understand that this could be a good thing?'

Her defence surprised him, but he could see it was hopeless.

'I see nothing of the sort.'

The stricken look in Selina's eyes gave Ian a pain in his gut.

Albright, his arm linked through his wife's, turned and walked heavily up the steps. 'Come now or come not at all, Gilvry.'

Much as he would have liked to stay and comfort Selina, he had to get this business done. He gave her a quick hug. 'Wait here.'

She looked ready to argue.

'Wait.'

Chapter Sixteen

Selina stared up at the old stone walls that were about to become her home. Permanently.

Years ago, dazed by his kisses, she'd dreamed of this. Now the dream of a foolish schoolgirl had come true. But not in the way she had imagined. There was no love involved. Just advantage.

What a fool. One smile, one look at his face and the defences she'd built up over the years had instantly crumbled.

What if Father never forgave her for this last piece of folly? What if he refused to see her ever again?

Perhaps Chrissie could soften his anger.

She looked up at her father's study window. No doubt her husband and father would be engaged for a while. She ran up the steps and headed for Chrissie's chamber with hope in her heart.

She passed through the chamber with the oriole window overlooking the courtyard that would have once been the lord's chamber and now served as Chrissie's sitting room and into the bedchamber where she heard sounds of movement.

Chrissie was directing her maid with the packing.

She looked up at Selina's entry with a small gasp. 'Oh, Selina,' she said, looking sorrowful. She glanced at the maid and walked into the sitting room before speaking. 'Your father was out of his mind with worry. And now this?'

'I know he's upset and disappointed, but perhaps in time he will forgive me, don't you think?'

Chrissie looked at her. 'Not for a long while, I think. His heart is wounded, he had great hopes of Dunstan.'

It was more likely it was his pride she had wounded. A footman knocked. 'Come for the baggage, my lady.' They remained silent as he carried out Chrissie's trunks and boxes, the maid following along behind admonishing him to be careful.

'Will you write to me?' Selina asked. 'Tell me how he fares from time to time?'

'If he does not forbid it.' Chrissie smiled her sweet smile. 'But then, I will not ask his permission, I shall assume it. And I will speak to him on your behalf, when he comes down from the boughs.'

It was time to say farewell. Selina held out a hand. 'Oh, Chrissie, I am truly sorry for spoiling your visit to Scotland.'

Chrissie shook her head a little ruefully. 'It has certainly been a good deal more…exciting than I expected.'

Chrissie clasped her hands together and paced to the window, then swung around to face Selina. 'I wish I'd never asked Melville to bring us.'

'Me, too,' Selina said. She couldn't help her sigh. 'I thought I had the future so carefully planned.' And she had given it all up for a devil's kiss.

A noise at the open door brought her head up. She winced as she saw Ian standing there looking like thunder. 'I thought I told you to wait,' he said.

'I wanted to bid Chrissie farewell.'

'Well, do it now. Her ladyship's carriage awaits.'

Tears glinting in her eyes, Chrissie threw her arms around her and hugged her close. 'I'll speak to him for you.' Head down, not looking at Ian, she whisked out of the room.

Ian's hard expression softened. 'Your father doesn't like this wedding any more than does my family. We can only hope they both come around. Come.' He held out his hand. 'We will watch them depart from the ramparts.'

He tucked her hand under his arm and walked her along the corridor to the door that opened onto the winding staircase that led up to the small platform behind the tower's crenellation.

The narrow steps meant they had to go single file. She pressed the latch on the door at the top and stepped outside. She hadn't been up here for a very long time and gasped at the strength of the wind and the way it buffeted against her ears. Her father's carriage was already passing through the arch.

Gone without so much as a farewell and certainly no blessing. She had the sense she might never see him again. Prickles stung the back of her eyes. Her vision misted. She swallowed the lump in her throat and stared at the receding carriage, wishing with all her heart things could have been different.

Had she known what would come of her attempt to help, would she have rushed out into the night? The answer wasn't quite as clear in her mind as she thought it should be.

Ian looked at her straight back and the way the skirts of that shockingly red skirt clung to her slender legs, held there by the wind, and didn't know what to say as she watched her father's coach disappear.

He wanted to offer comfort, but her straight back and stiff body shut him out. He had the feeling whatever he said would be wrong.

He was married, but somehow, at this moment, he felt lonelier than he'd ever felt during all his years as Laird. Being in charge of his people was a duty he could not share with anyone else. Except a wife, perhaps. The right sort of wife.

In the past he'd made decisions he wasn't proud of, made mistakes, too, and those were his burdens to shoulder. But he'd always imagined that marriage would give him someone to share in his joys and, damn it, his sorrows in a way that brothers or clan members could not.

But the clan didn't seem at all ready to accept her. And they could be cruel to outsiders. A shudder passed down his spine as he recalled what his brothers had said to her when they were younger.

He would do all he could to protect her from their anger. In time they would come to accept the idea. They must. While this marriage had not started off on the best of feet, surely it could only get better from here.

He put a hand on her shoulder. She stiffened beneath his fingers, but then turned to face him.

His gut lurched. She'd been crying. He could see the moisture in her eyes.

An emotion he hadn't expected rose in his gorge. 'Are you so sorry for losing Dunstan, then?'

Damn, why did he have to ask that?

She looked at him for a moment, blinking back her tears before she spoke. 'He would have made a perfect husband. He was my choice.' She bit her lip and turned her face away as if appalled at what she'd said.

The words shouldn't hurt, because they were honest, but they did.

He let go a sigh. It didn't matter what she wanted. She was stuck with him now.

She looked so beautiful with strands of her dark hair whipping around her face. And so vulnerable. He wanted to kiss away the shadows in her eyes. Allay her fears. If she would let him. He offered her a smile of encouragement. 'It will be all right. You will see.'

Her expression softened for just a moment, her lips parting. He leaned closer, inhaling her scent, feeling her breath on his jaw. This was their common ground. This was where he would win the battle.

She frowned. 'Why didn't you tell the men at the inn about the keep being part of the settlement?'

This was a trap. No doubt about it. He'd need to tread warily. 'I wasna' sure your father would give me the same terms as Dunstan.'

Her mouth turned down in a bitter grimace.

Wrong answer, he realised. He opened his mouth to say more, but she tossed her head back and looked at him full on, her gaze hard and cold.

'It seems you got everything you wanted.' She swept an arm around to encompass the surrounding hills. 'Let me go. To Alice. As we planned.'

The words landed on his chest like one of the stones from the castle wall, hard, cold and heavy. 'You are my wife.' My wife. It sounded like ownership. It sounded medieval. He was feeling pretty medieval right at that moment as a primitive urge to claim her blasted though his veins.

'In name only.' She spoke so calmly, she might have been discussing the weather. She smiled then, a brittle little curve to her lips. 'You don't need me. You have what you Gilvrys have always wanted. Dunross Keep.'

'Your place is here.' Och, now he *sounded* medieval.

He reached for her hands and almost cursed when she tucked them behind her.

'Give it three months,' he said. 'If you are still of the same mind then, I'll let you go.' If he could not win his wife in three months with the kind of passion they shared, he did not deserve to keep her.

She didn't look happy. Because she knew he would win, he thought with a surge of triumph.

'A week,' she said.

Oh, yes, she knew he would win. He shook his head. 'A month. No less, or we will forget all about this nonsense.'

She glared at him. 'It isn't nonsense to want to leave a place where everyone hates you.'

'They need time to become accustomed to the idea.' And in the meantime, he would do his best to make sure she never wanted to leave.

Anger followed by determination chased across her face. 'Very well. A month.'

Now why did he suddenly have the feeling the trap had closed? He reached out a hand. 'Then we have a bargain.'

She took it. Instead of shaking her hand, he brought her small cold fingers to his lips, turned them palm up and kissed the inside her wrist. He felt her shiver, slight though it was, and saw the flush of heat in her face. He smiled. He was worrying for nothing. A month would be plenty of time. He released her. 'Let us go down.'

She made to push past him.

He barred her way. 'Let me go ahead, lass. The stairs are steep and twisty.'

'You might be wiser to give me a good hard push from behind. Perhaps I'd obligingly break my neck, then you can marry someone of whom your clan will approve.'

Red veiled his vision. He caught her arm, held her immobile while staring into her flashing dark eyes, noting the petulant set of her full lower lip. She tipped her chin in defiance. Taunting him. Daring him to prove his baseness. Winning her might not be as easy as he thought.

He took a deep breath and smiled with what he hoped was calmness and not quite the grimace he felt on his face. 'As long as I have breath in my body, you will suffer no harm from me.'

'No more harm, you mean,' she said with an overly sweet smile of her own.

He wasn't going to pursue that, not now. 'Come, let us go down, supper will soon be ready.'

And then would come the night and the battle would commence in earnest. His body hardened. This war between them definitely had its compensations.

He headed down the stairs, holding her hand fast in his all the way.

Chapter Seventeen

Supper was done and cleared away, the candles and the fire were lit, and they were alone in the old solar, the room off the bedroom Chrissie had used. Across the blackened wooden planks of the ancient trestle table, Ian sprawled in a carved wood chair, sipping his whisky like some medieval knight and watching her from heavy-lidded eyes.

As if she was some choice morsel he had yet to taste.

He'd got his precious keep. Why did he have to want her, too? Thank God she hadn't blurted out foolish professions of love the previous night. That would have made him impossible. She just had to survive a month of him and then she could go her own way.

It was even a better arrangement than she would have had with Dunstan. They would have lived together. With Ian, she would have freedom and respectability. She should be feeling pleased, not miserable.

There was no reason to feel miserable. Not once had he indicated he cared for her no more than he might care for any other woman. Attraction, yes. Lust, yes. But nothing more. And look how quickly he'd agreed to let her go in a month if they did not suit. No doubt he wanted to make sure the marriage could not be disputed. But for that, he would have let her leave with her father.

Not that Father would have taken her. She didn't quite understand why he'd been so angry. She could have understood disappointment, but it was as if there was something of importance riding on her marriage to Dunstan.

Ian rose.

Her heart beat faster. Her mouth dried. She felt flustered. Unsure.

In London, this would be the moment when she would retire to the drawing room for tea and he'd take his port in some male dominion. His study, if he was alone, the dining room if he had company. But this room was the domain of the lady of the keep. She had nowhere to go except to her bedroom.

He held out his hand. 'Come. We will sit by the fire.'

Two deep chairs flanked the merrily blazing hearth.

So he intended to prolong the evening. Continue the pretence of married bliss. No doubt for the sake of appearances, with half his clansmen now employed in the keep. With a sigh she rose to her feet and strode for one of the chairs.

Before she could sit, he swept her up in his arms and sat down with her on his lap.

'What are you doing?' she gasped.

'Enjoying a pleasant evening with my wife.'

The way his deep voice caressed the word 'wife' sent a shiver down her spine. She stiffened against the traitorous trickles of heat that sparked in her veins.

She gazed at the fire, trying to pretend she felt nothing, that the strong arms holding her against his chest were not warm or protective. That the feel of his heartbeat against her shoulder didn't send little thrills of anticipation through her body.

But she was his wife. And she could not deny him her body, a little voice whispered with a bit too much glee and excitement.

'I'm tired,' she said. 'I would like to retire.'

'Bed sounds like a good idea.' Amusement coloured his voice, along with desire.

Heat rushed through her. Anger. Defiance. 'It has been a long wearing day. Surely you will not force yourself on me tonight?'

She winced at the brittleness in her tone. Clinging to her anger was not easy when cradled so softly in his arms. But his utter stillness said her barb had reached its mark.

His chest rose and fell with a long breath. A man trying to hold on to his patience. Perhaps if she made him angry enough, he'd let her go sooner than later.

Fingers calloused by work grasped her chin with gentle force and brought her face around. Blue eyes dancing with the light of the fire gazed into her face. He didn't look particularly angry. Indeed, he looked as he always did, handsome, alluring, manly.

Then a seductively dark smile curved his lips. 'That's better,' he said. 'Your face is lovely by firelight. I have not yet looked my fill.'

He wasn't the first man to praise her beauty, but his softly spoken words warmed her more than any before. Somehow the power she'd always drawn from her beauty leached away in his presence. He made her feel weak. Needy.

Needing anyone was a mistake.

She returned his smile with one of her own. 'La, husband, you flatter me.'

His gaze darkened a fraction. 'It is not flattery to

speak the truth.' His lips descended on hers, gentle, wooing, teasing.

She tried to resist, to pretend his kisses did not make her dizzy, did not rob her of reason. Indeed, she even went so far as to place the flat of her hand on his shoulder to push him away, but instead her fingers closed on the lapel of his coat, clutching as if she would hold on to him. Her lips parted and his tongue stroked with a soft silken slide. And she was lost.

Lost in passion. Her body clenching at the thought of the pleasure to come.

A soft groan rumbled up from his chest as her tongue tangled with his in a shocking dance of intimacy she'd learned only one night before, yet now seemed to know the steps by heart. The give and take of pleasure.

Her hands cradling his head, the silk of his hair brushing her skin, she pressed into his hard wall of chest, while his hands wandered across her back, her buttocks, her thigh. Beneath her, the evidence of his desire pressed against her.

She let the passion carry away her fears and her anger, let physical sensation fill all the corners of her mind. Her body trembled at the sensual onslaught of his mouth, his hands, his body.

Heat rolled off him in waves. His scent filled her nostrils, the clean smell of the Highlands, the tang of soap, but more powerful yet, his essence.

And then he stood up, rising from the chair with her in his arms as if she weighed nothing.

Released from the magic of his kiss, she scrambled to pull herself back together. 'What are you doing?'

'Taking my wife to bed.' He gave her a wicked grin that curled her toes in her slippers. 'That was what you wanted, was it not?'

'Not quite,' she managed, though it was hard enough to breathe, let alone speak with any sense.

He cocked an arrogant brow. 'Tell me I did wrong after it is done, lass.' He strode for the bedchamber, kicked open the door and deposited her gently on her feet.

Now was the moment to tell him to leave, before she succumbed to him utterly. Before he stole her sense of self.

The resolve in his face, the determination in his eyes said he would not be gainsaid his rights as a husband. Nor did she want to gainsay him. Damn it. In the matter of attraction, of physical desire, it seemed they were of one mind. Yet she still resented the way he'd played her for a fool.

Well, she was a fool no longer. And she had her own arsenal of weapons. As long as she shielded her heart, as long as she kept him at a distance, she would be safe.

He had proposed the bargain, and in all honour he had no choice but to keep to it, just as she'd had no choice but to agree to this marriage. She would enjoy her month of married life and at the end of it she would walk away.

Without regret. Or very little.

She stood on her tiptoes, twined her arms around his neck and drew his head down. His eyes widened with surprise and flared with banked heat.

Then she tasted him in a slow measured kiss, teasing his lips with her tongue, nipping with her teeth. His hands skimmed her body as if they knew just how to touch and where so her bones would melt and her mind turn to mush.

One large warm hand came to her breast, gently circling and teasing, while the other explored the shape of her hips and her buttocks.

With each stroke of his tongue, each caress of his hand, he stoked the fires within until her body took on a will of its own, melding into him, demanding more.

Flames of desire leapt within her, heat flushed through her and the tension within her tightened. When he broke the kiss to pull at the laces of her bodice, she fumbled with the buttons of his coats.

When he knelt to remove her stockings, she fought with the knot of his cravat. When he untied the strings of her petticoats, she undid the buttons of his shirts. Urgency made each article of clothing a barrier to be conquered.

Finally she stood before him in nothing but her chemise. And he was naked. Beautiful. An aroused pagan warrior.

He stood still and proud and let her look. The sight stole her breath. Too bad she had to let him go. A pang twisted her heart.

He stepped towards her. 'Selina,' he murmured and there was comfort in his voice, along with the husky rasp of lust.

Now was not the time for comfort. That was not what she needed from him. It came too close to emotions she would never admit to. Not ever.

She undid the ties of her chemise and let it slip down her shoulders and slither its way to the floor. She could not hold back her smile as his hot dark gaze followed its progress, stopping only for a second to linger at her breasts and belly and finally the heart of her femininity.

On a groan he pulled her close, his mouth coming down hard on hers, ravishing and plundering and pleasuring.

She gave herself up to the pleasure of his hard strong body pressed against hers and rejoiced when he eased her back onto the bed, never breaking the kiss for a moment.

This was all she needed. All she would ever accept. She wasn't a child any longer and he would not break her heart again.

She stroked her hands over his shoulders, across the plane of his strong wide back. He felt lovely beneath her palms, skin like silk, muscle like bands of iron rippling beneath her hands. His soft indrawn breath let her know he enjoyed her touch as much as she enjoyed his. Perhaps she wouldn't be the only one to suffer loss when she left.

The thought pleased her. Gave her a surge of confidence, returned a little of the feminine power she had always relied on.

When he finally broke the kiss, he raised himself up to look into her face, as if he had noticed something different and was puzzled. She smiled at him.

He swallowed. '*Leannan,*' he breathed. 'My lovely wife.' There was awe in his voice.

It was nothing new, her beauty, or male admiration, but there was something of awe in the way he said the words that seemed to caress a soft place in her heart.

She didn't want tenderness. She reached up and clasped her hands around the back of his neck, drawing herself up to tease his lips with her tongue and her teeth. A soft groan filled her ears and he pressed his thigh between her legs. She shifted, parting her thighs, welcoming him into the cradle of her hips, telling him she was ready for their joining and the pleasure she had learned it would bring.

'Selina, love,' he rasped against her mouth. 'Slow down. You'll unman me.'

'Is that a bad thing?' she asked with a teasing note in her voice.

He took a deep ragged breath. 'It might be.' And then he was pressing hot kisses to her throat, licking the rise of her breasts, laving her nipples with his tongue, making her writhe and squirm beneath him as the pull of tension tightened within her.

His hand went to the apex of her thighs and he parted the soft folds and she felt his fingers slide within her slick passage. She cried out as a shudder of desire swept through her as he teased her with his touch.

She wanted to curse him, when he stopped and raised his head to look into her face with a dark smile of satisfaction. She let her hands slide down his back to the rise of his buttocks and pulled him tight against the heart of her that ached with a need for his flesh against hers.

The expression on his face tightened to one of painful intensity.

To see the effect of her actions on his face jolted through her like lightning, a hot spark of lust that darkened the edge of her vision and brought her close to the edge of bliss and yet keeping it just out of reach; she wanted to scream her frustration.

The inner core of her fluttered and tightened and she lifted her hips, wrapping her legs around his waist. And then, as if in obedience to her will, he drove home. Deep within her, he filled her and remained utterly still.

On a moan, she twisted her hips, fought to find the deeper pleasure waiting just beyond reach. One large hand went beneath her, bringing her body tight against his. The other curved around her breast. He bent his head and took her nipple in his mouth.

And then he suckled.

The sharpest sweetest pain she could ever imagine pierced her to the core.

He drove into her again and again as she shattered in

a fiery burst of light behind her eyes as her core pulsed around his shaft. A deep sound in his throat and the convulsive shudders of his body heightened her bliss.

It seemed like hours before her heartbeat returned to normal and she noticed the hot weight of him on her body. It could not have been more than a moment or two, but the warmth went on and on, waves of it making her languid and content. When he eased off her and pulled her close against his chest, she felt replete and complete.

Dangerous, she thought, but undeniably wonderful.

After a week, Selina's life at Dunross Keep settled into a rhythm. Tumultuous passion at night, followed by long, hellishly boring days.

Tonight, as usual, her husband sat with his dram of whisky beside the hearth, reading the news from London, while with a stomach tied in knots she pretended to read a book.

From beneath her lowered lashes she couldn't help but watch him, the way he sprawled in his chair, his long legs stretched out before him encased in a pair of buckskins, his shirt closed by a practical stock, rather than a cravat, and his shirtsleeves rolled up. He'd discarded his coats because of the warmth of the evening.

He looked handsome, relaxed and very much the Laird of Dunross.

He belonged here. Unlike her. There was nothing for her here. No society. No friends. No purpose. She was nothing but a china ornament to be admired and caressed and put away at the beginning of each day.

Three more weeks and she'd be free to leave. No matter how he wooed her in the bedroom, she was determined to make him stand by their bargain.

Chapter Eighteen

Ian had tricked her into thinking there was more between them than there was, and she wasn't going to pretend it was otherwise.

Every day he left her alone and went off to the mill. Each day, she carefully erected reasons why she should not give herself to this man. And each night it was ridiculous how easily he tore down those objections with his lovemaking.

She had no illusions about why they had married, and he might torment her body each night until she cried out with the pleasure of it, but he was not going to touch her heart. Not a second time.

He must have sensed her looking at him, since he glanced up.

She bit her lip.

'Out with it, lass,' he said quietly. 'What troubles you?'

'How do you know something troubles me?'

'There's an expression you get on your face.' He shrugged. 'I can't quite explain it.'

'I am troubled by the idea that you are smuggling again. Not that I care if you endanger yourself, understand, but I think the people of Dunross deserve better.'

His lips twisted wryly. ''Tis kind of you to worry, but the people of Dunross are my concern.'

'Don't you think I have a right to know if you are involved in a criminal activity? Something that might bring the law down on my head, too?'

He folded his paper and put it on one side with a sigh. 'We are turning the mill into a commercial still,' he said quietly.

'An illegal still, you mean. Are you mad?'

He grimaced. 'My family, my people, have been making whisky for centuries. It is our right.' He gave a hard laugh. 'Anywhere else in Britain, apart from the Highlands, what I am doing would be perfectly legal.'

'How so?'

'When they passed the law delineating the Highlands, the English Parliament also passed a law that no still beyond that line should have a capacity of less than five hundred gallons. Anything less is outside the law.'

'And that is what you are building?' She felt a flicker of relief. Not for him, he could do just as he wished, she assured herself, but for the people of Dunross.

'That,' he said flatly, 'is well nigh impossible. We can't grow enough barley for a still of that size.'

'Surely if the farmers all got together?'

He nodded. 'We might come close. But if we don't, we are still taxed as if we did. And even so, we can only sell what we produce in the Highlands. Pointless, when every man worth his salt makes his own. We are being penalised for the sins of our forefathers.' He frowned. 'Not to mention that distillers in England don't like the competition because they know our whisky is better than any geneva they can make.'

'Why make whisky at all? Or is it your dearest wish to go to prison?' Or worse.

'You don't understand.'

'I understand well enough that you are taking risks with other people's lives.'

A crease formed between his brows. 'You were out today. Where did you go?'

Changing the topic, because her opinion mattered not one wit.

'I went for a ride. What else is there for me to do?' She winced, knowing she sounded like a sulky child. 'I rode to Balnaen Cove. Topaz needed the exercise.'

He frowned. 'You should not go so far from the keep.'

'Why? Are you afraid I might see more smugglers?'

He cast her a dark glance. 'We still don't know who betrayed us to the gaugers. Or whether they intend more mischief. If you wish to exercise your horse, you will do it in my company.'

'You are never here during the day.'

A seductive smile curved his lips, his eyes becoming heavy-lidded and lighting with a wicked gleam. 'Are you telling me you are missing me during the day, lass?'

Heat flashed through her. Unwelcome little stirrings trickled through her blood. She stiffened against them. 'Certainly not. I am telling you I do not intend to sit inside these walls all day long with nothing to do.'

He frowned. 'You have things to do. The running of the household.'

'It pretty well runs itself. It isn't as if we have a vast number of servants and nor do we have guests to entertain. I tried visiting your mother, but was turned away at the door.'

His gaze shuttered. 'You know she isn't well.'

'I thought to ask her to live here at the keep. She would be more comfortable. She could have her own suite of rooms.'

''Tis kind of you, lass,' he said and there was warmth in his expression, but he shook his head. 'She's still not used to the idea of our marriage. You have to give her more time.'

'Not used to it? She hates it.' She shrugged. 'It doesn't matter to me. I'll be gone soon enough.'

The warmth in his eyes fled, replaced by a look of hurt. Or was she mistaken, as she was mistaken in so much about this man? For now it was determination on his face. His gaze dropped to her breasts and then rose again. Heat flooded through her.

Her body tingled.

She fought the sudden rush of desire. To no avail. He was already rising to his feet, a hand held out for hers. It seemed that conversation was over.

Ian wanted to curse as he looked at his beautiful wife. Every day she grew less and less happy. A woman like her should be dancing at balls, be the centre of society instead of stuck in a backwater like Dunross.

What had he expected? That she would be happy here, because she was with him? Four weeks she had given him. And every night he did his best to bind her to him. And every morning he knew it wasn't working.

Yet.

A Gilvry never gave up.

Sitting with her after dinner in her sitting room always helped him relax. Made him forget the day's worries in the anticipation of the night to come.

But his guilt over Andrew was always there, a looming shadow between them. He didn't blame her for what he'd done. She'd only asked for his help. The urge to win her gratitude had made him act against his brother more harshly than was warranted.

Thank God no one else knew what he had done. Nor would he ever let her influence him that way again. He would not let her twist him around her little finger. He was the Laird of Dunross and she would abide by his decisions as did the rest of his people.

Even so, he was gnawed by guilt, a feeling in his gut, that Drew had died so Ian could have everything he ever wanted. Dunross. Selina.

Except he didn't really have Selina. She clearly still had every intention of leaving. He should just let her go. It would be easier on them all. But the thought of her returning to her London friends, a married woman, free to do as she pleased, drove him to the madness of trying to win her.

And God knew they were compatible in bed. Blissfully so. Not that she came like a lamb. Each night he had to woo her anew. But the pleasure was not all one sided. Not in the least.

Lust surged through him. And something else. A kind of softness he did not want to examine too closely. He was already weak enough when it came to this woman.

He swept her up in his arms, gazed down into her face and saw her eyes were the colour of whisky. No shadows now. Only desire. Whatever the differences between them, in their desire for each other they were equally matched. And that was enough for him. Wasn't it?

It had to be. It was more than he deserved.

Heat raced through his veins and he strode for their bed.

'What are you doing?' she said, clearly knowing very well what he was doing, but bedevilling him none the less.

'I've had enough of arguments for one night. And talk of leaving.'

He set her down on her feet and pulled her into his arms, kissing and nibbling at her full lush lips, teasing them with his tongue until he felt her body start to melt beneath his hands, the way she always did. He just wished that once she would initiate their lovemaking. His body hardened to granite at the thought and he almost groaned aloud just imagining such a thing.

Sometimes she did things with her hands and her mouth that sent him far too quickly over the edge and he wondered if it was intentional. But he doubted it. She was too angry with him for tricking her into this marriage for her to care about his pleasure. He wasn't sure she would ever let go of that anger, but he would continue to attempt to convince her. As long as she'd let him.

Just as he would try to make her forget Dunstan.

He plundered her mouth with his tongue and she slipped her arms around his neck in sensual surrender. Perhaps tonight would be the night he'd win more than her body.

The next morning it was pouring with rain so Selina was surprised when a grim-faced Angus brought a message to the breakfast table that Mr Tearny urgently wanted to see Ian in the hall.

'Is something wrong?' she asked.

'That is for the Laird to say.' Angus didn't like the land agent, who was employed by both Carrick and the Dunross estate, and had remained after her father left. As Angus had. By choice.

Ian put down his knife and fork. His face took on hard lines as he rose from the table. 'I had better see him right away.' He followed Angus from the room.

Selina frowned at her toast. He hadn't asked her to

join him. Nor had he said she should not. And Angus's grim countenance had aroused her curiosity.

It was a large space, once used by the Laird for his men-at-arms and the keep's servants. It still had the raised dais at one end where in the old days the lord and his family would have taken their meal. Now the space was primarily used for storage.

Her father had also used it when in residence as a place to fulfil his responsibilities as Justice of the Peace. It seemed that Ian was doing the same. A solitary chair and small table held the centre of the dais and Ian was already seated by the time Selina reached the bottom of the stairs behind him.

She remained in the shadows. Silent. Watching. It was the first time she had seen him in the role of Laird. He looked stern, perhaps even harsh, where the light from a window high in the wall cast his face in shadow.

Tearny stood before him with a firm grasp around the arm of a young lad. A brace of rabbits lay at his feet. The boy brushed his russet hair out of his green eyes with defiance. There was a large red mark on his face, like a recent blow from a fist. Selina had a sense of recognition, yet she did not think she knew the lad.

'Well, Tearny?' Ian said without expression. Strange how both Scotland and Ireland spoke Gaelic, yet neither could understand the other in their native languages. It meant they had to resort to English.

'Caught young McKinly poaching, Laird,' Tearny said, his Irish lilt unmistakable.

McKinly. Selina stifled a gasp and pressed a hand to her chest. This must be the older boy she had not met. That was why she thought she had recognised him. He had the look of Marie Flora.

The land agent pushed the rabbits with his foot. 'He didn't deny it.'

'On whose land did you catch him?' Ian asked.

What did it matter whose land? No one cared about a few rabbits.

'He was on your land, Laird, when I caught him. But he could have caught them Carrick side. He won't tell me.'

Carrick's land abutted theirs to the south.

Ian frowned at the McKinly boy. 'What do you have to say for yourself?'

'My wee brother Tommy has been sick with the ague. Grannie McDonald said he needed a broth to make him well.' He glowered at Tearny. 'I only took what we needed for a stew.'

'Who hit you?' Selina asked, then winced as all eyes turned on her. She held her ground as Ian gazed at her with lowered brows.

He gestured to a stool beside his chair. 'Lady wife, you are welcome to watch the proceedings, but please do not interrupt.'

She flushed, but, shoulders straight, she climbed the steps up on to the dais and perched on the stool.

'Who hit you?' Ian said gently to the boy.

'I did,' Tearny said before the lad had a chance to reply. 'He kicked me in the shins, trying to escape. He knew he was in the wrong.'

'You hit me before I kicked you,' the boy muttered.

Ian looked at the rabbits. 'If they were discovered on my land,' he said, looking at Tearny, 'then we must assume they are my rabbits. Unless you have evidence to the contrary?'

The Irishman shook his head. 'Doesn't matter whose

land. He stole them. If he wants rabbits, he should go to the common land and hunt them there.'

'The common land no has a rabbit to be seen,' the boy said.

Tearny glared at him, then turned to Ian. 'There's gratitude for ye. I told you it would do no good to give them free land for grazing their beasts. They just want more.'

Ian's eyes narrowed. 'Poaching is a serious crime, young man.'

Selina couldn't repress her gasp at the severity in his tone. 'It is only a few rabbits,' she said.

Ian glared at her.

'Well, it is,' she said. 'We could do with a few less of them, too. They make holes everywhere.'

'It seems my wife has no fondness for rabbit holes, Tearny.' His voice held a touch of wryness.

Selina frowned. Was he referring to the time she'd twisted her ankle in one of their burrows? The first time he kissed her. She flushed red. If not for that rabbit hole, it was unlikely they would ever have spoken at all.

She glared at him. He raised a brow in response, then turned back to the matter at hand.

The bruise on the boy's face was turning purple. It wasn't right for a man Tearny's size to strike a boy.

'Ye need to make an example of him, Laird,' Tearny said heavily. 'They'll be clearing the land of game birds next.'

Anger, hot and wild, rose up inside her. She shot to her feet. 'What are you suggesting? That he be hanged? Or transported?' She turned on Ian. 'He's only a child. He needed meat for his brother. You can't do such a wicked thing.'

The young lad's mouth dropped open. Tearny looked shocked, then looked at Ian with a sneer on his lips.

Ian's face darkened to thunderous. 'Be silent, woman.'

She rose to her feet. 'I'll not sit here and listen to such…such inhumanity.'

'You will sit and listen to my judgement,' Ian said quietly, and there was more danger in that quiet tone than there was in all of Tearny's bluster.

But she didn't care. What he was doing was wrong. Blindly she leapt down from the dais and hurried out of the chamber into the courtyard and the driving rain. She didn't care what kind of sentence Ian imposed, she was going to find a way to send the boy back to his father, before anything bad happened to him.

Ian half-rose in his seat, then realised he'd have to let her go. Tearny thought him weak enough already with the concessions he'd given to the clan, without him chasing after his wife, a woman who had just flayed him with her tongue. He could almost imagine a strip of skin a yard wide ripped off his back.

So much for wifely respect. Somehow he would have to make her understand that it was important that they present a united front to the world. In private, they could argue. The clan would turn against her completely if they thought she was trying to rule the roost. It was the way they were. She needed to give them time to become used to her, to see her as the wife of the Laird, not an outsider, before she handed out her opinions.

It was a discussion they would have later, behind closed doors. Right now he had a more important matter on his mind. One that would set the tone with the clansmen for the future.

'Well, lad,' Ian said sternly, 'what do you have to say for yourself?'

'We are not like thieving Irish,' the boy blurted out.

Ian focused in on the boy. 'Say what you mean.'

The boy darted a glance at Tearny's dark frown and shook his head.

Ian switched to Gaelic. 'I am your Laird. You must answer the question. Be a man. If you have right on your side, no harm will come to you.'

The boy straightened his spine. 'Everyone knows Tearny—'

'In English, lad,' Ian said.

The boy took a deep breath, glanced at Tearny, then started to speak. 'Everyone knows Tearny sells grouse and snipe to a butcher in Wick and pockets the money.'

'Is this true?' Ian asked.

The Irishman shuffled his feet. ''Tis one of the perks. Lord Albright gave me permission. As does the Carrick. It has no bearing on him stealing rabbits.'

'I am Laird here now and I did not give you permission,' he said quietly. 'The estate requires the income from all the birds it raises.'

'As you wish. But I'm not the one on trial here. The boy is.'

Ian turned his gaze back to the boy, who shrank a little.

Stone-faced, Ian leaned back and folded his arms across his chest, regarding the man and boy before him. He had to make the right decision here, prove he was the Laird in truth, not just in name.

The boy squirmed a little, but held his gaze. Tearny, on the other hand, looked anywhere but his face. For some odd reason he had the feeling the man was out to make trouble.

'I suppose the boy should count himself fortunate you

didn't shoot him first and ask questions afterwards.' He kept his voice neutral.

Tearny grinned. 'Aye, but question him, Laird. You'll find the father knew what he was up to. Encouraged him. He's the one who should be standing before ye.'

'No!' the boy yelled. 'Pa didn't...' He looked at Ian, then flushed bright red. He pressed his lips together.

'But you did hit the boy?' Ian asked mildly.

'Gave me some lip, kicked me, then tried to run off.'

Ian nodded. 'Mr Tearny, I do not approve of grown men striking boys.'

Tearny's fists clenched. 'Very well, Laird. I'll remember that in future.'

'In fact, I don't approve of any of your methods. I think it is time Dunross dispensed with your services. You will attend me in my office in one hour when we will settle matters between us. You may go.'

Tearny's face turned brick red. His jaw worked as if he would argue, but he must have thought better of it because he gave a jerk of his head. 'As you wish.' He glared at the boy. 'Be assured Lord Carrick will not welcome your trespass, boy. So make sure you do not stray onto his land.' He spun on his heel and stomped out of the hall.

The McKinly boy grinned and made a rude gesture at Tearny's departing back.

'Enough,' Ian said grimly. 'Why have you no been attending the school at the tythe barn?'

The boy shrugged. 'I'm too old for school.'

'No man is too old to learn something new,' Ian said. 'As your punishment for not asking permission to trap rabbits on my land, you will attend every afternoon after you have finished your chores for your father. Now get those rabbits home.'

The boy ducked his head, obviously relieved. 'Yes, Laird.' He picked up the carcasses and ran for the door.

'Oh, McKinly,' Ian said. The boy stopped and turned, anxiety written all over his face.

'No more than a brace every two weeks, do you ken? And that goes for everyone else or they'll be no rabbits left this side of Edinburgh.'

His face brightened. He shot out of the door and was gone.

Ian let go a long sigh. Now he had to deal with his angry wife. It made him feel a little sick to know that she thought so badly of him that she thought he would harm the boy.

He went out into the courtyard. Rain splattered his face as he glanced around.

Angus, talking to one of the grooms, gestured with his chin towards the stables. With a heaviness in his chest he hated, he ducked into the barn. It took a moment for his eyes to adjust to the gloom, then he saw her in the stall with her gelding, rhythmically stroking his glossy coat with a brush. What would he give for that kind of attention from his wife?

He strode towards her and she turned at the sound of his footfall. A frown appeared and she turned away to continue her brushing.

'Planning on going somewhere?' he asked and was aware that there was an edge of anger in his voice, despite his attempt to sound pleasant.

'I thought I might go for a ride.'

'And when were you intending to come and ask me to go with you?'

She kept on brushing. 'I was going to ask Angus.'

Another nice hit to his pride. Of course she'd sooner go with his steward.

'And where were you planning on going? McKinly's croft, by any chance?' This time he made no effort to keep the bitterness from his voice.

'Perhaps.'

'To what purpose?'

'To tell him that his son is here. That he should come and...and...speak for him. Rescue him. Something. Couldn't you see the boy was terrified out of his wits?'

'You ran off before I was done with him.' The insult to his integrity rankled.

'I thought I should go to his father, at once.'

'Then why are you still here?'

She swung around and glared at him. 'Because Angus wouldn't let me leave without your permission. It seems I'm a prisoner.'

Tears welled in her eyes, and he felt like a tyrant. 'It is for your own safety. I told you that.' He let out an impatient sigh. He had intended to let her believe the worst, let her think he was hard-hearted as she seemed to think, and let her find out on her own that he wasn't. But that would put her in a very embarrassing position. And he could not do it.

'I let the boy go with a warning,' he said.

She flattened herself against the stall, as if she didn't trust her legs to hold her up.

'I turned Tearny off,' he continued. 'He's too harsh. I've no truck with men who hit boys. You should have known that, Selina. You should have given me the benefit of the doubt. I'm not your father. These are my people.'

Her face paled. She looked down at the brush in her hand and back up at his face. 'I...I am sorry.'

He gave her a grim smile. 'I am sorry I could not explain my intentions, but I do expect you to support me, at least in public, if you want the clan's acceptance.'

'I see.'

He wished he was sure she did see. There was still a stubborn set to her jaw. 'We can talk about this later. Right now I have Tearny waiting in my office.'

Selina stood looking after him long after the door closed. Feeling deflated. Empty. Very much in the wrong. Because he was right. She should have known he wouldn't do anything to hurt McKinly's boy. She'd just wanted to believe the worst because it fed into her determination not to trust him. If she trusted him, then other softer emotions would creep under her guard and take her unawares. She could not allow it. It would become too easy to give in, to easy to give him her heart and let him trample it.

She stroked Topaz's nose. 'I don't think we'll be going riding today.' She sighed. 'But I will swallow my pride and ask him to go with us tomorrow.' After all, she couldn't live in a state of war with him. He didn't deserve it.

Chapter Nineteen

The next two weeks passed quickly. Too quickly for Selina's peace of mind. Each morning they sat in the solar taking breakfast, reading their letters, planning the day's activities. Like a happily married couple.

The time was coming when she would leave and she was wishing she had given him the three months he had asked for. Not because she wouldn't leave—she would not go back on her word—but because she was learning so much about the Highlands and its people.

She and Ian rode out together on the days he wasn't busy at the mill, riding through the village and around the estate, visiting outlying crofts. The welcomes she received were rarely effusive, but the clansmen were polite in Ian's presence.

She couldn't help feeling that he would have been much better off marrying one of the local women. Some of them were quite lovely. And they all spoke Gaelic. Although she had learned a few more words, she could not follow any of the rapid conversations Ian had with his tenants so she always had to ask him what was said as they rode away. She had the feeling he only told her the parts that wouldn't upset her.

She certainly hadn't made any friends, unless you counted Marie Flora McKinly. So without their nights of passion, she might have gone mad with no one to talk to but the cook, who came in from the village every day and with whom she decided the menus, and her occasional conversations with Angus about the supplies she needed for the household.

She glanced at her husband on the other side of the breakfast table. So handsome. The longer she stayed the more affection she felt for him. He was a kind and just Laird. And she could only admire him.

Right now he was frowning at a letter he had received that morning. He'd seemed more abstracted than usual the past couple of days. More remote.

Ian looked up and caught her watching him. 'What troubles you?'

Did he have to pretend he cared? These gentle enquiries of his always disarmed her. In one more week she would leave. She could not afford for him to see any chink in her armour. 'Do you like this way of arranging my hair? I saw it in one of the fashion plates Chrissie left behind.'

His frown deepened. 'You sighed. Twice in the last ten minutes.'

Had she sighed? 'I was just tired of your head being buried in that letter. Is it bad news?'

He glanced down at the paper. 'No.' He shook his head as if trying to convince himself. 'It just isn't as good as I had hoped.'

She waited for him to say more. Not that he usually did. He told her not to worry about clan business. He had it all in hand. She was like a porcelain doll, all right to look at, but easily broken.

An expression of horror crossed his face. 'I'm sorry,

I forgot.' He pulled a crumpled letter from his pocket. 'Logan brought it up from the post this morning. I meant to give it to you right away.'

'But you became engrossed in your own letter, which contains matters of little importance.' He looked at her blankly and she wondered why she bothered.

He slid the note across the table and her heart lifted at the sight of the familiar crest on the seal.

'It is from Alice!' She couldn't keep the excitement from her voice, but then remembered it was probably better not mentioning Alice. Her name always made him grumpy. Probably because it brought back memories of Drew. The man's shade seemed to hang over them enough as it was.

She broke the seal and read eagerly, filling her mind with images of Alice and Hawkhurst and the recent addition to their family. She chuckled at Alice's description of Hawkhurst rowing his son around the lake and playing pirates. He had been a pirate once. Or at least a privateer, which was as close to a pirate as one could come these days. He had captured the ship on which she and Alice were returning to England from Lisbon. In the end, he was the one who had ended up in irons. But the war was over and all that was behind him.

When she finished, she had a smile on her lips. She looked up to find her husband watching her intently. The expression on his face was carefully blank.

'Your friend is well?' he asked in a non-committal voice.

'Yes. She writes of her son. Nursery stories. She begs me to visit.'

'I can't take you now, or any time soon.'

In one week's time she had the right to choose whether to leave or whether to stay. 'I will visit them later, after we…' She shrugged as his lips thinned to a straight line and his jaw hardened.

He glowered and picked up his letter.

'There is nothing to keep me here, Ian,' she said, feeling the need to explain when she saw hurt in his eyes. Deep hurt. Something she thought she had glimpsed from time to time when she spoke of leaving. This time she was sure of it. If only he would say something. Tell her what he was thinking. 'Ian?'

He pushed to his feet. 'Since being my wife isn't a reason to stay, what more is to be said? Excuse me. I have a busy day ahead of me and must cancel our planned ride this afternoon.'

He strode out, leaving her staring after him. It was all in her imagination. If he wanted her to stay, if there was anything beyond their physical attraction, surely she would know by now? He would have said something. And after all, what did he have to feel hurt about? He'd got everything he wanted out of this marriage. She was the one who had been tricked. She was the one who had lost everything she valued because she'd tried to help him.

Sometimes, at night, when they were alone, when he was making love to her, she sensed he cared for her more than he would say—but if that was the case, why did he shut her out of the rest of his life?

No, it was Dunross he had wanted, not her. And now he had it.

Their marriage was purely for convenience. His. He had established the rules and she had abided by them. Now it was coming to an end. A few more days and she could head south as he had promised.

Something twisted in her chest.

* * *

'Did you hear what I said, Ian?' Niall's voice was sharp with impatience.

Ian shook his head. 'I'm sorry, I was thinking about something else. Say it again.'

Niall huffed out an impatient breath. 'I've let everyone know to bring their harvest to the mill over the next two days. The weather looks ready to hold fair for at least a week. We could take in some from farther afield if they can bring it in.'

'They know to bring it at night?' Ian asked, looking down at the two drawings of two stills Niall had spread out on a bench in the stables. Designed to fit one over the other, it might fool the authorities if they didn't look too closely.

Niall nodded. 'I gave them all the trails being watched by the gaugers. They know to avoid them.'

Logan grinned. 'And the militia are watching the coast after my visit to the tavern at Wick.'

Ian nodded. Dunstan wasn't a complete idiot, but since he expected them to smuggle brandy, he seemed ready to believe his eyes and ears. Still it would not do to underestimate the man. 'Have Tammy keep an eye on Dunstan and his men over the next couple of days. Once the barley is in, things should be quiet again until it is time to distil.'

Niall glanced down at the drawings. 'It is too bad we can't apply for a licence and do all this legally.'

It was too bad. But five hundred gallons at a time was beyond their meagre resources.

'We can't. Not with the law as it stands. I heard from Carrick the other day that, even with Lord Gordon's support, there is no hope of the English Parliament changing its mind. We proceed as planned.'

The sound he had been listening for, the reason for his abstraction, came to his ears. Coach wheels on cobbles. He straightened his shoulders. Saying goodbye to her was going to be the hardest thing he had ever done. But after careful thought, he had decided she would be safer with her friend. If she wanted to go, it was better she went now, before they ran the still, then she could claim she knew nothing if he was caught. She would be tainted enough as his wife; he would not want her to witness his disgrace.

And the clan didn't want her here. No matter how often he defended her and no matter how often he argued, there were still some who blamed her for the last fiasco. Her presence undermined his authority.

Their marriage was doomed from the start. Their worlds were too far apart.

He glanced up to see her walking down the steps dressed for travel. Her trunks were already at the bottom of the stairs. Even though he'd steeled himself for this moment all morning, her appearance came as a shock.

What, had he thought that when it came to it, she wouldn't go, when he wasn't the man she wanted?

The slight hesitation in her gait as she descended caused a painful tug in the region of his chest. She looked so beautiful and calmly remote, yet he knew she was vulnerable, fragile, and the need to protect her overcame regret.

The coachman and his guard hurried over to load her luggage in the boot. He joined her at the bottom of the steps.

'You are making an early start,' he said, for something to fill the silence between them, when he wanted to ask her to stay. Oh, that would be a fine sight for his men, the Laird begging his wife not to leave him. Especially if she went anyway. And he had no doubt she would.

'I don't wish to make more stops on the road than necessary.' Her voice was cool, emotionless, light.

As loneliness stretched before him, he gazed at her face. There was a glittering brittleness about her determination this morning. The same brittleness she'd used to keep the world at a distance at Carrick's ball, and when she fell from her horse. It dazzled, like her beauty.

It left him in awe and feeling rough and awkward. The way he'd felt as a lad, when he'd found her stoically hopping her way back home after she had fallen in a rabbit hole and twisted her ankle.

He had never seen such a pretty girl. Or heard one talk so boldly. He'd been unable to resist her pretty full lips and had stolen a kiss. How many times had they met that long-ago summer? Four. Five. They all blurred together in one happy memory he thought he'd forgotten. They had all come crashing back the moment he got her letter about Drew. Along with the guilt. When his brothers had come across them on the beach he'd been ashamed of being caught consorting with his family's enemy. He'd said some pretty cruel things. At least he had stopped his brothers from throwing rocks at her as she ran off.

An urge to tell her he needed her here, with him, rose in his throat. Angry at himself, angry at his inability to think logically when it came to this woman, to be the Laird he was raised to be, he cut himself off from his feelings and focused on what had to be done.

He opened the door and held out his hand to Selina. No gloves. Her hand nestled in his like a small broken bird. He had broken her. He saw it on her face, in the shadows in her eyes. He had taken away her freedom to choose and now he should be pleased to give it back, instead of feeling as if someone had reached into his chest and plucked out his heart.

A flash of understanding hit him hard.

While he had been busy trying to woo her, he had fallen in love, not with her beauty, though he dearly loved that, too, but with her courage and spirit, her caring heart.

Love. Was that what all this turmoil in his chest was about? Apparently it was a brutal taskmaster, for it turned a sensible man into a fool and had him wanting things he couldn't have. Like her loving him back.

How could she? He'd crushed her dreams to further his own. Well, he would not do it any longer.

So while it went against every instinct he had—indeed, he found that his hands were actually shaking as he helped her into the vehicle—he closed the door.

She sat back against the squabs.

A man ran down the steps from the keep. Angus. 'Fire!' he yelled. Breathless, his chest heaving, he struggled to speak. 'At the mill,' he panted. 'I was up on the battlements looking out for yon chaise when I saw a pillar of smoke. It can be nothing else. You need men down there right away.'

Everyone looked at Ian, their mouths agape. 'I'll take Beau to the Barleycorn and gather as many as I can there. You go on down in the chaise, Niall, please. Take Logan with you. Do what you can until we arrive.'

His brothers were already leaping onto the roof of the coach as he finished speaking. The coachman swung the carriage around as Ian ran for his horse. He glanced over his shoulder.

Damn it. Selina was in there. And in for a rough ride. He just had to hope she would understand this was important.

As the carriage rocked to a stop and the three men leaped down, Selina peered out of the window at the mill. Stunned, she watched as smoke poured from under the eaves and rose up for a few feet, only to be whipped away by the wind.

Two figures, one small, one large, ran up from the stream to throw the contents of their leather bucket through an open door into the heart of the blaze. Greedy red flames.

The coachman yanked the door open as Niall and Logan rushed to help. 'Out you come, my lady, in case these beasts panic.'

Heart racing, she jumped down. 'Go. I'll be fine.'

Outside, the roar of the fire was overpowering and so was the smell of smoke. She glanced around, wondering what she could do to help. More men were pouring over the hill and women from the village. They carried buckets of all shapes and sizes, running to form a chain from the stream to the mill. Another chain formed beside the first. Selina joined it, squeezing in beside a small girl who was sobbing with the effort of passing the heavy containers.

Selina added her strength to the child's and they soon had a backbreaking rhythm of lift and heave and pass, until her back ached.

The supply of water-filled buckets stopped for a moment.

Were they winning? She stood and stretched her back, looking towards the head of the chain. Flames licked around the doorframe. A familiar figure ran inside. Ian?

She hadn't seen him arrive, but he must have been with the rest of the men. What on earth was he doing?

One of the younger boys, his face covered in soot, ran towards the stream with several empty buckets. And the woman behind her tapped her on the back. The rhythm started again. A pause several buckets later gave her another chance to look up. Ian and several of the other men were rolling barrels out through the doorway, wet jackets pulled over their heads for protection. Spirits. They were risking their lives for smuggled liquor?

Again.

She might have guessed. Anger stirred in her stomach. How could they be so stupid?

At any moment, the militia might see the smoke and ride up and arrest the lot of them. They should have let it burn.

The child beside her tugged at her hand. 'My lady?'

Beneath the soot and the tears tracking down the child's face were thousands of freckles. 'Marie Flora? What are you doing here?'

'Pa brought his barley. Then the fire started.'

Selina turned to take the next run of buckets from the woman behind her and the backbreaking work began again.

'It's out,' someone yelled.

Cheers rang out.

Selina looked up. Smoke, acrid and choking, still swirled around the cobbled courtyard, but it was lessening, being cleared out by gusts of wind.

'Keep the water coming,' someone shouted. 'Just to be sure.' She passed on the next few buckets until there were no more to grab and walked out of the line.

Marie Flora ran off, no doubt looking for her father.

Selina surveyed the damage. Part of the roof had

fallen in, but most of the stone building remained intact. The fire had been confined to the end where the waterwheel turned the great millstones.

Thank God they had arrived in time.

She glanced around. There was no sign of Ian. Or the barrels. Then she realised the coachman was whipping up his horses.

It was leaving without her? As the coach moved off it revealed Ian on the other side of it, sooty-faced and with a hand raised in farewell.

Blast them. No doubt the coach was full of their precious barrels. Her stomach sank. She wouldn't be leaving the village tonight, after all. She wasn't sure if she was sorry or glad. Glad, damn her soft heart.

Chapter Twenty

Looking as wild as some ancient warrior, Ian set the men to shoving the ashes outside where the women poured water every time they saw smoke rising.

A tug on her skirts drew Selina's attention away from the work. 'Tommy's gone,' Marie Flora said.

For a moment the words didn't sink in. 'Your brother, Tommy?'

'I told him to wait beside the stream while I helped my father. He's not there.' Ignoring her aching back, Selina crouched down so she was eye to eye with the child. 'Do you want me to help you look for him?'

Relief flooded her wide eyes. She nodded. With a groan Selina rose and took the child's hand. 'Show me where you left him.'

Pray Heaven the little lad hadn't fallen into the stream.

She walked along beside the child, heading upstream from the mill, aching all over from the unaccustomed heavy work, limping more than usual.

'There,' Marie Flora said, pointing to a flat rock. 'I told him to sit there with Milly and wait.'

'Milly?'

'Grannie gave him one of her chicks. Pa didn't know he had it until we were halfway here.'

'How did you get here?'

'We borrowed Grannie's cart. It is in the barn. We were going to walk to the village after, to visit.'

The barn lay on the other side of the courtyard, but a small door led out the back on the side facing them. The door was ajar. 'Do you think he would be hiding in there?' It didn't seem likely even as she said it. The place would be full of smoke. Or not. The wind was blowing in the other direction.

'If he's hidin', Pa will warm the seat of his breeches,' the girl said.

As one they marched down the hill to the open door, two angry women ready to do battle with one recalcitrant little boy. Selina was already feeling sorry for little Tommy.

She pushed open the door.

'Tommy,' Marie Flora called. 'Get out of here. Wait till I tell Pa.'

No answer. Just the soft noises of animals in their stalls.

'Tommy,' Marie Flora called again and there were tears in her voice. She was afraid he wasn't here.

'Tommy, come out now,' Selina said, 'and we will say nothing to your Da.' She stepped deeper into the barn, her eyes adjusting to the dim light streaming in from this door and the opening to the courtyard.

She could see the cart and the donkey. And the pony Ian had hitched to the cart he had brought her home in when she fell off Topaz.

Something scuttled across the floor. A rat? She squeaked a protest.

'Milly,' Marie Flora said, diving forwards to catch

the chick. 'Tommy,' she shouted. She rattled off something in Gaelic, but the scold in her tone made translation unnecessary. The warm breeches again, no doubt.

Peering into the gloom, Selina expected at any moment to see Tommy step out of hiding with a sneaky little grin on his face.

Holding the chick close to her chest, Marie Flora spun around. 'Tommy.' Now she sounded furious.

Little bits of straw floated down from above to fall on the child's shoulder and in her hair. Some landed on Selina's face. She looked up. A loft! A ladder rested against an opening in the upper floor.

She touched her fingers to her lips and pointed upwards, then at the ladder. Comprehension filled the girl's eyes. She pursed her lips and lowered her brows.

Oh, dear, Tommy was going to be in trouble.

'I suppose he is not here,' Selina said loudly. 'We shall have to look elsewhere.'

'He'll catch it when Pa finds him,' Marie Flora said, with quick understanding. She tucked the chick in her grimy apron pocket.

They stomped their feet and opened the door as if they were leaving, then crept to the ladder.

Marie Flora clambered up quietly and her head disappeared, then the rest of her. Selina followed more slowly, her skirts hampering her movements. When her head cleared the opening, she stopped in shock.

Both children were staring at her, their eyes wide and terrified in the light streaming in from the gable window. A knife glinted wickedly. The breath left her lungs in a rush and she grabbed for the edge.

The man who held the children in one arm, tight against his chest, and the knife in his hand against Marie Flora's throat, smiled.

'It seems luck is with me, after all. Do come right up, Lady Selina,' Tearny said.

Ian stared around at the mess. The fire had been quite deliberate. Yet who on earth among those who knew about the still would want to see it damaged? Even if the success of the mill hadn't meant good money for the clan, no Highlander in his right mind would want to see good whisky go up in flames.

He could imagine them stealing it and drinking it, but not this. He ran his gaze around the courtyard. Everyone here was covered in soot and working hard to clean up the mess.

Niall joined him, also looking around. 'Anyone hurt?'

Ian shook his head. 'No. And the damage is minimal. Whoever set the fire must not have realised that it is not the mill where we have been putting all our efforts.'

'Do you think Albright might be behind it?'

He took a deep breath. His father-in-law had seemed more saddened than angry, though he had been that, too. 'I don't know, but it doesn't make any sense. What good would it do him?'

'Revenge.'

Ian glanced around for his wife. The last time he saw her she was passing buckets of water.

A group of women stood nearby, washing up in a bucket. He tapped the nearest one on the shoulder. 'Have you see Lady Selina?'

The woman smiled. 'Aye, Laird. Going up the hill behind the barn with the wee McKinly girl, not more than five minutes ago.'

McKinly wandered over then; his face was grim. 'The mill should nae take too much to repair. We were lucky to save my whisky.'

'Aye, lucky. But how the hell did it start?'

''Tis the oddest thing. My wee lad said he smelled the smoke of a pipe when we pulled up. I ne'er smelled a thing. I unloaded the barrels as you'd instructed and took the sacks of barley into the stable to unload it there when my wee Tommy yelled fire from outside.' He rubbed at the back of his neck. 'The mill door was open. I could have sworn I barred it behind me, but I'm that bluidy tired from harvesting... I'm sorry, Laird. It must have been a spark from the donkey's hooves, or maybe my boots. I canna think of aught else.'

Had the other man been smoking and was now trying to lay the blame elsewhere? The clear gaze meeting his showed no signs of guile. A spark from a hoof hardly seemed likely, though.

'Did Tommy see anyone?'

'I didna' ask him. I sent the bairns off to wait up the hill and ran for water. It took hold verra fast. Almost seemed like it had started in several places at once. I just thank God the barley is safe in the barn.'

Ian clapped McKinly on the shoulder. 'And I thank God you acted so quickly. I can never repay you.'

The other man smiled a shy smile. 'Glad to do it, Laird.' He looked around. 'But now I can't find Marie Flora. I told her to care for her brother. Next thing I see her passing buckets.'

'Apparently she is with the Lady Selina. Come, man, we will find them together.'

The hillside behind the barn was deserted. Ian frowned. 'One of the women said she saw them head in this direction.'

McKinly pointed to a flat rock. 'This is where I told her and the boy to wait.'

* * *

Forced at the point of a knife to stand in a corner with the children, Selina watched Tearny scatter straw from a pile of bales all over the floor in little heaps. Her body was still trembling with the shock of seeing the knife held to Tommy's scrawny little neck. She tried to swallow the lump in her throat.

Tearny laid his knife down at his feet and pulled out his tinderbox.

Dear God. Her stomach roiled. 'You fired the mill.'

He smiled with terrible triumph. 'Indeed. I told Gilvry when he paid me off he'd have his just deserts one of these days. The best of it is it comes with a reward. A good one.'

'What are you talking about?'

His answer was a grin. He struck flint against steel. The click sounded terribly loud in the strained silence.

Tommy turned his face into her skirts. Marie Flora was looking up at her expectantly, relying on her to save them.

The tinder didn't spark. She breathed a sigh of relief. Tearny fiddled with the flint.

Selina eyed the distance to the knife and knew it was too far. Somehow she had to distract him.

'Come, Mr Tearny, whatever grudge you hold against my husband, you surely do not wish to harm a woman and two children.'

'Mr Tearny,' he mimicked. 'How are you today, Mr Tearny? You never expected an answer, though, did you, you haughty bitch. I saw how pleased you were, though, the day he gave me notice. You married the wrong man, my lady.'

This wasn't making any sense. 'I don't see what my marriage has to do with you, Mr Tearny.'

'No, I'm sure you don't. Ian cock-of-the-walk Gilvry shouldn't have brought you here today. You can blame him for this.'

His gaze went back to his tinderbox. 'He should never have got his hands on Dunross.' He struck the flint against the steel. Again no spark.

A horrid thought entered her mind, one she didn't want to believe. 'Are you doing this on my father's behalf?'

He looked surprised, then he sneered. 'This has nothing to do with your father. Still, I won't be sorry to know he'll also be grieving his loss.'

Her heart stopped at the callousness of his words. 'My father won't care one way or the other.' She slid one foot forwards.

'Do you think not? It is not the impression he gave me when he thought you were abducted. What a slut, going off in the night with Gilvry and letting everyone worry.' He shot her a glare. 'If he'd been picked up by the gaugers that night, we would all have been better off.'

'Someone paid you to betray him.'

'Quick, aren't you?'

She inched forwards another step. 'Thank you. Who was it?'

His glanced up, his eyes gleaming with cunning. 'Wouldn't you like to know?'

Blast the man. 'As soon as you walk out of here, they will know you are to blame. Let us go and I'll say nothing.'

His lip curled. 'No one saw me come and no one will see me leave. I might not be a Scot, but I know my way around these hills better than most.'

Two more steps and she'd be close enough to dive for

the knife—if she could just keep him talking. 'Don't I have the right to know who is behind my death?'

He struck the flint again. The straw caught.

Little Tommy cried out. Tearny's eyes snapped to the child. He picked up the knife and waved it. 'Enough talk. It is time I was finished here. I have a purse to collect.' He tucked the knife in his waistband.

Her heart pounded. Her voice shook. 'If it is me you want to hurt, let the children go.'

He glanced at Marie Flora. 'Well, little girl? Would you know me again?' He spoke so kindly, so mildly, he sounded almost harmless.

'Aye. I know you,' Marie Flora said, her curls springy with defiance. 'You are a bad man.'

Selina groaned. Wrong answer, child. Not that she believed the right one would have done them any good. Tearny had made up his twisted mind.

He crouched and blew gently on the spark. The small pile of straw between his knees smouldered, then flared. He picked up the bundle and backed down the ladder, until all they could see was his face like some grinning devil emerging from the pit of hell. He touched the flames to the straw encircling the hole in the floor and tossed the bundle at them, making them back up. In that brief second, they lost any chance of getting out.

'Scream all you want, Lady Selina,' he said. 'Hopefully Gilvry will rush to save you and it will be the end of him, too.'

As he disappeared, she rushed for the opening. The heat of the flames drove her back. While she whirled around, looking for another way out, the flames spread, racing outwards. The dry timber of the floor started to catch.

Smoke filled her mouth and her nose. It was hopeless.

Chapter Twenty-One

Ian and McKinly had walked a good distance up the hill and still no sign of Selina or the children.

'She's a grand lass, your wife,' McKinly said. 'Marie Flora has done nothing but talk about her since she left. How she peeled the tatties and mended my shirts. And the way she joined the women on the buckets, you would never know she was a lady born. You should be proud of her.'

'I am,' Ian said. Proud enough to realise she was far too good for the likes of him. His biggest fear right now was her being caught here by the gaugers or the local militia. He had to get her away. 'Where in hell's name did they go?'

McKinly glanced back down the hill towards the mill and froze. 'Dear God, not again,' he muttered. 'The barn is on fire.'

Startled, Ian turned.

Wisps of smoke were curling up from the roof. He cursed. 'Fire,' he roared racing downhill. He had to get the animals out. And the barley, or all of their earlier efforts wouldn't mean a damn thing.

'I don't get it,' McKinly panted, jogging alongside

him. 'The smoke is from inside the roof. Perhaps we should have looked there first.'

Holy hell. 'You think the children are in there?'

The look of terror in McKinly's eyes was answer enough.

Ian increased his pace. If the children were there, then... He didn't dare finish the thought.

He ducked through the low-arched door as a male figure ran out through the open double doors into the courtyard opposite. He hesitated, looking around.

'Up there!' McKinly yelled. Two small legs dangled from the trapdoor where the ladder should have rested. It lay on the floor. A moment later, the rest of Tommy appeared, in his shirtsleeves, his hands above his head, dangling far above the floor.

Ian and McKinly ran beneath the opening where Selina's head and shoulders were now visible. She was holding the lad, her hands gripping the boy's elbows, smoke writhing around her. 'Let him go,' Ian called. 'I'll catch him.'

She raised her face, the effort of holding the boy etched on her features, along with the flash of relief when she realised help had come.

The boy dropped with a screech. Heart in his throat, Ian caught him and handed him off to his father. He heaved the ladder up against the edge of the opening and dashed up.

Heat hit him in the face like a wall. Nearby, bales of hay were on fire. The floorboards were smouldering. Somehow Selina and the child were standing in a small area free of flames, the remains of a singed boy's coat in her hands. They were coughing and gasping, the fire crowding in on them. She batted at the flames with the coat.

He grabbed the child and handed her down to her waiting father behind him on the ladder, then, without really quite knowing how it had happened, he had Selina on his shoulder and was making his way down to safety.

As he reached the floor, men were running in with buckets of water. Another was leading the animals out of the barn and others were manhandling the sacks of barley. It looked like they'd be in time.

He carried Selina out and up the hill away from danger. Away from the flames to safety. This was where he wanted her. Safe in his arms.

He set her down, inspected her hands, her face covered in soot, her reddened bare arms, saw the singed hem of her gown and a bone-deep shudder went through him. Another few moments and it might have been too late.

He pulled her close against his chest. 'Tell me you are all right.' His heart was beating so hard he thought it would make a hole in his chest.

She struggled against him and he loosened his grip. 'I'm all right,' she said, gazing up at him, her eyes full of shock. 'The children.'

'They are in fine fettle,' McKinly said from right behind him. 'Tommy, don't tell me you did that?'

Ian whirled around to stare at the cringing boy.

'No,' Selina said. 'It was Tearny.'

The man he'd seen running out. He'd all but forgotten him in the haste to get to Selina.

Anger burned in his veins at the danger she'd been in. Fury hotter than the flames in that loft. There was only one way to be rid of it. He raked his gaze over the courtyard and saw no one who looked like his erstwhile land agent. He pushed Selina towards McKinly. 'Take care of them.'

'Ian, wait!' she called out. 'He's dangerous.'

He couldn't help the smile that came to his lips. 'So am I, lass.'

Leaving her with McKinly, he went in search of Tammy McNab. 'Did you see Tearny pass you by?'

Tammy looked puzzled. 'He ran up towards the road. To get more help, he said.'

The rodent was running back to his burrow. Ian would catch him long before then. He lengthened his stride and headed up the cart track leading to the road. It wasn't long before he saw his quarry bent double, catching his breath a few yards from the main road. So he thought he'd escaped.

A smile touched his lips.

The other man must have sensed he was not alone, because he straightened, turning to look back. His jaw dropped. Shock. Horror. He put his head down and ran, but with his paunch, he was no match for Ian's long stride. Realising his danger, he cut off the road and headed downhill, no doubt thinking to lose Ian among the heather. In his haste, he stumbled over the rough terrain, his feet catching in tussocks that in places were up to his knees.

Within moments, Ian was upon him.

Tearny pivoted, pulling a knife, holding it in front of him, his chest heaving, his eyes wild.

Ian put a hand to his sock and pulled out his dirk. 'Give it up, Tearny. You can't get away with it.' He lunged.

Tearny dodged, then slashed out with the knife. It sliced through Ian's shirt. It stung like the devil. Blood ran warm down his chest. A quick glance showed little more than a scratch, but the man was quick with a knife. He would have to be more careful.

Tearny grinned. 'How good of you to come after me. I can finish what I started.'

None of this made any sense. 'What are you after? I paid your wages in full.'

The man's grin didn't falter.

'Did Albright put you up to this?'

'The answer won't matter to a dead man.'

Ian lunged again. If he could get behind his opponent, he could get an arm around his neck.

Tearny twisted away, thrusting with his blade as he went. He missed. His eyes turned wary. Then his gaze shifted. He looked past Ian. His jaw dropped. His eyes widened.

An accomplice? Ian backed around to see what had caught the other man's attention.

He groaned at the sight of Selina running towards them. Alone. The strength of purpose in the set of her shoulders made him feel proud. And angry. The word wait didn't seem to exist in her vocabulary.

But she wasn't alone. McKinly appeared over the brow of the hill, followed by Tammy. He turned to Tearny. 'Seems you are outnumbered.'

The man turned and fled.

Idiot. There was nowhere to go. Ian raced after him and stared in surprise as the man tripped and went flying. He almost felt sorry for him as he lay in the grass, too stunned to get to his feet.

He didn't move when Ian reached him. Warily he turned the man onto his back by the shoulder. His eyes were wide open and full of pain.

For a moment, Ian didn't understand. Then he saw the hilt of the knife sticking out of his chest. He'd fallen on the blade. Ian's gut churned. He dropped to his knees.

Tearny's gaze focused on Ian and he seemed to rally.

'It is not over, Gilvry. You'll see. I've paid my debt, but yours awaits.'

'What the hell are you talking about?' Ian said, pulling off his jacket, thinking to somehow staunch the wound.

Tearny's breath rattled in his throat and then his eyes were staring sightlessly up at the sky.

Selina came up behind him. He rose and blocked her view of the body as the other men arrived. 'He's dead. By his own hand.'

Selina turned her face away, her expression full of doubt.

'I swear it. I did not touch him.'

'I know.'

Then why the doubt?

Her gaze dropped to his chest. 'You are hurt.'

'A scratch.'

'Did he say who was behind him in this?' she asked.

'No.' Ian didn't want to give voice to his suspicions. 'He admitted to me it wasn't my father.'

Could she read his mind?

'I asked him, just before he left us in the barn. He thought my question a great joke. But he wouldn't say who it was.'

Ian pulled her close and tipped up her tear-streaked face. 'Then we have something to be glad of, right?'

She nodded and gave him a wobbly smile.

Tammy was staring at the man on the ground. 'He used to come in the Barleycorn. None of us could understand why he came night after night. It wasn't for the company. We rarely spoke anything but the Gaelic. Stupid Irishman never could understand a word.'

Selina lifted her head. 'He threatened Tommy McKinly in Gaelic. I heard him.'

Tammy looked scandalised. 'He never once showed he could speak the Gaelic.'

'I think his mother was Scottish. He was some distant relative of Carrick's. He recommended him to my father,' Selina said.

Tammy turned pale. 'The scoundrel. He must have overheard us talking. He betrayed us to the gaugers.' His face crumpled. 'Laird, I never guessed he understood a word.' He cursed.

'One mystery is solved,' Ian said, glad it wasn't one of the clan. But Tearny wasn't working alone if his last words could be believed. The back of Ian's neck prickled. He wished like hell he'd been able to get more out of the man. 'Whoever was behind him might try to strike again. We will have to be careful who we trust. I hope he was paid well, because he has paid the ultimate price.' Yet the threat was still there. Selina might have been killed, for the sake of whisky and his clan. And if Tearny had told the truth, the danger wasn't over.

It was good that she was leaving. Going somewhere she would be safe.

He turned and gestured to the corpse on the ground. 'Tammy, get him back to the village. We'll need to inform the coroner. I'll be back in time to speak to him.'

'I'll fetch the cart,' McKinly said.

Ian put an arm around Selina's shoulders, wanting to hold her and offer comfort, and take it, too, in the knowledge she was safe, though he knew it was the last thing he should be doing.

She shivered, not from cold, but from the blaze of awareness between them. He felt it course through his blood. 'The chaise should be back any moment,' he said.

She didn't answer.

He slowed his walk, waiting for McKinly and Tammy

to get a little ahead of them. He stopped and swung her around to face him. 'Tearny could have killed you. It is not safe here.' As he looked down into her face he found himself catching her nape and seeking her lips. A farewell kiss. It was probably the last time he would see her.

She turned her head at the last moment and his kiss landed on her ear. Ears were good. And even though he could smell the smoke from the fire on her, he could also smell the perfume she favoured. Something light and floral.

He glanced over her shoulder and saw the carriage a few yards away, waiting. He had to let her go. It was the right thing to do. He caught her chin between thumb and finger and turned her face.

Anger glowed in her eyes. 'No, Ian. I won't let you do that to me again.' Her lips thinned. 'It was always about Dunross. I wish you joy of it.'

Startled, he stared at her. Then he realised the truth. It really was over.

He clenched his teeth hard. Balled his hands at his sides. His heart twisted with the knowledge of how badly he had used her. He'd had his chance; if she no longer responded to his kisses, then he had nothing to offer. 'I'll walk you up there.'

He took her arm and walked her slowly up the hill to the waiting chaise. His heart felt as heavy as lead. He wanted to say something to fill the silence, but the longer it went on, the more difficult it became, as if the closer they drew to the carriage, the greater the distance between them.

The gap had always been too wide to conquer, even when they were younger.

Once settled on the squabs, Selina leaned forwards

and lowered the window. He let himself imagine that she was having trouble leaving.

'I really do wish you well, Ian,' she said softly. 'I wish it might have been different.'

Over the past few weeks he'd watched her smiles become brighter, heard her laughter become more and more brittle. And if it was Dunstan she wanted, then no matter how he felt he must make things right. He must.

Looking at her now, the smudges of soot on her cheek, the wild tangle of jet hair around her beautiful heart-shaped face, she didn't look at all out of place here in the wilds of the Highlands, but he had tricked her into this marriage for the sake of his clan. He owed her a debt he could never repay, but, as much as he wanted her to stay, he wanted her happiness more. Since he could not change the past, he had to let her choose how to live her future. He had to give her that gift.

A band tightened around his chest. The pain of loss. But she deserved better than a penniless Laird. She deserved to shine among her own people. To find love. He rubbed at a smudge on her lovely cheek. 'You look like you've been to hell and back.'

Her smile was blade sharp. 'I'll repair the damage when we stop to change the horses.'

She couldn't wait to be gone.

He had only himself to blame. He shouldn't have let his weakness for her, his desire, influence his decision the night she came to warn him. He should have left her at the keep and trusted her to keep silent.

'You'll find a welcome at my hearth any time you choose to seek it,' he said, his voice sounding hoarse. He hoped he didn't sound as pathetic as he felt.

Her gaze searched his face. 'Thank you.'

He fought the urge to drag her from the coach and

kiss her into staying, seducing her into forgetting how he'd played her false. Passion was the one thing they had between them that was honest. But passion only lasted until the morning. In the cold light of day he'd once more be faced with the truth.

He made her unhappy.

He covered the small hand gripping the window with his and found it chilled to the bone. She was so fragile, so delicate, so incredibly strong.

'Are we to leave then, gov?' the coachman called down from the box.

'A moment more,' he said as she began to withdraw into the carriage. There was one thing more to tell her, one gift he had to give, no matter how it tore him in two. He drew in a deep breath. 'There is something I must tell you.'

She raised a brow.

Was that hope he saw in her eyes? Hope for what? He shook the thought aside. Hope had no place in what he was about to say. 'I'm sorry I tricked you into marrying me. Our marriage was…well, it is on pretty shaky ground, even for Scotland. We could probably have it annulled.'

She gasped. Looked shocked.

'I know.' He shook his head. 'It might not work. But a divorce is not out of the question, either.'

Her face looked pale beneath the grim of the smoke. 'You said nothing of this before.'

'No.' He'd kept hoping she would want to stay. But he'd been thinking only of himself. 'I'll talk to a solicitor as soon as I can and send you word.'

Her gaze clashed with his and he thought he saw regret in the depths of her eyes. He hadn't expected that. Was that cause for hope?

'I see,' she said coolly. 'It would have been a whole lot easier if you had let me go the same day my father left, as I suggested.'

Never had he heard her sound so cold. And now he knew the reason for her regret. 'Yes. I'm sorry. I will set up an account for you at Coutts's Bank. Draw on it as you find the need until things are settled. I will write and let you know the details.'

She nodded gravely and for a moment she was the large-eyed sprite he'd fallen in love with as a boy and, feeling like a knight in shining armour, had carried home to his castle.

So soft and sentimental. So weak when it came to this woman. And he'd let his weakness bring her harm.

He stepped back.

'Promise me you will be careful.' He heard tears in her voice, but when he looked into her eyes, they were clear and dry.

Too full of emotion to say more, he raised a hand and walked to the front of the carriage.

'Drive carefully,' he warned the coachman. 'Or deal with me.'

The coachman touched his hat with his whip. And the carriage moved off. He watched the dust rise behind it until it was only there in his imagination. He was doing the right thing for her. She could change her mind any time she wanted. He'd always be here, waiting.

He smiled wryly. Love was a very strange thing. It made you do the one thing you didn't want to do, so the one you loved could be happy. And it hurt like hell.

Now he knew how Drew must have felt when he'd forced him to get on that ship for America. Loss. Despair. Anger. Unending loneliness.

Just deserts, then.

Chapter Twenty-Two

Selina had been at Hawkhurst for two weeks and was sitting with Alice in the drawing room dandling her friend's four-month-old son and heir, David, on her lap.

'He is such a good child,' Selina said.

'At the moment he is.' Alice, her freckles more noticeable than ever, smiled her quiet smile. 'At three in the morning, he turns into a hungry monster and reminds me of his father.'

Selina tickled the satin-soft cheek and he smiled sleepily. So adorable.

'You must marry again as soon as you are divorced from that dreadful Highlander,' Alice said. 'You should have children of your own.'

The note of censure in her friend's practical voice caused her to stiffen. Words in defence of Ian hovered on the tip of her tongue. She kept them behind her teeth. Alice was only reflecting her own anger. The hurt she'd poured out into her friend's ears when she'd arrived at Hawkhurst's front door.

The anger had gone, but the hurt still remained at being his dupe.

But did she really want to sever all ties? Her marriage to Ian hadn't caused much of a stir. It seemed that Dunstan had said little or nothing about the end of her understanding with him and nothing about Ian's criminal activities had come to light so far.

She and Ian wouldn't be the first married couple to live estranged, each going their own way. It wasn't as if he needed an heir. He had his brothers for that.

The thought reminded her of something. 'Oh, I meant to tell you, Chrissie is expecting a happy event. Perhaps my father will finally get his son.'

Alice, like the good friend she was, let her change the subject. 'Please give her my congratulations when next you write. How is your father?'

'In alt. Very proud of his accomplishment, according to Chrissie. She asked me if I would like to visit them.'

Alice looked at her sharply. 'With your father's agreement?'

'Apparently so.'

'That is good,' Alice said with a smile. 'Families belong together.'

And Ian wasn't family, was he? He was her inconvenient husband. She just wished she didn't miss him.

She held back a sigh. Ian had his own family. They also only wanted Dunross. They were welcome to it. She just wished she could be rid of the ache in her chest.

Time. It would take time for the wound to heal.

She just wished she didn't have the feeling that she would never feel whole again.

The door swung back. A tall dark-haired man strode across the room to kiss Alice on the lips.

'Back so soon?' Alice said fondly.

'I invited Jaimie to tea,' Hawkhurst said, greeting Selina, then taking his son from her arms and lifting him high above his head. 'And how is my feisty son?'

Two more men entered the room at a more leisurely pace. Alice's father, Alex Fulton. He wasn't a well man, but there was joy in his eyes as he watched Hawkhurst kiss his grandson. The other man was Hawkhurst's cousin, Jaimie, Lord Sanford. Fair haired, slender and impeccably dressed, he spent most evenings with the Hawkhursts when he wasn't in town, Alice had explained.

'That child is ready for a sleep,' Alice scolded her husband.

'Let me take him,' Alex Fulton said.

Hawkhurst handed the child over to his grandfather and watched him leave the room. 'Your father is having a good day today,' he said to his wife.

Alice's expression became sad. 'They are few and far between these days, but he seems happy.' Alex Fulton had suffered badly from his overindulgence of alcohol, but in the last few years he hadn't drunk a drop of liquor. It was only that abstinence that had prolonged his life.

Simpson, their butler, who had once been Hawkhurst's steward at sea, carried in the tea tray, set it beside Alice and left, his rolling-seaman's gait still in evidence.

Jaimie brought Selina her cup and sat down beside her, balancing his cup and saucer precariously on his knee.

'May I say how ravishing you are looking today, Mrs Gilvry,' he said. His green eyes were warm with admiration. He'd been engaging in a mild flirtation with her ever since she had arrived. He was quite the rake, according to Alice, and Selina had felt just a little flattered by his attentions.

She'd enjoyed their verbal sparring. It stopped her from thinking about Ian. At least for a few hours in the day. Her nights were a very different story.

She missed him all the time, but at night, when she was alone with her thoughts, she felt the full force of her misery.

'You are very kind to say so, Lord Sanford.' She gave him a brilliant smile. 'Is that a new way of tying your cravat?'

'Don't encourage him,' Hawkhurst said. 'He's already far too dandified.'

The sound of someone pounding on the front door echoed through the house.

Alice glanced at her husband, who rose to his feet.

'What the devil?' Hawkhurst said.

Jaimie went to the window. 'I don't recognise the horse, but it's a fine bit of blood and bone. Probably some irate shipowner from your past,' he said to Hawkhurst.

The butler scurried in. 'There is a barbarian at the door, my lord,' he said, all out of breath and mopping at his brow. 'Shall I fetch your shotgun?'

The pounding started again.

'Are you saying you left this man on the doorstep?' Sanford asked.

'He looks ready for murder,' Simpson replied.

'What do you mean, a barbarian?' Hawkhurst asked frowning.

'He is wearing some sort of skirt.'

Heart pounding, Selina rose to her feet. 'What does this barbarian look like?' She found she could hardly get the words out, she felt so breathless.

'As to that, my lady, it is hard to tell, for he has a black beard covering most of his face.'

A beard. That didn't sound like Ian, then. Her heart dipped. Perhaps he'd sent one of his men with a message. Perhaps he was in trouble. 'What colour is his kilt and plaid?'

'My lady?'

'His skirt.'

'I didn't notice the colour, my lady, but he was demanding you come to the door if I wouldn't let him in.'

It had to be someone from Ian. Her mouth dried. 'Perhaps we should at least find out what he wants?'

''Tis a good thing your doors are solid,' Jaimie observed, returning to his seat beside her. While he seemed insolent enough—indeed, he seemed very much the fop—there was a lethal quality about his movements that occasionally made her wonder if he wasn't more than the man milliner his cousin often called him.

The butler looked to his employer. 'Shall I set the dogs on him, then?'

'Certainly not,' Alice said, her gaze on Selina. 'Send him up.'

Hawkhurst's brow lowered and he sent his wife a considering look.

She shrugged and he said nothing, but walked to the hearth and leaned one elbow on the mantel, watching the door.

Selina clasped her hands together, sure it couldn't be Ian and praying nothing had happened to him. Like being arrested. Or deported. Or, bile rose in her throat, hanged.

If so, she hoped his people were suitably grateful, she thought with a surge of bitterness.

The door burst open.

She gasped. The man towering in the doorway indeed looked like a ruffian. 'Ian,' she choked out.

Never had she seen him look so dreadful. A beard covered his jaw beneath gaunt cheeks. Purple smudges beneath sapphire eyes snapping with fury made him look as if he had not slept for days. His blazing gaze honed in on Sanford.

'Are you the lordling trifling with my wife?' he asked in a dangerous voice.

Jaimie aimed a brief glance at Hawkhurst, who hadn't moved, and shrugged, his mouth mocking. 'Since we haven't been introduced, I'm not sure which one of the ladies I'm trifling with is yours.'

Ian clenched his fists. 'She is sitting beside you, you little cur. Outside with you, so I can teach you some manners.'

'How very rustic, old chap.' Jaimie pushed to his feet.

Selina leapt in front of him. 'Ian, stop it, this instant. No one is trifling with me. Where on earth did you get such a notion? And besides, if they were, why would you care?'

His gaze left Jaimie and focused on her. 'Because you are my wife.'

'Dear Lady Selina, did you really marry such a dreadful boor?' Sanford drawled. He raised his quizzing glass and inspected Ian from head to toe.

'Enough, Jaimie,' Hawkhurst commanded, moving into the centre of the room.

Ian turned and looked surprised, as if he hadn't seen Hawkhurst until that moment. And then he took in Alice. Some of the rage in his face lessened. 'I beg your pardon. I was under the impression that this…this dandy was alone with my wife.'

Jaimie picked a piece of lint from his sleeve and watched it drift to the floor before meeting Ian's gaze. 'Does that mean you don't want to engage in fisticuffs on the lawn?'

Ian's eyes narrowed. He looked at Selina. 'It means

I'm reserving judgement, so don't be going anywhere just yet a while.'

He sounded so very Scottish when he was angered. The sound of those rolling *r*s and the lilting cadence made her feel weak inside. Not to mention the way he was looking at her as if he wanted to eat her whole.

'I believe introductions are in order,' Hawkhurst said mildly. 'Followed by an explanation.' Once more his gaze drifted to his wife, who was looking suspiciously innocent.

Selina stared at her. 'Alice?'

Alice shook her head.

Hawkhurst continued on as if Selina hadn't spoken. 'I am Hawkhurst.' He stuck out a hand. He was as tall as Ian, but nowhere near as broad, but he didn't look the slightest bit intimidated, whereas Selina could feel her knees wobbling in the strangest way.

'This is my wife, Lady Hawkhurst. We don't tend to stand on formality, so Michael and Alice will do.'

Ian bowed over Alice's hand and did it with such grace and charm that Selina felt proud.

'This young reprobate is my cousin, Jaimie, Lord Sanford,' Hawkhurst continued. His lips curved in a hard smile. 'I can assure you he would not be welcome in this house if his manners to my wife's guest were anything but impeccable.'

Ian shot a glance at Alice. 'It is not what I am hearing.'

'Nevertheless,' Hawkhurst said in a tone that did not brook argument, 'it is the case.'

Jaimie raised a brow and held out a languid hand.

Ian glared at it, then clasped it with his own. 'Sanford.' Then he grinned. 'You've a firmer hand than I expected.'

Jaimie bowed very slightly and made as if to return to his seat beside Selina. Ian glowered and he smothered a laugh and strolled to the chair at Alice's right hand.

'How can we be of service?' Hawkhurst asked.

Ian looked blank.

'I am assuming,' Hawkhurst drawled, 'you came with some purpose in mind?'

'I would have conversation with Lady Selina.'

'By all means,' Hawkhurst said, gesturing to the sofa.

'Alone,' Ian said. 'If you don't mind.'

'That is up to the lady, surely?' Hawkhurst said.

All eyes turned on her. Heat crawled up her neck and into her cheeks, where it stung painfully.

She swallowed the lump in her throat. 'I am not sure there is anything to say.'

'I have something to say,' Ian said. And he sounded very determined to get it off his chest.

'Very well. I will hear it.'

He glared around the room. 'What I have to say does not need an audience. I would like to be alone with my wife, if you do not mind.'

'I, for one,' Jaimie said, 'fear for the lady's safety. What assurance will you give us that you will not try to bully her when we are gone?'

'Or trick her,' Alice added.

Ian flushed.

Selina winced. He might not be pleased to learn she had been so frank with Alice.

'I give you my word,' Ian said, his gaze fixed on her face.

She didn't actually have the right to refuse him. He was her husband, but she was glad to see he did not force that issue. Though she had the feeling he might, if she turned him down.

'It is all right, Alice,' she said. 'Mr Gilvry has given his word. If he has something of a private nature to discuss with me, I am quite willing to hear it.'

Hawkhurst bowed and brought his wife to her feet. 'We will be in the library, just down the hall within calling distance, should you have need of us.'

'Such a pleasure,' Jaimie said, with a slight inclination of his head. 'Lady Selina, I look forward to seeing you at dinner tonight.'

Ian looked ready to strangle him as he followed his cousin Hawkhurst out of the door.

'Well, Ian,' she said, glad that the thump of her heart in her chest did not affect the calm of her voice. Or at least she hoped it did not. She was shaking much too hard to be sure.

He gestured to the sofa. 'Please, sit down.'

She sat. He did not. He towered over her, looking down with narrowed eyes as if he wanted to assure himself she was still in one piece.

Heat travelled up from her belly. Answering heat flared in his eyes.

But that had always been the best part of their marriage.

She took a quick breath. 'You wanted to speak with me. What was it you wanted to say?'

He straightened his shoulders. 'Did you want a divorce?'

Pain seized her heart and twisted it cruelly. She lowered her gaze to her hands, kept them fixed on her fingers so he would not see how his words wounded.

She forced a smile before she looked up. 'Is that why you came? La, sir, surely a letter to your solicitor or even to me was all that was necessary?'

'He's the kind of man you should have married. That

young puppy who just left here. Another drawing-room dandy.'

'He is a well-bred young gentleman, to be sure.'

'What happened to Dunstan? I thought you wanted him.'

'No.' Was he accusing her of something?

He spun away and paced the carpet in front of her. 'When your friend wrote to me last week saying how unhappy you were and how you ought to be free as soon as possible because there was a gentleman...' he paused to glower at her '...another gentleman, with an interest, I thought I'd come here and take the high road, offer you your freedom if that's what you wanted. But the closer I got, the less noble I wanted to be.'

'Alice wrote to you?' A feeling of betrayal rippled through her. 'I suppose she meant for the best.' Only right now she wanted to strangle her friend.

He stopped pacing and looked at her. 'I thought so, too.'

Her heart no longer seemed to be beating at all. It still hurt, but didn't seem to be working. 'You did?'

'So I will ask you again,' he said harshly. 'Shall I set the wheels in motion for our divorce?'

Should he? 'And Dunross?'

He took a deep breath. 'It goes back to you.'

She stared at him. 'It was the only reason you married me.'

He gave her a long look. 'It was not.'

'This is part of the settlement, isn't it? The arrangements you made with my father.'

He shook his head. 'Your father made Dunross over to me, free and clear. But I'm no that kind of cur, Selina. Yes, I wanted Dunross. Gilvrys have always wanted Dunross, but I never expected to get it. I wanted you, too, but I never expected to get you either. I do not deserve a woman as fine as you. And I'll not be robbing you of your dowry.'

It was a pretty long speech, but something in the middle of it was pretty important. 'What do you mean, you always wanted me?'

He let go a long sigh. 'I believe I fell in love with you when I was eighteen, though I never would admit it, given the history between our families. It was my own stupid pride that made me turn from you when my brothers came along that day at Balnaen. I was ashamed for not doing my duty and hating you the way they did.' He gave a short laugh. 'I have never done my duty where you are concerned. You muddle every proper thought in my head.'

She knew just what he meant. He only had to look at her to muddle her brain. 'Did you say you loved me?'

Red stained his cheekbones above the disreputable beard. He took a deep breath. 'Aye. I. Love. You.'

No mistaking that. Something like joy bubbled in her chest. And hope. 'Why did you never speak of this before?'

He stilled, looking at her, and in that startlingly blue gaze she saw his hope. Only it was stronger than hope. It was longing.

Mingled with dread. 'Would ye have believed me? Would it not have seemed a mite too convenient? And besides, you told me you loved Dunstan.'

Not exactly. 'I told you I had chosen him.' She had a bit of confessing to do on her own account. 'I picked him because I knew my heart wasn't engaged. I knew he couldn't hurt me the way you had.'

He blinked. 'When I saw you again at Carrick's ball, I wanted to hate you. Because of Drew.'

'You blamed me.'

'I blamed myself for wanting to please you. I vowed I would not let you twist me around your finger again.' He gave a short laugh. 'So you tied my heart in knots instead.' He inhaled a breath so deep she thought the seams of his jacket might split asunder. A ragged-sounding breath. 'Well. Is it to be a divorce?'

She shook her head.

'If you are to stay as my wife, then you will have to live as my wife. I'll not have it any other way. And I'll do all in my power to prove my love. I promise you that.' His voice ended on a low seductive note.

Heat raced under her skin as the thought of the benefits of being his wife came to mind in full force. But she wasn't quite done torturing him yet. After all, he had offered to divorce her and let her stay here for almost two weeks when all the time he'd known he loved her. 'And where would we live?'

His face twisted in a grimace. 'Wherever you prefer.'

Oh, the delicious sound of his *r*s as they vibrated all through her body and down to her toes. But did he mean what he said? 'In London, then?'

His expression became stoic. It reminded her of the time she had dressed the bullet wound in his arm. He was determined not to let her see how the thought irked him. 'If that is what you want.'

'Whatever I want?'

He nodded, albeit a little stiffly. He sat beside her and took her hand lacing and unlacing their fingers. 'I missed you.'

She almost didn't hear the words, he said them so softly.

'I couldn't sleep,' he said louder. 'Couldn't force a mouthful of food down my throat. All I could do was work and try not to think. Try not to wonder if things would have been different, if I had found the courage to tell you the truth of how I felt.'

'Oh,' she said, her heart lifting a little more than was seemly. 'And you did find the courage.'

'Aye. I did. For there was no denying it, no matter how hard I tried.' He brought her hand up to his lips and kissed it with a gentle kind of reverence that was so out of character for this big rough man, except around her. Her insides quivered with longing.

'I missed you,' he said. 'I missed your smiles and I missed your laughter. I even missed your frowns. My chest ached like a great rock was pressing down on it.'

His symptoms sounded much like hers.

'Oh, Ian. I did not mean to hurt you.'

'It was not your doing.' He stood up. 'Where you are concerned I have no strength at all.' He dropped to one knee. 'Selina, *leannan*, please, come back to me. I know I treated you badly. I did indeed trick you into marriage, but it was for your sake as much as mine. I swear to you I did not know about the dowry. You have to believe me.'

As he gazed into her face, she knew he did not lie. 'I believe you.'

'Then you'll come back to me?' He took another of those deep shuddering breaths and gazed into her eyes with longing and hope and a vulnerability that caused her poor heart to contract in the sweetest way. 'I love you, Lady Selina, and I will spend the rest of my life trying to make you happy. This I swear.'

The lump in her throat turned into hot prickles behind her eyes. She tried to breathe and the tears welled over.

A fierce grimace twisted his lips. 'Now I've made you cry. I'm sorry.'

He made to get up, but she flung herself at his chest,

clinging fast to his neck. 'You are a fool, Ian Gilvry,' she sobbed into his cravat. 'An idiot. I love you, too. I always have. I was afraid to tell you, in case I lost you. And it seemed that I had.'

Tentatively, his big hands came around her back, circling and patting. 'Aye, it would seem I truly am an idiot,' he said softly.

She pulled herself together with a small laugh, but he didn't let her go. Oh, no, the brute lifted her arm and sat down with her on his lap.

He gave a sigh of contentment. 'This is where you belong.'

She sat with her head on his chest while he dried her tears with his handkerchief. He kissed the tip of her nose. 'You always loved me?' he mumbled.

Feeling terribly shy, she smiled up at him. 'It was why I could never bring myself up to the mark. Every time I got close to accepting a proposal, I remembered our kiss, that little touch of your lips to mine and the thrill I felt. No other man ever made me feel that way, so I always backed out.'

'Until Dunstan.' His voice was harsh.

'Poor Dunstan. He was my forlorn hope. I had to marry someone. I could no longer live with Father and Chrissie. It was too painful to watch their love grow and know I would never have the same.'

'You will and you do. More.' He stroked her arm.

'I know that now.'

'I kept hoping you might be with child. My child,' he added quickly. 'I would have had you back, then.'

'I suppose we will have to try again.' She gave him a soft smile.

He captured her mouth in a kiss. 'I can't wait to get started,' he said when they finally came up for air.

'So you will take me to London?'

He nodded grimly. 'If it is what you want.'

'And who will look after Dunross and the people there?'

'Niall and Logan.' He sounded quite worried, but determined. 'Though I must tell you, after the fire, the people have been asking after you. It seems they miss their lady.'

She stared at him astonished. 'And your mother?'

'Not quite so much. I dinna understand it. She's not a vindictive woman. I am sure she will come around.'

Her mind drifted on dreams of the future. 'Ian, do you think we could have a proper wedding? In a church?'

'In St George's, Hanover Square, I suppose.' Again the stoic face and she had to force herself not to laugh.

Then she imagined the ceremony and the pomp and the *ton* all coming to gawk. 'No. I'd like it in the village church in Dunross. With those of your family who will come. And the McKinlys. And the rest of the clan, too, as long as they won't throw stones.'

'They wouldn't dare.' He looked deep into her eyes. 'Are you sure?'

'Yes. I've been talking to Hawkhurst about that law— you know, the volume of stills in Scotland. He thinks it is very unfair. He knows all about the smuggling and didn't express a bit of concern.' She frowned. 'Not about the brandy, but about moving whisky from Scotland to England. He said he couldn't see any other way of dealing with such a stupid law. He likes whisky.'

Ian gave her a quizzical look. 'If I'm not mistaken, Hawkhurst also thinks it's all right to be a pirate.'

She grinned. 'Privateer. And he's given it up. I'd be happy for you to give up smuggling, too, but not until Dunross's people are secure.'

He looked at her intently. 'Are you telling me you want to come back with me to Dunross? We still don't know who was behind Tearny, or whether they will strike again. I am not entirely sure I can keep you safe.'

She took a deep breath. 'I love you, Ian. Dunross is where you belong and it is where I belong as your wife. But only if you don't shut me out. My father shut me out of his life when my mother died. And again when he married Chrissie, though Chrissie tried to prevent it. You kept me at a distance too, and I won't be locked out of your life. Whatever we do, we do together.'

He gave a soft groan and kissed her mouth, long and slow and lingering. It felt like a promise. And when he was done, he set her back on the sofa and once more went down on one knee. 'Lady Selina, to thee I plight my troth for ever and always and from this day forth will share with you all that I am, if you will do the same.'

She cupped his beloved rough-bearded face in her palms and pressed a kiss to his lips. 'I will, Ian,' she whispered.

'You know you have made me the happiest man alive, *leannan.*'

She took a shaky breath. 'I'd like to invite Alice and Hawkhurst to the ceremony.'

He nodded.

'And my father.'

'Invite the world, love. I want them all to see my beautiful wife and what a lucky man I am.' He leaped to his feet. 'And now to get you home where you belong.'

Belong. It sounded like such a sweet word to her ears. And he was right. She did belong there, with him.

'You came on Beau?' she asked.

'Aye.'

'Well, since it is too far to ride on your saddle bow, I

think we need to ask Hawkhurst for the loan of his carriage. And since it is too late to set out today, I think perhaps you should stay the night. We can set out in the morning.' She cast him a wicked look.

His blue eyes danced with amusement. 'Only if you have room for me in your bed.'

'What, before we are married, sir?'

She laughed as his face fell comically and rose up onto her toes and put her arms around his neck and pressed a kiss to his lovely sensual mouth. 'I have missed you so much, my dearest Ian. I waited for you for years and years, even though I didn't realise that is what I was doing, and I am not going to wait another moment.'

He picked her up. 'Thank God for that. Now, which way to the bedroom?'

She let out a squeak of surprise, as he carried her out of the room to the staircase, but she did not hear the door down the corridor open or the whispers and laughter from the library.

She was too busy looking at the love shining in her husband's eyes and trying to kiss his lips, while he took the stairs two at a time.

* * * * *

Haunted by the Earl's Touch

Chapter One

The wind keened outside the ancient walls of Beresford Abbey. Bane, following on the heels of the ancient butler along the stone passageway, noticed that only one sconce in five had been lit. Blown out by draughts? Or a sign of his welcome? No matter which, the gloom suited his mood.

'You should have left the dog in the stables,' the butler muttered over his shoulder.

Bane glance down at Ranger, part-lurcher, part-wolfhound, pressed to his left side. 'The dog stays with me.'

The butler tutted. 'And how shall I announce you, sir?' He gestured to the open door a few feet along the gloomy corridor.

A wry smile twisted Bane's lips. Was there a protocol to be followed? If so, he didn't know it. 'I'll announce myself.'

Looking shocked, but also relieved, the doddering old man turned back, shuffling down the dim stone corridor shaking his head. A wise old bird for whom discretion was the better part of valour.

Bane approached the doorway on feet silenced by carpet. He paused at the entrance to the cavernous chamber. The flickering light from ten-foot-high torchères on each side of the heavily carved four-poster bed fell on the features of the shrunken man propped up by pillows. A face lined by dissipation and framed by thin strands of yellowing grey hair straggling out from beneath a blue silken nightcap. Bony shoulders hunched in silk valuable enough to feed a family of four for a year shook with a spasm of coughing.

A dead man breathing his last. Finally. The chill inside Bane spread outwards as he took in the others clustered at the edge of the circle of light. Two women, three men, some of whom he recognised as family. He'd investigated all of his relatives to avoid unnecessary surprises.

The older woman was his aunt, his grandfather's daughter, Mrs Hampton, returned home as a widow. Her gown was the first stare of fashion as befitted her station. Tight curls of grey hair beneath a lace cap framed a middle-aged but still arresting face. As a young woman she'd been lovely, according to his mother, and too proud to make a friend of a lass from Yorkshire. At her side stood her son, Gerald, an almost too-pretty lad of seventeen with a petulant mouth and vivid blue eyes. The other young man was a distant fourth cousin. A Beresford through and through, slight, dapper, with blond hair and light blue eyes and a man his grandfather would have been happy to see as his heir had Bane not stood in the way.

An aspiring tulip of fashion in his early twenties, Bane had seen Jeffrey Beresford in town. They had no friends in common, but they bowed in passing—an acknowledgement of mutual distrust.

The other woman he did not know. Young, with a willowy figure, standing a good head taller than Mrs Hampton, she had inches on both young men. A Beresford also? She had the blonde hair and blue eyes to match the name, though she was dressed simply, in some dark stuff bespeaking modesty rather than style. The desire to see that statuesque body in something more revealing caused his throat to close.

Surprised him.

As a boy he'd had lusty thoughts about anything in skirts. As a man, a businessman, he had more important things on his mind. Women like her wanted home and hearth and a man to protect them. His life was about taking risks. Gambling all, on the chance for profit. No woman should live with such uncertainty. They were too delicate, too easily broken as his mother had been broken. The pain of her death had been unbearable. Not something he ever intended to experience again. Nor was it necessary. He was quite content to avoid the respectable ones while enjoying those who only wanted money in exchange for their favours, the *demi-monde*.

So why couldn't he keep his eyes from this most respectable-looking of females? Who was she? He wasn't aware of a female cousin, close or distant. Not that there couldn't be a whole host of relatives he didn't know about, since he didn't give a damn about any of them. But as his gaze ran over the girl, a prickle of awareness raised the hairs on the back of his neck. A sensation of familiarity so strong, he felt the urge to draw closer and ask for her name.

Yet he was positive they had never met. Perhaps it was the wariness in her expression that had him intrigued.

A blinding flash of lightning beyond the mullioned windows lit the room in a ghostly light. An image seared on Bane's vision. Stark otherworldly faces. Mouths dark pits in pale skin as the air moved with their startled gasps. They looked like the monsters who had peopled his childish nightmares. His enemies. The people who wanted him dead, according to his uncle. His mother's brother.

In truth, he hadn't expected to see family members here. He'd preferred to think of the old man alone and friendless as he gasped his last.

Just like Bane's mother.

If not for this man, his mother might be alive today and the guilt of her death would not weigh so heavily on Bane's shoulders. No matter how often he tried to put the blame where it belonged, on the man in the bed, he could not deny his own part in the events of that day. His thoughtless anger that had put her at risk. Hell, even his very existence, the reason she had run from this house in the first place.

Power and wealth brought invulnerability. His mother had drilled it into him since the day he could understand his place in the world. And that was why he was here. That and to see the old man off to the next world. He simply couldn't pass up the chance to see the dismay in the old earl's gaze.

He could count the number of times he and the old man had met face to face on one hand. But he had always been there, in the shadows, a threatening presence. Forcing his will where it was not wanted. Guiding Bane's education, trying to choose his friends, but his mother's brother had been more than a match for the earl. Bane still remembered his horror as he stood with his uncle on the doorstep of this house and listened to an argument over him, about money, about cruelty and murder. Accusations that had haunted him as a youth. Fed his anger at this man.

But his temper was not the hot flash of his youth, the kind that brought trouble to him and those around him. It was a cold burn in his gut, controlled, and carefully directed. Guilt over his mother's death had taught him that lesson.

Since then, Bane had striven to be the gentleman his mother always wanted him to be. He had battled for the respect of the scions of other noble houses at school and held his head high. But at heart he was the son of a coalminer's daughter. And proud of it. Mining was in his blood and showed in the scars on his knuckles and the muscles in his shoulders developed at the coalface.

He was more Walker than Beresford, whether or not he had any Beresford blood.

The lightning faded. Shadows once more reclaimed all but the man in the bed. As his coughing subsided, the earl's gnarled fingers clawed at the bedsheets, then beckoned.

Resistance stiffened Bane's spine. He wasn't about to be called to heel like some slavering cur. But, no, apparently this particular summons was not for him. The old man must not have seen him yet, since it was the two women who moved towards the bed, Mrs Hampton nudging the younger one ahead of her, making her stumble.

Bane took a half-step, a warning on his lips, but the girl recovered inches from the earl's warding hand, mumbling an apology.

Who was she? Some indigent relative looking for crumbs in the final hours? There would be no crumbs for any one of them. Not if Bane had a say.

'So you are Mary.' The old man's voice sounded like a door creaking in the wind. 'She said you were no great beauty, but not that you were a beanpole. You take after your father.'

'You knew my father?' the girl asked, and Bane sensed how keenly she awaited his answer. Her body seemed to vibrate with the depth of her interest.

The old man grimaced. 'I met him once. Kneel, girl. I'm getting a crick in my neck.'

Like a supplicant, the girl sank down. Anger rose hot and hard in Bane's throat on the girl's behalf, but she seemed unperturbed by the command and gazed calmly into the dying man's face.

She spoke again, but her low voice did not reach all the way to Bane in the shadows beside the door.

The old man glared at her, lifted a clawed hand to twist her chin this way and that. Glimpses of her profile showed strong classical features, a straight aristocratic nose. Lush, full lips. A narrow jaw ending in a decided chin. Not a classical beauty, but a face full of character.

The sight of the old man's hands on her delicate skin caused Bane's hands to fist at his sides, made him want to go to her rescue. An impulse he instantly crushed. A weak old man could do her no harm. And Bane had no interest in her, despite her allure.

She was not his type of woman.

Ranger growled, more a vibration under his hand than a sound. Bane glanced down at the dog and signalled him to settle. By the time he looked back, the old man had released his grip on the young woman. 'No,' the old man said, answering the question Bane had not heard. 'My reasons are my own.'

The girl's shoulders seemed to slump, as if she had hoped for a different response.

Bane remained still in the shadows, content to watch a little longer, content to choose his own moment to reveal his presence.

The old man peered into the shadows on the other side of the bed. 'She'll do,' he said with a triumphant leer. His smile was a mirthless drawing back of lips over crooked yellow teeth.

The woman, Mary, jerked back. 'I have given my thanks, my lord, I do not need your approval.' Her words rang with defiance. Brave words, but the voice shook.

Bane ruthlessly quelled a tiny surge of pity. He had no room for pity or mercy.

Beresford wheezed a laugh. 'Bold piece, ain't you. No milk-and-water miss. All the better.' He flicked his fingers in dismissal. The girl rose to her feet and turned.

Bane knew the moment she saw him. The widening of her eyes, the hesitation, the flare of recognition in her gaze, not recognition of him as a person, but of his presence. The connection between them was a tangible thing, a twisting invisible thread that kept their gazes locked. And he felt…something. A tightening of his body. The kind that heralded lust. Not something he wanted or needed right now.

He shook his head, a warning to remain silent, and it seemed she understood for she strode back to Mrs Hampton's side as if she hadn't seen him at all. An unwanted trickle of admiration for her quiet calm warmed his veins.

He dragged his gaze back to the man in the bed. It was time to be done with this farce. Bane forced himself not to square his shoulders or take a deep breath. He was no boy worried about his acceptance. He belonged here and he cared not a whit if they thought otherwise. He signalled Ranger to lie down, yet still he hesitated to take the first step.

The earl again looked over into the shadows on the far side of the bed. 'You said he would come,' he quavered.

A man trotted up to the bed. Tight lips. Eyes that darted hither and yon, never resting long enough to be read, bald pate shining. 'He is expected, my lord. I sent word as you ordered.' A dry, officious voice. A clerk of some sort. Solicitor, Bane decided.

'The storm must have delayed him.' The solicitor rubbed his palms together with a papery sound. 'Perhaps tomorrow.'

'Tomorrow will be too late.'

A flash of lightning punctuated his words, the room once more a colourless tableau of frozen players.

Bane stepped into the lamplight in that moment. His shadow loomed black over the bed and up the wall behind the dying man like some portent of evil. 'I am here.'

The old man's gasp was eminently satisfying. No doubt he had carried the hope his elder grandson would miraculously die at the eleventh hour.

Thunder rolled beyond the window, drowning out the old man's muttered words.

Bane's lip curled. It no longer mattered what the old man said. Beresford Abbey was a few short breaths from being passed on to a man who likely had not a drop of Beresford blood.

Oh, the old man had tried to make the best of an heir he despised once he'd discovered Bane had survived to stake his claim. He'd tried to force the twelve-year-old Bane into the appropriate mould. The right sort of school, the right education. As much as his mother's family would permit. And Bane had used what he needed to take back what was rightfully his. His mother had fled the Abbey because she feared for Bane's life. She had lost her own, trying to keep him safe. The powerlessness he'd felt that day still haunted him. He'd fought. How he'd fought. And those men, they had laughed at him. Mocked him. After that day he had sworn he would never let anyone make him feel weak and helpless again. He never had. And never by the man lying in the bed.

He'd used the best of both his worlds. The strength of the coalminers he'd worked alongside in summer holidays and the power of the nobility given by the title he would inherit. He'd taken control of his life.

No one would ever manipulate him again. Not his mother's brother, or the earl.

Bane glanced over at the watchers. If one of them, just one of these relatives, had taken pity on his mother, offered her their support, he might have been able to find a little mercy in his heart. But they hadn't. He bared his teeth in a smile that would do Ranger proud.

The old earl looked him over, his red-rimmed, faded blue eyes watery, his face a picture of scorn. 'So, the scavengers are circling.'

'You sent for me, Grandfather,' he said his tone mocking.

The earl's gaze lingered on Bane's face and he shook his head. 'A curse on your mother for sending my son to an early grave.'

Bitterness roiled in his gut at the vilification. A drunken lord driving his carriage off the road was hardly his mother's fault. His chest tightened until his lungs were starved. Not that he was surprised by the accusation, just by his own visceral reaction, when there was nothing this decayed piece of flesh could do to her any more. 'But for you, my mother would be alive today.'

Yet even as he spoke the words, the old guilt rose up to choke him. The knowledge that he had done nothing to save her. 'But she beat you in the end.'

The old man sneered. 'Did she now?'

The urge to stop the vile tongue edged his vision in red. Involuntarily his fists clenched. His palms tingled with the desire to tighten around the scrawny neck, to feel the flesh and bones crush in on his windpipe. Watch the life fade from those cruel eyes and silence his lips for ever.

He reached for his hard-won iron control over his temper, shocked at how close it was to slipping from his grasp at this long-awaited moment, grabbed a breath of air and let the heat dissipate. He would not let his anger overpower his reason. He knew the penalty for doing so. It would rob him of his victory as it has robbed him of his mother. There was no need for anger, not now, when he'd won. He shrugged.

The old devil grinned a death's-head smile. 'Look at you, apeing the gentleman in your fine clothes, with not an ounce of nobility in your blood. It is a wonder decent society tolerates you at all.'

He smiled his own mocking smile. 'They welcome me with open arms. It is the prospect of a title that does it, you know.'

Something flashed in the old man's eyes. If Bane hadn't known better, he might have thought it was admiration. It was more likely rage at being defeated in his plan to be rid of his cuckoo in the nest. Thanks to his rough-and-ready upbringing by his maternal uncle, and later his years of misery at school and university, Bane had no doubts about his ability to withstand any torment his grandfather might devise. He'd spent his life preparing for this moment.

He moved closer to the head of the bed, lowering his voice. 'You sent for me, old man, and here I am. Speak your piece. I am a busy man.'

'A coalminer. A labourer for hire.' Scorn dripped from the old man's thin lips like poison. Spittle spattered his chin and the lapels of the silken robe bearing the Beresford emblem in gold.

'Aye,' Bane said. 'I know how to earn my keep.' Not that he laboured with his hands any more, but he could if need be. He let his gaze drift around the worn bed hangings and worn furniture. 'And I know how to follow your example, spending money on idle pursuits in town.' He'd done his share of playing the debauched nobleman since making his bows at court, much to the displeasure of both sides of his family. But he hadn't been wasting his time, no matter what they thought.

The old man raised a hand and pointed a crooked finger at the young men nearby. 'They are real Beresfords.' His whispery voice flicked like a whip at Bane's pride.

He bared his teeth in a hard smile. His was, after all, the final triumph. 'Too bad. There is nothing anyone can do about it.'

'No?' A calculating gleam entered the faded blue eyes and his lips twisted. His gaze darted to the far side of the bed, to the huddle just beyond the lamplight. 'Jeffrey. Gerald. Come to me.'

The two young men came forwards. The dandy, Jeffrey, at a saunter, meeting Bane's gaze surprisingly coolly. The younger cousin, Gerald, known to Bane only as a name, ran to the old man's side and knelt, clutching one of those misshapen hands. 'Grandfather, do not upset yourself.' The boy looked up at Bane. 'Leave him in peace.'

Beresford pulled his hand free and stared at the two young men with a wry expression. 'These are my grandsons. True nobility. Real Beresfords.' He turned his head on the pillow to look at Bane. 'But whose spawn are you?'

Whose bastard, he meant. It wasn't anything Bane hadn't heard before. It barely registered, but the soft gasp coming from somewhere in the shadows cut at him like a whip. The girl. He knew it instinctively. He forced himself not to look her way, despite feeling the intensity of her gaze grazing his skin. 'It doesn't matter,' he said coldly. 'I am your legal heir, so that pair of spoiled ninnyhammers had best crawl at my feet if they want crumbs from my table.' He took pleasure in speaking in the rough tones of his mother's people.

The old man grunted and struggled up on to one elbow, pointing at Bane's face with a crooked finger. 'Think you've bested me, do you? You've got nerve, I'll credit you that. I've watched you. I've got your measure. If you want the wealth and power that goes with the title, then you'll dance to my tune.'

Ranger, by the door, rumbled low in his throat.

'Grandfather!' the young lad at his side said, trying to ease him back down on to the pillows.

His grandfather brushed him aside. 'It takes a clever man to best a Beresford.' His laugh crackled like tearing paper. 'I'm only sorry I won't be here to see it.'

Bane shot him a considering look. The old man seemed just too sure of himself. 'I won't be controlled, old man. You should know that by now.'

As the dying man collapsed against the pillows, his gaze sought out the young woman he'd spoken to earlier. 'Don't be so sure.'

Who the devil was she? Bane sent her a baleful glance. She inched deeper into the shadows, but her blue eyes, her Beresford-blue eyes, never left his face and they held a kind of fascinated horror.

The earl's gaze dropped to his other grandsons and moisture ran down his cheeks, glistening, running into the crevasses on his cheeks. Then he drew in a shuddering breath, his jaw working. He turned his head and his eyes, still wet with tears, fixed on Bane. 'You'll do your duty by the family.'

'I have no family in this house.' Bane let his scorn show on his face. 'You failed to be rid of me when you had the chance and they bear the consequence. The sins of the father will be visited upon these children of your line. And there will be no more.'

The old man chuckled, a grim sound in the quiet room.

'Cocksure, aren't you. And proud. Yet you hold the losing hand.'

The wry amusement gave Bane pause. Intimidation. The old man excelled at terrifying those weaker than himself. Bane was not his or anyone else's victim. He'd made himself too strong to be any man's punching bag. He leaned over, speaking only for the old man to hear. 'You forget, it will all be within my control. My only regret is that you won't see the desecration of your family name.' He flicked a glance at his cousins, the coolly insolent one who hid his true nature from the world and the half-scared boy. 'It would do them good to work at some low honest task for their bread.'

The old man groaned, but there was something odd in his tone, as if he wasn't so much in agony, but stifling amusement. 'You think you are such a cold devil,' he muttered. 'I will be sorry to miss the heat of your anger.'

Bane drew back, searching that vindictive face. 'What have you done?'

'You'll see.'

A resounding crack of thunder split the air at the same time as lightning flickered around the room. The storm's last violent convulsion.

Ranger howled. The old man jerked upright in that wild blue light, the colour draining from his face, from his clothing, from the twisted hand clutching his throat. He sank back with a sigh.

The kneeling boy uttered a cry of despair. Jeffrey leaned over and felt for his pulse. Mrs Hampton rushed forwards. The tall girl remained where she was, a hand flat across her mouth, her eyes wide.

Bane curled his lip as he looked down on the empty shell of what had once been a man who had wielded his power to harm the innocent.

Bane was the earl now. And to hell with the Beresfords.

He spared a last glance for those gathering close around the bed and shrugged. Let them weep and wail at the old man's passing. It was of no import to him.

Weariness swept through him. After travelling hard for three days, he needed a bath and a good night's sleep. He had a great deal to do on the morrow if he was to set his plans in motion. He had debts to pay and a coalmine to purchase.

As he turned to leave, he caught sight of the young woman hanging back, her expression one of distaste. What mischief had the old man planned for her? Nothing his grandfather could do from beyond the grave could harm Bane. But he did not like to think of yet another innocent female destroyed by his machinations.

Unless she wasn't as innocent as she appeared. Was anyone in this family innocent? It was hard to think so. And if she wasn't, then Bane was more than a match for her, too.

He snapped his fingers for Ranger and headed down the corridor, hoping like hell he could find the way back through the maze of passages to his assigned chamber.

While the family members hovered and wept around the body of the old earl, Mary made good her escape. Her brain whirled. Her stomach cramped. And she ran like a cowardly rabbit.

When she'd been invited to meet her benefactor, the man she'd recently learned had paid for her schooling, her every meal, for most of her life, she had wondered—no, truly, she had dreamed that at last some family member, some distant relative, had decided to claim her as their own. A childhood fantasy finally fulfilled.

She'd certainly had no idea that the man was at death's

door until the butler guided her into that room earlier this evening. And when she'd asked her question with breathless hope and seen the surprise in those watery blue eyes and the wry twist to his lips, she'd felt utterly foolish.

Was she a member of his family? The answer had been a flat *no*.

Sally Ladbrook had been right. The man had viewed her as a good work, a charitable impulse, and was looking for recognition before he met his end. Unless he intended to impose the obligation on his heir.

She shivered. Just the thought of the new earl's overwhelmingly menacing presence in that room made her heart race and her knees tremble. She'd been transfixed by the sheer male strength of him, while he had stood in the shadows as still as death.

She halted at the end of the corridor and glanced back. A sliver of light spilling on to the runner revealed the location of that horrid room. Never in her life had she witnessed anything so morbid. She rubbed at her jaw, trying to erase the sensation of cold papery fingers on her skin and shuddered.

To make it worse, once the heir had stepped out of the shadows, the hatred in the room had been palpable. Like hot oil on metal, hissing and spitting first from one direction and then another, scalding wherever it landed.

And the man. The new earl. So dark. So unexpectedly large, even handsome in a brutal way. A powerful man who had overshadowed his dying grandfather like some avenging devil.

He didn't walk, he prowled. He didn't speak, he made utterances in a voice composed of velvet and sandpaper. And his eyes. His eyes were as deep as an abyss when he had stared directly at her. That look owed nothing to the gloom in the room, for it was the same when he stood within the light of the torches. Worse. Because she could see the pinpoints of flickering light reflected in his gaze and still make out nothing in their shadowed depths.

She—who prided herself on being able to stand in front of a class of spoiled daughters and hold her own, at least on the surface, and who, as a charity boarder, had suffered pity and sly comments about her poverty all those years—had managed to stand up to the gloating way the old man had looked at her and crushed any hope that she might have found her place in the world.

But when that piercing gaze looking out from the shadows in the doorway had tangled with hers, it had sapped her courage dry. She'd scuttled ignominiously back to her place without a shred of dignity remaining.

The sooner she left this place, this house with its dark undercurrents, the better. She'd done her duty. Offered her thanks. Surely she was free to go? She would leave first thing in the morning.

She glanced left and right. Which way? The maid who had brought her to the dying man's room had found her way with unerring ease, but Mary no longer had a clue which way they had come, there had been so many twists and turns on their journey from her chamber. Not to mention the odd staircase.

Part-dissolved abbey, part-Tudor mansion, part-renaissance estate, it sprawled and rambled inside and out. She'd glimpsed the house at dusk, perched high on a Cornish cliff, crenulated towers and chimney pots rising to the sky. A complete muddle of a house.

Her room was in one of those square towers. At the north end, the butler had told her when he escorted her there upon her arrival. The tower nearest the abbey ruins. She could see them through her small window. She had also heard the muffled rumble of the ocean somewhere deep below the house, in its very foundations. A very ominous sound. She shuddered as she imagined the house undermined by the force of the sea.

She eyed her two choices and selected the one that seemed to amble north. Picking up her skirts for speed, she hurried on, wishing there was more light, or a servant to show her the way.

Another corridor branched off to her right, going south? Or had that last corner she had turned set her off course? The maid had turned off the main corridor, hadn't she? More than once. She plunged into the new hallway. It looked no more familiar than the last.

She needed help.

She tried the first door she came to. A bedroom, its furniture huddled beneath holland covers. If there ever had been a bell rope, it had been removed.

Blast. She returned to the corridor, heading for another room further along.

Footsteps. Behind her. Thank God. Help at last.

She turned around.

A light flickered and stopped. Whoever held the candle remained masked in shadow.

The wind howled through a nearby crevice, lifting the hair at her nape. Her heart picked up speed. The girls at school had told late-night stories of ghosts and hauntings that started like this. Deliciously wicked in their frightening aspects and heroic deeds. Figments of imagination. She did not believe in ghosts. People like her, practical people, did not have the luxury of such flights of fancy, yet she could not quite quell the fear gripping her chest. 'Who is there?' She was shocked at the tremble in her voice.

The light drew closer. A candle held in a square-fingered hand joined to a brawny figure still in the darkness. Him. The new earl.

How she knew, she wasn't sure, but her skin prickled with the knowledge. Heat flushed up from her belly. 'My lord?' she said. Her voice quavering just a little more than she would have liked. 'Lord Beresford?'

The candle went upwards, lighting his harsh face.

'Great goliaths,' she said, letting go of her breath. 'Do you always creep around hallways in such a fashion?' Oops. That sounded a bit too much like the schoolteacher taking a pupil to task.

The eyes staring down at her were not dark as she had thought in the old earl's bedroom. They were as grey as storm clouds. And watchful.

'Are you lost?' he drawled in that deep mocking voice with its hint of roughness.

'Certainly not,' she replied, discomposed by his obvious indifference. Heat rushed to her cheeks and she was glad the dim light would not reveal her embarrassment. She let her gaze fall away.

'Liar,' he said softly.

She bristled.

'That's better.'

A snuffling sound drew her gaze down. The dog. It sank to its haunches and watched her with its head cocked on one side. It was enormous. 'What is better?' she asked, keeping a wary eye on the dog.

'It is better when you stand up straight, instead of hunching over like a scared schoolgirl.'

As a schoolgirl, she had tried to disguise her ungainly height. It spoke to her discomfort that she had fallen back into that old habit.

She looked up past the wide chest and broad shoulders, past the snowy cravat and strong column of throat, his full mobile mouth at eye level, then up to meet his gaze. Most men were either her height or shorter. This one was taller than her by half a head—he must be inches above six foot tall—and he reeked of danger.

What snatches of conversation she'd heard between him and the dying earl had been positively menacing. And, unless she was badly mistaken, some of the venom shifting back and forth between them had been directed at her.

'If you will excuse me, I must be on my way.'

'On your way where?'

'To my room.'

He shot her a wolfish smile. 'So that was not your room. The one you just left.'

'No,' she muttered, making to step past him.

'What were you doing in that chamber?'

Did he think she was trying to steal? She stiffened her spine, meeting his gaze full on. Such directness usually sent men running for the hills. On this one it apparently had no effect. Or none visible, though she did sense a sharpening of interest in those wintery eyes.

She huffed out a breath of defeat. 'I will admit I am a little turned about. My chamber is in the tower at the north end of the house. I thought I would ring for a servant to guide me, but there was no bell pull in the first room I tried.'

'A clever thought.'

'I am clever.' She bit her lip. That was just the sort of quick retort men did not like. A habit of bravado honed in the schoolroom.

He didn't seem to notice. 'Follow me.' He strode past her down the corridor, the dog following at his heels, leaving her to trot along behind as best she might.

He took a flight of stairs down and then passed along a stone corridor that smelled of must and damp. She was sure she had not come this way.

He hesitated at yet another intersection of passageways.
She huffed out a breath. 'Don't tell me, you are lost too.'
He gave her a scornful look. 'I never get lost.'

Doubt filled her mind. 'Have you ever been to this
house before?'

'North is this way.' He set off once more with the dog
padding beside him.

Hah. Avoidance. He was just as lost as she was. More
lost. Because she was quite sure from the increasingly
dank feel to the air that they were now in the cellars. The
sea growled louder too. Typical. Why would men never
admit to being lost?

About to insist they stop, she was surprised when he
took off up a circular flight of narrow stairs she hadn't
noticed. At the top, he turned left and there they were, at
her chamber door. How irritating. And she still had no
idea how she got here. It didn't matter. She had no reason to learn her way around, since she would be departing at once.

'Thank you, my lord.' She dipped her best curtsy and
prayed he would not hear the wry note in her voice.

He held his candle high and caught her chin in long
strong fingers just like the old man had done. But these
fingers were warm with youth and strong with vigour and,
while firm, they were also gentle. She jerked her head,
but he held her fast.

She stared up at his face, at the beautifully moulded
lips set in a straight line hovering above hers. His head
dipped a fraction. Angled. She could feel his breath, warm
on her cheek, inhaled a hint of cologne, something male,
mingled with leather and horse and briny air that made
her feel dizzy.

She drew in a deep breath as his gaze fell on her
mouth, lingering there, until she thought he would kiss

her. Longed that he would to break this dreadful tension between them.

Nervous, she licked her lips.

His eyes narrowed and he raised that piercing gaze to meet hers as if he would read her mind. Stroked her chin with his thumb and, she shivered. He leaned closer and for a wild moment, she thought he really did intend to kiss her and her body hummed at the thought.

Instead, he spoke. 'Who are you?' he rasped softly.

'Mary,' she managed to gasp in a breathless whisper, her breathing beyond her control. 'Mary Wilding.'

'Wilding?' A brow went up. 'And what brought you here, Miss Wilding?'

She swallowed. 'I was invited. By the earl.'

'The late earl.'

She nodded.

He stepped back, releasing her face. 'And what is your purpose here, I wonder?'

'It doesn't matter. I will be leaving first thing.'

'I see. Well, Miss Wilding, I bid you goodnight. We will talk before you go.'

She remained frozen as he disappeared back down the twisting stairs and she was left alone, in the silence, not hearing even his footsteps and feeling strangely giddy.

Breathless, from…fear? The fluttering in her belly, the tremble in her hands, could be nothing else. Though what made her fearful, she wasn't sure. Perhaps her reactions? To him? Would she have actually let him kiss her, had he wanted to do so?

Could she have stopped such a powerful man taking whatever he wanted? A little thrill rippled through her. Perverse. Unwanted.

All he had wanted was to question her.

She pressed cold fingers to her hot cheeks and hauled

in a deep breath before stepping inside her small chamber. While thanking her benefactor had been one of the less pleasant experiences of her life, meeting the new earl had been something else entirely. Disturbing and exciting. It might be as well to avoid him before she left.

Coward.

Chapter Two

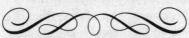

The maid Betsy, assigned to help Mary dress, arrived at nine the next morning.

Mary didn't needed help dressing. Just as always, she'd been awake and dressed by six, before light touched the grey wintery sky. At school, it was her task to see that the girls were washed and dressed before they came to breakfast. The maid had to content herself with drawing back the curtains and putting coal on the fire. 'This room is always cold,' the girl announced cheerfully. 'Will there be anything else, miss?'

'I would like a carriage to take me to St Ives.'

'You will need to speak to Mr Manners,' the girl said, her Cornish vowels hard to decipher.

Of course. The butler. He would be in charge of such things. 'Where will I find him?'

The small brown-eyed girl raised her brows. 'In the breakfast room. Serving the family.'

The grieving family. She wanted nothing to do with any of them, especially the new earl. But since she needed to order the carriage, she straightened her shoulders and smiled. 'Perhaps you would be good enough to guide me there?'

Betsy bobbed a curtsy. 'Follow me, miss.'

It wasn't long before she was deposited in front of a large oak door off the entrance hall. 'In there, miss.'

'Thank you.' Mary sailed through the door as if she had been making grand entrances all her life. Or at least she hoped she gave that impression.

What a relief. No brooding earl awaited her in the oak-panelled room with its polished furniture and gleaming silver. Only his cousins sat at the table. Blond and handsome, they rose to their feet as she entered.

'Good morning,' she said.

'Good morning, Miss Wilding,' they replied gravely.

The older one, Mr Jeffrey Beresford, gave her a swift perusal. A slightly pained expression entered his vivid-blue eyes. No doubt he thought her dreadfully shabby in her Sunday-best dress, but it was grey and she'd thought it the most appropriate under the circumstances. The younger one nodded morosely.

Both young men wore dark coats and black armbands. Of Mrs Hampton there was no sign. No doubt she preferred to breakfast in her room on such a sorrowful day.

'Miss Wilding,' the butler said, pulling out a chair opposite the Beresford cousins. She sat.

They followed suit.

'Did you sleep well, Miss Wilding?' Mr Beresford asked, assuming the duty of host in the earl's absence.

'Yes, thank you.' She certainly wasn't going to admit to her mind replaying the scene with the earl outside her chamber door over and over as she restlessly tossed and turned.

'Really?' Mr Hampton said, looking up, his face angelic in a shaft of sunlight that at that moment had broken through the clouds and found its way into the dining room to rest on him.

'Is there some reason why I should not?' she asked a little stiffly, surprised by his sudden interest.

He looked at her moodily. 'They do say as how the White Lady's ghost haunts the north tower.'

'You are an idiot, Ger,' the other cousin said. 'Don't listen to him, Miss Wilding. It is an old wives' tale.'

''Tis not,' Gerald said, his lips twisting. 'One of the servants saw her last week.'

'And that is a bouncer,' his cousin replied repressively. 'One servant saw her fifty years ago.'

The younger man scowled.

Mary felt sorry for him. Boys liked their ghost stories as much as foolish young girls did, no doubt. 'It would take more than a ghost to scare me,' she said calmly, 'if I actually believed in them.' It would take a tall dark earl with a sinful mouth to make her quiver in fear. Or quiver with something.

The young man looked a little insulted. 'If you see her, you will tell me, won't you? I've been keeping track of her sightings.' He pushed his food around with his fork. 'They say she appears when there is to be a death in the house.' The utter belief in his voice gave her a strange slithery sensation in her stomach. It also reminded her of last night's events with a pang of guilt.

'Although I had never met your grandfather before last night, I hope you will accept my deepest sympathy for your loss.'

Both young men nodded their acceptance of her condolence.

'Coffee, miss?' the butler asked.

She usually had tea in the morning. And only one cup. But there was another scent floating in the air, making her mouth water and her stomach give little hops of pleasure. 'Chocolate, please, Manners.' She'd had her first taste of chocolate this morning when Betsy had brought her tray and really couldn't resist having it one last time.

The man poured a cup from the silver chocolate pot on the sideboard and added a generous dollop of cream. Such luxury. Wait until she told Sally. Her friend and employer would be so envious. Chocolate was one of those luxuries they dreamt of on a cold winter's night.

The butler brought her toast on a plate and offered her a selection of platters. Deciding to make the most of what was offered—after all, she was an invited guest—she took some shirred eggs and ham and sausage and tucked in with relish. Breakfast at Ladbrook's rarely consisted of more than toast and jam and porridge in the winter months. Ladbrook's School for Young Ladies was rarely full to capacity and the best food always went to the paying pupils. As a charity case, she had managed on leftovers. Since becoming employed as a teacher things had improved, but not by much.

Hope of improving the school was why she had agreed to travel all the way from Wiltshire to meet the late earl. If he had proved to be a distant relation, she had thought to convince him to provide funds for improvements, to make it more fashionable and therefore profitable, as well as enable the taking in of one or two more charity boarders like herself.

She let go of a sigh. The earl's death had put paid to all her hopes, including any hope of some family connection. She ought to speak of the school's needs to the new earl, she supposed, but his behaviour so far had led her to the conclusion that, rather than a man of charitable bent, he was likely to be one of the scandalous rakes one read about in broadsheets and romantic novels.

'What do you think of the Abbey, Miss Wilding?' Mr Hampton asked.

'It's a dreadful pile,' his cousin put in before she could answer. 'Don't you think?'

Tact seemed to be the best course between two extremes. 'I have seen very little, so would find it hard to form an opinion, Mr Hampton.'

'Call me Gerald. Mr Hampton was my father. That pink of the *ton* is Jeffrey.'

His older cousin inclined his head, clearly accepting the description with aplomb. Mary smiled her thanks, not quite sure what lay behind this courtesy for a virtual stranger.

'What shall we call you?' he asked. 'Cousin?'

She stiffened. Had they also formed the mistaken impression they were related, or had they heard the earl's mocking reply to her question and thought to follow suit? Heat rushed to her cheeks. 'You may call me Miss Wilding.'

Gerald frowned. 'You sound like my old governess.'

'I am a schoolteacher.'

Jeffrey leaned back in his chair and cast an impatient glance at Gerald. 'Miss Wilding it is then, ma'am. At least *you* are not claiming to be a Beresford.'

Mary caught her breath at this obvious jibe at his absent older cousin. She had heard some of his conversation with the old earl and gathered there was some doubt about the legitimacy of his birth. She hadn't expected the issue addressed so openly.

Last night she'd had the sense that the old man's barbs had found their mark with the heir. Not that he'd had shown any reaction. But there had been something running beneath the surface. Anger. Perhaps resentment. And a sense of aloneness, as if he too had hoped for acceptance from this family.

She certainly did not approve of sniping at a person

behind their back and their family quarrels were certainly none of her business, so she ignored the comment and buttered her toast. She had more important matters on her mind. Getting back to school. Preparing her lessons. Helping Sally find ways to reduce expenses still further if the earl's munificence was indeed ended.

She smiled at the butler as he added chocolate to her cup. 'Manners, may I request the carriage take me to St Ives after breakfast? I would like to catch the stage back to Wiltshire.'

'I can't do that, miss,' Manners replied stone-faced.

Startled, she stared at him.

Gerald frowned. 'Why not?'

'His lordship's orders. You will have to apply to him, miss.'

The heat in her cheeks turned to fire at the thought of asking his lordship for anything.

'Damn him,' Jeffrey said with more heat than he seemed wont to display. 'He hasn't been here five minutes and already he's acting...' His voice tailed off and he reddened as he realised Gerald's avid gaze was fixed on his face.

'It isn't fair,' Gerald said. 'You should be the heir. He should have the decency to withdraw his claim.'

'He can't,' Jeffrey said. 'The heir is the heir. The proof is irrefutable.'

'It still isn't right,' Gerald muttered.

Jeffrey gave Mary an apologetic smile. 'Gerald takes things too much to heart. And I am sorry about the carriage, Miss Wilding. Would you like me to speak to...to his lordship?' He stumbled on the last word as if he was not quite as sanguine as he made out.

'I would certainly hate to inconvenience anyone,' Mary said. 'Perhaps I shall walk.'

'There's a path along the cliffs,' Gerald said. 'I've walked it often. Take you a good while, though.'

'I advise you not to try it, Miss Wilding,' Jeffrey drawled. 'The Cornish coast is dangerous for those who do not know it.'

Another roadblock. Her spine stiffened. She gave him a tight smile 'Thank you for the warning. Perhaps I should seek the earl's permission to take the carriage, after all.'

Or not. How difficult could it be to walk along the coast? Sea on one side, land on the other and no earthly chance of getting lost. Unlike her experience in this house. And she had absolutely no intention of asking his lordship for anything. The thought of doing so made her heart race.

'Where is the new lordship,' Gerald asked, his lip curling with distaste.

'I believe he rode out, sir,' the butler said. 'More coffee?'

Gerald waved him off.

'I wonder what he is riding?' Jeffrey said. 'A man like him probably has no idea of good horseflesh.'

Like him? Now that was pure snobbery. She wondered what they said about a woman like her, a penniless schoolteacher, behind her back. No doubt they had thought she had come to ingratiate herself. How mortifying that they were very nearly right. She felt her shoulders rise in that old defensive posture and forced them to relax, keeping her expression neutral. These young noblemen were nowhere near as vicious as schoolgirls, nothing to fear at all.

'Aye,' Gerald said. 'A man like him will be all show and no go.'

Jeffrey raised a brow. 'As if you would know, cuz. Isn't it time your mother let you have a decent mount of your own?'

Gerald hunched a shoulder. 'I'm to get one on my birthday. And a phaeton.'

'God help us all,' Jeff said *sotto voce*.

The door swung back and the earl strode in. His silver gaze swept the room, taking in the occupants in one swift glance before he made for the empty place at the head of the table.

The new earl was just as impressive in the grey of morning as he had been in the glow of lamplight. Perhaps more so. His black coat hugged his broad shoulders and his cravat was neatly tied. He was not wearing an armband. Perhaps he considered the black coat quite enough, though the rich fabric of his cream waistcoat, embroidered with blue sprigs, suggested he hadn't given mourning a thought when he dressed.

The shadowed jaw of the previous night was gone, his face smooth and recently shaved. He was, as her girls would say when they thought she could not hear, devilishly handsome. Devilish being the most apt word she could think of in respect to the earl, since his face was set in the granite-hard lines of a fallen angel who found his fate grim.

Oh, jumping Jehosophat, did it matter how he looked? After today, she would never see him again.

'Good morning,' he said to the room at large.

The two young men mumbled grudging greetings.

'Good morning, my lord,' Mary said with a polite calm. It wasn't right to treat him like some sort of pariah in his own house. She wouldn't do it. She would be civil. Even if it was hard to breathe now he took up so much of the air in the room.

His eyes widened a fraction. 'Miss Wilding. Up and about so early?'

'As is my usual wont,' she replied, sipping her chocolate, not tasting it at all any more, because all she was aware of was him.

Heat rushed to her cheeks and she hoped he did not notice.

After responding to Manners's enquiries about his preferences for breakfast, he picked up the newspaper beside his plate and disappeared behind it.

A strained silence filled the room. It demanded that someone break it. It was just too obvious that they had stopped talking the moment he entered. He would think they were talking about him. They weren't. At least, not all of the time. It made her feel very uncomfortable, as if her skin was stretched too tight.

She waited until he had eaten most of his breakfast. Sally, widowed by two husbands and therefore an expert, always said men were not worth talking to until they had filled their stomachs. 'My lord?'

He looked up, frowning.

Perhaps he hadn't eaten enough. Well, it was too late to draw back. 'May I request that your coachman drive me to St Ives this morning? It is time I returned home.'

He frowned. 'Not today. Your presence is required in two hours' time for the reading of the will.'

The will? What did that have to do with her? 'That is not necessary, surely?'

He gave her a look that froze her to the spot. 'Would I ask it, if it were not?'

She dragged her gaze from his and put down her cup. A tiny hope unfurled in her chest. Perhaps the earl had left something for the school after all. Had she been too hasty in thinking her quest unsuccessful?

The earl was watching her face with a cynical twist to his lips, as if she was some sort of carrion crow picking over a carcase. Guilt twisted in her stomach. She had no reason to feel guilty. The school was a worthy cause, even if it did also benefit her. And if she had previously hoped the earl's summons had signified something more, something of a familial nature, those expectations had been summarily disabused and were no one's concern but her own. 'If it is required, then I will attend.'

The earl pushed his plate aside and pushed to his feet. 'Eleven o'clock in the library, Miss Wilding. Try not to be late.'

She bristled, but managed to hang on to her aplomb. 'I am never late, my lord.'

He gazed at her for a long moment and she was sure she saw a gleam of amusement in his eyes, but it was gone too fast for her to be certain. 'Unless you become lost, I assume.'

Once more heat flooded her face at the memory of his rescue the previous evening and her shocking responses to his closeness. Her incomprehensible longings, which must not recur. It was ungentlemanly of him to remind her.

He departed without waiting for a reply, no doubt assuming his orders would be carried out. And if they weren't then no doubt the autocratic man would find a way to rectify the matter.

'I'm for the stables,' Jeffrey said. 'I want to take a look at his horseflesh.'

He wanted to mock.

'Can I come?' Gerald asked, his expression pleading.

'If you wish,' his cousin said, kindly, which made Mary think a great deal more of him. He bowed to Mary and the two of them strolled away.

Now what should she do? Go back to her room and risk getting lost? Sally hadn't expected her to spend more than one night here at the Abbey, no matter what hopes Mary had secretly held. What she should do was despatch a let-

ter to Sally telling her what was happening and why her
return might be delayed by another day. She could while
away the two hours before the appointed time in writing and reading more enjoyably than spending the time
wandering the chilly corridors of this rambling mansion
looking for her room.

'Will you direct me to the library, Manners? I assume
there is paper and pen there?'

The butler bowed. 'Yes, miss. It is located further along
this hallway. You cannot miss it.'

If anyone could miss anything when it came to directions, she could and would. But that was her own personal
cross to bear. 'Thank you.'

He gave her a kind smile. 'There is a footman going to
the village this afternoon, if you would like a letter posted,
miss. Ring the bell when you are finished and he'll come
and collect it. You will find sealing wax and paper in the
desk drawer, and ink on the inkstand.'

She smiled her thanks and made her escape.

The library proved to be exactly where the butler had
said and she found it without difficulty.

Nirvana could not have looked any more inviting.
Shelves, packed with leather-bound books in shades of
blue, red and green, rose from floor to ceiling on three
dark-panelled walls. Wooden chairs strategically placed
beside tables of just the right height encouraged a person
to spread books out at will. Deep overstuffed sofas and
chairs upholstered in fabrics faded to soft brown tempted
the reader who liked to curl up with a novel. Cushioned
window seats offered comfort and light on dark winter
days. All was overseen by a large oak desk at one end.

The delights on offer tested her determination to write
to Sally first and read afterwards. But she managed it, sit-

ting at the heavy desk, putting out of her mind what she could not say about the new earl as she wrote of the demise of their donor.

She flicked the feather end of her quill across her chin. Should she mention a possibility of some small sum in the will? It seemed a bit presumptuous. She decided to write only of her delayed return. A mere day or two, she said.

Having rung the bell and sent off her missive, she turned her attention to the feast of books. She selected a book of poems by Wordsworth and settled into one of the window seats.

She didn't have long to indulge because, within the half-hour, Mr Savary, the solicitor who had been at the earl's bedside, arrived with a box full of papers and began fussing with them on the desk.

Mary decided she would remain where she was, at the furthest point in the room from where the family would conduct its business.

At a few minutes past eleven, the family members straggled in. First Gerald with his mother. Mrs Hampton looked very becoming in black. It suited her air of delicacy. She would have been an extraordinarily beautiful woman in her youth. She and her son, who took after her in the beauty department, sat beside the blazing hearth not far from the desk.

Jeffrey, his saunter as pronounced as any Bond Street beau, came next. Not that Mary had ever seen a Bond Street beau, but she'd seen cartoons in the paper, read descriptions of their antics and could use her imagination. He struck a languid pose at the fireplace, one arm resting on the mantel while he gazed pensively into the flames. Regretting being cut out of the title? He didn't seem to care much about anything. Perhaps it was the idea of the earl holding the purse-strings that had him looking so thoughtful.

The upper servants gathered just inside the doorway: the butler, the housekeeper and a gentleman in a sombre suit who could have been anything from a parson to a land steward. They must all have expectations. The old earl had proved generous to her over the past many years, so why not to his servants? Though, in truth, on meeting him, she had not liked him one little bit. There had been an air of maliciousness about him.

She was relieved they were not related. She really was.

But if he left the school a small sum of money, an annuity, or a lump sum, it would be a blessing for which she would be suitably grateful, no matter her personal feelings. She put her book on the table at her elbow and folded her hands in her lap, trying not to look hopeful.

But where was the earl?

Ah, here he came, last but definitely not least. He prowled into the room, looking far more sartorially splendid than the dandified Jeffrey. Perhaps it was his size. Or the sheer starkness of a black coat against the white of his cravat. The room certainly seemed much smaller upon his entrance. And even a little airless.

His hard gaze scanned the room, missing nothing. Indeed, she had the feeling his eyes kept on moving until he discovered her whereabouts. He looked almost relieved, as if he feared she might have *loped off*, as Sally's cockney coachman would have said.

Ignoring the group at the hearth, he swung one of the plain wooden chairs near her window seat around and sat astride it. Arms across the back, he fixed the solicitor with a grim stare. 'Get on with it, then, man.'

The fussy little solicitor tugged at his neckcloth, then

broke the seal on a rolled document. He spread it out on the desk. 'This being the last—'

'No need to read all the curlicues and periods,' the earl interrupted. 'Just give us the details.'

'Yes, my lord.' He took a deep breath. 'Basically, the title goes to you, but all the unentailed income goes to Miss Wilding on condition that she marry within the year.'

The earl's gaze, steel hard beneath lowered brows, cut to her face. A muscle jumped in his jaw.

What had the solicitor said? No, she knew what he had said. But what did it mean? The unentailed income?

'There are ten guineas for Manners, five for Mrs Davis and another ten for Ragwell for his excellent stewardship this past many years.'

The servants mumbled and sounded pleased. They shuffled out of the room at the solicitor's wave of a hand.

Mrs Hampton put a hand to her throat. 'What about my son? And Jeffrey.'

'It is my understanding that the late earl passed on any personal trinkets prior to his…his—'

'His death,' the earl growled.

'I got his ring,' Gerald announced, waving his hand about for everyone to see.

'The seal of the Beresfords belongs to me,' the earl said with almost a snarl.

Gerald thumbed his nose. 'This was my grandmother's ring.'

The earl scowled. 'Then where is the seal?'

Gerald shrugged.

'With the earl's effects,' the lawyer said stiffly.

Mrs Hampton's pallor increased. 'I thought there was to be some—' She caught herself.

The earl stood up and looked down at the little solicitor. 'How much of the income from the estate is unentailed?' His voice was soft, but no one in the room could possibly doubt his ire.

'All of it,' the little man squeaked.

The ensuing pause was charged like air before a storm. The earl's gaze shifted to her and the heat in their depths flared bright before he turned back to the lawyer. 'And you permitted this abomination? This dividing of the money from the land? What man in his right mind does such a thing?'

'The late earl was not always rational when it came to the matter of...' His breathless voice tailed off.

'His heir,' the earl said flatly.

'I followed instructions,' the lawyer pleaded.

The earl's silver gaze found hers again. This time it was colder than ice. 'Very clever indeed, Miss Wilding.'

She stiffened. Outrage flooding her with heat. 'I do not understand what this means.' At least she was hoping that what she understood was not what was really happening.

'You got the fortune,' the earl said. 'And I got the expenses.'

Then she had interpreted the lawyer's words correctly. How was this possible?

Beresford turned on the solicitor. 'It can be overturned.'

The man shook his head. 'If Miss Wilding marries within the year, she gets all income from the estate. If not, the money goes to the Crown.' He glanced down at his papers. 'That is, unless she dies before the year is up.'

'What happens if she dies?' the earl asked harshly.

Mary froze in her seat. A shudder took hold of her body. The hairs on the back of her neck rose. The man spoke about her death without the slightest emotion. He was positively evil.

'In that case, it goes to you, or to your heir, currently Mr Jeffrey Beresford, if you predecease him,' the solicitor said. He smiled apologetically at the young man who was watching the earl with icy blue eyes and a very small smile.

The wretch was enjoying the earl's shock.

The earl said something under his breath. It sounded suspiciously like a curse. 'Clearly the man was disordered. What will the courts think of that?'

'My father was not mad,' Mrs Hampton said haughtily. 'Madness does not run in the Beresford family. But you wouldn't know that, since you have had nothing to do with any of us.'

Mary listened to what they were saying, heard them perfectly well, but it all seemed a great distance off. She didn't think she'd taken a breath since the earl had explained. She worked a little moisture into her dry mouth. 'The will requires that I marry in order to inherit?'

The lawyer nodded gravely. 'Indeed. Within the year.'

'Marry who?' she asked.

The earl's mouth curled in a predatory smile. 'That is the question, isn't it?'

Irritated beyond endurance, she rose to her feet. 'You are hardly helpful, sir.'

Forced to rise also, the earl gave her a mirthless smile. 'I thought you said you were clever, Miss Wilding.'

She looked at him blankly.

'He means you must marry him,' Gerald said, scowling. 'But you could marry Jeffrey or me. That would put a spoke in his wheels.'

The earl glowered, but said nothing.

She strode over to the solicitor, whose forehead was beaded with sweat. He pulled out a kerchief and mopped his brow. 'Well, Mr Savary, is it true?' she asked. 'Does the late earl's will require me to marry...' she waved an arm in the earl's direction '...him?'

'It is silent on the issue, Miss Wilding.' He swallowed. 'Under the law, no one can require your marriage to any particular person. However, if you wish to inherit the money, you must marry someone. Perhaps there is someone....' His words tailed off at a low growl from the earl.

Someone. She wanted to laugh. And then she wanted to cry. Someone. She was a schoolteacher. A charity case. And a beanpole to boot. Suddenly a very rich beanpole. She glanced over at the earl. 'No doubt there will be many someones lining up at my door on the morrow.'

The earl glared at her. 'Over my dead body.'

'Or over mine,' she said as the full enormity of it all solidified in her mind.

'There is that,' he agreed.

'Are you saying you intend us to marry?' she asked.

He looked at her for a long moment and she had the feeling that sympathy lurked somewhere in those flat grey eyes, then they hardened to polished steel and she knew she was mistaken. 'Marry to suit my grandfather?' he rasped. 'Not if I can help it.'

She flinched at the harshness of his reply and was glad that he did not see her reaction as he turned at once to the solicitor.

'There must be some loophole you have not considered. Bring those papers to my study. I will review them in detail.'

He strode from the room.

Mrs Hampton gave Mary an accusatory glare. 'Come, Gerald. Jeffrey. We need to talk.' She departed in what appeared to be high dudgeon for some unknown destination with the two young men in tow.

Unsure what else to do, Mary gathered herself to return to her chamber. She needed time to think about this new development. She could only pray the earl would find a way out of the conundrum. She certainly did not want to, nor would she, marry him. Or anyone else for that matter. She'd put away the hopes for a husband many years before

'Er, miss?' Savary said.

'Yes?'

'There was one thing I forgot to mention to his lordship.'

She gazed at him askance. Forgetting to mention something to his lordship sounded like a serious mistake given the earl's present mood. She had not thought the man so stupid. 'What did you forget?'

'He should have let me read things in order.' He fussed with the papers on the desk. 'You must have his permission. Whoever you choose to marry, he must approve.'

A burst of anger ripped through her at being required to bend to the earl's wishes on this or any matter. Especially one so altogether personal. Proving herself to be suitable to work as a teacher, to gain her independence, had taken years of hard work. She wasn't about to give it up on some stranger's whim. 'I suggest you hurry and tell his lordship the good news. I expect it will make him feel a great deal more sanguine about what has happened here today.'

'Do you think so?'

A laugh bubbled up inside her. Hysteria, no doubt. 'I have not the slightest idea of what goes on in his lordship's mind.' That much was certainly true. 'Please excuse me.'

She stalked out of the room. Whether anger improved her sense of direction, or she was getting used to the Abbey, she found her way back to her room without any problem.

The room was chilly. It was the stone walls, she thought, rubbing her arms with her hands, then wrapping her old woollen shawl around her shoulders. Stone walls needed tapestries and blazing fires. She poked at the glowing embers and added more coal. Then she sat on the edge of the bed and stared through the diamond windowpanes. From here she could see the crumbling walls of what had been the abbey church. And beyond it, the sea pounding on rocks.

Finally, she allowed herself to think about what had happened back there in the library.

Oh, heavens! Marry and inherit a fortune? How could this be?

Not for years had she imagined she would ever be married. She was not the kind of woman men took to wife. They liked little dainty things, simpering girls like the ones she helped train at Ladbrook's School. Years ago, the idea of being a wife and a mother had made her heart miss a number of beats. How it had raced when she thought that Mr Allerdyce who had been so attentive, walking her home from church, treating her like a lady of importance, would come up to scratch, until Sally had discovered it was all a front. He was currying favour with Mary in order to get close to one of her pupils. An heiress. His parting words had made it very clear just what he thought of her as a woman. As hurtful and mortifying an experience as it had been, it had forced her to realise she would never be a wife.

Instead, she'd decided that her true vocation lay with her girls, being a teacher. That they were her family. She only had them for a short while, it was true, and their departures were always a wrench, but they were planned. It was not as though they abandoned her, but rather that she sent them out into the world with her blessing.

Now, this stranger, this deceased earl, had somehow engineered her into a marriage to a man she knew nothing about. She swallowed. What would it be liked to be married to such a man? He'd want an heir. Children. A family, just as she'd always dreamed. Her heart raced. Her chest tightened at the thought of being a mother.

It wouldn't be a marriage born of romantic love. It would be for convenience. A practical arrangement such as people from the nobility entered into all of the time. For mutual gain.

He'd hardly been thrilled at the idea of marrying her to obtain what was rightfully his, now had he? He'd looked positively horrified when he realised what the will intended. As if he faced a fate worse than death.

She gripped her hands in her lap to stop them from shaking. Oh, great heavens, please let this all be a bad dream. Please let her wake up and discover it was a nightmare.

But she was awake. And it was horribly real.

What would Sally advise? Don't trust a man like him an inch. Mary could imagine the hard look in her friend's eye and the knowing edge to her voice. She'd been right about Allerdyce. And look at how easily her father had abandoned her after her mother's death. But she couldn't ask Sally for her opinion. She had to rely on her own judgement. And, so far, nothing the earl had said or done made her want to trust him.

Gradually she became calmer, her breathing less shallow, the trembles less pronounced. One thing she knew, she wasn't going to force any man to the altar. Especially not a man like the new earl.

Her heart gave an odd little kick. The sort of pang that someone less practical might describe as disappointment. Not her, though. Let other women have their romantic notions. There was no room for them in her life.

There had to be some way out of this dilemma. And

no doubt the earl would find it. Once more the uneasy prickles of a ghost walking across her skin rippled across her shoulders.

The earl did not come down for dinner, nor did any of the other members of the family. Mary dined in splendid solitude in the dining room and felt like an idiot. Three footman and a butler wasting their time serving her. If they had told her, she could have taken a tray in her room. She finished as quickly as she could and waved off an offer of tea in the drawing room.

'Do you know where the earl is, Manners?'

'In his study, miss.'

'And where is that?'

'In the south wing, miss.' He bowed and withdrew, leaving her none the wiser, but determined to seek him out and try to come to some agreement with him about the future.

Outside the dining room, she turned right, because left was the direction towards the north tower and her room. It stood to reason the south wing must be in the opposite direction, if the corridors were straight. But they weren't.

After a half an hour of criss-crossing various parts of the house, and once arriving back at the dining room, she was ready to give up.

There was one hallway she hadn't explored yet, because it looked narrow and darker than most of the others. She took a deep breath and gave it a try. It had only one door.

A door that was ajar and throwing a wedge of light into the corridor. She peeped through the crack. Aha. She had found the study and the earl. It was a small room, filled with ledgers on shelves rising to the ceiling behind a battered desk covered in papers. The earl was standing with one foot on the brazier in the hearth and his elbow on the mantel, staring into the flames of a merrily burning log fire. His dog lay prone at his feet.

He wasn't an elegant man, his physique was too muscular, his shoulders too broad, his features too large and square, but there was nothing about him to displease the female eye, especially not now when his expression was pensive rather than hard and uncompromising. He looked not much older than she was. Early thirties, perhaps. And not really so very overpowering from this distance.

Her heartbeat picked up speed and her mouth dried. All right, he was really intimidating. Afraid that if she dallied longer she would flee, she tapped sharply on the door.

Both he and the dog looked up. Thankfully, the dog's head dropped back to its paws and its eyes slid closed.

But his lordship was a whole different matter. His whole attention focused on her. She could feel it like a touch on her face. For a moment, a very brief moment, warmth flickered in his eyes as if he was pleased to see her.

His gaze shuttered. His jaw hardened.

Perhaps not, then. Perhaps he had been expecting someone else, for a moment later his lips formed a flat line and his eyes were icy cold. Almost as if he was angry. And yet she did not feel as if his anger was directed at her. It seemed to be turned inwards.

He left the hearth and strode to the middle of the room. 'Miss Wilding,' he said with a stiff bow.

She quelled the urge to run and dipped a curtsy. 'Lord Beresford.'

'Have you once more lost your way? Did you need an escort back to your chamber? Allow me to ring the bell for Manners.'

The irony in his tone was not lost on her even as his

deep voice made her heart jolt, before continuing its rapid knocking against her ribs. Never in her life had she been so nervous around a man. Not that she met very many men in her line of work. Fathers, mostly. In a hurry to depart. Or men pursuing her girls and needing to be kept at bay.

She decided to ignore his jibe and boldly stepped into the room. 'May I have a word with you, please, your lordship?'

He frowned darkly, but gestured for her to sit in the comfortably stuffed chair in front of the desk. He went around and sat on the other side, clearing a space before him, stacking papers and account books to one side. His face was almost entirely in shadow, while she sat in the full light of the lamp. 'How may I be of service?' he asked, politely enough to almost settle her nerves.

'We must discuss this will.'

She sensed him stiffen, though his hands, linked together on the ink-stained wood, remained completely relaxed. He had strong hands with blunt-tipped fingers. Practical hands, bronzed by wind and weather and scarred across the knuckles. Labourer's hands rather than those of a gentleman.

After a small pause, he sighed, a small exhale of air, as if he had been holding his breath. As if she had caught him by surprise. 'I suppose now is as good a time as any.' His voice was expressionless.

'Was the lawyer able to provide any advice on how the terms might be broken?'

'No. You are perfectly safe on that score.'

He thought her a fortune hunter. The desire to bash him over the head with something rose up in her breast.

But how could he not, given the terms of the will?

The chill in the air was palpable. The suspicion. 'Perhaps you would like to explain why the earl…my grandfather,' he choked out the last word, 'would leave the bulk of his fortune to you?'

'He is the benefactor of the school where I grew up and now work. He supported me there when I was orphaned. That is all I know.'

The earl made a soft sound of derision.

She bridled. 'It is true. I swear it.'

His hands flattened on the table. 'Then he was not your lover?'

She gasped. 'You are jesting.'

The silence said he was not.

'How dare you suggest such a thing?' She shot to her feet.

He followed. 'Sit,' he said coldly. 'You wanted to talk. Let us have this out.'

'Not if you are going to insult me.'

'Sit of your own volition or by my will.' His voice was soft but the menace was unmistakable.

She did not doubt for a moment that the brute could overpower her. 'Touch me and I will scream.'

His face darkened. 'And who will come to your aid, do you think?' he asked softly.

No one. She swallowed.

He let go a displeased sigh. 'Please, Miss Wilding. Take your seat. You are right, we have things we need to discuss.'

For a moment she hesitated, but it was foolish to dash off having worked up the courage to face him. She sat and folded her hands in her lap. 'Very well, but do not cast aspersions on my character.'

His gaze didn't waver from her face. 'Look at this from my perspective. I am trying to understand why my grandfather left you his fortune. Lover is an obvious answer.'

Her hackles rose again. She hung on to her anger. 'Isn't

it more likely I did him some favour? Perhaps rescued him from danger.'

He snorted. 'What sort of danger?'

'He could have ridden past Ladbrook's School where I teach one day and been set upon by footpads. Seeing him from the classroom window, I might have charged out to save him with my pupils at my heels. As you know, there is nothing more daunting to the male species than the high-pitched squeals of a gaggle of females, particularly when armed with parasols.'

Oh dear, now where had all that ridiculousness come from? Her stomach tightened. Rarely did she let her tongue run away with her these days. It seemed she needed to get a firmer grip on her anger.

He picked up a quill and twirled it in those strong fingers. Fascinated, she watched the only sign she'd ever seen that he was not completely in control. 'But it didn't happen that way,' he said drily.

'No. But you must admit it is just as plausible as your scenario. He was a very old man.'

'You think to toy with me, Miss Wilding? I can assure you that is a very dangerous game and not one you are equipped to play.'

'I have no idea why he left his money to me in this fashion.'

'Let us hope you do not. If I discover that you are a willing instrument in this plot of his, things will not go well for you.'

The air left her lungs in a rush at the obvious threat. 'I can assure you…'

'You need assure me of nothing. There will be no marriage.'

'You must have done something to deserve so terrible a fate?'

He didn't seem to notice the irony in her tone. 'I drew breath when I was born.' The quill snapped.

She jumped at the sound.

He tossed the two pieces aside.

A shiver ran down her back. She fought her instinct for sympathy. 'A little melodramatic, isn't it?'

'Much like your tale of rescue.'

She frowned. It was time to play the one and only card in her hand and hope it was a trump. 'Why don't I just sign over the money to you? I need only a very little for myself.'

'The perfect solution.'

She let go a sigh of relief. She really had not expected him to see reason so quickly. 'Then I will leave in the morning, once the papers are signed.'

'No.'

'Why not?'

'It can't be done. The money only comes to you if you marry. I will put the best legal minds to work on finding a solution, and in the meantime you will remain here.'

'I can't stay. I am expected back at the school.'

'Then tell me what connection you are to the earl.' His fingers drummed an impatient tattoo. 'His by-blow, perhaps?' he said flatly.

'I beg your pardon?' She stared into the shadows, trying to see his expression, trying to see if he was jesting, while her mind skittered this way and that. 'You think me the late earl's daughter?'

'You look like a Beresford.'

He thought they were family? Her chest squeezed. Her heart struggled to beat. The air in the room seemed suddenly thick, too dense to breathe. That had been her first thought, also. Her wild hope, but not in the way he was suggesting. Good Lord, did he think the earl was requiring his grandson to marry his aunt? Technically incest, even if he carried not a drop of Beresford blood. 'That is disgusting.'

'Exactly.'

She leaped to her feet and made for the door. 'I will leave first thing in the morning.'

Before she could reach the door, he was there, one hand holding it shut while he gazed down into her face. For a big man, he moved very quickly. And surprisingly quietly.

Judging by the tightness of his mouth and the flash of steel in his eyes, he was not pleased. 'You, Miss Wilding, are not going anywhere until I say you may.'

She shrank back against the door. 'You have no authority over me.'

'Apparently, I do.'

She gasped. 'What are you talking about?'

'According to the solicitor, you are my ward.'

Chapter Three

'Utter nonsense.'

'Savary informed me that he told you that you need my permission to wed.'

'That does not make you my guardian.'

'No, but since I have taken over the responsibilities of the earldom, *that* makes me your guardian.'

'The late earl was not my guardian. I have no need of a guardian, I have lived by my own efforts for years.'

'You have lived off this estate.' He pointed to a ledger on the desk. 'Each quarter a sum of money was paid to a Mrs Sally Ladbrook for your keep and education. A very princely sum, I might add.' His gaze dropped to her chest, which she realised was expanding and contracting at a very rapid rate to accommodate her breathing.

His eyes came back to her face and his jaw hardened. 'And then you show up here in rags hoping for more.'

Damn him and his horrid accusations. Her hand flashed out. He caught her wrist. His fingers were like an iron band around her flesh. 'You'll need to be quicker to catch me off guard.'

'What kind of person do you think I am?'

His expression darkened. 'A Beresford.' He cast her hand aside.

Never had she heard such hatred directed at a single word. It must have tasted like acid on his tongue.

'You are a Beresford.'

His eyes widened. 'I doubt there are many who would agree. Certainly not me.'

'Then you should not be inheriting the title.'

'You are changing the subject again, Miss Wilding.'

The subject was as slippery as a bucket of eels. 'I have had quite enough of your accusations.'

'Are you saying you didn't come here seeking money?'

She coloured. 'No. Well, yes, for the school. It needs a new roof.' Among many other things it needed. 'But I have never met the earl before last night. And there certainly have been no vast sums of money coming to Ladbrook's or to me.'

He glanced across the room at his desk, at the account book, clearly not believing a word.

A rush of tears burned behind her eyes, because she knew it could not be true, unless... No, she would not believe it. 'I need to go back to the school. I need to speak to Mrs Ladbrook.'

He stared into her face, his gaze so intense, she wanted to look away. But she couldn't. Didn't dare, in case he thought she was lying.

Why did it matter what he thought?

Yet she would not stand down. Once more there was heat in that grey gaze, like molten silver, and the warmth seemed to set off a spark in her belly that flashed up to her face. Her cheeks were scalding, her heart pounding against the wall of her chest as if she had run a great race.

Slowly his hand moved from the door to her shoulder, stroked down her arm, his fingers inexorably sliding over muscle and bone as if he would learn the contours of her arm.

His expression was grim, as if this was not something he wanted to do at all, yet he did not stop.

She tipped her face upwards, her lips parted to protest... Only to accept the soft brush of his warm dry velvety lips. Little thrills raced through her stomach. Chased across her skin.

And then his mouth melded to hers, his tongue stroking the seam of her mouth, the sweet sensation melting her bones until she parted her lips on a gasp of sheer bliss and tasted his tongue with her own. Feverishly, their mouths tasted each other while she clung to those wide shoulders for support and his hands at her waist held her tight against his hard body.

She could feel the thunder of his heart where his chest pressed against her breasts, hear the rush of her blood in her veins. It was shocking. And utterly mesmerising.

On an oath, he stepped back, breaking all contact, shock blazing in his eyes.

The thrills faded to little more than echoes of the sensations they had been a moment ago. What on earth was she doing? More to the point, what was he doing? 'How dare you, sir?' she said, pulling her shawl tightly around her.

At that he gave a short laugh. 'How dare I what?'

'Kiss me.'

'You kissed me.'

Had she? She didn't think she had, but she wasn't exactly sure what had happened. Unless... 'Don't think to force me into marrying you by ruining my reputation. You see, that kind of thing doesn't matter to me.'

His eyes widened. 'So that is your plan, is it?'

'Oh, you really are impossible.'

For a long moment his gaze studied her face, searching

for who knew what. 'I will discover what it is my grandfather put you up to, you know. I will stop you any way
I can. I have more resources at my disposal than you can
possibly imagine.'

She could imagine all right. She could imagine all sorts
of things when it came to this man. Resources weren't the
only thing chasing through her mind. And those thoughts
were the worst of all: the thoughts of his kisses and the
heat of his body. 'The best thing you could do is kill me
off. Then all your troubles will be over.'

The grey of his eyes turned wintry. His expression
hardened. 'Don't think I haven't thought of it.'

Her breath left her in a rush. Her stomach dropped
away and she felt cold all over. She ducked under his arm,
pulled at the door handle and was out the door in a flash
and running down the corridor.

'Miss Wilding, wait,' he called after her.

She didn't dare stop. Her heart was beating far too fast,
the blood roaring in her head, for her to think clearly. But
now he had shown his hand, she would be on her guard.

After a night filled with dreams Mary couldn't quite
recall—though she suspected from how hot she felt that
they had something to do with the earl and his kiss—she
awoke to find Betsy setting a tray of hot chocolate and
freshly baked rolls beside the bed.

'What time is it?'

'Nine o'clock, miss.'

So late? How could she have slept so long and still feel
desperately tired? Perhaps because she'd been in such a
turmoil when she went to bed. Perhaps because she could
not get those dark words out of her mind. *Don't think I
haven't thought of it.*

'The weather is set to be fair, miss.' Betsy knelt to rake the coals in the fire. 'Warm for this time of year.'

Mary hopped out of bed and went to the window. 'So it is. I think I will go for a walk.' She dressed with her usual efficiency in her best gown.

Betsy rose to her feet. 'The ruins are very popular with visitors in the summer,' she said, watching Mary reach behind her to button her gown with a frown of disapproval. 'Very old they are. Some say the are haunted by the old friars who were killed by King Henry.'

Mary tucked a plain linen scarf in the neck of her bodice and picked up her brush. 'Superstitious nonsense.' She brushed hard. 'Have you ever seen a ghost?' She glanced past her own reflection at the maid, who looked a little pale.

'No, miss.' She gave a little shiver. 'And I've worked here for three years. But I don't go out there at night.'

Mary coiled her hair around her fingers and reached for her pins. 'The ruins sound fascinating. I will be sure to take a look.' She wished she had used her time in the library the previous day looking at a map of the area instead of reading romantic poetry.

'Would miss like me to fix her hair?' Betsy asked, looking a little askance at the plain knot Mary favoured. 'I can do it up fancy like Mrs Hampton's maid does, if you like. I have been practising on the other girls.'

Mary heard a note of longing in the girl's voice. 'Why, Betsy, do you have ambitions to become a lady's maid?'

Betsy coloured, but her eyes shone. 'Yes, miss. I would like that above all. My brother works down Beresford's tin mine. If I had a better paying job, he could go to school.'

Her mine. Or it would be if she married. 'Is it a bad place to work?'

Betsy looked embarrassed. 'It's hard work, but the manager, Mr Trelawny, is a fair man. Not like some.'

'How old is your brother?'

'Ten, miss. Works alongside my Da, he does. Proud as a peacock.'

The thought of such a small boy working in the mine did not sit well in her stomach. But she knew families needed the income. As the mine owner, if she really was a mine owner, she could make some changes. To do that, she had to marry. And then the mine would belong to her husband and not to her. It was all such a muddle. Being a schoolteacher was one thing, but this…this was quite another. Besides, it was easy to see that if she married the earl, he would rule the roost. He was not the type of man to listen to a woman.

What she needed was some sensible counsel to see her through this mess. While Sally Ladbrook might not be the warmest of people, she had a sensible head on her shoulders. 'Perhaps you can help me with my hair another day. That will be all for now.'

How strange it sounded, giving out orders to another person in such a manner, but Betsy seemed to take it as natural, bobbing her curtsy and leaving right away.

Oh dear, Mary hoped the girl wouldn't be too disappointed that Mary could not offer her a position, but she really couldn't stay. Not when Lord Beresford considered her death a plausible option.

Besides, she desperately needed to speak to Sally about the other matter the earl had raised. The money. There had to be a plausible explanation, other than misappropriation. The earl was wrong to suggest it.

She sat down and drank the chocolate and ate as many of the rolls as she could manage. The last two she wrapped in a napkin and tucked in her reticule to eat on the journey.

She counted out her small horde of coins and was relieved to discover she had enough to get her back to Wiltshire on a stagecoach. After packing her valise and bundling up in her winter cloak and bonnet, she headed for a side door she'd noticed in her wanderings. She just hoped she could find it again in the maze of passageways and stairs.

After a couple of wrong turns, she did indeed find it again. A quick survey assured her no one was around to see her departure. She twisted the black-iron ring attached to the latch and tugged. The heavy door, caught by the wind, yanked the handle out of her hands and slammed against the passage wall with a resounding bang.

Her heart raced in her chest. Had anyone heard? Would they come running? Rather than wait to see, she stepped outside and, after a moment's struggle, closed the door behind her.

She really hadn't expected the wind to be so fierce. She pulled up her hood and tightened the strings, staring around her at crumbling walls and stone arches overgrown with weeds. The jagged walls looked grim and ghostly against the leaden sky, though no doubt it would look charmingly antiquated on a sunny day.

Clutching her valise, she picked her way through the ruins, heading north, she hoped. A green sward opened up before her. Not the cliffs and the sea. In the distance, a rider on a magnificent black horse galloped across the park, a dog loping along behind.

The earl. It could be no one else. Hatless, his open greatcoat flapping in the wind, he looked like the apocalyptic horseman of Death. She shivered.

No, that was giving him far too much in the way of mystical power. He was simply a man who wanted his birthright. And she had somehow managed to get in the way. The thought didn't make her feel any better.

Realising she must have turned south, she swiftly marched in the other direction, around the outside of the ruins, up hill this time, which made more sense if she was headed for cliffs.

The wind increased in strength, buffeting her ears, whipping the ribbons of her bonnet in her face and billowing her cloak around her. She gasped as it tore the very breath from her throat. It would be a vigorous walk to St Ives and no mistake.

She licked her lips and was surprised by the sharp tang of salt on her tongue. From the sea, she supposed. Interesting. She hadn't thought of the salt being carried in the air. Head down, she forged on, looking for a path along the cliff top. The upward climb became steeper, so rocky underfoot she had to watch where she placed each step or risk a tumble. She paused to take stock of her progress.

A few feet in front of her the ground disappeared and all she could see ahead of her was grey surging waves crested with spume. It was lucky she had stopped when she did.

But where was the path mentioned by Gerald? She scanned the ground in both directions and was able to make out a very faint track meandering along the cliff top. It looked more like a track for sheep than for people.

The wind seemed intent of holding her back, but she battled into it, following the track frighteningly close to the edge.

The strings of her hood gave way against a battering gust and her bonnet blew off, bouncing against her back, pulling against her throat. Strands of hair tore free and whipped at her face, stinging her eyes. A roar like thunder rolled up from below.

She leaned out to peer through the spray into the boiling churning water. Hell's kitchen must surely look and sound like this. As each wave drew back with a grumbling growl, she glimpsed the jagged rocks at the base of the cliff and off to her left a rocky cove with a small sandy beach.

Out in the distance, the sky and sea became one vast grey mist. The world had never felt this big in the little Wiltshire village of Sarum. She leaned into the wind and felt its pure natural strength holding her weight. She laughed. She couldn't help it. She had never experienced such wildness.

Something nudged into her back.

She windmilled her arms to regain her balance. Her valise went flying over the cliff. And the ground fell from beneath her feet.

She screamed.

Chapter Four

An iron band of an arm closed around her waist at the same moment her feet left the ground. She hung suspended above the raging sea for what felt like hours, but could only be seconds. That arm twisted her around and plonked her down. Not on the ground, but on a pair of hard muscled thighs gripping a saddle.

Teeth chattering, heart racing, she gazed up into the earl's hard face. With a click of his tongue he backed the horse away from the edge. Was he mad? They could all have gone over the cliff.

Clear of the edge, he halted the horse's backward progress and wheeled around so they were no longer facing the sea. Further along the cliff, a shepherd, crook in hand, was running towards them. The earl waved, an everything-is-fine acknowledgement, which it wasn't, and the shepherd stopped running and waved back.

'Put me down,' she demanded.

A grunt was all the answer he gave.

She felt his thighs move beneath her as he clicked his tongue. The horse headed down hill. Back the way she had come. The urge to protest caused her hands to clench.

'Are you mad?' she yelled over the wind. 'I almost went over the edge.'

His cold gaze flicked over her face. He took a deep shuddering breath as if to control some strong emotion. Fear? More likely anger. His next words confirmed it. 'It would have served you right, my girl. What the devil did you think you were doing?'

She shoved the annoying lengths of hair out of her face. Dash it, she would not lie. 'Walking to St Ives. Now I have lost my bag.'

'You are lucky that was all you lost,' he murmured like a threat in her ear.

He meant she could have lost her life. She swallowed and glanced back towards the headland, where the shepherd, a hand shading his eyes, was still watching them. It would have been the answer to all the earl's problems if she had gone over that cliff. She could have sworn something nudged her in the back. Had he changed his mind at the last moment?

A cold hand clawed at her stomach. She glanced at his grim expression. He'd been angry about that will. She could well imagine him taking matters into his own hands. But murder? A shiver slid down her back.

The further from the cliff they got, the less the sea and the wind roared in her ears. She lifted her chin and met his chilly gaze. 'You have no right to keep me here.'

'I have every right. I am your guardian.'

'Only in your mind,' she muttered.

He stiffened. 'You need a *keeper* if you think it is safe to walk along that cliff top.'

Now he was pretending he minded if she fell. Why? So she wouldn't guess his intentions? It certainly wasn't because he cared about what happened to her. The cold in her stomach spread to her chest. She readied herself to jump down and run for her life.

He hissed in a breath, as if in some sort of pain. 'In heaven's name, stop wriggling.'

'Then put me down.'

'I'll put you down when I am good and ready.'

The big horse pranced and kicked up his back legs. She instinctively grabbed for his lordship's solid shoulders. He tensed and she heard him curse softly under his breath. He pulled the horse to a stop and, putting an arm around her waist, lowered her to the ground. He dismounted beside her.

'No need to interrupt your ride,' she said brightly. 'I can find my own way.'

He grasped her upper arm in an iron grip. Not hard enough to hurt, but there was no mistaking she could not break free. 'How did you get out of the house without anyone seeing you?'

She gasped. 'What are you talking about?'

'I left orders that you were not to leave.'

'Orders you have no right to give?'

'Don't test my patience, Miss Wilding. I will have no hesitation in dealing with you as you deserve.'

She swallowed hard. 'Killing me off, you mean?' Oh, no. She couldn't believe she had just blurted that out.

He released her as if she was hot to the touch. His eyes flashed with an emotion she could not read—pain, perhaps? More likely disgust given the hard set to his jaw. 'I assure you, when I want your death, it will not occur in front of witnesses.'

So he had seen the shepherd and thought better of it. She tried not to shiver at the chill in his voice. 'I will keep that in mind, my lord. Thank you for the forewarning.'

He stared at her, his lips twitching, his eyes gleaming

as if he found something she had said amusing. 'You are welcome, Miss Wilding. Come along, I will escort you back to the house.'

So now they were to pretend nothing had happened? That he hadn't seriously thought about pushing her off a cliff? Perhaps she should pretend she was joking about thinking he wanted her dead. She quelled a shiver. She hated this feeling of fear. Anger at her weakness rose up in her throat, making it hard to breathe or think, when she should be finding a way to beat him at his own game. She gave him a look of disdain. 'Did no one tell you it isn't polite to creep up on a person?'

'I was riding a very large stallion over rocky terrain. That hardly counts as creeping.'

'I didn't hear you over the noise of the sea. Surely you could tell?'

He gave her a look designed to strike terror into the heart of the most intrepid individual. 'I had other things on my mind.'

Such as pushing her over the edge. She began striding down hill. Unlike most men of her acquaintance, he easily kept pace, the horse following docilely, while the dog bounded around them. Surprisingly, his steps matched hers perfectly. On the rare occasion when she'd walked alongside a gentleman—well, back from the village with the young man who delivered the mail—she'd had to shorten her stride considerably because the young man was a good head shorter than she. The earl, on the other hand, towered above her. A rather unnerving sensation.

All her sensations with regard to this man were unnerving. The fluttery ones when he kissed her, the shivery ones when she felt fear and the one she was feeling now, a strange kind of appreciation for his handsome face and athletic build when she should be absolutely terrified. It seemed that whereas her mind was as sharp as a needle, her body was behaving like a fool.

It was this silence between them making her react this way. It needed filling to distract her from these wayward thoughts and feelings.

'The Abbey is an extraordinary house, isn't it?' She gestured towards the sprawling mish-mash of wings and turrets.

His eyes narrowed. 'Highly impractical. Ridiculously expensive to run. It should be torn down.'

Aghast, she stopped, staring up at his implacable face. 'But think of all the history that would be lost.'

'A history of murderous brigands.'

'Rather fitting, don't you think?' The words were out before she could stop them.

He gave her a look askance, as if he found her a puzzle he would like to solve. Well, she had solved his puzzle. She knew exactly what was on his mind. Her murder. A bone-deep shudder trembled in her bones.

They reached the ruins near her tower. He stopped, his gaze fixed on the door through which she had left. 'You came through there.'

It wasn't a question. She shrugged and kept walking.

He caught her arm and halted her. 'Give me your word you will not try to leave again without my permission.'

'You have no authority over my actions. None at all.'

He let go a sigh. 'Very well, that door and all the others will from now on be locked and barred.' One corner of his mouth curled up, and if his voice had not been so harsh, she might have thought it an attempt at a smile. 'You might as well use it to go back inside.'

She pulled her arm free. Anything not to have to spend any more time in his company. Her runaway heart was going to knock right through the wall of her chest. She headed for the door.

'Miss Wilding,' he said, softly.

She turned back.

'Be in the library at eleven o'clock.'

'Why?'

'There is a funeral to arrange.'

Why would she need to be involved in family arrangements? Unless he still thought she was some sort of relation. The very idea made anger ball up in her chest, because while she had longed for it desperately, it wasn't the case. And that was just as foolish as the way her emotions seemed to see-saw around him.

She shot him a glare as he stood there, waiting for her obedience, one hand on a hip, the other gripping the horse's reins, watching her with those unnerving grey eyes as if she was a recalcitrant child.

With no other alternative in sight, she lifted the latch and went in.

As custom dictated, the ladies were not expected to attend the funeral. Mary also refused to attend the reception arranged for afterwards. She wasn't family and there had been quite enough speculation about her relationship to the deceased earl. She had no wish to run the gauntlet of local gossip. Besides, she had nothing suitable to wear now her valise was gone. Reluctantly the earl had agreed.

Heady with triumph at winning the argument, Mary had settled herself in the library with Maria Edgeworth's *Belinda*. Romantic nonsense, Sally would have called it, but it had a depth to it, too, that Mary found fascinating.

'What are you reading?'

Startled at the closeness of the voice, Mary looked up with a gasp. The earl, dark and predatory, loomed over her looking like a dark angel. Much as he had looked at his grandfather's bedside. Perhaps not quite as grim.

'Shouldn't you be at the reception?' she asked sweetly.

'It is over.'

A hot flush travelled up her face as she realised that evening was drawing in rapidly. The afternoon had flown by in unaccustomed idleness. She was already straining to see the words on the page, but she'd been too engrossed to get up and light a candle. She closed the book. 'I didn't realise how late it was.'

He glanced down at the cover. 'A novel. I should have guessed.'

The back of her neck prickled because he was standing so close. Because once more his cologne invaded her nostrils and recalled to mind her disgraceful response to his lips on hers. Her body warmed in the most uncomfortable way at the memory. How could she think about his kiss after he had practically dropped her off the cliff earlier in the day? Her mind must be disordered.

'Was there some reason for your interruption?' She gave him the frosty glance that had new girls quaking in their slippers.

It troubled him not one whit, it seemed. Indeed he didn't seem to notice the chill in her voice at all, since a flicker of amusement passed across his face. Hah! She should be glad he found her entertaining.

He held out a note. 'The post brought you a letter.'

Oh, now she felt bad for being rude.

He moved away to give her privacy and began browsing the shelves on the far side of the room.

She frowned at the handwriting. She had not expected Sally to write after such a short time. Sending mail such a distance was expensive. Now she would owe the earl for the cost of the postage and she had little enough money in her purse. She broke the seal and spread open the paper.

For a moment, she could not quite believe the words she was reading. She read the cold little missive again, more slowly.

Miss Wilding,
Ladbrook School is now closed as ordered by the
Earl of Beresford and the property is sold. I wish
you all success in your new life. Yours, Sally Lad-
brook.

Closed? How could the school be closed? Why would he do such a thing? How could he? Anger trembled through her with the force of an earthquake. The paper shivered like an aspen in her fingers. A band tightened around her chest as the enormity of what had happened became clear. She was homeless.

Abandoned by her only friend in the world. It hurt. Badly.

The earl, who was leaning against the shelves leafing idly through a book, looked up from the pages to meet her gaze. 'Bad news?'

The wretch. 'Bad?' She rose to her feet. 'You take away my livelihood and then ask if it is bad?' She gave a bitter laugh.

He straightened, frowning. 'What are you talking about?'

'You know very well what I am talking about.' Her voice shook with the effect of roiling anger. Everything inside her chest rocked and heaved. Her ribs ached from the force of it. For a moment it seemed she might never breathe again. But she did. And words followed. 'You need not think this will stop me from leaving.' She crumpled the note in her fist and threw it at him. Incredibly, he plucked it out of the air.

She marched for the door, not knowing where she was going, but knowing she could not remain in the same room with him without trying to do him a mischief.

'Wait!' he commanded.

She didn't stop, but once again he beat her to the door, holding it closed with his hand above her head, while she pulled on the handle. She swung around, glaring up at him. 'Open this door.'

He glanced down at the note. 'This school has no relevance now.'

'No relevance?' She wanted to hit him for his stupidity. Instead she dodged around him and went to the window, putting as much distance between them as possible. 'The school was my home.'

She turned to stare out of the window, wanting to bang her fist against the glass, break through it to freedom, like a trapped sparrow in a garden room.

Her stomach fell away. Even if she did, she had nowhere to go. No home. Not even a forwarding address for Sally. Was that his doing, too? Or did Sally blame her for the loss of her school? The selfish, horrid man.

Moisture burned in the back of her throat and pushed its way up behind her eyes. She bowed her head against the pressure and swallowed hard. Tried to regain her composure

The earl drew closer, his gaze puzzled. 'Miss Wilding, surely it is not as bad as all that? You will have enough money to buy a hundred schools when you marry.'

'Marry who?' She whirled around and stared at him. Was that guilt she saw in his face? Guilt because he'd taken away all her options as well as her only friend.

Or guilt because he had decided that marrying her was preferable to her death? Or guilt because he planned…?

A sob pushed its way up her throat. Tears welled up, hovering on her lashes, blurring her vision. She dashed them away, clinging to her anger. 'Ladbrook's is the only home I remember. Everything I owned was there. My books. My mementos from my pupils. Why? Why did you have to interfere?' She struck out at his chest with her fist.

The next moment she found her face pressed to his wide shoulder, her hand gripping his lapel and supressed sobs shaking her body.

'Mary,' he said, his voice achingly soft. A large hand landed warm on her back, tentatively at first and then patting gently. 'I will have your property recovered, if that is what disturbs you.'

The urge to give in to her overwhelming longing for someone who cared battled with her good sense and won. She leaned against that broad chest, felt his heat and his power, and the steady rhythm of his heart as he held her close.

For a moment, she lost all sense of self. Forgot it was his fault things had come to this pass and revelled in the sense of being protected.

'So, this is how it is.' The angry voice came from the doorway. 'What a cur you really are.'

'Gerald,' the earl said, loosening his hold and looking over her shoulder. 'Could you be any more *de trop*?' The sarcasm was back and the raspy drawl.

Apparently oblivious to the threat those soft words contained, Gerald stomped across the room.

Mary pulled away, turning her face to the window while she groped for a handkerchief. The earl planted himself between her and the intruder who was clearly bound and determined to have his say. 'Miss Wilding is distressed. Please leave.'

'Distressed?' Gerald said. 'Aye, I can believe it. And what did you do to bring her to tears?'

'It is none of your business,' the earl replied coldly. 'Go away.'

Mary blew her nose and dabbed at her eyes. A few deep breaths would set her to rights, but she needed to be alone, away from the disturbing presence of the earl, to work out what Sally's letter really meant for her future. 'Please, excuse me, gentlemen.'

The earl put out a hand as if he would stop her, then let it fall. She made for the door and Gerald stepped aside to let her pass as if he barely saw her. His gaze was fixed on the earl. 'You don't belong here, Bane Beresford. We all know what you are. A bloody coalminer stealing a title from the rightful heir.'

Mary felt her mouth drop open in shock. She glanced back at the earl. His body radiated tension. His fists at his sides clenched and released. His dark gaze shifted from Gerald to her and back and then he leaned against the window frame folding his arms over his chest with a cynical curl to his lips. 'And what do you intend to do about it, bantling?'

Colour crept into the younger man's face, still set in an expression of defiance. Did he plan to fight with the earl? He would be badly outmatched.

'Gentlemen, please. This is hardly the way for members of a family to behave to each other,' she said.

Both men threw her angry looks.

Clearly she wasn't helping. But then, what did she know of families? Or friends for that matter? Once more, thoughts of Sally's callous note made her stomach fall away. The hard hot lump she had managed to swallow while wrapped in the earl's arms returned with a vengeance. Tears. A river of them, if the burning behind her eyes was any indication. 'Please excuse me,' she said, ducking her head as she ran for her chamber and privacy.

No one, least of all the earl, was going to see her dissolve into a blob of self-pity.

It took a good four hours before she gained her composure. First there had been tears, then anger at the earl, followed by a new emptiness. It had always been there, the small cold kernel of knowledge that she was unwanted, but as the years had passed, she'd formed an attachment for Sally Ladbrook. First as her pupil and employee, and more recently as a friend. Until today, she hadn't realised how much she relied on Sally's advice and counsel, on that one constant in her life. Now, thanks to the earl, she was completely alone.

It was terrifying.

But why? Why had Sally abandoned her? Was she really so unnecessary to anyone? Or had the earl offered an irresistible lure? If so, then she would never forgive him.

With a final sniff, she rose from the bed and went to the glass on the dressing table. Yes, her eyes were red rimmed and bloodshot. Her cheeks were chapped and sore, and her nose looked like a cherry popped into the middle of her face.

But the storm was over. She was drained of all emotion. Empty.

And that was how she would proceed from here. From now on, she would take no one at face value. Trust no one and rely only on herself.

She straightened her shoulders and went to the basin to bath her face. Her stomach grumbled. She vaguely remembered Betsy knocking on the door, reminding her of dinner and finally going away. She could not have gone to dinner then, hating the thought of anyone seeing her in this state.

There were the rolls she had purloined earlier. She retrieved them from the dresser drawer where she had tucked them after her escapade on the cliff. Hard as rocks, but edible if washed down with water. She munched slowly on the stale bread and considered her options. Find Sally and let her explain what had happened? Or consign her to the devil and set her feet on a new path?

If only she had some money of her own, then she would not need anyone's help. She did have money under this will, but only if she married.

Marriage. A home. A family of her own. How shining and bright the dream had been in her young lonely heart. Mr Allerdyce had shattered those dreams of a knight in shining armour coming to her rescue and falling at her feet. In reality, the best she could ever hope for was a widower with a gaggle of children looking for a cheap housekeeper.

Now, the only candidate seemed to be the earl. Her heart gave an odd little thump, as if it welcomed the idea. But he didn't welcome it. She could not imagine being married to man as cold as ice, who was forced up to the mark. She'd likely find herself dead in a week. Or rather someone else would find her dead. Oh, no. Now that really was the kind of melodrama she discouraged in her pupils.

She mentally shook her head. It was time to move on. The earl might think he'd won by taking away her only sanctuary, but she had more gumption than to give in at the first obstacle. And the fact that he hadn't yet realised it was to her advantage.

Something crashed above her head. She jumped to her feet, looking up. She hadn't known there was a room above hers. Whatever had fallen continued to bang several more times as if it was bouncing and rolling across the floor.

And then it stopped.

How strange.

A servant at work had dropped something, perhaps? She tried to imagine what it might be. Large and heavy and seemingly round.

A low moan echoed through her chamber, then a shriek so piercing she put her hands over her ears. What on earth was going on up there? What on earth would make anyone cry out in such a dreadful way? Were they hurt? There was no other explanation. And if they were in that much pain, they needed help. Urgently.

She wrapped her woollen shawl around her shoulders, then picked up a candlestick to the sound of what now sounded like rattling chains and opened her door.

Then nothing. Silence prevailed. It was over, whatever it was. She went back inside and started to close her door. A bang. Another yell. Something heavy dropped on a toe?

Such a racket, she could not ignore it. She left her room and started up the circular staircase beyond her door. The air out here was strangely cold. As far as she remembered, it was usually the same temperature outside her door as in the rest of the house, now it chilled her cheeks. Had someone opened a window? Her candle was certainly guttering in what must be a draught.

The stairs wound upwards around a central column of fluted grey granite. The way ahead was only visible as far as the next tight curve and the steps were worn into smooth grooves by centuries of feet. They became narrower the higher she went. Clutching her candle in one hand, she put the other on the wall for balance. The stone was ice to the touch.

Now someone was sobbing. Much as she had sobbed earlier. Someone mocking her? Oh, that would be mortifying. She had assumed she was completely alone.

The crying stopped. Footsteps tapped across stone.

A warm breath grazed the back of her neck. Someone following? She whirled around. One foot slipped. She teetered on the step, clutching at the wall, desperately hanging on to her candle. Her heart was thundering like the hooves of a runaway horse. 'Hello?'

There was no one behind her, but she had not imagined that warm rush of air. Indeed, there was no cold draught at all now.

Sweat formed on her brow and upper lip.

Fear.

What did she have to fear?

Then she remembered Gerald's ghoulish tale of a lady in white. She didn't believe in ghosts. She didn't. There had to be a perfectly logical explanation.

She chuckled, laughing at her fears to give herself courage. The sound bounced off the walls and it was several seconds before it died away. The reason the sounds she had heard were so strange: echoes. That must be it. A distortion of normal sounds in the room above.

She rounded the next curve and found a landing much like the one outside her chamber door. Two of the walls had arrow loops high above her head. The source of the cold breeze? If so, there was nothing now. The other two walls had doors set within stone arches, much like the one she had taken to the outside earlier in the day. The first latch she tried didn't budge. The second yielded grudgingly outwards to her pull, requiring all her strength to push it back against the wall. About to step inside, a shadow fell across the floor. A figure surged towards her.

Her heart stopped. She screamed and leaped back.

'Good God, Miss Wilding, what on earth is the matter?'

The earl, looking positively demonic in the flickering light of her candle, was staring at her as if she was mad. She pressed a hand to her breastbone, to quiet her rapid breathing. 'I heard a noise.' She swallowed. 'Why are you here?'

His brows climbed his forehead. 'You may hold the money in thrall, but surely I am entitled to go where I wish in my own home.'

The bitterness in his voice stung. It sounded like righteous indignation, as if he blamed her for this business with the will. He was trying to distract her from the noises she'd heard.

She peered into the room behind him, lifting her candle high. The chamber was completely empty. No sign of anything that could have rolled across the wooden planks. Not even any dust on the floor to show where it had been. 'Is this some sort of cruel game, then? Something to frighten me?' And, if so, to what purpose?

He tilted his head, regarding her intently. 'If you were scared, why did you come up here?'

'I heard a cry for help.'

'Quite the little Samaritan.'

'Hardly little.'

His eyes flashed amusement.

Was he mocking her?

'As you see, there is no one here but me,' he said in reasonable tones. 'Exactly what did you hear?'

If he didn't do it, he must have heard it. Why was he pretending he had not. 'Something rolling. Rattling chains, followed by a shriek. Right above my chamber. And now there is no one here but you.'

His eyes narrowed. 'You sound almost disappointed. Have the servants been telling you ghost stories?'

'Gerald said something about the White Lady at breakfast, but that has nothing to do with it. I know what I heard. You must have heard it, too.'

'I heard a noise,' he admitted grudgingly. 'Someone calling out.'

'It was more than that. Something bounced across the floor.' She gave him a suspicious look.

He gave a shrug. 'Perhaps it was my footsteps you heard.'

'And the chains rattling?'

He pulled a bunch of keys from his pocket. 'I used these to open the door. The stone walls must have magnified the sound.'

'It is not doing it now.'

'You would only hear it from below,' he said in the patient tones of an adult to a foolish child. She knew exactly what it was, because she had used it on many similar occasions. But she was not a child. She knew what she had heard.

Perhaps she had let Gerald's stories colour her imagination, but she had heard something. 'Who was it who called out, then?'

'Again, it might be a trick of the way this place is constructed. Sound travelling through stone from somewhere else.'

He spoke almost as if he was trying to convince himself.

'But if you heard someone call out and came to see, how did you get up here so quickly? Why didn't I see you on the stairs ahead of me?'

'I didn't come up the stairs. I came across the battlements from the other tower. I was going down when...' He hesitated. 'I decided to take a look in here.'

The outside door opening and closing would account for the cold wind rushing past her. Perhaps it was only footsteps and keys echoing off stone walls she had heard. But it did not explain the shrieks and the moans or what had made him close himself inside an obviously empty room.

She bit her tongue. To say more would be to sound hysterical. He was deliberately making her feel like a fool.

'Then in the absence of anyone needing help, I suppose I should go back down,' she said finally.

He held out his arm. 'Allow me to escort you.' Masterfully, he took her candle and helped her down the stairs as if she was made of china. It made her feel strangely feminine—not something she should be feeling around him. He was just being polite. But even that seemed out of character. Perhaps he was trying to allay her suspicions.

Not for a moment did she think his explanations held water.

At her chamber door he paused, looking down at her. The air thickened and heated around them. Oh, no! Was he going to kiss her again? Her heart thudded wildly in anticipation.

His breathing hitched. His eyes widened as if he was startled by what was happening. He took a half-step back from her. 'Until tomorrow, Miss Wilding.'

Her stomach dipped in disappointment. How mortifying.

She sketched the briefest curtsy. 'Indeed.'

His face suddenly hardened into its normal stern lines. 'Do not wander about this house, Miss Wilding. You don't know what dangers may lurk.'

That sounded very much like a threat. Something inside her trembled at the idea. She stiffened her spine and ignored her racing heart. She reminded herself that she did not respond well to threats.

Chapter Five

To Mary's surprise, the whole family appeared in the drawing room before dinner the next day, although she had seen none of them during daylight hours. The earl looked sartorially splendid this evening in a cream-coloured waistcoat and dark-blue coat, the silver buttons winking in the light of the chandelier.

Whatever the Beresfords said about him not being a gentleman, his linen was impeccably starched and his crisp dark curls artfully disarrayed. The moment she entered, she felt the touch of his steely gaze from where he was standing slightly apart from his relations.

Unwanted colour rose to her cheeks. It had nothing to do with that considering look. It was embarrassment at how poor she looked compared to the rest of them.

With her valise gone, she only had the dress she'd worn yesterday, a fine merino wool decorated with Brussels lace at neckline and cuff. Small pieces of lace, to be sure, but their purchase had been wickedly extravagant for a poor schoolteacher. And hardly worth the investment, once she'd realised Mr Allerdyce's true intention.

Gerald ceased listening to his mother and looked over at her. 'Feeling better, Miss Wilding?'

The boy was as graceless as a puppy to remind her of the scene he'd interrupted the day before. She smiled coolly. 'Quite fine, Gerald.'

His mother's head came up like a hound scenting a fox. 'Not well, Miss Wilding?' She was beautifully dressed, her gown of rose silk and the peacock feather in her turban more suited to a ball than an evening at home. Or were they? What would a country schoolteacher know of the style nobility employed *en famille*, apart from what she read in the fashion magazines?

'She was crying,' Gerald declared with a glare at the earl.

'I received some unwelcome news in the post. The earl had nothing to do with it.'

An expression chased across the earl's face. Surprise? Had he thought she would expose his dastardly plot to his family? Still, she wasn't quite sure why she felt the need to defend him, except that they held him in such disdain, it set up her hackles.

'Dinner is served, my lord,' Manners said.

Mrs Hampton moved smoothly to take the earl's arm. An undeniable flash of annoyance darkened his eyes. He was lucky to have a family. Mary would have loved to have an aunt or two. And as the older and most senior woman present it was only polite that he should escort her into dinner.

He gathered himself quickly, she was pleased to see, walking ahead of the party with all the grace of a courtier. Indeed, his innate elegance continually surprised her.

Jeffrey held out his arm. 'Miss Wilding?'

She took it and instantly became aware of her height. Jeffrey wasn't short for a man, but she was ridiculously tall for a woman, and she looked down on the top of his head. She could see the whorl of hair at his crown. If he noticed the disparity, he didn't show it and seated her opposite his aunt, taking the place at Mary's side. Gerald settled in beside his mother.

The footmen served the first courses and retired. Conversation was desultory. The weather, which was threatening snow. An invitation to be declined because the family was in mourning.

During a lull, Mrs Hampton turned to Mary with a condescending smile. 'You know, there are several Wildings among my acquaintance, my dear. Might you be a relation, perhaps? They are from Norfolk.'

Her heart stilled. Could she indeed have relatives somewhere? How would she ever know? Since soup required careful attention, as she'd always taught her girls, she sipped at her spoonful of leek and potato before she attempted a reply. The delay gave her a smidgeon of time to think how to word an answer that did not make her seem to be asking for sympathy. 'I hale from St John's Parish in Hampshire. I know nothing of my relatives.'

'Perhaps a junior branch, then,' she said. 'Had you belonged to one of the great families, they no doubt would have claimed you.'

'Certainly no family members came forward,' Mary said calmly as if she had never dreamt of an aunt or an uncle searching England for their lost niece.

'I doubt Grandfather would have lifted a hand to help, if there were others with the responsibility,' Jeffrey drawled. 'Can I cut you a piece of this excellent fowl, Miss Wilding?'

'Thank you.'

Jeffrey filled her plate with the chicken and some buttered parsnips.

The earl scowled darkly. 'St John's Parish in Hampshire, you said?'

She met his gaze. 'You have heard of it?'

'No.'

'Nor me,' Mrs Hampton said. 'My brother, now, he is an archdeacon at York Minster.'

'And likely to bore a fellow to death with his sermonising,' Gerald muttered.

His mother appeared not to notice.

Mary had the feeling that Mrs Hampton did a great deal of not noticing when it came to her son. It was one way to avoid unpleasantness, Mary supposed. No wonder he seemed spoilt.

The servants entered to clear the table and added a remove of game pie.

'It must come as a welcome change, Miss Wilding,' Mrs Hampton continued, 'to find yourself visiting such a noble seat as Beresford Abbey. It has been in our family since the Dissolution, you know. The house is quite distinctive, I believe.'

Mary caught herself glancing at the earl for his reaction, but he seemed intent on the wine in his glass, his expression inscrutable. 'It is a very interesting house,' Mary said. 'Full of strange sounds.'

Both Jeffrey and Gerald fixed their gazes on her face, both with expressions of innocence. Gerald more angelic than his older cousin, whose shirt points were so high his neck all but disappeared in the starched white cravat.

'Have you heard strange sounds?' Jeffrey asked. Was his tone a little too innocent?

'What struck me as strange,' she said, 'was how loud the sea sounds in some of the passageways. And sometimes in my chamber.' She had forgotten until this moment that not long before she had heard the racket above her head, the low rumble of the sea had been most distinct.

The earl did look up then. Instead of offering his earlier plausible explanation, he was watching his cousins.

Gerald waved an airy hand. 'Likely the tide was high. Caves run all through these cliffs. Very useful for smuggling or sedition, depending on who holds the crown.'

'The Beresfords are loyal to the House of Hanover,' Mrs Hampton announced.

'They are now,' Jeffrey said with a cynical twist to his lips.

Mary imagined a network of caves beneath the house. 'Is the house likely to collapse?'

'Not likely,' Jeffrey scoffed. 'Or not for centuries.'

Mary didn't like the sound of it at all.

The earl was looking at Jeffrey very intently. 'Do you know the way into these caves?'

'From the sea. I have seen them from the sailboat we use in the summer,' Jeffrey said. 'Never attempted a landing. Too many rocks. The tunnels were blocked up years ago. Isn't that right, Ger?'

Gerald nodded.

The thought of smugglers, or anyone, being able to make their way secretly into the house was downright disturbing.

With a change of tablecloth, the final course appeared. Jeffrey and Gerald descended into an argument about the merits of the local hunt. The earl leaned back in his chair sipping his burgundy and listening with a bored expression. For some odd reason, Mary felt as if he was watching her, but every time she looked his way, his gaze was idly fixed on the two young men.

Which was good. She did not want his attention.

Mrs Hampton gave a little sniff and dabbed at her delicate little nose with a handkerchief and leaned closer to the earl. 'Now the funeral is over I must think about finding a new home. His lordship was very fond of Gerald and insisted we stay here after my dear husband's demise.' She sighed. 'I could go to my brother, naturally. But the demands of his position—archdeacon, you know.'

The earl grimaced. 'Actually, madam, I was hoping you would stay. Miss Wilding needs a chaperon.'

Mrs Hampton visibly brightened. 'Miss Wilding is staying?'

'Naturally,' the earl drawled. 'She has nowhere else to go.'

Mary felt prickles run across her shoulders and down her back. Prickles of anger. Prickles of pain at his cool dismissal of her loss. She opened her mouth to deny his assertion, then closed it again. He was right. For the moment, she did have nowhere to go. But that didn't mean she couldn't formulate a plan.

'I suppose I could remain for a while, if I can be of assistance,' Mrs Hampton said, her brightening expression giving the lie to her begrudging words. 'You would like that, would you not, Gerald? If we stayed?'

Gerald looked at his mother and his eyes lowered as if shielding his thoughts. 'I wanted to go to London.'

'Not until we are out of mourning,' his mother said.

'Then it doesn't matter where we go,' her son replied with a shrug.

His lordship ran a fingertip around the rim of his glass, his hard gaze fixed on his aunt. 'Miss Wilding needs help with her wardrobe.'

'My wardrobe is fine,' Mary said quickly.

The earl's grey gaze settled on her and she wanted to squirm under that intense scrutiny. 'I understood your luggage went astray. We cannot have the Beresford heiress tramping around the countryside in rags, now can we?'

His glance flicked over her person and heat flushed to her hairline at that critical regard. He must think her such a dowd, but, more to the point, he seemed to have decided he had the right to make decisions on her behalf.

Mrs Hampton smiled at her son. 'Then it is settled. We will stay.'

Her son flushed. His eyes flashed fury. 'I don't see why we want to stay now he is here.'

'A common refrain,' the earl said coolly. He didn't look at Mary, but her stomach dipped all the same. Sympathy in the face of his cousin's rejection, when it really was none of her business.

'I could stay with Jeffrey. At his lodgings,' Gerald said with a defiant look at his mother. 'Couldn't I, cuz?'

Jeffrey almost choked on a mouthful of food.

The earl's lip curled in distaste. 'What about it, cuz?' he asked in silken tones. 'Will you take him in? I for one would be for ever in your debt.'

It seemed the earl didn't need her sympathy.

'Gerald. You would not desert me at such a time,' Mrs Hampton said.

Gerald shot her a sulky glare.

'You could, of course, old chap. Always welcome,' Jeffrey said, recovering his voice. 'But my apartments have only one bed.'

'I could sleep on the floor.'

Mrs Hampton made a sound of horror.

Jeffrey shook his head. 'My man wouldn't like that above half,' he pronounced, as if it trumped all objections.

'Your constitution is far too delicate for such hardship, Gerald,' his mother said. 'I could not permit it.'

'My dear madam,' the earl said clearly tired of the conversation, 'the decision is made. You will chaperon Miss

Wilding and see to her dress. And Gerald will of necessity remain at your side.'

'You cannot do better than my aunt for advice on style,' Jeffrey added, joining the ranks of traitors siding with the earl.

Mrs Hampton simpered.

Mary dipped her head meekly. As a reward she received a suspicious glance from the earl which she met head on with a cool smile.

Gerald, who had subsided into his own thoughts for the previous few moments, raised his head and turned to look at her. 'What of the White Lady, Miss Wilding?' he asked. 'Have you heard any screams or clanking chains?'

Oh, the wretch. It must be he who had made those noises. Though how, when there had been no sign of him, she could not begin to imagine. She couldn't keep her gaze from darting to the earl, to see if he shared her opinion.

He shook his head very slightly. Because he didn't want Gerald to know he was suspected? Perhaps he intended to catch the boy out. She certainly felt better at this proof she had not imagined those unearthly noises, as well as the proof that the earl was finally taking them seriously.

She narrowed her eyes, looking at Gerald's face for signs of guilt, and received a glance of innocent interest.

The butler entered at that moment. 'A gentleman to see you, my lord. Lord Templeton. He says he is expected.'

The earl leapt to his feet. 'Expected, but not this soon.'

'I have taken the liberty of showing him to the library, my lord, since he declined to join the family in the drawing room for tea.'

'Very good. I will join him there immediately.'

It was the first time Mary had seen him looked pleased about anything. His delight made him look decidedly more handsome, but his pleasure only added to her resentment that he still had a friend who would come to visit. Hopefully he would be too busy with the man to notice when she slipped away on the morrow.

'How rude,' Mrs Beresford said, looking at the door that closed behind him. 'I suppose one can't expect manners from a coalminer's son, even if he does have a title.'

'I think he has shown a great deal of forbearance,' Mary muttered.

Gerald grinned at her. 'You did hear the White Lady, didn't you?'

'Certainly not,' she said truthfully, giving him a bland look. It wasn't a lie, because she was now certain it had been Gerald all along.

Jeffrey raised a brow. 'I'm glad to hear it, Miss Wilding. As Gerald said this morning, any sighting of her ghostly form usually heralds a death in the family. And one is enough, don't you think?'

He looked so dashed innocent that perhaps it was him playing cruel jokes and not his younger cousin. Or they were in it together. Her stomach dipped. 'Then we certainly have something to be grateful for,' she replied and put down her knife and fork at the loss of her appetite at what felt like a threat. Another one. 'One is certainly enough for any family.'

'Will you take tea in the drawing room, Miss Wilding?' Mrs Hampton asked with what she must have considered a great deal of condescension to one as so far down the social scale.

Mary gave her a polite smile. 'No, thank you. I find I am quite tired. I think I will retire.'

'Oh, but we should really pull out some fashion plates. Discuss colours, if we are to go shopping tomorrow.'

Discuss fashion plates after all that had been implied? 'Another time.' She hurried from the room.

* * *

Back in her own chamber, she held her hands out to the fire and then rubbed her palms together. Her room seemed even colder than usual. In fact, there was a definite draught. She got up and went to the window to see if it had been left open, although with the curtains so still, it hardly seemed likely.

No. It was closed. She tugged at the latch just to be sure. Put her palms to the edges. Nothing.

Then where was the chill coming from?

Frowning, she toured the perimeter of the room, trying to feel the direction of this strange blast of cold air.

Here. Beside the fireplace.

She ran her palm along the corner beside the chimney-breast and distinctly sensed cold pressure against her skin. Was there something wrong with the chimney? Bricks coming loose, walls falling down? Like those old tunnels?

She probably should report it to the earl. Or his steward. But not now. It was far too late and the earl would be busy with his guest.

She reached out again just to be sure she was not mistaken, running her palm up the wall. The draught stopped at eye level and was forceful enough to send the adjacent candle in the wall sconce flickering and smoking. She pulled her scissors from her reticule and on tiptoes trimmed the wick, grasping the base of the brass sconce for balance.

A grinding noise. Vibration under her fingers. She jumped back, her heart in her throat.

She could have sworn the wall moved towards her. It wasn't moving now and the odd noise had stopped. It had definitely come from inside the wall, not from above like before.

Or at least she was fairly certain it had. And the wall looked odd, out of line.

Once more she put her hand on the base of the sconce. It moved, twisted under her hand. The grinding started again.

The sconce turned upside down as she pushed harder. Quickly she blew out the candle. The last thing she needed was to start a fire.

A section of wall slowly swung inwards, stopping at right angles. Cold air rushed past her. She wrinkled her nose at the musty smell. In the distance she could hear the sea, much as she had done when the earl had led her to her room by way of the basement. And again before those strange noises above her head. Pulling her shawl tight against the sudden chill, she stared into pitch blackness.

A priest's hole? It would make sense for a house with a connection with the Roman Catholic Church to have such a thing. She'd heard about them countless times when reading history books. She also read about such things in Gothic novels. They always led to something bad for the heroine. Only this wasn't a Gothic novel and she wasn't a heroine. She was a sensible schoolteacher.

Hopefully, whoever had used the priest's hole had managed to get out, though, and it didn't contain their wasted bones. She shuddered at the thought of someone trapped inside the darkness behind that wall. Nonsense. Anyone who went in must have known how to get out when the coast was clear.

She peered in. The space appeared larger than one would expect. How odd. She went to the bedside table for her candlestick and marched back to the gaping hole. She held the candle out in front of her and revealed what looked like a passage into a tunnel that branched left and right. A tunnel? One of those that led to the caves de-

scribed at dinner tonight? It didn't look in the least like
a ruin. And why did it lead straight to her chamber? Her
stomach gave a sickening lurch.

Who else knew about this? And exactly where did it
go? Down to the sea? To the outside? Could she use it to
escape the earl's high-handed edict that she might not
leave? Her heart beating loud in her ears as she held her
breath, she stepped over the threshold.

The hairs on the back of her neck stood to attention.

What if the door closed behind her, leaving her
trapped? She backed out into her room, set her candle on
the mantel and dragged over the chair from beside the
hearth. She stood it in the opening. The door would be
unable to close with that in the way. Not completely. She
picked up her candle once more and plunged into the dark.

The candle's flickering light illuminated rough-stone
walls glistening with damp. Creeping along one step at
a time, she wondered what on earth she would find. The
passage took a turn and came to a set of stairs leading up.
Stairs that seemed to mirror those just beyond her chamber door, only narrower and the steps rougher-hewn. She
climbed upwards carefully and came to a blank wall. She
raised her candle high and saw a sconce much like the one
in her bedroom. She twisted the base and started back as
the wall shifted inwards, revealing the chamber above her
room and in the corner, against the passage wall, a length
of chain and a rusty cannonball.

In that instant she was sure the earl had lied. This was
how he had got into that room. He was the one making
the unearthly noises. But why? Did he plan to drive her to
madness and have her locked away, thereby taking control of the money? Or did he want to frighten her into his
arms? Into marriage? Or did he think to blame a ghost
for her death?

Her mouth dried. The air wouldn't seem to fill her lungs. She swallowed hard. Inside she was trembling. Weak. Wishing she knew just what he was up to.

Surely Gerald and Jeffrey knew about this passageway? It was the sort of thing no self-respecting boy would miss. Unless they truly believed that the tunnels had collapsed long ago. If their grandfather had told them it was so, would they not have believed him?

Whoever knew about this had ready access into her chamber. Suddenly her skin felt too tight and her scalp tingled. That person could come and go into her room at will.

Hastily, she closed the secret door and hurried back down the steps, pausing outside the entrance to her room to make sure everything was just as she had left it.

She let go a breath she hadn't realised she was holding. Should she explore further, or simply face the earl with her findings in the morning? It would be good to know if it led outside to freedom. She took a quick breath and continued on past her room. Darkness closed in around her, apart from the small circle of light cast by her candle.

At the sound of a deep low rumble of male voices she froze. Was someone else in the passageway? There was no glimmer of light ahead. No footsteps accompanying the voices. She continued on more slowly and came to a fork in the tunnel. By heavens, it seemed there was a veritable rabbit warren inside the walls. And they looked in good working order, too. Was there something else going on here? Was the old earl involved in smuggling? French brandy was smuggled all along the coast of Cornwall at great profit.

The voices were louder now, though still indistinct. If she could hear them, they would be able to hear her if she called out. But that would give her discovery away and she wasn't ready to do so. Not yet.

With one hand on the clammy wall and the candle held out in front of her, she pressed on, slowly, one step at a time. This part of the tunnel was not quite high enough for her to stand upright, but as long as she kept her neck bent, she managed not to give the top of her head more than the odd scrape.

She turned another corner. Now the voices were as clear as if she was standing in the room with the earl and, she supposed, his visitor, Lord Templeton.

'To speedy success. Hopefully it won't take too much time away from your duties,' the earl said. A chinking of glasses ensued.

What on earth could they be talking about? Whatever it was, it was not her business.

'What more do you know about her?' Lord Templeton asked.

'Nothing, except he left her a fortune.'

They were talking about her. Then it was her business.

'What is she like?'

Her breath caught in her throat. She winced. She did not want to hear this, but for some reason she could not move.

There was a long pause, as if the earl was taking his time considering the question. Oh, she really should go.

'Tall. Stubborn to a fault,' he said quite softly, sounding almost bemused. 'Certainly not my type,' he added more forcefully.

Nor was he hers.

'I suppose you have thought about the other solution,' Templeton said.

She stilled. Another solution would be a very good thing, wouldn't it? Some way out of their predicament?

The earl made a sound like a bitter laugh and said

something indistinct. Then continued more clearly. 'I want know what I am dealing with before taking drastic action.'

Drastic? What did he mean by drastic? She recalled the push that had almost sent her over the cliff. Her mouth dried. Her heart knocked against her ribs. She leaned against the wall for support. A sick feeling churned in her stomach. Fear.

An overreaction? Drastic could mean anything. The fact he stood to inherit by her death didn't mean he would actually plan it.

Surely he couldn't be that evil.

'I'll do anything you want,' Templeton said. His next words were too low for her to hear.

If they were plotting against her it would help to know what they had in mind. She put her ear to the wall.

A piece of rock crumbled against her fingers and rattled to the floor.

'What was that?' Templeton asked.

She held her breath, frozen to the spot. If the earl knew about the passageway, would he guess someone was inside, listening?

'Ranger heard it, too,' the earl said. His voice drew closer. 'What is it, old fellow?'

The dog whined, then she heard a snuffling sound as if he had his nose pressed against the stonework.

'It's either a mouse or a rat,' the earl said, so close to her ear that she recoiled. 'I wouldn't be surprised if the inside of the walls weren't crawling with vermin. Something else to eliminate when I have the money situation resolved.'

Something else to eliminate? The tunnels and her? Her stomach pitched. She had to get away from this place. As soon as possible. Sooner.

'Another brandy, Gabe?' The earl's voice moved further away.

'Thank you. That had better be the last though, if I am to leave at first light.'

She didn't dare wait to hear more in case she made more noise and he decided to investigate. And besides, she'd heard all she needed to know.

Terror blocking her throat, her legs almost too weak to hold her up, she walked through the dark and the damp holding on to the rough stone for support. At the sight of the light streaming into the tunnel from her chamber, she ran the last few steps. Panting with the effort of not collapsing in a heap, she sent the wall back to its proper place.

Her heart knocking hard against her ribs, her stomach in a knot, she leaned her back against the wall. She squeezed her hands tightly together as the words went round and round in her head. *Drastic action. When I have the money. Another thing to eliminate.* There was only one conclusion she could draw from his words.

Her mind refused to focus. *Think, Mary. Think.* She took a deep breath. And another. The trembling eased. Her breathing slowed. She looked around at the bed, the door, the window. Stepped away from a wall anyone could open from the other side.

Anyone. The earl or his friend could walk in on her as she slept and take drastic action. Panic clawed its way back into her throat. Then she must not sleep.

It would not work. No one could remain awake all day and all night. She had to find a way to block off the entrance.

She tried putting a chair in front of it, then the dresser, but nothing seemed substantial enough to hold back a chunk of stone wall.

Perhaps she needed a different tack. Something that would warn her the moment the door started to open. Give her time to hide. Or run. Something loud. The crash of a set of brass fire irons like the ones standing on the hearth, perhaps. She gave them a push and they went over with a satisfying clang and a clatter.

Perfect. She stood listening, waiting to see if anyone had heard. Would the sound carry down that tunnel to the earl? Would he come to investigate?

Not by the secret tunnel, surely? She glared at the now-perfectly positioned wall. Oh, no. He would not come that way. He would not want her to learn he had easy access to her room. She strode to the chamber door and turned the large iron key.

Her panic started to fade and her mind cleared. She looked at the fire irons from several angles. They needed to fall at the very first movement, but they had a wide base and needed a good push at the top to make them topple. Something more precarious was required.

The slender vase on the dressing table, perhaps. She stood it beside the crack in the wall and carefully balanced the fire irons on top. It took a few tries to get it to stay in place. She nodded grimly. One push and it would topple.

She flopped down on the edge of the bed and stared at her odd structure. Now what?

Now she needed to plan her escape. Where she would go, she wasn't quite sure, but anywhere was better than here. Anywhere was better than the house of a man who talked of drastic action and getting his money, when the only way the money would go to him was if she died.

An ache filled her heart. Everything she'd ever known was gone. Sally. The school. Her girls. She would have to start all over again.

For a moment, she'd let herself hope she might belong here. That she might actually have found a family. The old longing clutched at her heart. Such a childish thing, to want what could never be.

She must have bats in her belfry. Her father hadn't wanted her—why would anyone else? Certainly not Beresford. All he wanted was his rightful inheritance. And who would blame him? She really wished there was a way she could give it to him before he resorted to drastic action.

She climbed beneath the sheets, fully clothed, ready to run at a moment's notice, and lay concocting a plan of her own. A way to turn the trip to St Ives to her advantage.

Chapter Six

The visit to St Ives had turned into a family outing. The earl had ridden ahead with his cousins, while Mary and Mrs Hampton had travelled by carriage. Mary spent most of the journey parrying the older woman's questions about her past and she could not have been more glad when they arrived at their destination.

The carriage pulled into the courtyard of a small hostelry. 'We always walk from here,' Mrs Hampton announced.

The footman let down the steps and Mary followed her companion out of the carriage into a bustling courtyard. The air smelled of the sea and fish. At any other time, she would have been eager to explore the town, but finding a way to depart claimed her immediate attention, since on the other side of the inn courtyard a sign proclaimed 'Ticket Office'.

While the men saw to their horses and Mrs Hampton chatted with an acquaintance who had rushed over to offer condolences, Mary wandered casually over to the wicket below the sign and, with her heart picking up speed, smiled at the man inside.

'Can I help you, ma'am?' he asked.

A quick glance told her the earl was busy seeing to the horses. He looked every bit the Earl of Beresford today, in his close-fitting riding coat and muscle-defining doeskin breeches. She was positive, if she tried, she could see her face in the highly polished Hessians. To the manor born. Though it was the intensity of his expression as he dealt with the head groom, the square jaw and firm mouth, that drew her attention. It was too bad that such an attractive exterior hid a villainous heart. 'Does the stage leave from here for London?' she asked the clerk in a low voice.

'Not London miss, Exeter, every day, at six in the morning. You can pick up the stage to London from there.'

'But is there nothing that leaves later in the day? Say this afternoon?'

'There's a coach to Plymouth at two this afternoon. You'd have to stay overnight there and pick up the mail coach to London.'

Plymouth. 'How much does it cost?'

'One shilling and six pence.'

She had that much and a little more. And the earl would never think to look for her in Plymouth. She raked around in her reticule and put the required amount down on the counter. 'One, please. For this afternoon.'

'Planning a journey, Miss Wilding?' The deep voice from behind her held amusement and an edge of steel.

She gasped.

'The young lady bought a ticket to Plymouth,' the clerk said.

'No,' the earl replied, scooping up her money. 'She did not.'

The ticket man shook his head. 'Young women today...'

The earl gave him a tight smile. 'Precisely.'

Heat rushing to her face, Mary glared up at him. 'You have no right to say where I may or may not go.'

The earl gave her a bored look. 'I thought we had already discussed this,' he drawled. He took her arm and gently and firmly drew her away from the wicket.

She pulled her arm free. 'You cannot force me to stay. Please return my money.' She held out her hand.

'Until the matter of the will is settled,' he said in a low murmur, 'I require your presence here.' He took her hand in his and his fingers closed around hers in an unbreakable grip. Not hard, or painful, but firm. 'Now let us to our purpose for coming here today, shall we?' He gave her a pleasant smile so that anyone watching would see a most kindly expression. Looking at him now, at his large frame blocking her way, his cold eyes making his point, she could not help but remember his words from the night before. *Drastic action.* A shiver ran down her spine.

And if she screamed? Called attention to her plight? What then? Would anyone come to her aid? The only person left in the yard was Mrs Hampton, who was looking at her impatiently. No, it would be better not to make a scene where the earl would have the upper hand. She would find a chance to slip away quietly.

She inhaled a deep breath. 'Very well. Let us go shopping.'

If she hadn't known better, she might have thought the earl gave a sigh of relief.

'You do not seem like the sort of man who would enjoy a visit to a mantua-maker, my lord.'

'Oh?' He looked at her with one brow cocked in question. He gave her such a heart-stopping smile, her jaw dropped in wonder. 'And what sort of man do I seem to be?'

A dangerous one, if the way her heart was beating in her chest was to be believed. And a scoundrel who kissed unsuspecting maidens, too. 'I suspect you are interested in more manly pursuits. Shooting at things and riding roughshod over people.'

He laughed. In that moment his face changed and her heart tumbled over at how attractive he looked with those silver eyes alight and a genuine smile curving his lips. 'I see you do not hold me in any high regard, Miss Wilding,' he said.

Oh heavens, was that regret she heard in his tone? Or was it her own longing colouring her judgement? She could not afford to let him charm her. To weaken her resolve.

'I just assume you are like most men, for whom a trip to the dressmaker would be torture.'

'It seems you don't know me at all, Miss Wilding.'

'Are you ready, Miss Wilding?' Mrs Hampton asked at their approach.

Mary nodded her assent.

'Then let us be off.' The widow strode briskly out of the courtyard with Mary and the earl following behind. The streets were so crowded, they were soon forced to go single file, like a crocodile of schoolchildren, Mary thought wryly, very aware of the earl hard on her heels. She also noticed that other pedestrians moved out of their way the moment they saw the three of them coming towards them. She suspected it was the earl's looming presence behind them causing the wide berth given to their party.

Mrs Hampton stopped outside one of the shops lining the street and turned back to speak to Mary. 'Mrs Wharton is not of the same calibre as a London dressmaker, you understand, but she is not bad and her prices are reasonable.'

As the earl ushered them inside, a bell above the door tinkled.

A thin-faced woman, with her hair pulled back beneath

her cap and bonnet, curtsied. 'Why, Mrs Hampton, how good to see you and after such a long time, too. Come for your mourning clothes, have you?'

'Certainly not. The ones from last year are perfectly adequate. No. It is Miss Wilding who requires your services.'

The woman's surprised gaze swivelled to Mary and then up to the earl. She frowned. 'A family member, miss? Needing black?'

'Goodness me, Wharton, you do jump to conclusions. Miss Wilding is…' her face took on an expression of dismay '…a family friend.'

The woman's eyebrows rose. 'What can I do for you, miss?'

'A complete wardrobe, if you please,' the earl said. 'To be charged to the Earl of Beresford.' He removed his gloves and toured the shop, touching the bolts of silks and muslins displayed on the shelves.

What on earth must the woman think of a man purchasing a wardrobe for a woman not a relative? Mary knew what she was thinking from the knowing gleam in the other woman's eyes.

Mary felt the heat crawl up her face. This was too much. And it didn't make sense. Why would he be purchasing clothes for her, if he was planning her demise, unless it was to draw people off the scent?

Whatever his purpose, she would not put herself under such an obligation. 'Two morning gowns are all I require,' she said firmly. They would replace what the earl had caused her to lose. That was fair.

Mrs Hampton glared at her. 'Nonsense. Every young lady needs walking dresses. A dress for the opera. A ball gown. A riding habit. At the very least. Not to mention gloves, bonnets, and—' she shot a wary look at the earl '—other items of apparel.'

Mrs Wharton's jaw hung open.

Mary understood exactly how she felt. 'I would prefer to see what you have already made up,' she said with a feeling of desperation at the silken trap closing around her.

'Something we can take with us today,' the earl agreed, bestowing so charming a smile on Mrs Wharton, she simpered. 'The rest can follow along later.'

The seamstress rubbed her hands together, a dry raspy sound like snakeskin over rock. 'A complete wardrobe it is then, your lordship.' She ran a critical eye over Mary. 'No frills or bows.'

Tall girls couldn't wear frills or bows. It made them look like mountains. It seemed Mrs Wharton and Sally agreed on that score. 'Come this way, miss, so I can take your measurements. A glass of wine for you, sir? Tea for you, Mrs Hampton?'

The earl nodded his agreement. The woman scurried behind a curtain, no doubt to relay her instructions.

'Surely there is no reason for you to stay, my lord,' Mary said as he settled himself in one of the visitors' chairs and stretched out his long legs. He looked altogether too comfortable. Too much at home, as if this wasn't the first time he had participated in the dressing of a female.

An idea that gave her a nasty little wrench.

'Ah, Miss Wilding, but there is. I wish to see you attired in the first stare of fashion.' The hard look in his eyes warned her not to argue.

'But surely Mrs Hampton—'

'It is a long time since I was in town,' the widow said. 'I am sure his lordship has a much better idea of what is all the crack these days than I. My dear Miss Wilding, everyone knows that gentlemen have discerning taste when it comes to ladies' fashion.' She blinked rapidly, as if she realised just what she'd said.

Mrs Wharton reappeared. 'This way, miss.' She gestured to a door at the back of the room.

With a glare at the earl, Mary stepped through the door into a small dressing room containing a looking glass, a low stool and a young woman standing ready with measuring strings.

'Daisy, while I take miss's measurements, run and fetch the blue dimity and the yellow silk. With a little alteration, I think they will fit perfectly.'

The girl scurried off.

Gritting her teeth, Mary let the seamstress strip her down to her stays and chemise, and held still while the woman measured and tied her knots in the string. And all the time Mary stood there practically naked, she kept thinking about the earl sprawled in the chair only a few feet away.

Daisy returned with the gowns requested over her arms. They looked far too expensive and not at all practical.

'They do not seem to be what I had in mind,' she said. 'I prefer something more…similar to the gown I wore in here.'

The seamstress made a little moue of disgust. 'Perhaps we should let his lordship be the judge.'

Mary gasped. 'Certainly not.' She wasn't going to parade herself in front of him.

'Help her into the blue one, Daisy,' the seamstress said. 'I am going to look and see if we have anything more akin to miss's taste.' She disappeared out of the door.

The young woman unlaced the blue gown and held it ready. 'If miss would bend a little…'

The usual problem of her height was what the girl meant. With a sigh, Mary ducked and the dress was slipped over her head. It went on with a whisper. Such light airy fabric. So silky to the touch.

The girl made a couple of adjustments to the bodice with pins and glanced down. 'We will have to add some trim to the hem.'

Mary glanced in the mirror and recoiled. The figure in the mirror wasn't her, surely. This woman wore a gown cut shockingly low across the bosom and edged in vandyke lace. So much skin. And the tops of her breasts were clearly visible. She tugged the fabric higher to no avail, not to mention that the sleeves did not reach her wrists and the skirts were well above her ankles. She looked ridiculous.

Daisy opened the door. 'All ready, Mrs Wharton.'

'There is something missing, surely,' Mary said, staring at her chest. 'A fichu. Or a shawl. You need to find something else. This one will not do at all.'

'I think it looks perfect,' a dark male voice said. She swung around, startled to see his eyes roving her body from her head to her heels. Heat flared in that silver gaze.

Answering heat rushed through her blood. Her insides fluttered alarmingly. A blush rose up her chest to her face. 'You can't come in here.'

Mrs Wharton swept in with swathes of lace. 'Why ever not? You are fully dressed. Let us see, now. Up on the stool, now, please, miss.'

The earl's charming smile was directed fully at her. He looked utterly gorgeous and was clearly enjoying himself. 'Allow me.' He held out his hand.

A large hand and as steady as a rock, when she was trembling inside like an aspen and her knees had the consistency of butter.

She glanced up at his face and saw his jaw tighten as he realised she intended to refuse his aid. Why she did it, she wasn't sure, but she gave him her hand, felt the warmth of his fingers around her cold ones.

He raised her hand to his lips, all the while keeping his gaze locked with hers. A startlingly warm brush of his mouth against her skin felt far too familiar, and terribly unnerving. A shiver ran down her spine, a special little thrill.

'I am glad to see we have come to an understanding,' he said in a murmur meant only for her.

She almost moaned at the way that deep rasping voice made her insides clench. The impression of strength when he supported her as she stepped up left her feeling weak.

Now their eyes were on a level, their gazes locked in a breathless awareness. Her skin tingled all over. Her heartbeat unsteady, out of rhythm, made her breathing unnaturally fast.

His gaze drifted downwards from her eyes, to her parted lips, down her throat to her chest and, God help her, what she saw in his expression was a powerful hunger. Her breasts tightened under his scrutiny.

A sensation of being utterly feminine swept over her, warming her from the inside out, making her limbs feel suddenly languid.

'Let me take a look at that hem,' Mrs Wharton said, dropping to her knees.

And the spell, or whatever it was that had occurred between them, broke. The earl stepped back, his face in its usual taut lines, his gaze guarded.

Did he fear she'd seen too much?

Mary closed her eyes. She was imagining things. He was here to make sure his money didn't slip out of his grasp. That was all there was to it.

While the dressmaker pinned lace to the bottom of

the gown and added matching fabric to the sleeves, Mary avoided looking at his lordship.

After a few minutes he said, 'Alter the other one the same way.'

'I would prefer a higher neckline,' Mary said.

'No,' his lordship said and walked out.

'It is perfect the way it is, miss,' the seamstress said, handing her down. She twitched at the skirts, checked the bodice and nodded. 'Perfect. Let us see to the rest of your order now, shall we?'

Daisy returned to help her into her own gown.

By the time Mary was dressed and back out in the shop, his lordship was nowhere to be seen.

'He bethought himself of an urgent errand,' Mrs Hampton said at her look of enquiry. 'He left orders as to the rest of the items to be purchased, however.' She pointed to a pile of fine linens and gloves on the counter.

Mary tried not to feel disappointed he had left. She should be pleased, because while she was being buttoned into her gown, she'd had another idea.

'I'll have the two gowns sent up to the livery before the hour is up,' Mrs Wharton finally said, when all the choices had been made. 'I'll parcel these up to go home with you now.'

'I still think you should have that military-style riding habit made,' Mrs Hampton said, sounding quite weary, but there was a sparkle in her eye, likely because Mrs Wharton had thrown in a gown for her as commission for bringing Mary to her shop.

'I don't ride,' Mary said quickly. Her only experience on a horse had been sitting on the earl's lap and, while the thought of it made her blush, it certainly didn't count as riding.

Mrs Hampton glared. 'You don't play the pianoforte either, I'll be bound, but that is no reason not to visit the music room.'

As a metaphor it didn't really work. And Mary did play. Very well. It was one of her few ladylike accomplishments. But Mrs Hampton didn't need to know that. She smiled sweetly. 'If I decide to visit the stables, I shall be sure to order a riding habit ahead of time.'

The widow sniffed. 'I will speak to the earl about it.'

'It is none of the earl's business,' Mary said resolutely and prayed Mrs Hampton would leave it there.

Outside the shop, the street was bathed in the light of a sun that had barely lifted itself above the horizon and was already on a downward path. It hung so low that facing into it caused everyone to squint.

'Do we return to the carriage now,' Mary asked, 'or is there time to explore a little? I would love to walk down to the quay.'

'Certainly not. It reeks of fish. Next we go to the haberdasher. I am in need of some ribbon and a paper of pins.'

They walked a few yards down the hill to the next shop Mrs Hampton wanted to visit.

Mary glanced longingly down the hill where boats lay off shore. Boats carried passengers. It would take but a moment to slip aboard one of those waiting for the tide to turn.

'I have never visited a seaside town before. It will take but a moment to walk down to the shore and back while you complete your purchases.'

Mrs Hampton looked doubtful. 'If only one of the males of our party were on hand, I would be less concerned. The men on the wharf are dreadfully rough and ill mannered.'

'I will just go as far as the next bend in the road, look at the harbour and walk back.'

Her companion let out a sigh. 'You are a very determined young woman, Miss Wilding. I really do not have the energy to argue. If the earl does not like what I cannot stop, then let him take you to task.'

She disappeared inside the shop.

So, the earl had instructed Mrs Hampton to act as not only her chaperon, but as her guard. How annoying. In that case, she did not feel so bad about not telling her the truth.

She walked down to the corner and the harbour spread out below her. Fishing boats drawn up on the beach; nets drying in the sun; men and women plying their trade along the waterside. Just like the landscapes she had seen in books. Out on the sea, waves rippled, catching sunbeams and tossing them back with a glitter that would outdo a diamond necklace.

Breathtaking. Enchanting.

Nothing like the wild sea she had seen the other day from the top of the cliff near the Abbey. This sea looked friendly and enticing. After a quick glance over her shoulder, she hurried down to the wharf. A young man in uniform stepped in front of her. 'Can I help you, miss?'

Surprised she stared at him. 'I don't think so.'

'Lieutenant South, miss. Revenue officer. May I know your name?'

'Miss Wilding,' she replied, surprised. 'I thought I might hire a boat.'

The young man winced. 'His lordship said you might find your way down here. I regret that there are no boats for hire today.'

Mary gaped at him. 'His lordship?'

'The Earl of Beresford, miss.' He coloured. 'You really should go back to your family. The earl said he was sorry for your disagreement and that he would buy you the bonnet you wanted.'

'Bonnet?' She almost spluttered the word, but she could also see there was no sense in arguing with the young man. The earl had been before her. How could he have guessed her intention, when she'd had no idea of coming down here until but a few moments ago? And this young lieutenant was looking at her as if she was some spoiled miss sulking over a bonnet. It was really too much. She was going to have strong words with his lordship. Very strong words indeed.

'Good day, Lieutenant,' she managed through gritted teeth. He bowed and she turned and marched back up the hill to her…to her gaoler. This was intolerable and so she would tell him.

The hill seemed a great deal steeper on the way up. She was required to lean into the slope and watch where she put her feet on the uneven pavement, not to mention dodging people headed downhill.

She glanced up to catch her bearings. Ahead of her, a brewer's dray blocked half the road. Pedestrians were manoeuvring their way around it.

'Careful, miss,' a man with a handcart said when she almost ran into him.

'I beg your pardon,' she said, sidestepping out into the road to avoid him.

'Look out!' a male voice cried.

She looked up, expecting to see yet another cart heading down the hill. She gasped. Not so. A barrel hit the cobbles and bounced. Behind it stood a tall broad-shouldered familiar-looking figure, hand outstretched. A slighter figure darted into the alley, barely avoiding the barrel when it landed.

A woman screamed. A man shouted and leapt clear.

The barrel was rolling right for her, rumbling and banging over the stones. She picked up her skirts and ran for safety against the wall of the nearest building. She slipped, falling to her knees. Pain shot through her foot and up her shin. Sickening.

The barrel was upon her.

She struggled to get to her feet. A hand grabbed her under the arms and pulled her clear.

The barrel slammed into the wall two feet from her with a resounding bang—into the very spot she had thought to take refuge. Splinters flew. Beer showered the cobbles and nearby pedestrians. One of its iron hoops bowled on down the street, clanging and bouncing wildly, scattering people in its path, disappearing around the bend, terrified shouts marking its passage.

'Are you all right?'

A youngish man, decently dressed but hatless, was holding her against his chest, looking thoroughly discomposed, his hair ruffled and his cheeks pink. 'Are you all right, miss?' he asked again.

'I'm fine,' she croaked, trying to ignore the throb of pain in her ankle.

A hand grabbed her and pulled her away. 'Miss Wilding,' the earl said, his voice full of anger, his chest rising and falling as he fought to catch his breath. His gaze raked her person, his eyes wide with anxiety. He blinked and then all she could see in his expression was the usual stern disapproval. 'I see you are like a cat, Miss Wilding. You have nine lives.' He turned to her rescuer with a frown. The man stepped back and put a respectful distance between them.

She stood on one foot, not daring to test her weight on the other. 'This gentleman saved my life. Thank you, sir.'

Her rescuer bowed. 'It was nothing.'

The earl frowned. 'Then I owe you my thanks also.' He didn't sound terribly grateful. He sounded annoyed.

The young man took another step back. 'I was glad to be of help.'

'Did you see what happened?' the earl questioned, looking at him intently.

'I saw nothing until I saw the barrel bowling down hill and the young lady falling. I acted without thought.' He glanced up the hill. 'Jack Bridges should be whipped at the cart tail for letting a barrel go like that.'

Mrs Hampton puffed up to their small group. She glared at the crowd gathered around the smashed barrel, some on their hands and knees sopping up beer with whatever came to hand. ''Pon rep, what a dreadful hullaballoo.'

'Free beer will do that,' the young man said.

'Why,' Mrs Hampton said, smiling, 'it is Mr Trelawny, is it not?'

He bowed. 'My condolences on your loss, madam.'

'Thank you. Let me introduce you to the new Earl of Beresford,' she said, gesturing to the earl. 'And his ward, Miss Wilding. My lord, this is Mr Trelawny, manager of the Beresford mine.'

The earl's expression eased a fraction. 'Well met, Trelawny, even if the circumstances are not ideal. I had planned to visit the mine later in the week.'

The young man shook his hand. 'I would be delighted to show you around, my lord.'

'And me, too,' Mary said. 'After all, I am the owner.'

The earl's face darkened.

Trelawny's cheeks reddened. 'It is not really a suitable place for a lady,' he said. 'It is much too dangerous.'

'I will view it on your behalf,' the earl said.

Mary smiled sweetly at the foundry manager. 'Do you employ children, Mr Trelawny?'

He swallowed. 'A few.'

'Then I will definitely want to see for myself.'

The earl looked as if he was biting back the urge to argue. 'We will discuss this later,' he said finally. 'Right now I am more concerned with getting you ladies off this street before a riot breaks out.'

Indeed, the men and women crawling around in the road looked ready to come to blows over the rivulets of beer running down the hill, as they jostled and pushed each other.

A burly individual joined the fray. 'Get back from there,' he yelled. 'That's my beer.'

'Let 'em be, Jack,' a man shouted. 'You can't pick it up. Don't be a dog in the manger.'

The man swore.

'Bridges, you fool,' Trelawny called out. 'That barrel could have killed someone. It knocked this lady down.'

'No,' Mary said. 'It didn't. But it would have if you hadn't acted so swiftly.'

Trelawny coloured. The earl glowered.

The publican, an apron tied around a belly as round as the barrel, wandered down to join the milling scene. 'I ain't paying for that 'un, Bridges,' he shouted. 'It were still on your cart.'

Bridges rounded on him. 'A barrel can't just fall off. One of your men dropped it.'

'Did not.'

'Did.'

'My men weren't nowhere near it. They were rolling old barrels out. Someone give it a push.'

Mary recoiled. Had that outstretched hand been pushing, rather than trying to hold the barrel back? She glanced up at the earl to find him watching her face, his eyes narrow, his jaw tight. A band seemed to tighten around her chest. Was he worried about what she had seen? Was that the cause of his earlier anxiety?

'Who is to pay for it, then?' the carter asked, putting his fists on his hips. He glared at the thinning crowd, snatched his hat off his head and waved it at the people still sopping up the last dregs. 'If I finds out one of you did it on purpose, I'll have you in front of the beak, so I will.'

The crowd jeered and then melted away.

Jeffrey sauntered up to them, his hat at a rakish angle. 'What is going on?'

'Never mind,' Mrs Hampton said. 'Where is Gerald? It is time we headed home.'

'I don't know where he is,' Jeffrey said. 'He decided not to come with me to the gunsmith's shop.'

Gerald emerged from a nearby alley. 'Here you all are.' He gave them an angelic smile.

It seemed the whole party was now back together and the earl was still glowering. At her. 'Why were you out in the street alone?'

She felt her face heat as she remembered her mortification at the quay. 'I went to look at the harbour and was making my way back to meet Mrs Hampton.'

'She was never out of my sight,' Mrs Hampton declared.

Mary had no intention of giving her the lie. Indeed, she felt grateful that the widow had decided to support her story even if it was only to protect herself.

'If you will excuse me,' Mr Trelawny said, 'I have an appointment. I will look forward to your lordship's visit,' he said to the earl. 'And Miss Wilding. Please send word to the mine as to when I should expect you.' On that he bowed and strode off.

'Good man, Trelawny,' Mrs Hampton said. 'According to the earl.' She bit her lip. 'The late earl, that is.'

The current earl said nothing. He was still looking at Mary with suspicion in those slate-grey eyes. But the throbbing in her ankle was growing worse.

'Miss Wilding, you have had quite a shock, I think,' Mrs Hampton said. 'You are looking quite pale.'

She was also feeling dizzy. 'Yes, I would like to return to the Abbey.'

She took a step. Pain lanced up her leg. Nausea pushed up her throat. The world did a cartwheel. She clutched at the nearest solid object. The earl's arm. He caught her, held her up, the warmth of his body permeating her clothes, the scent of his cologne, something dark and musky, making her senses swim even worse.

She leaned against his strength.

'You are hurt,' Jeffrey said accusingly.

'It is nothing,' she said, flushing hot, pulling away from the earl. 'I twisted my ankle when I fell.'

The earl's eyes widened—something hot flared in their depths. Shock? Or annoyance that her injuries were so minor? 'Jeffrey,' he barked out, 'do something useful. Ride for the doctor and have him come to the Abbey right away.'

Jeffrey's blue eyes flashed resentment. His lips compressed. Then he gave a stiff nod. 'I will see you there.' He marched off up the hill.

'Are you able to walk, Miss Wilding?' the earl asked in an unexpectedly gentle tone of voice. 'If I support you?' He offered his forearm. His large well-muscled forearm. It looked like a lifeline from where she stood with all her weight on one foot. Yet, was it not the same arm that had pushed the barrel at her in the first place? She wished she knew for certain, so she could charge him with his crime.

But she wasn't sure. Had he actually seen his chance and decided to put his drastic plan in action?

'I am sure I can manage.' She took a step and stifled a gasp at the sudden arrow of pain.

'Apparently not,' he said drily.

Before she knew what he was about, he had swept her up in his arms and was striding uphill. Never had she ever been picked up by a man. She could not believe the strength of him. Or how weak the sensation made her feel. And not just because of her injury. It was a strange softness. One from the inside out.

The intensity of it made her gasp. She clutched at his shoulder for balance and he glanced down at her, his gaze a blaze of silver as if he somehow sensed her strange re-action.

Her blood ran hot at the thought.

He lifted his head and looked straight ahead, his mouth tightening, his chest rising as he took a deep breath. 'Not long now, Miss Wilding.'

He sounded relieved. Clearly he couldn't wait to be rid of her. The thought was dreadfully lowering.

There was certainly nothing in his rigid face of the skilled seducer who had kissed her hand in the dressing room. Perhaps he had been merely toying with her, as a cat toys with a mouse. Seeking to put her off guard.

It had almost worked. Her stomach dipped. 'I am sure I could walk, given time,' she said stiffly.

'You would only make matters worse,' he said grimly. 'And who knows what would befall you next?'

'It wasn't my fault the barrel broke free.'

'You should have remained with your chaperon and nothing would have happened. Next time, perhaps, you will listen.' His voice was silky soft with menace.

He'd known she wouldn't stay with Mrs Hampton, otherwise why he had warned the Revenue man down at the dock? And then he'd been right there, at the top of the hill, waiting beside the cart. She had recognised him, even though she'd only caught a quick glimpse. And he was the only one who would profit by her death.

A shudder rippled deep in her bones. And her heart ached as if it had received a blow.

Chapter Seven

'Well, doctor? Is it broken?' The earl stood in the doorway of her chamber, watching the doctor's every move while Mary lay supine on her bed. His voice was unnecessarily harsh, Mary thought, trying not to wince as the doctor poked and prodded at the swollen flesh of her ankle, then gently rotated her foot.

Pain. She hissed in a breath and closed her eyes.

'Be careful, man,' the earl said, his voice sounding strained.

Mary opened her eyes and saw his fist clenched on the doorframe, his face filled with concern.

Sympathy. Something she had not expected from him. And for a moment it warmed her, until reason prevailed. While her heart might be fooled into thinking he cared, she was far too realistic to be taken in. The only person he cared about was himself and the stupid inheritance. Now he would have to think of some other way to be rid of her.

Once more that painful squeeze in her chest. Foolish hurt.

Mentally, she gave herself a shake. At least she knew the truth. At least she was now thoroughly on her guard. But it seemed as though her plans to leave would have to be put off until her ankle was better. It seemed she was well and truly trapped. And at the earl's mercy.

He must have sensed her scrutiny, because his glance flicked to her face. He tensed, his expression becoming guarded, as if he feared she might read his thoughts.

'I am sorry to be such a nuisance,' she said bitterly.

Beresford folded his arms over his wide chest with an implacable glare. 'You should have thought of that before wandering off alone.'

'Not broken,' the doctor announced, apparently oblivious to the animosity. 'Badly sprained. I recommend binding it up and plenty of rest.' The doctor smiled at Mary. 'No dancing for a while, I am afraid, Miss Wilding.'

Dancing was another thing she didn't do. Or at least not well. What man wanted to dance with a woman who could look right over his head and who had a tendency to want to lead? She smiled, albeit a little wanly. 'Thank you, Doctor.'

With quick efficient movements, he bandaged her ankle and foot.

Jeffrey peered around the earl. 'How are you feeling, Miss Wilding?'

The doctor flicked her skirts over her lower limb. 'She is well enough.' He smiled down at her. 'I will give you some laudanum for the pain.'

She shook her head. 'Laudanum makes me feel sick.'

'Then I'll have the housekeeper make you some willow-bark tea.'

'You will take the laudanum as the doctor ordered,' his lordship snarled.

'Cuz, if she doesn't want it, she doesn't,' Jeffrey said in placating terms.

Not placating at all apparently, for the earl bared his teeth. 'Thinking to rule the roost, are you, bantam?'

Good Lord, were they fighting over her? Nothing like an injured woman to bring out the protective side in men, she supposed. She'd heard of it, but never experienced it for herself. Being the target of such discord created a very odd feeling in her breast, to be sure. A sort of warm glow. How irrational.

Unless the earl was hoping to have her drugged and helpless. The warm glow seeped away, replaced by ice in her veins.

'Willow-bark tea will do just as well,' the doctor said absently, packing up his bag. 'Not everyone responds well to laudanum, my lord.'

A triumphant gleam lit Jeffrey's eyes, but she didn't think the earl could see it since Jeffrey stood behind him.

'Let me show you out, Doctor,' the earl said. 'I have some questions for you.'

Mary glowered at his back as he left. No doubt he was planning to get a more detailed prognosis. Or to convince the doctor to leave the laudanum.

'Is there something I can get for you, Miss Wilding?' Jeffrey asked. 'Tea? Something to read?'

Oh dear. He was also going to treat her like an invalid, when she would really rather just hop around and do for herself. Still, she would go mad sitting here staring into space if they insisted she remain lying on her bed. 'A book, if you please. I was reading one in the library. It might still be on the table where I left it.'

'At your service, madam.' He flourished a bow and sauntered off with a jaunty whistle. He'd forgotten he was a man about town, at least for the moment. It was nice to see him with a little less cynicism.

She relaxed against the pillows, resigned to wait for his return. From where she reclined, she could see blue sky and clouds out her window. This was the closest she was going to get to the outdoors for a while. There would be no escape for several days. Provided she survived that long.

Her mouth dried.

A prickle of awareness at her nape made her glance up. She expected to see Jeffrey with her book. It was the earl, his expression far from happy.

'There is no need to fuss over me, Lord Beresford. Please, do continue about your business. I am sure you have many important matters requiring your attention.'

He recoiled slightly. And she had the strangest sense she had hurt his feelings. A pang of guilt made her regret her sharp words.

'What happened back there in St Ives, Miss Wilding?' He didn't sound hurt, he sounded as if he thought she was lying.

She frowned. Was he worried that he had aroused her suspicions? She decided to play innocent. 'I don't know what else you expect me to say.'

'So you did not see what caused the barrel to break loose?'

Again the flash of memory of his hand outstretched as the barrel left its mooring. And a slender man darting away. A man who could have been anyone. She recalled the conversation she had overheard from behind his wall. Perhaps Beresford's friend, Lord Templeton, had not left for Hampshire and the earl was worried that she might have seen his friend. That she was on to his plan to be rid of her?

She shook her head. 'I was too far away.' She tried not to wince at the lie.

His jaw flexed. 'Why do I have the impression you are not telling me everything, Miss Wilding? Don't you trust me?'

At that she couldn't help but chuckle under her breath.

'I scarcely know you, Lord Beresford, and so far you have done nothing but issue commands and edicts.' And talk about drastic measures in private. 'Where might trust be found in that? Please, believe me, there is nothing more to add to what I have already told you.'

An odd expression passed across his face. A mix of frustration and disappointment, as if he actually hoped she would believe he deserved her trust.

Guilt stabbed her. He had rescued her from the edge of the cliff. He had carried her most tenderly up to the carriage. And sometimes she had the feeling, when she looked at him, that he was dreadfully lonely. Like now. A painful pang squeezed her heart.

A small sneaking sensation inside her said she should trust him. A small fragile feeling that would be easily bruised if he proved her wrong. She would have trusted Sally with her life. It seemed that trust had been completely misplaced. What reason did she have to trust the earl?

No, trust was not something she needed to hand out willy-nilly at the moment. Not if she was using her head instead of her emotions.

'Here are some books, Miss Wilding,' Jeffrey said, breezing past his lordship and setting the pile down on the bedside table. 'You here again, Beresford?'

The earl glared at him. 'Not for long. Miss Wilding needs her rest.' He looked pointedly at the younger man and raised a brow.

Jeffrey curled his lip as he bowed. 'I will see you later, Miss Wilding,' he drawled. The cynic was back.

But she did not see the earl at dinner, nor anyone else, because she took a tray in her room. She had no wish to be carried about by his lordship or a footman. She told

Manners she would stay in her room until she felt able to walk with a cane. Jeffrey had provided her with a mountain of books to read and she had managed to hop across her room after Betsy finished preparing her for bed, to set up her makeshift alarm. As a further means of defence, she kept one of the heavy iron pokers alongside her beneath the counterpane.

For all her worries, nothing disturbed her sleep, except dreams of the earl's strong arms around her, which annoyed her considerably.

By the next afternoon she was able to dress and sit in the chair by her bedroom window, reading until the light began to fade.

Betsy bustled in with some packages. 'Two gowns arrived from Mrs Wharton and his lordship says you are to join the family at dinner.'

Mary frowned at the parcels, wishing she could refuse them outright, but she'd been wearing the same dress for three days and it didn't make any sense to get on her high horse after they'd been altered to fit. The earl had refused to wait for their delivery to the carriage after yesterday's accident, so Mrs Wharton must have sent them by carter today. 'I prefer to take a tray in my room.'

Betsy looked anxious. 'He said he would come for you in an hour and, dressed or not, he would carry you to the dining room.'

A little thrill fluttered through her at this masterful statement. A thrill she should not be feeling. Heat crawled up her face. 'How dare he—?' She pressed her lips together. One did not shoot the messenger. If she had words to say, she would say them to his lordship.

Betsy held up the blue muslin, the one with the dreadfully low neckline. 'This one, miss?' Betsy asked. 'Or this. Such a pretty shade of yellow. And silk, too. Much more suitable for dinner. There's a feather dyed to match for your hair.' She held up an ostrich plume, then glanced at the clock. 'We should hurry, miss. His lordship will be here in no time.'

Ready to carry her to the dining room, dressed or not. He wouldn't dare. Or would he? She had the distinct impression his lordship would dare anything at all, if it suited him.

'Very well, the yellow.'

Betsy made short work of getting her into the shift and stays that had accompanied the gowns. They were beautiful garments, much nicer than anything Mary had ever bought for herself. They felt wonderful against her skin.

'And now for the gown,' Betsy said, gently bunching up the fabric in her arms so she could slip the dress over Mary's head.

It went on with a whisper. So light and silky and a perfect length. Betsy fastened it at the back, handed her a pair of lacy gloves and gestured to the chair in front of the mirror. 'If miss will sit down, I will do your hair.'

Mary could see from the girl's face that she was dying to be given free rein. She shook her head with a smile. 'Do what you can, then.'

Her hair was too straight and to heavy for anything fancy.

She sat down and glanced at her reflection. She winced. This gown was worse than the blue one. Never had she felt so exposed. 'Give me my shawl, please.'

Betsy looked scandalised. 'You can't wear that old thing with such a pretty gown, miss.'

She could and she would. 'I will surely freeze otherwise.'

With a sigh Betsy handed her the shawl and picked up the hairbrush. In minutes the maid had artfully twisted her hair into clusters of braids on each side of her head and anchored the feather on her crown. She stepped back. 'You look beautiful, miss.'

Beautiful? The girl had stars in her eyes. She looked like a carthorse dressed up as a thoroughbred. Just as Sally always said she would.

A firm rap sounded on the door. It opened without giving her a chance to answer. Blast. She should have had Betsy turn the key.

Lord Beresford stood staring at her for a moment. His hooded gaze ran from her head to her heels and, if she wasn't mistaken, lingered on her bosom for more seconds that was polite. His gaze met hers and his eyes lit with genuine pleasure. Her stomach gave a funny little hop. 'Ah, Miss Wilding. I see you are ready and waiting.'

For a man whose plan to do away with her had failed, he looked remarkably at ease and splendidly handsome. Had her imagination played tricks on her, after all? But as he came towards her, clearly intending to lift her in his arms, it dawned on her that while he might not have succeeded in St Ives, now, unable to walk, she was well and truly at his mercy.

Cold slid down her spine. She opened her mouth to refuse to go to dinner.

His gaze sharpened, his expression tightening as if he had guessed her intent. She could almost see him distancing himself and she felt terribly guilty for letting her prejudices show. 'Yes, I am ready.'

He looked relieved. Did she really have the power to hurt his feelings? It was hard to believe.

In the next moment, he swept her up in his arms and carried her out of the room. Her mind scrambled to catch up with her body's pleasure of once more being in his arms.

He glanced down at her. The earlier gladness had leached from his face, replaced by cool remoteness. 'I won't have poor old Manners dashing from one end of this labyrinth to the other when it is so easy for me to bring you to the dining room.'

So this was all for Manners's benefit. Well, that put her in her place. He was right about the Abbey being a labyrinth. A labyrinth with secrets in its walls. And she ought to be glad of his thoughtfulness for the ancient butler, but perversely she wished it had been the pleasure of her company that made him come to fetch her.

Now that really was illogical.

Just as illogical as the way something in her chest gave a painful squeeze each time she saw him anew. Fear. That was all it could possibly be. They were enemies, fighting over a fortune she had never wanted in the first place.

And still she could not help her admiration for his male beauty as she stared at his freshly shaved jaw and inhaled the scent of rosemary and lemon of his soap. It was a lovely manly smell that went well with all that strength.

Strength enough to push a full barrel of beer off a wagon and into her path. Her stomach tensed, as she realised she'd let him lull her into forgetting.

Why did the man who wanted her death have to cause her heart to flutter? There was obviously something wrong with her. She was turning into one of those desperate spinsters who flung themselves into the arms of any man who showed them the least bit of attention. Good or bad.

Her throat dried. Her insides quaked with the knowledge that, in his case, the attention was all bad.

She stiffened. Held herself as aloof as possible in such an awkward position. And was still aware of the steady rhythm of his heart against her ribs and the warmth of his lithe body.

He glanced down at her briefly, his expression one of regret, heaved a sigh and shifted his grip, holding her a little less close. 'Better, Miss Wilding?'

Clearly he'd sensed her discomfort.

'Much,' she said quietly, because it actually wasn't better at all. Not really.

And when his long rapid stride brought them to the drawing room she could not help her pang of disappointment when he gently put her down on the sofa. She fought the insidious longing to be wrapped in this man's strong arms.

She had learned that such longings led only to misery.

Jeffrey handed her a glass of sherry. 'Feeling better, Miss Wilding?' he asked with a charming smile.

Her heart was fluttering, her stomach in knots, yet she managed a small smile. 'Yes, thank you.'

Mrs Hampton gave her a cool nod. 'I am glad to hear it, Miss Wilding. You gave us quite a scare.'

She had given them a scare? What did the woman think, that she had deliberately sat down in front of the barrel?

'Look what I found,' Gerald crowed, racing into the drawing room. He bowled into the centre of the group surrounding Mary, pushing, of all things, an odd-looking three-wheeled chair. 'Grandfather's bath chair. He bought it the year he went to take the waters for his gout. He never used it. It was kicking about at the back of the stables. It will be perfect for wheeling Miss Wilding about. Come on, Miss Wilding, give it a try.'

Such enthusiasm was hard to squash, Mary thought, warily looking at the contraption.

'She doesn't want to be pushed about in that,' Jeffrey

said with a grimace. 'All she needs is one of us fellows
to carry her to the table. I can do it.'

The earl's gaze narrowed.

Gerald's face fell, the triumph of moments before
dashed down by disappointment. It was almost painful
to watch.

'I think it is a fine idea,' she said. 'Much better than
being carried.'

The earl gave her a humourless smile. 'As the one who
has so far done the carrying, I suppose I must also express my appreciation.' Far from sounding please, there
was a note of disapproval in his voice. Did he think she
could use the wheeled chair to escape him? She looked
at it with renewed interest.

'It might work in the main part of the house,' Mrs
Hampton said with her habitual sniff. 'But many of the
passageways are narrow. And who on earth would carry
it and Miss Wilding up and down the stairs? That is why
my father didn't use it, you know.'

The woman had a point. 'Perhaps it would be better if
I stayed in my chamber until I can use a cane,' Mary said.
'I really don't want to put people to all of this trouble.'

'Dinner is served, my lord,' Manners intoned from
the doorway.

'No trouble at all,' the earl said and she was airborne
again. 'You can use the chair when there are no beefy
fellows to cart you about.' He cast a very pointed look
at Jeffrey.

Once more she was deposited on a chair. This time the
earl placed her beside him at the head of the table where
Mrs Hampton usually sat.

The other woman eyed her askance for a moment, then
took Mary's usual place.

Mary did her best to eat her dinner, but her ankle had begun to throb abominably. It must be the way she was sitting. Or because the effects of the willow-bark tea had worn off.

During the second remove the earl leaned closer. 'If it is not an insult to say so, Miss Wilding, you are looking quite pulled. You have been moving that piece of fish around on your plate for the past five minutes. Have you had enough?'

'Yes. I find I have eaten my fill.'

'I wasn't talking about food,' he said. 'I meant this.' His glance took in the group around the table. 'Would you feel more comfortable in the library? Sitting with your feet up on the sofa by the fire and reading your book until it is time to retire?'

The way he described it, he made it sound heavenly. The thought of putting up her foot was almost too tempting for words. 'I should probably go to bed.'

'No, I insist.' He raised his voice. 'I am sure Gerald would jump at the chance to push you along to the library.'

Gerald's enthusiastic expression agreed.

The earl gave her a conspiratorial smile. Had he guessed she would not hurt the young man's feelings by refusing? She had the feeling she was somehow playing into the earl's hands by agreeing to his plan. Nonsense. What could happen to her in the library? Besides, she was tired of the four walls of her chamber. A change of scene would do her good. 'Very well.'

Gerald wheeled the chair close. 'Hop in, Miss Wilding.'

Hop being a most appropriate word.

The earl didn't allow it. He stood and lifted her in. Once more that strange languid sensation weakened her limbs and her heart picked up speed. Oh, the man was attractive all right, but what did that matter when he meant her nothing but harm.

No matter how alluring he might be, she must remain on her guard.

As promised, the library was cosy, the fire blazing and the candles all lit.

Gerald came to a halt beside a *chaise longue* that had not been beside the hearth earlier. If she remembered correctly, it had been near the window. It seemed the earl had indeed planned this. But why? Now she wished she had insisted on going straight to her room.

'You should return to your meal,' she said to Gerald, manoeuvring out of the chair and on to the sofa.

He strolled along the bookshelves, his face moody. 'Such dullness. I was supposed to make my bows at court in the spring. We won't be going now that we are in mourning again.' The petulance was back. His moods seemed too volatile for such a young man.

'I know it will seem like for ever, but there is always next season,' she said in a matter-of-fact voice. She did not believe in encouraging the histrionics of young girls and felt the same must apply to boys equally. 'The year will pass before you know it.'

He stopped, pulled out a book and rifled absently through the pages. 'No doubt there will be some other reason not to go. Something concocted by Mama, yet again.'

'Oh, you are in the dumps,' she said, smiling.

He put the book back with a sigh. He didn't look quite so angelic in this mood.

'Do you like to read?' she asked, thinking to turn the conversation to pleasanter topics.

'I used to. I was quite sickly for a time. It was my only company.'

The memories seemed less than happy.

He swung about, his face alight once more. 'I forgot. I promised Jeff I would play billiards after dinner. You don't mind, do you? If I go?'

'Not at all.' She rather thought she'd be glad of it. Keeping up with his mercurial moods wasn't at all entertaining.

He grinned charmingly. 'Miss Wilding, I don't care what the earl says, you really are a brick.'

What the earl says? 'What—?'

Too late, he was already on his way out of the door.

What would the earl have said? That she was an antidote of a schoolmistress. Or that she was here on sufferance? Or he wished her to Jericho? While mortifying to think that he might have said any of those things, it wasn't difficult to imagine him saying them in that biting tone of his. That he would have said them to his cousin, though, that hurt. It hurt behind her ribs in a way she hadn't felt hurt in a very long time.

Because no matter how she tried not to, she had the feeling that, had circumstances been different, she might have liked him.

Oh, now that was pure foolishness. The man was pleasant to look at. He was strong. He was tall. And he was intelligent. He was in all ways…perfect.

For someone else.

He didn't want her any more than she wanted him.

Nice as it would be to live in a house like this, to have a real family, she didn't fit. She belonged with her girls. Educating them about things their families would never teach them: geography, mathematics, philosophy. Let someone else teach them deportment and drawing-room accomplishments. She wanted to expand their minds to the world.

Not that she would ever see much of it. But they might. And she could read about it.

Oh, bother. She had left her book in her chamber. Now this really was torture. Surrounded by the most magnificent selection of books she had ever seen in her life and nothing to read. Could anything else go wrong?

Really? Was she just going to sit here and bemoan her fate? She rose, standing on her uninjured foot and grasping the handles of the bath chair, hopped her way across to the shelves. Where there was a will, there was always a way.

What to choose?

She ran her eye along the titles in gold leaf on the spines of the books at eye level. Sermons. Well, she didn't mind a sermon occasionally, but tonight she needed something lighter, something to sweep her into another world. To help her forget the throbbing in her ankle and the fears lurking at the forefront of her mind. The fears that kept getting tangled up with ridiculous hopes.

The next shelf up held Shakespeare. His tales were wonderful, but difficult to read. Higher up? Novels. Some she had read. *Mysteries of Udolpho. Tom Jones.* A bit *risqué* to be sure, but fun. A slim volume, and much shorter than the others, jammed between them, caught her eye. 'A history of Beresford Abbey'. Now surely that was in the wrong place?

She reached up, but it was beyond her fingertips. She could touch the shelf, but not the book, no matter how she stretched. Ah, here was the answer. A rolling ladder tucked in the corner.

With a clever bit of work with her rolling support, heretofore known as a bath chair, she managed to get the ladder in place. She only needed to go up one step.

Tentatively she put her injured foot on the ground, gripping on to the sides of the ladder for support. Just one step up.

Her ankle gave a protesting throb. Jehosophat, that still hurt, but she was up and the book was within her grasp. It was jammed in tightly. She pulled. The ladder shifted. She grabbed at the shelf.

'Miss Wilding. What in the devil's name do you think you are doing?'

She started, then gave a little cry of alarm as the ladder moved sideways.

The next moment, the earl's large capable hands were around her waist and he was lifting her down as if she weighed nothing. Again. Making her stomach flutter and her heart bang against her ribs. Again.

And now he was glaring down at her as he held her at arm's length, making her feel no bigger than a pea.

'Well?' he said.

'I was trying to reach a book.'

He raised his eyes to the ceiling for a second. A plea for help, or a plea for patience? 'There are hundreds of books you can reach without climbing a ladder.'

'Not one I wanted.' Oh dear, she sounded as sullen as Gerald.

He huffed out a breath. Looked at the shelves. 'Which one did you want?'

'The one I was just about to take down when you scared me half to death.' She pointed at the blue leather-bound book jutting outward from its fellows. 'Stop sneaking up on me.' Her heart couldn't stand it.

'I was not sneaking.' He reached up and took the book down. Before she realised what he was about, he put an arm around her waist. He couldn't possibly...

But he had. With one arm. The man had the strength of ten. It left her feeling completely in his power. A good way to let her know she could not win with him. Not a feeling she liked.

He deposited her on the *chaise* with a small grunt. So he didn't find her as quite light as he made out. Showing off, no doubt, though to what purpose she could not imagine. Unless to serve as a warning of his superior strength.

A strong mind was a match for a strong arm any day of the week.

She held out her hand for the book.

He was staring at the words on the cover. 'This is what you wanted? A history book?'

'I like history. I thought I might find out a little more about the house.'

He raised his gaze and his rare smile made an appearance. 'I am glad you are starting to feel at home, Miss Wilding.'

The warmth of that smile sent butterflies dancing in her stomach. She repressed them with a frown. 'There is no sense in going somewhere and leaving again without finding out something about it.' She sighed. 'And besides, it caught my eye because it was out of place, pushed in there with the novels.'

His smile broadened. His grey eyes danced with amusement. 'Did you ever hear the saying, curiosity killed the cat?'

Now he was teasing her. 'Without curiosity we would be no better than the beasts of the field, my lord.'

He laughed out loud. 'Then I hope you find this worth another fall.'

'The first fall was hardly my fault.' Perhaps he was thinking that if she hadn't fallen and been whisked out of the way by Mr Trelawny she might already be out of his way. The lightness she'd been feeling dissipated in a rush.

Sensing the change of mood, he huffed out a sigh. 'The

rest of them went to play billiards. Even Mrs Hampton.
I came to see if you wanted to join them. To be truthful, I had thought they would come here after dinner.'
He sounded disgruntled, as if they had spoiled his plan.
What, had he expected them all to gather in the library,
like some sort of close-knit family? The kind of family
she had always dreamed of having. Or had dreamed of
once, a long time ago. Now, she only wanted her job back.
Her classes to teach. Her girls.

He handed her the book and wandered around the
room, looking at titles, poking around in cupboards. He
looked large and restless, as if he couldn't breathe in the
confines of the room. How could she possibly read with
him pacing around like a caged lion? To be truthful, with
his dark looks, he reminded her more of a panther than a
lion. But just as dangerous.

Perhaps he was eager to play billiards and felt obligated
to see to her welfare. In which case, it would be easy to
set him free. A little stab of disappointment caught her
by surprise. What, did she want him to stay? Surely not?

'I am quite happy to sit here and read,' she said, tacitly
giving him permission to depart. She glanced down at
the little book and flipped through the pages. It was not a
printed book. It was handwritten and there were sketches
of the abbey looking very different to how it looked today.
The paper was old and yellowed. Parchment? At the back
of it were what looked like maps. She quickly turned to
the middle of the book. She wanted to look at those maps,
but not in the presence of the earl.

'Do you consider yourself a blue-stocking, Miss Wilding?' he asked idly, riffling through the pages of a volume he had pulled from the shelves. He held it up. 'A
Mary Wollstonecraft acolyte? You have read her work,
I am sure.'

'*A Vindication Of The Rights Of Woman*? I think astonishingly far-sighted.'

He looked at her for a long moment and she had the feeling he was considering his options. 'You agree with her, then?'

'On many counts.' She swung her legs to the floor to face him. Her hands clasped tightly in her lap. 'Why should girls not receive the same education as their brothers? Not everyone is destined to be a wife or a mother. And even in those roles, surely an educated woman is a valuable addition to any family.'

'You are passionate in your beliefs, I see.'

And she had exposed herself to his mockery by the intensity of her response. She stiffened against her desire to back down, to please him. 'Why should I not be, since it is of importance to me as a person?'

'And it is your opinion that a woman need not, by definition of her sex, suffer from an excess of sensibility. You would not consider romantic love as a requirement for a contented marriage?'

Was this a proposal? Her heart gave a painful lurch. 'It is a sound principal from which to begin.' A painful flush rushed to her cheeks, because it was only partly the truth. Whatever she believed in her rationale mind, her heart wanted more than mere friendship or affection.

In her youth, it had yearned for love.

Yet she was not the sort of woman men fell in love with. She had accepted that. And now he was stirring up all those old emotions, those longings. Resentment rose against his probing into old wounds.

'And what of yourself, my lord?' she countered. 'What are your thoughts? You must marry, produce an heir.'

An emotion she could not read flickered across his face. Not a happy one though, of that she was certain.

'My business affairs leave little time for wooing. Besides, I have an heir.'

'Jeffrey.'

He nodded.

She remembered his vow that the Beresford line would end with him. 'So he is, after all, to provide the next generation of Beresfords? Your grandfather would be pleased.' It was an unfair jab, but she could not help but defend herself.

'It won't happen.'

He spoke with such surety, she stared at him in surprise. 'You cannot be sure he will not marry and have children. He is a young man.' Unless he planned to do away with him, too? The idea filled her with sick horror. First that she had even thought of the idea and second that she even thought it plausible. 'It is a rare man who does not marry,' she finished weakly.

He gave her a sharp look. 'You do not then eschew marriage?'

'I do not seek it for myself. But I do not eschew it for others.'

'You believe in choice, then.' A heaviness weighted his words. As if they held an underlying significance.

'Yes. I do.'

'Did you know your father was a vicar?'

She gasped.

Chapter Eight

After a moment of shock, Mary took a deep steadying breath. 'May I know what else you have learned, sir?' How she spoke with such calm, she couldn't be sure, for her pulse was racing so fast that she could feel the thunder of her heart against the press of her stays.

He gave a slight shrug. 'It is of very little help in this bind in which we find ourselves.'

The will was his only concern. Hers ran much deeper. 'My lord, this is my family we are discussing.' How rarely had she used those words, *my family*. It always seemed false to talk about family when one had none. 'I deserve to know all you have learned.'

'As you wish. Lord Templeton has established to his satisfaction that there is little or no chance that you and I are related. On either side of the blanket.'

She stiffened. 'You make it sound as if that is not a good thing.'

'It would have ended this farce immediately.'

She stared at him.

'The laws of consanguinity, Miss Wilding.' He drew up a chair and sat on the opposite side of the hearth. His expression was pensive, but the contrast of flame and shadows on his skin were unnervingly menacing. 'You must be aware of the required degrees of separation for a couple to be permitted to marry.'

Marry. There was that word again. Her face flamed, but he was looking into the fire and fortunately did not see her reaction.

'I—yes, of course I am aware.' She was proud of the way she sounded as if this was purely an academic discussion, even if inside she was as taut as a bowstring. 'Are you thinking you will submit to the terms of your grandfather's will?' Was that the point of his questions? Was he deciding what sort of wife she would make? She held her breath.

He turned away from the fire to look at her, his eyes wide with surprise and silver with intensity. Expressions flickered across his normally impassive face—longing, she thought, and perhaps loneliness. Things that pulled at her too-soft heart. Finally he settled on mockery, which seemed primarily directed at himself. 'Submission. Is that how you see it, Miss Wilding? Without knowing what is behind it all, I'd consider myself a fool to submit.' His voice was a low velvet murmur. A seduction of the senses, when the words, the unspoken criticism, flayed her heart.

She straightened her spine. 'As would I.'

Again something like regret reflected in his eyes as he acknowledged her answer with a sharp nod. 'So you would,' he agreed without inflection.

He rose to his feet. 'May I return you to your chamber? I find I am not inclined for sociability any more this evening.'

Bored with her company, he meant. 'I can ring for a footman.'

'Oh, no, Miss Wilding. Why would I deny myself the pleasure of holding you in my arms?'

Heat bathed her skin. 'Sir, you are impertinent.'

'Yes. I am, am I not?' And without another word he lifted her from the sofa and carried her to her room.

Pleasure. The word rippled through her, leaving her breathless. It was an admission that he, too, felt the attraction between them. And now he was carrying her to her bedroom. Little shivers chased across her skin.

Pleasure indeed. The feel of strong arms cradling her body, the beat of a heart against her chest, for without thinking she had curled her arm over his shoulder. To support herself, naturally. Her fingers itched to test the silkiness of the hair at his nape. Her head longed to lean against that powerful shoulder. Her body yearned to curl into him. All in the name of pleasure.

Little though she knew of it.

Too soon they arrived at her door and he set her down on her feet. Without a word, he reached around her and opened the door to her chamber. She fought the strange sense of disappointment as she turned to enter her room. 'Thank you, my lord.'

He caught her arm, holding her back, and she looked up at him. There was a strange expression on his face. A sort of wry twist to his mouth as he trapped her against the doorframe with one hand above her head and the other resting on the wall beside her cheek.

'My lord,' she gasped.

In the light from the sconce, his face was all hard angles and smooth planes. There was a loneliness about him, she was sure of it this time. An impossible bleakness as he stared into her eyes. His lids lowered a fraction, his mouth softened and curved in a most decadent smile when she nervously licked her lips.

She intended to speak, to warn him off, to push him away, but her fingers curled around his lapel as her knees felt suddenly weak and the tightness in her throat made it impossible to do more than breathe shallow sips of air.

A flash of hunger flared in those storm-grey eyes.

An answering desire roared through her veins. Shocked, heart pounding, she stared into his lovely face, waiting, wondering.

Slowly he bent his head, as if daring her to meet him halfway. Unable to resist the challenge, she closed the distance and brushed her mouth against his. His hand came behind her nape and expertly steadied her as he angled his head and took her lips in a ravenous kiss.

Large warm hands held her steady, one at her waist, the other cradling her head. A storm of sensation swept through her: tingles in her breasts, flutters in her core and the silken slide of his tongue tangling with hers. Delicious. Decadent. Bone melting. Heart stopping.

Thrills chased along her veins, making her tremble and long for more.

A sort of wonder filled her as her fingers finally explored the hair at his nape and wandered the impossible width of those muscled shoulders. Conscious mind disappeared into the hot darkness of desire.

A heavy thigh pressed between her legs, a steady pressure that offered ease to a growing ache. She shifted, parting her thighs to that insistent pressure, only to feel the torture, the aching need for something more. She tilted her hips into him.

On a soft groan, he broke the kiss. His chest was rising and falling as rapidly as her own, his gaze molten. 'Would it really be so bad to be married to me, Miss Wilding?' he asked in a low seductive growl.

Blankly she stared at him, her mind dizzy from his sensual assault.

His short laugh was low and slightly incredulous as

he swept her up and set her on the bed. He stood over her like some pillaging Viking.

Finally, some sense of preservation took control of her mind. 'You must not do this.'

His silver eyes were cold. 'Think about it, Miss Wilding. The alternative is not all that attractive.'

He turned on his heel and the door closed quietly behind him.

She swallowed. The alternative was death.

Shivering, she struggled to sit up, then pressed her fingers to her mouth, where just a few moments ago his kisses had wooed her to the point of insensibility. Had the unthinkable just happened? Had she practically given her virtue to this man? This stranger who to all intents and purposes, would be better off if she died? She gave a small moan as the delight of that moment echoed through her body and her feminine flesh gave a little pulse of pleasure.

Wanton female. Fool, more like.

Was he actually proposing marriage, or had he simply been carried away by the moment, by lust?

According to Sally, men promised many things in the throes of desire, only to go back on their word when they achieved their aim.

And he hadn't asked her to marry him. He'd asked her if marriage to him would be all that bad. She couldn't imagine anything worse, because clearly she could not keep her wits about him when he kissed her. And their marriage wouldn't be about kisses. It was about him getting his hands on his money.

He didn't even want children.

The lawyers in London must have told him there was no other way.

She went hot, then cold. Embarrassment. At him being forced to marry her. At his pretence of desire. Although it had not felt like pretence. Not at all. It had felt deliciously wicked and enticing.

Which was his whole purpose. To entice her into a marriage neither of them wanted.

If only she could get to the bottom of why the old earl had placed them in this ridiculous predicament, perhaps it would help them find a way out of it. Sally Ladbrook was the key. She was sure of it. Should she tell the earl where his friend might look for her, since it seemed unlikely she could go looking for herself any time soon? It was a question she would have to ponder carefully.

It would mean trusting him.

She did not see the earl at all the next day. Likely he was plotting his next move, after her refusal to succumb to seduction. After a night of restlessly tossing and turning, she'd spent most of the day wondering why she had.

He did not join the family for dinner, either. He was closeted with the lawyer, Mr Savary, and his steward, Manners said. He had requested a tray in his study for all three gentlemen. Not something an earl would normally do, Mrs Hampton announced in arctic tones.

Perhaps he was avoiding her. Perhaps he wasn't quite as in control as he made out. Perhaps he regretted last evening's encounter as much as she did.

So much for getting all dressed up for him. Mentally she gave herself a reproving shake. She was glad he had not come for dinner. Imagine the embarrassment of having to converse with a man whose body her hands had roamed the day before. She should be grateful for his consideration. Not that she thought he cared about her feelings.

He was no doubt busy trying to find a way to break the will.

Conversation throughout the meal was desultory, hinging around the visit the two young men had paid to a neighbour that afternoon and catching Mrs Hampton up on local gossip. Since none of it meant anything to Mary, she listened with only half an ear.

The meal was just about done and she was beginning to think she could retire to her chamber unscathed when Gerald turned his angelic-blue eyes in her direction. While he looked utterly angelic, she often had the feeling that the glimmer in his eyes was vaguely malicious. She braced herself for what might come out of his mouth.

'Did you find out anything about our ghost in that history, Miss Wilding?'

She frowned.

'The history of the house. I saw it on your bedside table when I brought you more books.'

She hadn't looked at the book, preferring the novels instead. She had set it aside and forgotten all about it. 'I did not.'

'I can't believe there isn't something in there about her,' he said, sounding disappointed.

'Let me give you the book, so you can look for yourself,' she said calmly.

The sly look was back. 'I would far rather you tell me what it says.'

'I say, old chap,' Jeffrey drawled. 'If Miss Wilding ain't interested in reading about ghosts, then she ain't. It is all speculation and gossip. I've never once seen hide nor hair of a ghost and I've explored every inch of the place.'

Including the tunnels behind the walls? He'd pooh-poohed the idea earlier, but he could have been trying to mislead her. And where had the heir to the title been when the barrel tumbled down that hill?

Could he be the one who wanted her dead? And not the earl?

Or was that her body's wishful thinking, a hope she could absolve the earl, so she could what? Encourage his seduction? Let it sway her common sense? Did she have no shame any more? No intelligence when it came to her thoughts about this man just because he had set fire to longings she had no business thinking about, let alone having?

'Would you care to take tea in the drawing room with me, Miss Wilding?' Mrs Hampton asked.

The woman sounded almost friendly, not the least bit condescending.

'I could fetch your book,' Gerald offered. 'And you could read aloud from it.'

Puzzled at his determination, Mary frowned at him.

His mother gave a little shudder. 'I am not sure it is quite an appropriate topic for the drawing room.'

'Do you believe in this ghost story, Mrs Hampton?' Mary couldn't keep the surprise out of her voice.

'It is a story passed down from generation to generation,' the widow said. 'A warning from our ancestors.'

A chill breeze seemed to pass through the room. Mary glanced up, expecting to see the door open and the curtains lifted by an errant breeze, but there was nothing, only Gerald staring at his mother with an avid expression.

His older cousin looked bored. 'He won't stop until you read it, Miss Wilding,' he said with a weary sigh.

'Very well, fetch the book. We will read it by firelight and scare ourselves to death.'

Gerald gave a whoop of triumph and shot off.

Mary, aided by Jeffrey's arm, limped the few steps to the drawing room. By the time they were settled, Gerald was back with his prize. He turned the pages until he found the chapter he wanted. 'Read from here.'

It was only as he was riffling through the pages that

Mary remembered the maps she had glanced at. The passageways and tunnels, and the caves to which they were connected.

Gerald was clearly familiar with this book, so he must be aware of them, too. But did he know that the tunnel behind her wall was in a state of good repair? Accessible?

She took the book. The handwriting was in the old style, the hand cramped, the letters *f* and *s* almost indistinguishable.

Legend tells us that tales of the ghost of a lady in white go back to the earliest days of the Reformation. Who she is, is lost in the mists of time. That she appears before the death of the Beresford earl is taken as fact by the inhabitants. The predominant tale has her as the wife of the first earl, killed by her lord so he could take another, richer wife. He was hanged when her body was found by his younger brother in the caves below the house.

'She came before Grandfather's death,' Gerald declared,

At his cousin's snort, he glowered. 'I heard her moaning and clanking around on the battlements. Old Ned said he saw her.'

'Old Ned would say your head was shaved and the hair in your pocket, should it lead to a pennyworth of beer,' Jeffrey said.

At Mary's enquiring look, he grinned. 'Old Ned is a gardener. Older than dirt, he is, and twice as thirsty.'

'Ned saw her,' Gerald said, his voice cracking awkwardly, reminding all of his youth. 'I told Grandfather.'

'Not well done,' his mother said.

The hairs on Mary's arms lifted. When she looked up, her gaze found the earl's. He had entered as quietly as a cat and, just as he had the first time she had seen him, he had paused in the shadows beyond the light of the fire and the candles. This time, however, when he caught her gaze, he immediately strode into the light.

'And what did your grandfather say?' the earl asked in such quiet mocking tones everyone in the room strained to hear him.

Gerald flushed. 'He said it was hardly a prediction, when he'd been ill for weeks. But then how do we know it was his death it portended?' He glowered at the earl.

Who ignored him. Instead he crossed to Mary's side and held out his hand. His eyes were the colour of a lake in winter and just as cold. He was back to his normal self. 'What are you are reading from?'

'The history of the Abbey, my lord.' She held it out. 'The book you kindly reached down for me.' She watched his face as he flipped through the pages.

He paused for a moment, frowning, then closed the book with a snap. 'It is hardly a work of erudition if it resorts to ghosts and tales of death.'

'It is a legend, my lord,' Mrs Hampton said, looking up from her embroidery. 'Well known to all Beresford descendants.'

Mary winced at the obvious slight, though the earl seemed oblivious, since he remained looking at her.

'It is foolish nonsense,' Mrs Hampton continued. 'But you have a good voice for reading, Miss Wilding. Clear as a bell. No mumbling, like so many of the misses of today. Read something else.'

'She reads well because she's a schoolteacher,' Gerald said.

He didn't mean it as a compliment.

Mary took a leaf out of the earl's book and ignored him. 'Why, thank you, ma'am. Unfortunately, this is the only book I have to hand, so I fear I must decline.'

Mrs Hampton scrabbled in her reticule. 'I have a book

of sermons written by my brother.' She held it out. 'I
haven't had a moment to open it since it arrived. It would
be a treat to hear it read.'

The earl stepped between them, ostensibly to save
Mary the trouble of rising, and glanced at the title. '*Re-
flections upon St Paul's Epistle to the Philippians*. It
sound most edifying, ma'am.' The wry note to his tone
made Mary look at him again. She could have sworn she
saw the chilly gaze warm with a spark of amusement. It
made him seem more human, somehow, and she barely
repressed an answering smile. It wouldn't be polite. She
took the book from his hand.

Jeffrey groaned. 'Not more of his ramblings. Forgive
me, ma'am but I'd rather blow my head off with a pistol.'

Gerald shot him a glance. 'Target practice? In the old
hall?' He looked ecstatic.

Mrs Hampton frowned. 'I don't know what your grandfather was thinking, letting you shoot guns indoors.'

'Every gentleman should know how to fire a weapon
accurately,' Gerald said. 'And that requires practice. I
should be shooting at Manton's, but since we never go
to London...'

His mother pressed her lips together, but Jeffrey
nodded his agreement. 'He's right. I'll join you, Cuz. You
coming, Beresford?'

'I prefer the pleasure of hearing Miss Wilding read,'
he said, his voice a shade more raspy than usual.

That rough sound sent a thrill down Mary's spine. An
unwelcome chill. Only it wasn't chill, there was a feverish
quality to it that once more sent colour rushing to her face.
She didn't have to see it to know her face had turned red,
she could feel the prickle of it all the way to her hairline.

'Let them go,' Mrs Hampton said, flapping her embroidery hoop in dismissal. 'They will only laugh and

carry on. Foolish boys. But be careful, my son. Pistols are dangerous.'

'I know what I am doing, Mother,' Gerald huffed. He bowed. 'I will see you in the morning. No doubt you will be abed from boredom ere long.'

Jeffrey made a more elegant departure, kissing each lady's hand in turn as he bid them goodnight, then he followed his cousin from the room.

The earl watched him go with narrowed eyes. Mary could not quite tell if he disliked his cousin or merely did not understand him. The two men were very different. It certainly did not appear as if they shared any blood, which might be the reason for their apparent mutual dislike. Perhaps Jeffrey really had hoped that somehow his claim to the title would be recognised.

Mary waited for the earl to sit down, but he did not. Instead he disposed himself with one arm resting along the mantel and his gaze fixed on the fire.

'Begin, child,' Mrs Hampton said. She leaned back against the cushions and closed her eyes.

Mary focused on the words and began reading. Hard as she tried to imbue the words with sense and meaning, the perorations and lengthy admonitions remained dreary and uninspiring. By the time she was done Mary could only pity the members of the archdeacon's congregation.

After only one paragraph a snore emanated from Mrs Hampton's end of the sofa. 'What?' she said, looking around her. Then her eyes cleared. 'Very nice. Wonderful, don't you think, my lord?'

He inclined his head. 'Entirely enlightening, ma'am.'

'Well, yes,' she muttered. 'Of course it would sound so much better in church. He has a wonderful baritone, my brother the archdeacon.'

So much for Mary doing her best.

'Would you like me to read more?' she asked with her heart sinking to her feet at the very thought.

'I think we have more than enough to reflect upon,' his lordship drawled. 'Is that your opinion also, Miss Wilding?'

Now that was really unfair, putting her in such a position, but there was a challenge in his eyes that she could not quite resist. 'I would dare to say one must take sufficient time to absorb such profoundness or it will lose its impact.'

The earl shot her a glance that just might have been tinged with admiration. She felt herself warm in the heat of that gaze.

He took a quick breath and once more his expression was guarded, his eyes cool. Once more he had distanced himself. So confusing and frustrating. Really? Why would she care?

Mrs Hampton beamed at her. 'Quite. Indeed. I shall be sure to relay your sentiments to my brother when next I write.'

'You are too kind, ma'am.'

Mrs Hampton made a great show of tidying up her embroidery, tucking it into the drawer in the table beside her. 'I believe it is time to retire, Miss Wilding.' She rose to her feet and the earl straightened.

Mary held out the book to her. 'Thank you for sharing this fine work with us.'

'Keep it. I am sure you will find it most edifying.' She darted a glance at the earl. 'Shall I write for another copy for you, your lordship? It has a great deal to offer a man in your position.'

Was that an insult? Mary felt a flash of heat on his behalf.

The earl gazed at the widow without expression. 'No

need, ma'am. I am sure Miss Wilding will be more than happy to lend me her copy. Indeed, I am sure I shall enjoy the pleasure of listening to her read on future evenings.'

Mary's jaw dropped.

'Very well, then,' Mrs Hampton said. 'I will say this. I do not as a general rule approve of blue-stockings, or young ladies earning a living, but the pupils at your school were fortunate to have you.' She gave Mary a tight smile.

Mary darted a glance at the earl, who raised a brow. She decided to accept the compliment. 'Thank you.'

Mrs Hampton headed for the door. 'Are you coming, Miss Wilding?'

Mary started to rise.

'Stay,' the earl commanded. An expression of surprise flickered across his face, as if he had not planned his request.

Startled, she stared at him blankly.

'It is early,' he added by way of an afterthought. 'Perhaps you would indulge me in a game of chess, Miss Wilding?'

It sounded like an excuse to get her alone. She swallowed, wondering what she should say.

'I am retiring.' Mrs Hampton gave the earl a pointed glance. 'While Miss Wilding is your ward, my lord, and while in most instances no one should think anything untoward of it, I do think she should follow my example.'

The earl's mouth tightened at what was clearly a suggestion he did not know how to behave like a gentleman— a cruel blow to any man's honour. And a petty triumph for the widow if Mary followed her lead.

He awaited her decision impassively. Clearly his pride would not let him argue his case. Not that he had much of a case after his attempted seductions. She really should go.

'I will stay for a while,' she said impulsively and

flushed. Oh why would she care if she hurt his feelings? If, indeed, he had any feelings.

'Then I bid you both goodnight.' The widow swept out of the room.

Wondering if she had quite lost her senses, Mary watched her go.

'You do play chess, do you not?' the earl asked.

'Indifferently, I am afraid,' she said as calmly as her racing heart would allow. She and Sally had played occasionally, but Mary had the feeling that Sally made up the rules as she went along. Fortunately, it was not something they had been required to teach their pupils. 'I really should retire and leave you to your port.'

'Afraid, Miss Wilding?'

Of course she was afraid. She'd be out of her mind not to be. But it would be a mistake to let him see it. 'I just do not think you will find my chess game much of a challenge.'

He tilted his head. 'Then let us take up where we left off. Will you read for me?'

She glanced down at the book of sermons. 'I'd really rather not.'

The earl pulled a small book from the inside breast pocket of his coat. 'This may be more to your taste.' He held out a small volume bound in worn brown leather and lettered in gold.

She read the cover. 'Spenser's *Faerie Queene*. Not an easy read.'

'But not beyond you, I think.'

There was something in his tone that made her try to read his expression, but as usual his thoughts were shuttered, as he took up his previous stance at the hearth. Once more she was reminded of a dark fallen angel. Or a god cast out from the heavens, much as it seemed he had been cast out by his family. Not unlike her. Something in her chest squeezed. A pang of empathy.

She knew what it felt like to be abandoned.

She lowered her gaze and opened the cover to read: *To Laura, for ever in my heart, LBB.* The B could stand for Bane. If so, it was odd to realise she did not know his first name. And if he had given it to Laura, why was it returned? She glanced up, but he simply nodded encouragement for her to continue. She opened the pages at the beginning. The vellum pages were worn and well-thumbed. 'An oft-read story,' she murmured.

'Yes.'

She coloured at the cold indifference in his voice. He clearly wasn't going to give her any information. And she had too much pride to press him.

She scanned the first few lines, getting a feeling of the flow and the rhythm.

> *Lo I the man, whose Muse whilome did maske,*
> *As time her taught, in lowly Shepheards weeds,*
> *Am now enforst a far unfitter taske,*
> *For trumpets sterne to change mine Oaten reeds,*
> *And sing of Knights and Ladies gentle deeds;*
> *Whose prayses having slept in silence long,*
> *Me, all to meane, the sacred Muse areeds*
> *To blazon broad emongst her learned throng:*
> *Fierce warres and faithfull loves shall moralise my*
> *song.*

Hesitant at first, she struggled with the rhythm and the ancient spelling. But her difficulties were not entirely the fault of the text. She could not help but be aware of the earl's overwhelming presence. The very essence of him pulled at her mind. The intensity of his regard on her face made her tremble inside.

After a time, she lost herself in the lyrical words and the world of warriors. Stanza after stanza rolled off her tongue. Her heartbeat provided the rhythm and her indrawn breath the pauses.

Slowly, she became aware of the low male voice joining hers, at first a murmur and then increasing in volume, until they read together, but he was not reading, he spoke from memory.

She let her voice subside to a whisper, and then die away altogether, watching his face, his gaze fixed on a time and space not of this room. There was sorrow and bleakness in his expression, as if the words did not recall happy memories.

And there was a shade of anger, too, mirroring that of the Knight whose words he spoke.

When he reached the end of the first Canto, he seemed to come to himself and realised she had ceased reading. A faint colour stained his cheekbones.

'You read very well,' he said.

'And you know it by rote.' She let her question go unspoken, but it hung in the small distance between them.

'I heard it read so often I think it is engraved on my brain.'

He reached for the book and tucked it back in a small pocket in the breast of his coat.

She felt a pang in her chest with respect to this Laura, whose book he carried close to his heart. Not jealousy, surely?

'It was my mother's.' His usual rough-edged voice was more raspy than usual, as if it cost him something to speak of it. 'It was the only thing she brought from this house, apart from me.'

She could not quite believe her feeling of relief that it was not something he had given a lover. 'And the giver?' she dared to ask.

'Her husband.'

She noticed that he did not call him his father.

'She read this book over and over,' he continued. 'Long after we heard he had died.' He looked away, clearly not wanting to share his emotions. 'It reminds me of her. Thank you for indulging me.'

There was no sentimentality in his voice and she had the sense the reminder was uncomfortable. She wanted to say more, even to offer comfort, but she had the sense he had said far more than he wished.

'Thank you. I have not read that work in an age.'

'It was not part of the school's curriculum?' he said, his voice sounding normal again.

She sighed. 'There is only so much time in the day and there are other subjects which must be covered.'

'Like chasing off footpads with parasols?'

She glanced just in time to see the faintest quirk to his lips. Was he teasing? Or mocking? She preferred not to know.

'The things people deem it important for women to know,' she said matter-of-factly. 'Needlework, French— with which I agree, by the way—drawing, deportment.'

'All useful attributes, surely?'

'Useful for those seeking a husband, no doubt.' She got up. He rose with her.

'You must excuse me, my lord, I am ready to retire.'

'I notice your ankle is considerably better.'

It was. She had healed far more quickly than the doctor expected. In a day or two she would be walking normally. But she had not intended for him to realise how well she progressed. 'It is well rested. No doubt by the time I reach my room, it will be aching again.'

'Then you must permit me to help you.'

Oh, she had fallen very neatly into that trap, hadn't she? 'Thank you, but I manage fine with my cane.' She bent down and retrieved it from the floor beside her chair.

His mouth was tight when she stood up and the faint warmth of earlier had gone from his eyes. They were as cold as granite. Was he somehow hurt that she had refused his aid?

'It is good for me to walk,' she said, in a feeble attempt to lessen the blow, if indeed she was interpreting his expression correctly. 'I have been sitting too long.'

A muscle jumped in his jaw. He bowed. 'As you wish.'

'Then I bid you goodnight, my lord. Thank you for a pleasant evening.'

'I see good manners were also a part of the curriculum,' he said drily as she passed out of the room.

As she limped back to her chamber, she had the strangest sensation of being followed. A sort of prickling at the back of her neck, but each time she turned around to look, there was no one there. She shivered, thinking of Gerald's tales of hauntings.

Or was it something much simpler—was his lordship following her to make sure she did not stray? Somehow she felt much more comfortable with the first idea.

Chapter Nine

A wisp of light floated above the uneven floor. The nearby rocks lining the tunnel wall and ceiling were shown in glistening relief, the darkness beyond impenetrable. The ground sloped downwards beneath Mary's feet. Steep. Rough. And Mary could hear the sea, a roaring grumbling vibration through the rocks.

The figure ahead beckoned. 'Don't be afraid,' it whispered softly.

Sometimes it was right in front of her, sometimes it disappeared around a corner, leaving only a faint glow in its wake, but as long as Mary kept moving forwards, it was always there, just ahead. The White Lady. It could be no one else.

The chill was unearthly. Mary rubbed her bare arms and realised she was dressed only in her nightrail. Her bare feet were numb. She glanced back down the tunnel. She should get her shawl and slippers. Behind her there was only blackness. How far had she come? It seemed better to go on.

A long low moan echoed around her.

Rattling chains.

The glowing figure headed towards her, twisting like

smoke. Fear caught at her heart. She turned and ran. Into the black. Ahead she could see a small wedge of light. Her chamber. Her stomach dropped away. She was falling. Into the dark.

A shriek split the air.

Mary jolted. Sat up, shaking.

Where was she? The last of the embers in her fire swam into focus. She shivered and looked around.

She was on her bed, her bedclothes on the floor. The only light in the room was a low red glow from the fire. Shadows clung to the walls. The air was freezing. Was that wretched door to the tunnel open? She shot out of bed. Rummaged for the poker among the sheets.

There. The comforting shape of iron. She grabbed it and held it high above her head. 'Who is there?' she quavered.

Her door burst open.

She screamed, backing away, grasping the poker in two hands, staring at the shadowy figure menacing her from the doorway.

'Get out,' she warned, her voice full of panic.

The man, for it was a man and not a ghost, plucked a candle from the sconce outside her door and stepped boldly into the room. The light revealed the earl, dressed in naught but his shirt and breeches.

'You!' she said.

'Miss Wilding. Mary. I heard you scream.' He drew closer, his gaze fixed on her face. 'Give me that.'

He could not possibly have heard her from his room in the south tower. She gripped her weapon tighter. 'Stay away.'

In one swift movement he wrested the poker from her hand and flung it aside.

She pressed her back against the wall.

He stared at her as if shocked, then stepped back, hand held away from his side. 'Take it easy, Miss Wilding.' He replaced the unlit stub in the candlestick on her dressing table with the lit one in his hand.

Her body was shaking. Her heart racing. She put a hand on the bedside table for balance. 'What do you want?'

He recoiled, as if startled by her vehemence, but as he looked at her, his eyes widened, and a sensual longing filled his expression as his gaze drifted down her body. Her insides tightened at the heat of the hunger in his eyes.

She gasped and, glancing down, realised how little she was wearing. She shielded herself with her hands. 'Please. Leave.'

'I think not.' He strode for the chest at the end of her bed and picked up her robe that Betsy had left there, ready for the morning. He threw it at her. 'Put this on.'

She caught it against her, but couldn't seem to move. He huffed out an impatient sigh, came around the bed and threw it around her shoulders, wrapping it around her. ''What the devil is going on here?'

He sounded genuinely perplexed. And perhaps even worried.

He had come through the door. Not from the tunnel. She had locked her door. She stared at the fire irons sitting neatly on the hearth. No longer her alarm, but simply fire irons. Someone had moved them since she had fallen asleep. Betsy? The light of the candle also showed the wall was exactly where it should be. How could she explain her fear without giving away her knowledge of what lay behind the wall?

Her breathing slowed. And although her body continued to tremble, she managed to catch her breath. If only she could think. She shuddered.

'Was it a nightmare?' he asked.

A nightmare. That would explain the vision of the ghost. The sensation of falling and yet awaking to find herself on her bed. It didn't explain the freezing temperature.

His eyes shifted to the window, then shot back to her face. His jaw hardened. He crossed the room, closed the casement and spun around to face her. 'What is going on here, Miss Wilding? A midnight visitor?'

She stared at him in astonishment and then at the window. 'Certainly not. Fresh air is healthy.' So healthy her teeth were aching with the urge to chatter—but she did not remember opening it.

'Not in the middle of winter,' he growled. 'Why do I have the sense you are not telling me the truth?'

'What reason do I have to lie?'

'Because you answer a question with a question.'

He was lying, too. There was no earthly way he could have heard her cry out and arrived so quickly unless he was in the tunnel behind the wall.

She tried to keep her gaze away from the chimney. He must not know she was aware of it. He must have entered her room from there, closed it and gone out by the door. That would explain how he had entered when the door was locked. It did not explain the window.

'Why did you cry out?'

'I had a bad dream. I was asleep. Something was chasing me. I fell.' She shook her head. 'I thought I fell. A long way down. But when I opened my eyes, I was here. And you came through the door.'

She started shaking again. It had all seemed so real. Felt real.

'Then it was your scream I heard.'

'I suppose it must have been.' But she'd heard the

scream, too. It had come from somewhere else. Above her head. Hadn't it?

Or had she screamed in her sleep and frightened him off before he could do whatever it was he had intended? Before he could take drastic action. Before she could disappear in the tunnels below the house. Had he then pretended to burst in to allay her suspicions?

She didn't dare give voice to her thoughts, in case she was right. Or in case she was wrong. She was just so confused. She pressed her hands together, staring at his face, trying to read his expression.

'Mary,' he murmured. Then muttered something under his breath. 'Miss Wilding. Sit down before you fall.'

When she didn't move he took her hand and led her to the bed. His large warm hands caught her around the waist and he lifted her easily on to the mattress. He looked down at the tangle of covers at his feet and then back at the window. His mouth tightened.

'Someone was here,' he said. His voice harsh. And it wasn't a question.

She shivered. You, she wanted to say. 'I saw no one,' she forced out. She could not let him know what she suspected. Nor could she accuse him without proof. 'I saw no one. Only…only the White Lady. In my dream.' It had to be a dream. She did not believe in ghosts. Would not.

He cursed softly, then took one of her hands in his, clearly intending to reason with her. His hands curled around her fingers. He frowned. 'You really are freezing.'

He crossed to the fire, stirred up the embers and added a few lumps of coal, then came back to her, taking her hands in his and rubbing them briskly. He rubbed at her upper arms and she could feel the warmth stealing through her body. Not just because his rubbing, but because of his closeness, because of the heat from his body.

He stared into her face. His breathing was also less than steady and there was fear in his eyes, as if she had somehow unnerved him. Fear for her? The very idea of it plucked at her heartstrings, made her want to confide in him. She just didn't dare.

His hands stopped their warm strokes and one came to her chin, tipping her face up, forcing her to either close her eyes or look at him. She chose to be bold, to return stare for stare. She would not show him how much she feared him, or how much she feared her responses to his touch.

'Mary,' he whispered, his rough voice containing a plea, as his warm breath grazed the cold skin on her cheek and his hungry gaze sparked heat low in her belly that seemed to trickle outwards.

'My lord,' she replied, shocked at the husky quality of her voice, at the difficulty she had breathing around the panicked beat of her heart.

A soft groan rumble up from his chest. Then his mouth covered hers. The storm of sensation racing through her body could not possibly be a dream. The way his hands roved her back, the way hers felt the muscle beneath the linen of his shirt. Nothing in her experience could lead her to imagine anything so wildly exciting.

Slowly he sank backwards on to the mattress. And heaven help her, she followed, not willing to break the magic of his wonderful kiss. His strong arms held her close against his body and he rolled her on to her back. He kissed her mouth, plying her lips softly at first, then his hunger grew more demanding, until she parted her lips and allowed him entry. He teased her tongue with little flicks and tastes until she dared taste him back. Such a heavenly silken slide. Deliciously wicked.

When his tongue slowly retreated, she followed with

her own, exploring the warm dark cavern of his mouth, tasting wine and him, mingled in one heady brew.

A sweet ache, trembling inside her with longing, built slowly—a hot, anxious longing.

A low groan rumbled up from his chest and he rolled over her, one knee pressing between her thighs, one hand steadying her at her nape, the other moving to stroke her ribs, to gently cup her breast.

She gasped at the shock of it, at the unfurling pleasure of it that made her breast tingle. As if that light touch was not enough.

She moaned.

He raised his head, looking down into her face. The fire and the candle gave just enough light to see the silver glitter of his eyes, the sensual cast to his mouth as his gaze searched her face, then skimmed down to where his hand rested on the swell of her breast. Slowly he moved his thumb over her nipple. It tightened beneath the fabric of her night rail. And her insides clenched.

Of their own accord her hips arched into him, seeking relief from the tender ache. He closed his eyes briefly, but there was pleasure in the brief wince of pain. And the hunger in his expression intensified.

Again his head lowered and her lips parted in anticipation of his kiss. Only this time his gentle mouth drifted slowly across her cheek in light brushes that made her want more. Until he found her ear and breathed hot moist air that sent shivers sweeping across her breast, down her back, into the very core of her.

She wriggled and moaned.

He laughed softly in her ear, sending another spasm through her body. Then his scorching mouth was moving onwards, to her neck where he licked her and her pulse spiralled out of control, to the hollow of her throat, where he breathed deeply, as if to inhale her essence, across the rise of her breast to the nipple he had stroked with his thumb.

She held her breath.

Then his mouth closed over it. Hot. Wet. His tongue flicking and tormenting while she wriggled and squirmed beneath him, seeking to break the ever-tightening cord inside her.

'No,' she gasped.

He raised his head, looking into her eyes with that penetrating stare as if he could see right into her mind, as if he knew what was happening inside her body. 'No? Shall I stop?'

'Yes,' she whispered, though it took all of her will.

But as he started to move, she couldn't bear it. 'I must not. It isn't right.'

'It feels right,' he said in that deep raspy voice. Seductive. Enticing. 'You feel right.' He cupped her breast. 'Perfect, in fact.' He squeezed his eyes shut. 'But you are right. This must wait until we are married.'

Married. But she hadn't agreed they would be married.

He kissed her mouth. Chastely. Sweetly. Preparing to leave.

Hot with desire and hunger, her lips clung to his. Her hands grasped his shoulders, pulling him down to her, as she lifted her body to press her breasts against his wide chest. It felt so good to be close to him. To feel his strength. To feel connected.

Her thighs parted to press her mons against that beautifully heavy and hard-muscled thigh. She rocked her hips. Sweet pleasure, stole her breath and made her want more.

He broke away.

'You must make up your mind, Mary,' he said, his voice a low growl. 'Marry me and finish this, or…not.'

She stared up at him. He was speaking of lust, not love. He was being forced into this by a grandfather he hated. Once they were wed, would he resent her? How could he not? But what was the alternative?

She turned her face away, trying to think, trying to make sense of it all.

The mattress shifted as he stood. The door clicked shut.

He had left without a word, quietly. Like a ghost. Did he assume she'd given her answer?

If so, what did that mean for her future?

The heat of her body slowly returned to normal and she rose from the bed, feeling the damp chill at her breast where he had suckled. The heat of embarrassment washed through her. How could she be so wanton with a man who—who might well prefer her dead?

She limped across the room and turned the key in the lock. She balanced the fire irons on the vase and stepped back. Had she forgotten to set them there last night? Had Betsy moved them? She couldn't seem to remember.

Could she have moved them herself and wandered down the tunnel? In her sleep? Was she indeed hysterical, her fears getting the better of her once she fell asleep? Could she also have opened the window?

She swallowed the dryness in her throat. Was it her mind playing tricks? Or was she just trying to find an excuse for him, for the earl, because she didn't want to believe he intended her harm?

Was she foolish enough to want to say yes to his offer of marriage?

She crawled back into her bed, her mind going around and around with questions she couldn't seem to answer.

The next morning she felt so listless, so tired, she had asked Betsy to bring her breakfast in bed. She just could not face the Beresford family. Not the earl. Not the cousins. And definitely not Mrs Hampton.

Betsy returned with a tray looking as cheerful as always. 'Eat up, miss,' she said. 'You'll soon feel more the thing.'

'Thank you.' She glanced out of the window at a bright-blue sky. 'The weather looks fine today.'

'Snow's on the way,' Betsy said. 'The calm before the storm.'

Mary laughed, but said nothing. She was used to local predictions of weather. They invariably turned out wrong. There seemed to be this feeling among country folk that good weather heralded bad. She tucked into the tea and toast she had requested while Betsy set out her gown.

'His lordship is off to the mine,' Betsy said, shaking out the creases in the blue muslin. 'I heard him asking for that there black beast of his. Joe says it's a vicious animal. The stable lads are all scared of it.'

Mary frowned. 'The earl never mentioned he was going to the mine.'

'He arranged it with the manager, Mr Trelawny, yesterday.'

And both men knew she wanted to go, too. Did the earl think she wouldn't find out, or had he decided that she would be his wife and therefore the mine would soon be under his control? 'Has his lordship left already?'

'I wouldn't know, miss.'

'Go and find out, would you? And ask him to wait, if he hasn't gone. Ask him to have the carriage readied for me.' And if he had left? Might it be an opportunity for escape? 'Betsy, if I missed him, please ask that the carriage be put to so I can follow on. He must have forgotten I was to go with him.'

Betsy stared at her. 'But your foot, miss.'

'It is well enough. Please hurry.' She'd taken off the bandage before Betsy had come back with the tray and, though her ankle was still discoloured by the bruise, the swelling had quite gone and it only really hurt if she moved carelessly. It was strong enough for a carriage ride and a short walk. She wanted to see the condition of the children at the mine. She'd read a great deal recently by some forward-thinking women about the cruel conditions of such places. She could not bear the thought that those kind of conditions existed at something for which she was responsible.

While Betsy hurried off to do her bidding, Mary dressed. Fortunately for her, she'd been wearing her front-closing stays when the rest of her things had gone over the cliff, so she managed fairly well, and only needed Betsy to fasten the back of her gown when she returned with the news that his lordship was waiting. But not for long.

'I can't say he was pleased, miss, but he ordered up the carriage.'

Mary wrapped her woollen cloak around her, tied on her bonnet and pulled on her gloves. 'And I am ready. Now if you would be so good as to lead me to the front door, I can make sure I am not delaying his lordship any more than necessary.'

She followed Betsy along the corridors and realised she no longer needed a guide. She was becoming quite familiar with the old house's twists and turns. But this morning it was better to be safe than sorry.

Losing her way and arriving late would be all the excuse his lordship needed to leave without her. And this would be a chance to survey the roads around the house. The next time she left, she intended to follow the road across the moors to Helston where his lordship had not warned the inhabitants they must not sell her a ticket for the stagecoach.

As much as she wanted to trust him when he was kissing her senseless, the answer had finally come to her just before she fell asleep. If she agreed to marry him, she would be wholly in his power. He would be able to do anything he wanted and she would not be able to object. A very bad idea while she had no idea why his grandfather had pushed them together.

The first order of business was to find Sally Ladbrook and find out what she knew. Then perhaps she could think about what to do in regard to the earl. Because the last thing she wanted was to be at the mercy of a vengeful husband in a damp and draughty house where ghosts seemed to roam at will and, according to legend, people could disappear without a trace.

Beresford was standing beside the carriage when she exited the house into the sunshine. His face was set in its usual grim lines as he looked up at her approach. There was no sign of his horse. 'Good morning, my lord,' she said brightly.

'Good day, Miss Wilding.'

There was nothing of the passionate man he had been in her room last night in the icy gaze he bestowed on her. She half-wondered if she had imagined the whole thing. But she hadn't. Nor had she imagined the scream that had awoken her from her horrible dream. 'You knew I wished to go with you, my lord. You might have sent word.'

'You weren't at breakfast, Miss Wilding,' he said, with a slight nod of his head, 'or I would have told you of my plans.'

Oh, yes, she really believed that.

His raised a brow. 'I thought you might prefer to wait until your ankle is perfectly well.'

By then it might be too late. By then she might have succumbed to his powers of seduction. 'I prefer to go today. And here I am. Ready to go.'

Something hot flared in his eyes. Anger, no doubt. No man liked a woman with a will of her own. He bowed slightly. 'Your carriage awaits, but time does not.'

One of the grooms leapt forwards to open the carriage door and she climbed inside and settled herself against the squabs. He climbed in after her.

Startled, she edged deeper into the corner. 'I thought you planned to ride?'

'I did.'

'Don't feel you must keep me company.' Oh dear, that sounded rude.

'I never do anything I don't wish to do, Miss Wilding,' he drawled and stretched out his legs, brushing against her skirts in a way that felt all too intimate. But what could she say? He was playing the perfect gentleman, sitting opposite her on the seat, facing backwards.

She winced inwardly. She had intended to make a note of any landmarks she saw as a means of finding her way—she'd brought along a notebook and pencil for the purpose. She could hardly do so with him sitting there watching her. She would just have to try to hold them in her memory.

She stared out of the window, trying to look as if her interest was idle curiosity. Here there was a large barn. There an oddly twisted tree, but they were moving so quickly it was hard to keep track.

'What do you think of Cornwall?' he asked.

Be quiet, I'm trying to follow our route, she wanted to snap. Instead, she pursed her lips as if giving consideration to his question. 'It's very different from the countryside in Wiltshire.'

'How?'

She turned to face him. 'The sea. The moors. The mining. Even the way the people speak. I can barely understand some of their words.'

'It is not so very different from Wales,' he murmured, as if remembering. 'They also have their own language.'

'Did you live in Wales?'

He nodded. 'For a while. When I was young.'

His willingness to talk about the past surprised her. 'Did you like it there?'

His eyes turned the colour of a winter sky. Bleak. Cold. Clearly she'd touched a nerve and she expected him to withdraw into his usual chilly distance.

'No.' He took a deep breath. 'Not true. There were good times as well as bad.' He turned his face to look out of the window as if he preferred to hide his thoughts, but the way the light shone on the window, she could make out his reflection. Not the detail, but enough to see him close his eyes as if shutting a lid on memories their conversation had evoked. 'It was a hard life,' he murmured. 'But I learned about mining and the men who risk their lives below ground.'

'Tin mining?' she asked in the awkward silence.

He turned back, his expression once more under control. 'Coal.'

'Did you work in the mine?'

'As a hewer?' He shook his head. 'I wasn't strong enough, then. I did later. Alongside the men in my uncle's mine. My mother's brother. He believed a man should learn every part of a business he intended to follow. The way he had.'

'Even the heir to an earldom?'

He smiled a little, as if amused by a recollection. The atmosphere in the carriage lightened. His face looked younger, more boyish. 'Especially the heir to an earldom. He is not a great respecter of nobility. He thinks they are all soft and idle.'

'Is that what you think?' she dared to ask.

He gave her question consideration. 'I think there is good and bad in every class of society.'

As did she. Strange how they were in accord on some things and so at odds on others. Like the inheritance, for example, she thought grimly.

He leaned forwards, picked up her gloved hand from her lap and held it his. He massaged her palm with his thumb. The bleakness was entirely gone from his face, and now his expression was pure seduction. 'Have you thought any more about our future?'

The stroke of his thumb was scrambling her thoughts. Her body was vibrating with longing, her pulse jumping. She swallowed. Forced her mind to focus. '*Our* future? I have certainly thought about my own.'

His eyes danced, as if she amused him. 'You cannot think about one and not dwell on the other. Don't take too long to come to a decision.'

'Why?'

The caress ceased, though he did not release her hand. If anything, his fingers closed tighter around it. He fixed her with his inscrutable gaze. 'It's a matter of life and death, isn't it?'

Dumbly she stared at him, taken aback by his frankness.

'What is holding you back?' He moved from his side of the carriage to hers and suddenly the seat felt a great deal smaller. The way his shoulders took up all the space and his thigh pressed against hers. He still had her hand, too. She gave it a gentle tug, but he didn't seem to notice. Instead, he eased down the leather at her wrist. 'You can't deny the spark of attraction between us.' He raised her hand to his mouth and breathed on the sensitive skin where he had pulled the leather apart. She shivered.

He kissed the pulse that now raced beneath her skin. Traced the fine blue veins of her inner wrist with his tongue. 'What can I do to persuade you?'

'You didn't want this marriage,' she managed to gasp.

'The benefits are becoming more and more apparent.' His voice was deep and dangerously seductive. Her eyelids drooped, her limbs felt heavy. She forced herself to straighten.

'I would never be your choice of a wife, if your grandfather hadn't drawn up his will this way. Would I?' Breathlessly she waited for his answer, hope a small fragile thing in her breast.

He raised his gaze from her wrist to her face. His silver eyes glittered. 'If we had met somewhere, you mean—in a ballroom in London?' His mouth quirked downwards. 'I will not do you a disservice and lie. I had no intention of marrying. Not yet. Not until the future was secure. But given the circumstances, it is not such a bad arrangement.'

Cold rippled across her skin. 'And what of love, my lord?'

He chuckled then, deep and low. It was a surprisingly pleasant sound. And his face looked more handsome, less of a devil.

'Miss Wilding. Mary. May I call you Mary?'

Breathless to hear his reply, she nodded her assent.

He tilted his head as if seeing her for the first time, then shook it. 'My dear Mary, you will not convince me that a rational logical woman such as yourself believes in such romantic nonsense.'

Oh, but she did. She did not think she loved this man, though she knew she was attracted to him. Desired him.

But was it enough on which to base a marriage? Others did. But she wasn't others.

She gazed up into his dark features, searching those silver-grey eyes, and realised that this was not the sort of man she had ever imagined in her life. She'd dreamed of a scholarly man. A gentle man, who would listen to her thoughts. Who would respect her ideas. Not this dark dangerous man who set her pulse fluttering and her body longing for wicked things.

Her insides gave a tiny little pulse of pleasure at the thought of those wicked things.

But she should think with her mind. Her rational mind. Just as a man would.

'What if at some time in the future you meet a woman you really wished to marry? Will not your resentment be great?'

He cupped her face in his hands, his large warm hands, and she felt the tremble in his fingers, as if he was struggling under some emotion as his gaze searched her face.

She could not help but look at his finely drawn lips before she raised her gaze to look at his face where she found the heat of desire in his eyes. 'My lord,' she whispered.

'Bane,' he rasped. 'Call me Bane.'

But she couldn't speak, because his mouth had taken hers in a ravening kiss and, lord help her, she was kissing him back, running her hands over his shoulders, tangling her fingers with his hair. He lifted her on to his lap and she felt his strong thighs beneath her bottom. The way he rocked lightly into her, and the deep groan from his throat, stirred her blood and made her heart beat too fast.

It felt as if his hot mouth was all over her and her skin was on fire from its touch.

'Marry me, Mary,' he whispered against her throat.

'Marry me,' he said, undoing the buttons of her coat and pressing his lips to her clavicle.

The carriage jolted, swaying over to one side, and he grabbed her around the shoulders to prevent her from falling. Then it came to a halt.

Bane cursed softly. 'We will continue this conversation later.' He lifted her off his lap and set her back on the seat.

The hard cold man was back. The man she recognised. And as she did up her buttons and straightened her hair, she could not help but wonder how much the passionate man was really him.

The groom opened the door. Bane picked up his gloves and his hat and stepped out. He reached up to help her down. His glance was swift and assessing. His brief nod assured her that she did not look as if she'd been ravished, though her lips still tingled from his kiss and her cheeks glowed from the scratch of his jaw.

And then the noises assaulted her ears.

A constant thumping she could feel vibrating under her feet and pounding through her head.

His lordship shook hands with Mr Trelawny, who was standing waiting for them. The poor man's eyes widened when they rested on her, but he smiled manfully. 'Miss Wilding,' he said, shouting to be heard above the noise of the great machine some distance away. 'I was not expecting you today, but welcome to Old Men's Wheal, as it was called once. I hope your…' He glanced down at her feet, then coloured. 'I hope you are quite recovered from your unfortunate accident.'

She smiled at the young man. 'But for you, Mr Trelawny, I doubt I would be here to tell the tale,' she said, leaning close to his ear to make herself heard.

The young man's colour deepened.

Bane surprised her by swiftly catching her hand, pulling her close and putting it on his arm. 'Show us the workings, Trelawny.' He did not raise his voice, but clearly the manager heard for he nodded and gestured for them to follow. He led them to the machine making all the noise.

'Stampers,' he yelled.

Bane's gaze swept over the monstrous structure, a beam supported on legs. Heavy metal tubes hanging from the beam on chains, rising up and down alternately, each one crashing down to crush the rocks shoved beneath it by a couple of men.

Driving the whole was an enormous waterwheel that clanked and creaked, adding to the cacophony. Beyond it three large pools were being stirred by women with long rakes and shovels.

Compared to the beauty of the countryside through which they had passed, it was ugly and dirty. And the noise was horrendous. She could not imagine working with that sound all day.

As far as she could see there were no children.

She put her hands over her ears, but it did nothing to lessen the noise. 'From here, the black tin is taken to the foundry at Hayle. You should visit it some time,' Mr Trelawny shouted.

Bane nodded. 'Where do they get the coal?' This time even he had to raise his voice.

'Wales.'

He grimaced.

'The mine is this way,' Mr Trelawny said. 'Up the hill. The carriage will take you up to the entrance, Miss Wilding.'

'We will all go in the carriage,' Bane said when they reached it.

How strange. She let him help her back in. Mr Trelawny climbed up with the driver, citing the dust and dirt he had gathered from his visit to the workings earlier that morning. Getting ready for the new owner's visit, no doubt.

Bane dropped the window and the noise of the stamper continued to assault their ears. 'Imagine living with that din day after day,' she said. 'Those poor men. They must go home with a headache.'

He cast her a sharp glance. 'They are paid well enough.'

She pressed her lips together. She had no wish to start an argument, but she had to be glad there had been no children working near that noisy machine.

As the carriage wound its way to the other side of the hill, the thumping faded to a bearable level. It was more like the sound of a heart beating loudly from this distance.

The carriage once more halted and they stepped down. The view of the surrounding countryside was breathtaking—open common, trees in the valley, sheep on the moor—but right here, on the side of the hill, industry was an ugly scar. Bare rock. Gravel. A horse walking steadily round and round a revolving drum. Every now and again, a bucket full of rocks would appear at the surface to be emptied into the back of a cart by a couple of workers. No doubt those rocks would end up at the stamper.

Another horse went round and round, pulling a chain, and beside it a strange-looking object spurted water into a ditch.

'A rag-and-chain pump,' Mr Trelawny explained, 'to remove water from the shafts. Let us go down. The men are expecting us. Please be careful where you walk, Miss Wilding. The ground is rough and there are some disused shafts here and there from the ancient workings.'

At her nervous glance, he smiled. 'If you stay close to me at all times, you will be fine.'

Bane shot him a glare and Trelawny flinched.

'This way,' he said, hustling them towards a stone structure. It looked a bit like a square Norman tower, without crenellations or arrow loops. He ducked inside and, after glancing around, Bane urged her to follow with his hand at the small of her back. The stone chamber was lit by candles.

Mary immediately recognised the greasy smell of melting tallow. They'd been forced to use tallow in the kitchens and working areas at the school when money was in short supply—or apparently in short supply. She felt a little trickle of resentment at the thought, but had no time to think about it, because Mr Trelawny was directing her to a wooden trestle around the wall. 'You'll need boots,' he said, sorting through a small pile. 'It is muddy down there.'

As she sat down and her eyes adjusted to the smoky light, she noticed the large gaping hole before her and the flimsy-looking rope ladder leading down into the depths.

'You will need a hat, my lord,' Trelawny said, handing him a battered-looking felt object with a candle stuck in a lump of something nasty-looking on the front of it. 'You, too, Miss Wilding.' He frowned. 'You will have to remove your bonnet.'

She looked at him and looked at the ladder and looked back at him. 'How far down does it go?'

'The first adit is about twenty feet down. Not far at all, miss. Old Jem is waiting at the bottom for us. There's other parts of the mine where the depth is close to one-hundred-and-eighty feet.'

She felt a little faint at the thought of going into the bowels of the earth a mere twenty feet. 'Why don't I wait up here for your return? I am not really dressed for climbing down ladders.'

'I should have loaned you a pair of my breeches,' Bane said and there was a teasing note to his voice.

When she looked at him, he was smiling. And looking quite at home. 'Come now, Miss Wilding, I thought you had more gumption. It was your idea to come.' He actually looked as if he was enjoying himself. And he seemed to want to include her. It was quite a revelation.

'I didn't know about the ladder,' she said weakly. 'I don't think my ankle is up to it.' It was the first thing that came into her mind.

'You haven't let that stop you in the past. I will carry you down.'

Why was he being so insistent? 'You couldn't possibly.' She shuddered.

'You are no heavier than a hod of coal and I have carried a few of them in my time. Come on, Miss Wilding. Buck up.' Before she knew what he was about, he had lifted her off her feet and tossed her over his shoulder. 'Don't move now, Miss Wilding, or we will both fall.' He heaved one leg over the side of the hole, grasping on to the railing. He paused. 'Light my candle for me, would you, Trelawny?' he said with great good cheer.

Never had she felt so undignified. Or so foolish. Oh lord, that was his hand on her posterior. Holding her steady? Was he going to climb down using only one hand? 'Really, my lord. I would be quite happy to wait up here for your return.'

'You must think I am a complete fool, Miss Wilding, if you think I am letting you out of my sight for more than a minute so far from the Abbey.'

Oh, drat. He thought she intended to run away. He began to descend and she pressed her teeth into her lip to stop herself from crying out in fear and clutched on to the tails of his coat. The walls of the shaft glowed softly in the light of the tallow candle on his hat and after a while she began to relax. His movements were lithe and sure and his body in perfect balance. She trusted him. In this, at least.

After what seemed like a very long time with his shoulder pressing beneath her ribs and making it hard to breathe, but was probably only a minute or so, another light appeared. Several, in fact, dotted here and there on ledges around a wide cave.

Her ears were filled with the sound of rushing water. It echoed off the walls, yet sounded far off.

Bane set her carefully on her feet, held her for a moment while she found her balance, then stepped back.

Mr Trelawny jumped down beside her.

A bent and bowed figure appeared out of the dark. He had a clay pipe in one hand and a disapproving expression. 'For what brought 'ee a woman down here? Bad luck it is.'

Mary stared back up the ladder and was able to see a faint glimmer way above them. The candles.

'Don't be foolish, man,' Bane said. 'Miss Wilding is the owner of this mine. If she wishes to look at her property, she has every right. Besides, women are only unlucky on ships.'

Mary's jaw dropped at his quick defence and at his announcement of her ownership.

The old man grumbled under his breath. 'She ain't got a light.'

'She does,' Mr Trelawny said, producing another of the hats. 'If you would just slip your bonnet off, Miss Wilding, let it hang by the strings, if you will, and you can put this on.'

She did as he suggested and he tied on the stiff felt hat, pushing it down hard, then lighting the candle. She was surprised at how much better she could see around her. 'Thank you.'

'Try to keep you head down as we go through the tunnels. They are low in places and while the hat will protect you somewhat, you can still get a nasty bruise if you are not careful. Follow Old Jem there and I will bring up the rear. Not too fast, now, Jem. I don't want anyone getting lost.'

'No indeed,' Bane said. 'Miss Wilding, hold on to my coat-tails if you please. I shall feel better if I know where you are at all times.'

The strange little cavalcade set off, stopping now and then when Mr Trelawny called out to Jem to stop so he could point out items of interest. Bane seemed greatly interested in each tiny detail.

'Where are the men working?' she asked on the third-such stop.

'Further along, Miss Wilding. They are hewing and hauling today. I thought it best we didn't use any black powder during your visit. We will find them near the horse-whim stope.'

When she looked at him blankly, he smiled. 'Whim means the drum turned by the horse to bring the buckets up. Stope refers to where we dig it out. There is a significant lode of ore in that part of the mine.' He pointed to a dark seam of rock running along the tunnel. 'This is also ore. Blue peach, we call it. But it is pretty well worked out and what is left is of poor quality. Further on, the lode is heavy with tin.'

'Then let us go there, since it is what Miss Wilding wishes to see,' Bane said.

And they set off again. In places the tunnel was narrow and low and both she and Bane had to duck to avoid the sharp rocks in the roof. Once her bonnet got hooked up on a promontory and Mr Trelawny had to set her free. They laughed about it, while his lordship, unable to help from where he stood, simply glowered at them. And what a glower it was with the flickering light of their candles bouncing off the rough granite walls and the brim of his hat throwing his eyes into deep shadow. Why, he looked almost jealous.

She shivered. And it wasn't an entirely unpleasant sensation. It seemed that his seductive words in the carriage had infected her body.

To prevent getting hooked up again, she untied the ribbons of her bonnet, retied them and hung it over her arm. 'I'm ready,' she said at his lordship's impatient sigh.

A short while later, the tunnel opened out and all around her were moving pinpoints of light and the sounds of shovelling overpowering the background noise of running water. It was a bit like watching Oberon's fairies, until you realised that the sparkling lights were attached to rough felt hats worn by men shovelling rocks into iron buckets. And lads running from smaller tunnels and crevasses with wooden wheelbarrows. Small boys of eight or nine.

Work stopped as they realised that their visitors had arrived. There were some startled looks between the miners as they realised they had a woman in their midst and then some touching of forelocks and awkward bobbing of heads at her and Bane.

'This is the shift foreman, Michael Trethewy,' Mr Trelawny said. 'Lord Beresford. Miss Wilding.'

Another very Cornish name. These people had lived in this isolated part of the country for centuries. The man himself was big and brawny. He bowed to Mary and looked surprised when Bane held out his hand, but shook it anyway with a ham of a hand. The two men stared into each other's eyes for a moment with a measuring look and then released the shake. Both looked satisfied with what they had discovered from that brief contact.

A meeting of like minds. Mary inwardly shrugged. Men had their own secret codes, Sally had said. This must be one of them. She was more interested in the condition of the boys pushing those heavy barrows. While the foreman introduced Bane to the other men and they talked about lodes and weights and percentages and even black powder, Mary followed one of the boys into a side tunnel. It came to a dead end. A man lying on his back picked away at the roof. Rock fell around him and the boy shovelled it into his barrow.

They looked up at the appearance of Mary's light. The man struggled to stand. 'Please,' she said. 'Don't let me interrupt, but the rest of the men are back there, meeting his lordship. The new earl.'

'Aye. I ought to have come.' He wiped his face on his sleeve. 'Me and the boy had a bet on that we could finish out this stope by day's end. I forgot about the visit.' To her surprise, he sounded a little resentful.

'Are we interrupting?'

'The lad is paid by the barrowful. He's the only one in his family working after his da's accident.'

The boy ducked his head. He looked healthy enough, if a little pale. So why was he anxious?

She crouched down to meet his gaze full on and to ease the ache in her back from stooping over. 'Do you find it hard, pushing that barrow?'

'I'm stronger than I look,' he said defensively. 'I don't need Peter to break the rocks, not really.' He looked anxiously at his companion.

'I do my share.' The man's face looked sullen.

'I am sure you do. Both of you.' She couldn't quite grasp why she was ruffling their feathers. 'Is it good working here at this wheal?' She was proud that she had remembered the correct word. 'Are you treated well?'

If anything the man looked even more sullen, perhaps even suspicious. Perhaps because she was a woman. Perhaps he was worried about bad luck.

'We haven't had our pay this month,' the boy blurted out. 'The men aren't happy.'

The man hushed him with a look.

'Why is that?'

'We hear the old earl's will is all tied up,' the man said.

Oh, Lord, did that mean there was no money to pay these men until she was married? She couldn't believe that was so. She would have to tackle Bane about it. No, not Bane, his lordship.

'I am sure Lord Beresford will sort something out as quickly as possible,' she said. Was this the reason for his emphatic proposal?

The man shrugged. 'We best be going to pay our respects, lad, or be found lacking.' He sounded a little bitter. 'After you, miss.'

She could do no more than make her way back to the cavern, where she found Bane and Trelawny deep in conversation with a couple of men as they stared at yet another of those blue veins in the rock. There were pink veins, too, she noticed, and white ones. The veins did not run straight along the walls but at an angle. She followed one of the pink ones with her gaze, it glistened in the light of her candle as it disappeared into another, even smaller tunnel. She decided to see where it led.

A short way along was another of those horrid shafts, with a ladder disappearing into the darkness above her head. No candles glimmering up there from this one. An old disused entrance, perhaps.

With her fingertips running along the rough rock, she

turned a sharp corner. Here the tunnel divided. Something about this configuration seemed familiar, as if she had been here before. Was that a light she saw in the distance? Another man working, unaware that the new earl had arrived and wishful to meet him?

Should she let him know? Would he be equally unfriendly? She decided to take the other fork.

This tunnel was much darker, the air stuffy, yet cold. The sound of running water drowned out any noises from the cavern behind her. The tunnel was getting lower and narrower and the terrain rougher under her feet. Time to go back. This must be a disused part of the mine.

As she halted, she saw the lip of yet another shaft. This one right in front of her feet, going down. Only a small ledge on one side allowed for passage. Ugh. She was not going to think about going around it.

The air stirred behind her. The hair on her nape rose. She started to swing around. 'Who—?'

'You little fool,' a harsh voice whispered in her ear. A hand shoved her in the middle of her back and she was falling.

Chapter Ten

She grabbed for the edge of the hole and managed to catch it. Heart in her throat, blood rushing in her ears, she dug with her toes, seeking purchase.

'Help me,' she croaked.

There was a soft laugh and then silence. Somehow she knew she was alone. And she could not hold on. Slowly, her weight was dragging her down. Where was the ladder? She could feel nothing but the smooth sides of the shaft. There. Her knee hit something jutting out from the wall. Her arms trembled with the effort of holding her weight. They weakened. Then gave out. Her fingernails scrabbled to hold on. She was slipping. Falling.

Only to stop with a jerk. She was caught. By her elbow. Not her elbow, the bonnet strings hooked over her arm. She was dangling from her bonnet. She grabbed on to the strings with her other hand.

Gasping for breath, sobs forced their way up into her throat. *No. Don't panic. Think.* Those ribbons were not going to hold her for very long. Carefully she turned her head, letting the light from her candle show her what her feet had missed. The ladder. Just off to her right. The ropes looked frayed and rotten. Not strong at all, but it was her only chance.

Carefully she inched one foot over to the closest rung. She got her foot into it. Then her other foot. She had to let go of the ribbons, her only lifeline, and reach for the ladder.

What if it wouldn't hold her weight?

Don't be afraid, a soft female voice said in her head. *Do it.*

It was the same voice she had heard in her dream.

She let go of the ribbons and grabbed for the rope with her right hand. Got it. Shifted her weight on to the ladder, then let go of the ribbons and grabbed on with her left hand. With a whisper, the strings, lightened of their burden, slid off the spike. Her bonnet fluttered into the darkness below.

The ladder gave an ominous creak.

She gasped and clung on for dear life, frozen in place.

Do not panic. Climb. Slowly. Three rungs. That was all she needed to climb. Gritting her teeth, swallowing her sobbing breaths, she made the painful ascent.

And then her head was above the lip of the shaft.

Oh, God, what if the person who had pushed her was still there? There was nothing she could do. She had to get up and out. She forced herself up the next rung and then threw her body over the edge. The next moment she was rolling away from that dreadful hole and lying gasping on the floor of the tunnel. Rocks were digging in her stomach. Her hands were burning. But she was alive. She dragged herself to the tunnel wall and sat leaning against it, gasping for breath.

And then she realised the way back was on the other side of that horrible hole. She gazed at the ledge and her body shook. She could not cross. She could not.

Slowly her pulse returned to normal and her breathing eased. She felt the chill of sweat cooling on her face and down the centre of her back. She could not stay here. She had to do something. Call for help? But she kept hearing that voice in her ear. The triumph. *You little fool.* That deep, dark whisper. It could have been anyone. Her heart clenched.

He wouldn't.

But he had. *Mary, stop being such a trusting idiot.* There was no other explanation. She hadn't agreed to marry him, hadn't fallen for his seduction, so he'd decided to take his drastic action.

She'd walked right into his trap. No wonder he had seemed so willing to bring her along to the mine, when previously he had seemed opposed to the idea. She should have known a man like him wouldn't really want her, a spinsterish schoolmistress. It had been all a ruse to get his own way.

And for some stupid reason, there was a terrible ache in her chest. It felt as if a hole had opened up and she wanted to cry.

The candle spluttered, then died.

Her misery was complete. Now she was alone and in the dark, with a murderer lurking somewhere about. She leaned back against the rough wall and closed her eyes, holding back the tears that wanted to run down her face. Why, oh, why had she given in to her longings for a home, a husband of her own, given in to the hope that somewhere in the world there might be a smidgeon of love just for her?

She swiped at her face with the heel of her hand. She'd shed enough tears over what she could not have. She would not shed any more.

She opened her eyes. To her surprise a light glimmered off in the distance, a soft sort of glow. Like the one in her dream. She pushed to her feet and, bent double at times, followed the source of the light.

It wasn't long before she realised that it wasn't men working and it wasn't the ghost of the White Lady leading her astray. It was daylight.

Wonderful daylight.

On her hands and knees now, splashing through freezing water that trickled down the walls and turned into a rivulet, she crawled out on to the hillside. She was out.

She collapsed and lifted her face to the sky, inhaled deep breaths of cold air and thanked God. Slowly her brain started to function. First, she took an inventory of her person.

Her knees were scraped, her skirts torn and soaking wet, her hands hurting. Her cotton gloves had been shredded by the rocks and her fingertips were raw and a couple of them were bleeding. She was still trembling inside, still shaken to her very core. But she was alive.

What had happened made no sense. Why had he been so seductive, talking of marriage on the carriage ride here, if he had intended to kill her? Or had he meant only to allay her fears?

Did she go back to the mine and face him? Or did she get as far away from here as possible? Wasn't now her chance to leave, when they would have discovered her missing and be busy searching in the dark?

You little fool. She'd be a fool to stay.

Hot moisture trickled down her face. She dashed the tears away. She didn't even know why she was crying, why she felt so betrayed. She'd known all along he hated the idea of their marriage.

The pretty words, the hot gazes, the kisses—they'd all been designed to allay her suspicions. And she'd let female sensibility overcome good sense, just as he'd no doubt planned.

She struggled to her feet, tossed her miner's hat aside and made for the nearest stone wall. For once, luck led her in the right direction. It was the wall that lined each side of the road up to the mine. After a while, she found a farmer's gate into the road. Now if she was really lucky a farmer would come along in a cart and offer her a ride.

She half-walked, half-ran along the rutted lane. How long would he search for her underground? How long would he keep up the pretence of looking for someone he already knew to be at the bottom of a deep hole?

At the sound of bridles jingling and the grind of wheels, she spun about. It wasn't the hoped-for farmer's cart, it was a carriage. His carriage. He wasn't searching the mine, he was sitting beside the coachman, driving his team straight towards her. He wasn't searching for her, at all. Why would he waste his time, when he had thought he knew where she was?

Dizziness washed through her, the world seemed to spin around her head, the grey clouds, the distant thumping of machines pounding in her ears. She should never have followed the road. She should have cut across country. And then she was falling. Falling into darkness.

When she came to her senses, she was in the carriage. It was rocking on its springs, tearing along at breakneck speed. And she was alone, lying on the seat with a blanket over her and a cushion beneath her head.

Where were they going? Where was Beresford?

She sat up, her head spun and she put a hand to temples that ached. A glance out of the carriage window told her they were pulling into the Abbey's drive.

Her stomach sank to her shoes. She was back in his power. Back where he could do with her as he willed.

The carriage pulled up outside the great door to the Abbey. The driver leapt down in a crunch of gravel and wrenched open the door.

Beresford.

She covered her mouth with a shaking hand at the look of fury he cast her. Anger flashed in his eyes. 'You little fool.'

The words were like a knife piercing her heart.

She should have gone across the fields when she had the chance.

'You are right,' she said in a low voice. 'I am a fool.' Because she hadn't wanted to believe he wished her dead. She looked at him. 'I was a fool to trust you.'

She ignored his hand and stepped down from the coach and, head held high, marched in through the front door held open by Manners.

The butler's eyes widened in shock at the sight of her. 'I'll send Betsy to your room, miss,' he said, sounding concerned.

'Thank you.' She didn't look back. Didn't care to. If she did, she might cry, and she wasn't going to do that. Not over him.

Nor would she go to dinner. Sit there being pleasant to a man who had tried to drop her down a deep hole in the ground? Certainly not.

But would he suspect that she realised that it was him? As it was, she should not have said that about not trusting him.

Very well, she would tell him she'd been angry because she thought he was leaving without her instead of searching. Again the bitterness rose like bile in her throat. And the fear. Of course, he wouldn't search when he assumed he'd succeeded.

She wouldn't let him get away with trying to kill her, now she was sure. She was going to find a constable. Or a magistrate.

What if they wouldn't believe her? What if they brought his supposed ward right back here? Then she wouldn't go to the authorities. She would just disappear. Tonight. It might be her last chance.

Betsy popped her head around the door. 'I brought some salve for your poor hands, miss.'

Betsy had been horrified at the sight of her hands and knees when she'd help Mary bathe. It was that soaking in the tub that had got Mary's brain working again. Returned her power of logic.

She smiled. 'Thank you.'

Betsy smiled back. 'A parcel came from Mrs Wharton while you were out today. A new gown. It is a lovely deep rose.'

Mary stared at her. 'I didn't order another gown.'

'His lordship did. He was tired of seeing you in the same gown for dinner, Mrs Wharton's girl said.'

His lordship was tired of seeing her. Full stop. She turned away, worried that her expression might give away the welling feeling of sadness. So his lordship had ordered her a gown. Then she would wear it. And let him make of that what he would.

After dressing in the low-necked, high-waisted gown with its pretty velvet ribbons, she gave Betsy free rein with her hair, as she planned her departure for after midnight.

'It has started snowing, miss,' Betsy said between teeth full of pins. 'We don't get snow very often in these parts. The children will be out playing in it tomorrow.'

'You sound as if you would like to join them,' Mary said looking up. She gasped at the sight of herself in the mirror. Betsy had turned her straight hair into a confection of ringlets and curls. 'Oh, Betsy, that is amazing.'

'Thank you, miss.'

'You really should be a lady's maid.'

Betsy beamed. 'Yours, I hope, miss?'

'We'll have to see,' she said, hating knowing she must disappoint the girl.

She got up from the stool in front of the dresser and gazed at the wall. How on earth could she escape, knowing that at any moment his lordship could walk through that wall and catch her out?

Her glance fell on the little history book on her side table. It had drawings of the old Abbey. And maps. She had forgotten about the maps. Perhaps they held the key.

She picked the book up and looked at the last few pages. There were plans of the house. Each floor in detail. And odd little markings, little dotted lines running along beside some of the walls. Along the walls of her room and the one above. Those dotted lines connected each of the towers, and then carried on to where the cliffs and the sea were marked.

The caves under the house.

It also showed a passage from the cellars to the old ruins.

Had the earl seen these maps, when he had glanced at this book? She hoped not.

'Gloves, miss,' Betsy said. 'It is a good thing you bought more than one pair. The ones from this afternoon were ruined.'

'Thank you, Betsy. Thank you for all you have done for me since I have been here.'

Betsy beamed. 'Do you need me to walk you down to the drawing room, miss?'

Mary smiled. 'No. Do you know, I think I have finally got the hang of it.' Right when she was ready to leave.

When she arrived at the drawing room, the Hamptons were there and Jeffrey, but there was no sign of the earl.

Manners entered shortly after she did. 'His lordship sent his regrets,' he said. 'He will not be dining tonight.'

A rush of relief shot through Mary.

Jeffrey held his arm out for his aunt and Gerald escorted Mary. 'How was your visit to the mine?' her dinner companion asked when they were seated.

'Very interesting.'

'Dangerous place, mines,' Mrs Hampton said. 'I am surprised his lordship let you go. You did not actually go inside, did you, Miss Wilding?'

The irony struck a nerve and she had to force herself not to laugh. 'I did.'

'I say,' Jeffrey said. 'Good for you. I shall have to ask old Trelawny for a tour myself. I didn't think they allowed people to walk around down there. Gerald and I used to sneak in there as lads, but the old manager wasn't nearly as particular as Trelawny.'

'I am a part-owner,' she pointed out.

Mrs Hampton gave a disapproving sniff.

'I heard you got lost down there,' Gerald said.

Mary stared at him. 'How did you hear such a thing?'

'Some of the men were talking in the inn. They said his lordship was in a proper temper that you had wandered off.' His gaze held speculation.

Anger rose hot inside her, but she filled her mouth with meat and let the act of chewing and swallowing before she answered cool her temper. 'I got lost.'

'There are a lot of old workings,' he said, looking at her rather strangely. 'Some of them go very deep. They are quite dangerous.'

'You were lucky you didn't fall down one of the old shafts,' Jeffrey remarked. 'I hear some of them date back to the dark ages. A couple of men from the village have lost their lives in them over the years.'

'Next you will be telling me the place is haunted,' she said with a sugary smile and a pretended shiver.

'Oh, no,' Gerald said blithely. 'I've never heard tales of ghosts in the mine.'

'Then perhaps it was a guardian angel who helped me find my way out.'

'I expect you just followed your nose,' Jeffrey said dismissively.

The door crashed open. The earl stood on the threshold.

Her heart gave a familiar jolt, then dipped as she recalled his perfidy.

'I hope I am not interrupting,' he said smoothly, looking at Mary.

'Not at all.' She gave him the benefit of that sugary smile and was pleased when his eyes widened. 'I thought you weren't joining us for dinner.'

His lordship gave her a piercing stare. 'I'm not.' He sat down at the head of the table. Mary was glad she was at the other end, opposite Gerald, for the earl had a glitter about his eyes and a set look to his jaw that did not bode well. He was looking at her with angry suspicion, no doubt frustrated at the failure of his plan. She focused on the food on her plate. If she looked at him, she might give away her anger. Her rage.

He waved off the plate that Manners offered him and poured himself a glass of the burgundy from the decanter near his elbow. He leaned back in his chair and, against her will, Mary found her gaze drawn to him, to the form of the man. The solid strength. The way his coat hugged his manly shoulders.

She forced her gaze back to her plate.

No one said a word.

It was as if his presence had dampened any pretence of civilised conversation.

Mrs Hampton signalled to Manners to clear the table. 'Will you take tea in the drawing room with me, Miss Wilding?' she asked as she rose and the gentlemen followed suit.

'Miss Wilding is otherwise engaged,' Beresford said. He glowered at the two younger men. 'Why don't you two fellows go off for your usual game of billiards and leave me and Miss Wilding to our conversation?'

The chairs went back and the cousins followed Gerald's mother out of the room.

Cowards.

But she didn't really blame them. She wished she could follow them, but she seemed to be pinned to her chair by that bright steely gaze fixed on her face. He gestured for the servants to leave.

Her mouth dried. She could hear her heart beating faster than she would like. He looked different tonight, less controlled. He sipped at his wine, watching her over the rim. A muscle ticked in the side of his face. 'What the devil did you think you were doing?'

She sat bolt upright in her chair. 'I beg your pardon?'

'Running off like that when my back was turned.'

It took a moment for her to understand. And then the answer came to her. He was making out that he thought she had tried to run away. How very clever of him. Did he think she would play along with his pretence? She pressed her lips together and lifted her chin.

He glared at her. 'Why go to such trouble, when you knew I would fetch you back?'

It would have been a miracle if he could have brought her back from the dead. She bit her tongue. She must not arouse his suspicions. Not let him know that she understood full well what he was up to. 'I got lost.' She watched his face for a reaction. All she got was a sound of derision.

'Believe what you will,' she said calmly, keeping her gaze steady with his.

'Then it seems I owe you an apology, Miss Wilding,' he drawled.

She could not imagine he was apologising for pushing her down a hole in the ground. 'Why?'

'Why what?'

'Why do you owe me an apology?'

He pushed his chair back and in a few lithe strides came to stand by her chair, looming, dark, still angry. He made her feel very small indeed. And that was quite a feat.

'I apologise for assuming you had broken your word and left without informing me.' He sounded as if he didn't believe what he was saying.

Because he knew it wasn't true. He knew she'd only wandered a little way down one of the tunnels. 'Apology accepted,' she said with remarkable calm. 'What made you seek me on the road?'

'One of the men said he glimpsed someone climbing the ladder. I was surprised not to find you in the courtyard.'

'Did he now?' She could not keep the sarcasm from her voice.

He gave her a puzzled look. 'He did.'

'All is well that ends well, then.'

He glowered. 'From now on, I will be keeping a very close eye on you, madam.'

She almost groaned out loud. 'If it will stop me from getting lost, I would much appreciate it.'

His eyes narrowed. 'Don't think to play your tricks off on me.'

'My tricks. What tricks would those be?'

'You know very well what I am talking about.'

'Was there anything else you wanted to say to me?'

He looked as if he wanted to throttle her. 'Not at this moment.'

'Then if you will excuse me, I will retire.'

'No.'

'I beg your pardon?'

'No I will not excuse you. We will go to the drawing room, take tea like sensible people, and enjoy some civilised conversation.'

'I don't believe you know how to have a civilised conversation. How to give orders, yes. How to impose your will on others, yes. But conversation? Sadly not.'

A pained look flashed across his face as if her words had the power to wound. Hardly. Annoyance was what she was seeing, nothing else. Annoyance that she wasn't just falling willy-nilly in with his wishes.

'You will excuse me, my lord. It has been a long and tiring day. I have no wish for conversation, civilised or otherwise.'

She rose to her feet. He stood up. As always, she was taken aback by the sheer size of him. The width of him. The height. She had to lift her chin to gaze into his eyes, to show him her determination. And he did not give, not one inch.

He gazed back, his eyes cold. 'You speak as if I am the one at fault for your weariness, Miss Wilding.' His mouth tightened. 'If you had stayed with your party—' He closed his eyes briefly. Took a breath as if mustering all of his patience. 'What is done is done. But understand, I will not have you wandering off again.'

'More commands? And where do you think I will go, my lord? I have no home, no relatives, no position of employment.'

'You do have one position.' His voice softened. 'Mary, after our conversation in the carriage I thought…I had the impression…'

She lifted her chin and allowed a chill to creep into her voice. 'What impression, my lord? That I had succumbed to your very obvious attempt at seduction?'

Pain filled his eyes. For once she had no trouble recognising his emotion and something horrid twisted inside her, like the blade of a knife slicing its way into her heart. Was she mad? She did not care if her words caused him pain. Could not.

She turned her face away, so she did not have to look into those fascinating silver-grey eyes, or to gaze on his handsome face. She was all too easily swayed by his wiles.

She was like a rabbit fascinated by the snake whose only intention was to make it the next meal. *Little fool.*

'If you will excuse me, my lord? I find myself exhausted by the day's events.'

He stepped back, frowning. 'Then I must bid you goodnight, Miss Wilding.'

He held out his hand for hers.

Reluctantly she accepted his courtesy, intending to rest her fingers lightly in his, but when his hand curled around it and he brought it up to his lips, she winced at the pain of it.

He tensed and glanced down. Before she could stop him he had gently peeled off her cotton glove and revealed the grazed skin and broken nails. His face hardened. 'These are the lengths to which you would go?'

The anger in his voice was unmistakable. He released her hand. Strode to the door, opening it. He paused. 'Miss Wilding, if there was any other way, believe me, I would not do this.'

Do what? Kill her? Was that supposed to make her feel better?

Her chest squeezed painfully.

Chapter Eleven

Back in her chamber, Mary picked up the little history book and turned to the maps. It clearly showed the tunnel to the old ruins. Hopefully it was in as good condition as the one running beside her chamber.

She put on her warmest gown, the last of the ones she had brought with her from Wiltshire, and donned her practical half-boots. She lay down on her bed to rest before it was time to leave, unable to stop herself from pondering Beresford's last words.

The bleakness in his voice had touched a chord deep inside her, started an ache. A feeling she was missing something important. Sometimes she felt as if he was speaking in riddles.

She shook the feeling off. He was playing her again, like a fish on a line. Turning her on her head. But each time she heard those whispered words in her head and what he had said when he jumped down from the carriage: *You little fool.* For some reason she could not match them up. It was as if the words were spoken by two different people, for two very different reasons.

Or was it simply his seductive kisses turning her upside down, making her want to believe he was not the cause of her fall? Her long, deliberately forgotten dreams of a home, a husband, children playing at her feet, a real family, conspiring to make her yearn to believe in his innocence, to believe the seduction and not the facts.

Why did she want to believe? Had her foolish heart done something she had sworn she would never do again—could it be possible she had fallen for him?

Despite everything she knew.

If so, she really deserved all that had happened.

A numbness crept into her chest. The sort of emptiness she'd felt after she'd learned the truth about Allerdyce, only deeper. Colder. It was the only way not to feel the pain of knowing he'd sooner kill her than marry her.

And so she must leave. Without regrets. Without feeling anything. She got up and carried her candle to the clock on the mantel. Two in the morning. The household would be asleep by now. She wrapped her cloak around her and pulled up the hood. She had no valise. Nothing to carry except her reticule and that she had tied around her waist under her skirts for safekeeping.

Quietly she opened her chamber door.

It creaked.

She held still, waiting, wondering if the alarm would be raised. Nothing. She opened it a little more. And then she saw him. Beresford. Sitting on the bottom of the circular stairs leading up to the room above.

She froze, waiting for him to leap up and force her back into her room.

His chest rose and fell in deep even breaths. She raised her candle higher and saw that his eyes were closed. He was sleeping, his head resting against the rough stone wall, his large body sprawled across the steps, in a sleep of utter exhaustion.

In sleep he looked so much younger, as if all the hard

lessons of life had been washed away and he was a boy again, with high hopes and sweet dreams. Her heart ached for that unsullied boy she had never met.

What was he doing here outside her door? Making sure she could not leave, obviously. Was that how he had arrived at her room so quickly the other night? No wonder he looked so weary if he had taken to sleeping here. One wrong sound and he would awaken and no doubt lock her up in her room.

She had to hurry, before he awoke and caught her. But somehow she could not drag herself away. She would never see him again and the sense of loss was almost more than she could bear.

Because, in spite of everything, in spite of the coldness he wore like armour against the world, she had glimpsed a softer and kinder side. And, yes, a vulnerable side that called to her in ways she did not understand, as well as a seductive side she found almost irresistible. Which she should not be thinking about now, but somehow she could not help it as she gazed at his face, at the small frown between his brows. He looked troubled and she wanted to smooth those cares away. She longed to press her lips to his lovely mouth and lose herself in his wonderful kiss.

She loved him.

The realisation filled her chest in the region of her heart with a sweet kind of ache.

Why not stay? Why not accept his offer of marriage? Perhaps in time, there would even be children despite what he had said. Had it not always been her dearest wish? A home. A family of her own.

And live her life knowing he would never return her love.

The thought sliced her heart to ribbons. She pressed a hand to her ribs to ease the terrible pain.

He stirred, shifting position, looking for ease he wouldn't find on the cold hard stone. If he awoke now, she would surely be lost. The next time he assaulted her with kisses and sweet seduction, she would be unable to resist.

To love and not be loved, it was all she had known. But with him it would be a disaster. She could feel it in her bones.

The was no other choice. She had to go.

Heavy-hearted, she crept over the threshold and closed the door behind her. Once more she glanced down at his sleeping form and had the wild urge to press her lips to his mouth. To bid him farewell. But she couldn't.

Instead she crept away, like a thief in the night, and took the stairs down to the cellar, the stairs he had brought her up that very first night, before either of them knew about the will. The first time he had kissed her.

She would never forget his kisses as long as she lived. When he was kissing her, she felt alive, like a different person, strong, sure and, heavens help her, beloved.

It was all a lie. A figment of her foolish longings. He didn't want her. He'd made it perfectly clear he didn't. He was being forced into this by a man he hated. And in time indifference might well turn to hate.

At the bottom of the stairs she turned left, away from the sound of the sea. Halfway along the wall, there was another sconce. Another entrance to yet another secret passage, if the map was correct. And this one would lead her outside to the old Abbey ruins.

She twisted the sconce.

Nothing happened.

Her heart rose in her throat. She'd got it wrong. Blast. She'd left the book in her room. She couldn't check the map. She'd been so sure she had memorised it correctly.

She glanced up and down the hallway, lifting her candle. There were no other sconces. She tried again. Twisting hard. She felt it shift. A little. It was stiff from disuse, perhaps.

She put the candle down and used both hands. The sconce turned painfully slowly. And the grinding noise echoed down the hallway. Heaven help her, Beresford would hear it. She had to hurry.

She wrenched it hard. The wall moved a little, then a little more, and then it opened fully. She picked up her candle and darted inside, found the mechanism on the other side and closed it behind her.

Now all she had to do was make it out to the ruins and run as fast as she could. And never look back.

The cold seeped into her bones. She felt as if she had been walking for hours, but she knew it was far less than that. Betsy had been right about the impending snow. It was up over her ankles and made walking difficult. And the wind seemed determined to impede her, too. It gusted this way and that, tearing at her cloak, blowing flurries of snow in her face so she couldn't see where she was going. Not that she could see much at all, it was so dark.

But if it was too dark to see her way, then it was too dark for anyone to find her. She clung to that hope and forged on. Going east. Keeping the wind on her right, as best as she could tell, because it constantly changed direction.

And she had to be correct, because the sound of the sea had faded away. She was heading into the countryside. Towards Halstead. Soon she should come across a road, with signposts and milestones and then she would be able to take her bearings.

She stopped to catch her breath, to look behind her for signs of pursuit. Nothing. Just the wind and the blowing snow. Hopefully his lordship was still sleeping outside her chamber door. He was going to be very angry when he awoke and found her gone. Hopefully that would not occur until later in the morning. She'd asked Betsy not to wake her too early, complaining of being tired.

It was all she could do.

She struggled on. The snow was drifting now. Getting deeper in some places and leaving the ground bare in others. And it also seemed to be lessening. She looked up at the sky and saw the glimmer of the moon through scudding clouds. Then a patch of stars.

The storm was over.

Her heart picked up speed. Even more reason to hurry. But now, with the moon casting light and shadow over the landscape at irregular intervals, she could see her way. See the line of a hedge that marked the edge of a field. See the moors rising in their white blanket off to her left. If she could just see the road. She looked around for a landmark. Something to tell her where she was. How far from the Abbey she had come.

Not far enough yet. She knew that. Not if his lordship was determined to find her. She would have to find a place to hide, somewhere he wouldn't look for her.

Again she glanced back over her shoulder. And gazed in horror. Oh, dear lord, what had she been thinking? That the snow would hide her? There, tracking across the field, was the dark imprint of where she had walked. She'd left the easiest trail for him to follow.

Wildly she glanced around her. She needed to find the road. Somewhere where other people walked and drove. Somewhere where her footsteps could not be identified.

She took careful stock of her surroundings and headed for the hedge where the snow was piling up on one side and clinging to the top and leaving the ground bare on her side.

Once in the lea of the hedge, with her footsteps no longer clearly visible to the most casual observer, she retraced her steps, going back on herself, hoping that he would not realise she would dare take such a risk.

She pulled her cloak around her, tried to ignore that her hands were freezing and her feet turning to blocks of ice and hurried on, taking the hedgerows, zigzagging in different directions, until she was dizzy, with no clue where she was. And still she did not find a single lane or road.

Yet there had to be one.

Had to be. She sank down to the ground to catch her breath, to think. She was exhausted. Tired. It would be just so easy to sleep for a while. To gain her strength.

Not a good idea, to sleep out here in the open. People froze to death under such circumstances. She had to find a place out of the wind. An inn. A barn. Any kind of structure. A flurry of snow stung her face. She frowned. Why was she panicking? The snow had been falling when she left the Abbey. It would have covered all traces of her footprints, and if these flurries kept up, then by morning there would be no sign for Bane to follow. Bane. She must not think of him as Bane. He was the Earl of Beresford. And a man who wished her at Jericho. Or worse.

She pushed herself to rise and took stock of her surroundings again. There. A barn. She could spend the rest of the night there and travel on in the morning. In daylight. She must have travelled five miles at least. Hopefully it was far enough for dawn would soon be upon her. Then she would get her bearings and move on. It would not be long before she was questioning Sally Ladbrook.

Filled with new purpose, she skirted the field, keeping to the hedges since they offered protection from the wind, and she was still concerned about leaving too easy a trail for the earl to follow.

The snow stopped again. The wind dropped, proving her caution correct. She inhaled deeply. There was something about the smell of the air. Cold. Crisp. Sparkling clean as it filled her lungs. She'd never inhaled anything quite like it. She rubbed her hands together to warm them as she walked.

Somewhere in the distance a dog barked. It sounded excited, as if it had been disturbed by an intruder. There must be a farmhouse or a village nearby. That was good news. Somewhere to aim for in the morning. Right now she just wanted to rest. To sleep. She shook her head to clear it. A few more yards and she would be able to lie down.

Another sound cut across the deep quiet. Hoofbeats. Travelling fast. She swallowed. Perhaps a traveller on a nearby road? In her heart, she knew it was not. She huddled deep against the hedge and looked back. A dark horse with its dark rider was cutting across the neighbouring field, heading straight for her, a dog bounding along at the horse's heels.

It couldn't be.

It was. It could be no one else. Hatless, his coat flying in the wind, it was Beresford. He hadn't seen her. He could not have. She picked up her skirts and ran for the barn, praying the door would be open. Praying he would not see her. Praying she could make it there before he cleared the hedge into this field.

And then she was there at the barn, huddled against the wall. The door was on her side. And closed.

She glanced over her shoulder. Beresford was coming up on the hedge. For the next moment or two he would be blind to her as he took the jump. She dashed to the door. To her great relief it opened and she slipped inside, closing the great door behind her. She scampered up the ladder to the loft, threw it down behind her and collapsed into the straw, breathing hard. Now all she had to do was remain as quiet as a mouse and pretend she wasn't here. She shivered. Despite her run, she was still freezing.

She took great gulping breaths of air in an attempt to fill her lungs and get her breathing back to normal as she listened to the sound of hoofbeats closing in on the barn. If she was lucky, he would keep on going, thinking she would have continued on without stopping.

The horse slowed and stopped.

Dash it. How had he guessed?

The dog whined, then barked.

The dog. He was using the dog to follow her. Inwardly she groaned. She had never considered the dog. That he would use it to hunt her like a wild animal had never occurred to her. And it should have. But she didn't know much about dogs and hunting. She had thought of Ranger as a pet, if she had thought of him at all. Since that first night the dog had not been seen anywhere in the house except his lordship's chamber.

Perhaps her disappearance up the ladder would fool the animal.

She lay still, jaw clamped, trying to stop her shivers, and listened to the barn door open, to the sound of a horse being led inside, to the excited barking of the dog.

'Mary,' Beresford called out in commanding tones, 'I know you are in here. Give up. Don't make me come and find you.'

She remained still, trying hard not to breathe. Trying not to let the sobs of fear welling in her throat and the cold seizing her limbs overcome her will to remain utterly silent.

'Down, Ranger,' he said.

The dog whined and was quiet.

She could imagine them down there, him in his great-coat glowering around the barn, listening, the dog at his feet. She strained to hear what he was doing over the sound of her banging heart.

Nothing. Not nothing—she could hear breathing. A laboured sort of panting. The horse. She held herself rigid, breathing in small sips of air, wondering if he could hear the pounding of her heart, while she knew he could not.

A click of metal against rock. An all-too-familiar sound of a tinder being struck. Light glowed through the floorboards. He must have found a lantern. She buried herself deeper in the straw, knowing in her heart it was hopeless.

She wanted to weep with frustration.

A thump.

She turned her head and saw, in the light cast by his lantern from below, the top of the ladder appear in the hole she had climbed through. If she pushed it away from the edge, it would pitch him to the ground.

She imagined his lifeless body sprawled on the paved floor beneath. It would be a fitting end. Except she could not make herself do it. She wasn't the murderer here.

His head appeared above the floor. He raised his lantern and she saw his dark ruffled hair, a face reddened by the wind, eyes filled with fury as he took her in. He leaped over the edge and stood before her. He set down the lantern, peeled off his gloves and stuffed them in his pocket.

Trapped. She backed up into the shadows, the blood rushing in her ears. They were all alone. What had he said that first day? *If I wanted to do away with you, I would not do it in front of witnesses.* There were no witnesses now.

She'd played right into his hands by running.

His expression softened. His mouth turning sultry as

he shook his head. 'You didn't think I would let you leave me, did you, sweetling?'

Bewildered by his words, she stared at him.

'You little fool,' he whispered tenderly. 'Why won't you trust me?'

She trembled at the sound of his voice. Shuddered from the cold in her bones. 'Say it again.'

He raised a brow. 'Trust me?'

'No.' Her voice shook. She could not imagine why she felt so desperate. So hopeful. 'Say "you little fool". Say it the way you did just now.'

A small smile curved his lips. 'You little fool,' he said softly.

It sounded nothing like the voice in the mine. His voice had its own special raspy quality she would recognise anywhere. He could not have been the one who had pushed her into the mineshaft. Could he? Her heart felt so certain, even if her logical mind refused to believe.

Which did she trust most?

There was a light in those pale-grey eyes, gladness mingled with the shadows of concern and something softer, more heartwarming. If she hadn't felt so cold, she might have been better able to understand what it was, but she was freezing, her body shaking, her teeth ready to chatter if she said one word.

She was too cold to feel fear.

'I—I'm s-s-sorry…' she got out.

'There will be time enough for sorry later,' he said, moving towards her.

Backing up, she tried a scornful laugh through her shivers. Pure bravado. 'I mean, I'm s-sorry you found me.'

His answering smile was so bright, steel-edged and glittering, her heart lurched. 'Not sorry enough, my dear. I can promise you that.'

He yanked her close, holding her tight with one arm around her shoulders, his mouth coming down hard on her lips. His tongue plundering the depths of her mouth. A punishing kiss. Searing. Possessive?

She certainly felt possessed, mind and body. Wild. Feverish as she responded to the hot pleasure of his kiss with a moan in the back of her throat. She didn't want to respond to him, to yield to the strength and his heat. Her mind knew it was a mistake, but he'd found her, and there was nothing she could do about it. It seemed she was helpless in the face of his seduction.

She couldn't fight the feelings inside her any longer. The traitorous longings. She twined her hands around his neck, felt his heat wash over her and breathed in the scent of snow among the essence of him. She loved the way he smelled. She let herself sink into the darkness of so many sensations she felt overwhelmed. Excitement. Longing. Desire.

His large hands roamed her shoulders, her back. It felt so good to be held. To feel the connection that strengthened with each passing moment. More especially delightful was his warmth. He pushed back her hood and cradled her face in his wonderfully warm hands. He pulled back from her, breathing hard. 'My God, you are freezing.' He touched her shoulders. 'And soaking wet.'

'It was snowing,' she said.

'I ought to put you over my knee and spank you,' he said through gritted teeth. 'Do you have any idea how dangerous it can be wandering the moors in weather like this?'

'It is safer than staying at the Abbey.'

His dark brows lowered in a frown. 'Are you saying I can't protect you?' He sounded furious. And frustrated.

She stiffened. 'Protect me from whom?'

'From yourself.'

Without another word he picked her up in his arms and made for the ladder. 'Put me down,' she gasped. 'You will fall.'

'Let us hope not,' he said through gritted teeth. 'Hold on.'

He let go of her with one hand, reached for the ladder and stepped on to it. There was not help for it, she put her hands around his neck and clung on. It was either that or fall ten or more feet to the floor.

Ranger wagged his tail in greeting when they hit the ground. Mary gave him a glare. 'But for your dog, you would never have found me.'

He gave a grunt in answer and put her down next to the stallion who was contentedly munching on hay. He pulled the horse away and mounted him with fluid ease. 'Give me your hands.'

She hadn't liked riding the horse the last time and she was sure she wouldn't like it any better now. She shook her head.

'It is either that or be tied on behind the saddle like luggage.'

That sounded worse. She approached the horse gingerly.

'Don't worry, he's calm after such a good run.'

She winced and held up her hands to him.

'Put your foot on top of mine,' he commanded.

She did so, with some difficulty, and then flew upwards. He somehow caught her under the arms and set her on his lap.

'Ready, Miss Wilding?' His voice wasn't offering an option.

She sighed. 'I suppose so.'

He urged the horse out into the night, setting it into a steady canter.

* * *

She couldn't believe how little time it took them to reach the drive up to the Abbey. Minutes. Not the hour or two she had been walking. 'How did we get here so fast?'

'You were walking in circles,' he said grimly.

Something hot rose in her throat. A hard lump of disappointment at her own inadequacy. She should have been miles from the Abbey. She sniffed the tears away.

She heard him mutter something under his breath that sounded like 'God save me', but she couldn't be sure with the wind rushing in her ears and the sound of hoofbeats. What she was sure of was the band of iron around her waist holding her firmly in place and the hard wall of chest at her back.

If she hadn't felt quite so cold, she might have enjoyed the wild ride in the wind and the dark. He rode the horse right into the barn where a sleepy-eyed groom was waiting with a lantern.

His eyes widened when he saw Mary, but he took the reins the earl threw at him and turned his back while Beresford helped her down.

'See him well rubbed down, if you please, Sol,' his lordship said. 'Some warm bran and not too much water. Ranger, with me.' He grabbed Mary around the shoulders and marched her into the house by the side door. The one by which she had left that very first day. Tonight it was unbarred and unlocked.

He walked her past the corridor leading to her chamber in the north tower.

She dug in her heels. 'Where are we going?'

'You'll see, soon enough.'

But she knew where they were going. He was heading for his rooms. 'You can't...'

'I can do whatever I please in my own home, as you will soon discover.'

He flung open a door to a chamber and pushed her inside. A room where a large four-poster bed took up most of the room. A fire blazed merrily in the hearth where a pot hung from the crane, and gave off a faint aromatic aroma. In front of a comfortable-looking sofa was a table. The two glasses said he was expecting company.

Startled, she turned to face him.

He kicked the door closed with his heel, took off his coat and flung it on a chair. He gave her a tight smile and began attacking the fastenings of her cloak.

She pushed his hand away. 'What are you doing?'

'Getting you out of these clothes before you are chilled to the bone.'

'I can undress in my own room.'

'You are not going anywhere before you and I talk.' He finally untied the knot at her throat and pulled off her cloak. He spun her around and started on the buttons of her gown.

'I can't undress in here.'

'You can and you will. Either you do it, or I will do it for you.'

A shiver ran down her back at the dark notes in his voice, the seductive promise laced with the heat of his anger. He might be completely in control, but she could still sense his anger running hot beneath the surface.

She folded her arms across her chest. 'I can't. Not with you watching.'

He walked around her, picked up a robe from across the foot of the bed and handed it to her. 'Put this on.' He locked the door and pocketed the key. 'I'll be right next door.'

He disappeared into what must be his dressing room.

'Close the door,' she said.

'My back is turned. I am not some errant schoolboy who needs to peek, Miss Wilding. I can assure you I have seen my share of women in various stages of undress.'

That was supposed to make her feel better?

She let her sodden gown slip to the floor, and stripped off her stays. She put her arms in his silk robe, so smooth and slightly cool against her skin. It was embroidered with dragons. It seemed very fanciful for such a dark man.

'Are you done?' he asked.

She picked up her gown and looked around for somewhere to hang it. He strode in without waiting for an answer. He took the garment from her hand and tossed it over a wooden chair.

'Now,' he said, with a hard smile. 'Sit there, Miss Wilding, on that sofa beside the hearth, and tell me what the devil you think you were doing tonight. Perhaps you can give me one reason why I should not punish you for setting the house in an uproar?'

Chapter Twelve

He was unbelievable. One minute he was kissing her with a passion that curled her toes inside her boots. The next he was treating her as if she was a child.

'I do not appreciate your tone of voice, my lord,' she said stiffly. 'Or your threats. Indeed, I find myself heartily irritated by them. And by you. I am not your ward. I am not anyone's ward. And what I do is my own concern. Now, if you will excuse me, I will return to my room.' She held out her hand for the key.

It was somewhat difficult to be haughty in a red robe covered in green and yellow dragons, but she thought she'd pulled it off tolerably well.

'Sit!' he snarled.

She jumped.

He spun away, raking his fingers through the hair at his temples. Clearly he was very close to losing his temper. It was the first time she'd seen him so close to losing control of his emotions. She eyed him just as warily as she had eyed his stallion earlier that evening, but she wasn't going to let him scare her. She was finished with being terrified.

'The key, if you please, my lord.'

Slowly he turned to face her. His eyes blazed fury. His fists opened and closed at his sides and he took a deep shuddering breath.

'We cannot go on like this,' he said with soft menace. 'I learned young that losing my temper only makes a bad situation worse, but you drive me to the brink of madness, to the point where I have no control.' He took another deep breath. 'So here it is, one last time. Please, Miss Wilding. Would you do me the very great honour of sitting down so we can talk like reasonable adults?'

What woman could resist a plea like that from such a man? Not Mary, even if she ought to. While his words were cool, his eyes were hot. The same heat she felt in her belly.

Slowly she sank to sit on the sofa, the heat from the fire warming one side of her body and face.

He bent over the flames and ladled out two mugs of the steaming aromatic liquid, the scent of cinnamon, cloves and oranges intensifying.

'Drink this,' he said, handing her one of the cups. 'It will warm you.'

He brought his own cup and sat beside her on the sofa. She had not expected that. She sipped at the steaming brew. It was delicious. 'What is it?'

'A hot toddy. A favourite with miners after a day in the damp and the cold. It is also known as punch.'

His words reminded her of the damp and the cold in the tin mine. She shivered.

He reached over and brought the cup to her lips again. 'Drink it all.'

She took another sip and another and soon it was all gone and her head felt a little muzzy.

He took the cup from her hand. 'How is that?' he asked.

He was right, she did feel warmer, inside and out. Relaxed. Her teeth were no longer clamped together to stop their chattering and her shoulders were not tight. 'Much better, thank you.'

He set the mug on the floor, then he reached out and touched her jaw with the tips of his fingers, urging her with that gentle touch to turn her face towards him. She did not resist, but she kept her gaze on her hands now lightly clasped in her lap.

'Look at me, Mary,' he whispered.

She forced her gaze up to his face. He dipped his head and took her mouth, sweetly, gently, his tightly controlled passion vibrating in the inch of air between their bodies.

He tasted of cinnamon and sweet oranges and night-time snow. A heady combination, when she was already feeling a little dizzy. His hand linked with hers in her lap, a strangely intrusive sensation, his wide fingers pushing hers apart, touching the sensitive skin in between her fingers. It made her breathe faster. It made her feel languid. Or was it the drink?

Did she care?

She was tired of running. Tired of being pulled hither and yon by her desires warring with her mind. Just once she wanted to experience the delights between a man and a woman.

It didn't mean anything, she knew it in her heart. He was simply seducing her into staying. He wanted to use her for his own purposes. Why should she not do the same? She had no doubt as to his experience as a lover. His touch told her he knew exactly how to make a woman's body hum with delight. She would never marry. So what did it really matter, this virtue, this strict adherence to the rules?

And if she was going to die, perish the thought, should she not have experienced something of the delights between a man and a woman? Discover for herself the joys lauded by poets and romance novels. Not that there was love involved on his part, but there could be great pleasure, according to Sally. He had given her pleasure, already. And she knew, instinctively, there had to be more.

She turned her body, to enable her better access to his mouth, to return his kiss, to twine her free hand around his neck, and kissed him back with all the art she had learned these past few days. The warm slide of tongue against tongue. The movement of lips that stirred her blood and tightened her core and made a rumble of approval rise up from deep in his chest. She liked that she had the power to move him as he moved her, that he was not completely unaffected by her touch. When she speared her fingers through his silky hair, he hissed in a breath. When she withdrew her tongue from his mouth and he followed with his, she captured it with her teeth and he groaned in the back of his throat.

She was also aware of his hand leaving hers and trailing a path up her arm to her shoulder. Aware of its stealthy path to the edge of the robe. Aware of the way he slowly eased it off her shoulder.

Aware with a sense of heart-pounding anticipation.

Each velvet stroke of his fingertips set a new inch of skin on fire. It felt delicious. Wicked. Wanton. And right. So very right. And when he pushed her back into the corner of the sofa, his chest pressing down on hers, his fingers teasing the rise of her breast, she closed her eyes and let the thrills ripple through her body.

Slowly, he broke their kiss, but his mouth didn't stop working its magic. He blazed a path of hot wet kisses across her cheek. His moist warm breath in her ear sent prickles of pleasure racing across her skin. Painful and delightful at one and the same time. She gasped.

He swirled his tongue around the edge of her ear, then nibbled her earlobe. When had her ear become such a centre of delight? Dazed by the sheer unexpectedness of the sensations searing through her body with each touch of his tongue, she lay immobile, breathing hard, waiting for what would come next.

He kissed his way down her throat, lingering to trace the hollow of her throat before moving on to the flesh at the edge of her robe, the swell of her breast.

Shocked to her very soul, she put up a hand to cover herself. He caught her fingers with his and kissed them one by one, until he reached her middle finger and closed his mouth around it, sucking on it.

Darkness edged her vision as something pulled tight inside her. An ache of unbearable sweetness.

'Bane,' she gasped, terrified and fascinated all at once.

Releasing her finger from its hot wet prison, he looked up at her, his eyes alight with fire and a sort of softness she didn't understand. His eyelids looked heavy. His mouth full and sensuous. He looked beautiful.

'Mary,' he whispered. 'Sweetling.' The word made her heart swell too large for her chest.

As he gazed at her, he gently rubbed her fingertip against the peak of her breast, inside the robe, where only the linen of her chemise protected her. The nipple hardened and furled into a tight little nub. It stood at attention. Not with cold, but with longing to be touched.

More thrills chased their way down to her belly. She felt that strange little pulse between her thighs and the jolt of pleasure it caused.

She moaned.

He pressed his lips to the place her finger had touched, kissing and nipping and laving with his tongue. The ache at her core intensified and she writhed beneath him, opening her thighs to cradle his body, seeking the pressure that would relieve the terrible unbearable need.

He unlaced the ribbon at the neck of her chemise and pulled down first one side, then the other to expose her breasts to his gaze. She could only see the top of his head, but she knew what he'd done by the feel of the air and his breath on her skin. By the tightness across her ribs. She tried to cover herself with her hands, but he grasped them in one of his and held them over her head, lifting his upper body to look down into her face.

'Would you deny me such bounteous beauty, my dearest?' he breathed and his expression held such a look of awe as he gazed down at her exposed flesh, at the mounds of her full bosom and at the tightly furled rosy peaks at their tips, she could deny him nothing.

She managed to shake her head and he gave a rough sort of laugh.

'Oh, Mary. You are every bit as delicious as my imagination said you were.'

'And wicked,' she mumbled as her face turned scarlet.

'How can anything so good be wicked?' he said, but his raspy voice was full of wicked seduction and passion. But it was his eyes that gave her pause. They were alive with something more than lust. There was tenderness and…affection. A warmth she had given up hoping to see in anyone's eyes.

She expected her girls to respect her, but she knew she could not command their affection.

But if her heart felt something stronger towards him, a deeper emotion she could not seem to freeze out of existence, there was no reason for him to know. Tonight was just about desire.

She pulled her hands free of his grip and flung her arms around his neck. She kissed his chin, his nose, his cheekbone with a rush of joy. He welcomed her kisses with a smile of such unusual sweetness it made her heart lurch. She had never felt quite so happy. And tears burned the backs of her eyes. His face wobbled out of focus.

His smile fled. 'Crying, sweetling?'

'Happy tears,' she said.

His laugh sounded a little startled.

Too much emotion for a man of his iron control, no doubt. 'It is nothing. Kiss me, Bane. Make me warm.'

His lips met hers and they sank into the heat of passion, his hands wandering her body, the silk of the robe sliding over her skin in a sensual dance. He undid the tie around her waist and it fell open, revealing her skin through her chemise, bathed in firelight.

And when he slid off the sofa to kneel beside her, this time she let him look his fill. Like a wanton woman. She watched his expression as his gaze roved over her from head to heel. A searing glance full of carnal longings. It sent her blood scorching through her veins.

Her thighs fell open at the gentle pressure of his hand. He stroked and kissed the inner bend of her knee, the delicate flesh high on the inside of her thigh and she closed her eyes and let the marvellous feelings wash away all thoughts from her mind. Thought had no place in this miracle of physical delight.

His touch left her. She forced her heavy-lidded eyes open and watched him strip off his shirt. She gaped at the magnificent breadth of him. The wide shoulders, the defined muscles of his chest with a dusting of crisp black curls around his nipples. The ridge of muscles across his abdomen.

So many muscles. So much unforgiving strength.

It would not matter how hard she fought physically, she

could never overcome such power. If she wanted to win, she would have to use her wits.

Right now, she had no thought of their struggle. Just the enjoyment of watching this virile male display his beauty. His hands went to the waistband of his pantaloons where they clung to firm, narrow hips and flanks. He paused.

She looked up at his face and realised he was await-ing her permission. Heat rushed through her body. She gave a quick nod and looked away. Looked at the back of the sofa, at the curtains covering the window, listening to the sound of him stripping off every stitch of clothing.

He gave a soft laugh. 'Coward.'

He picked her up and lay her down in front of the hearth. At her look of surprise, he smiled. 'I don't want you getting cold and that bed seems to sit in a draught.'

She glanced over at the bed and realised that beside the headboard was a sconce similar to the one in her room. Did it also open into a tunnel? For a moment, she tried to recall the map in the book, but when he lay down beside her, one heavy thigh across hers, his mouth plying her with kisses, the thought drifted away. Later. She would think about it later. For now, it was his hands and his mouth and the feel of his warm skin against hers that had all her attention.

The man was a master at seduction. He knew where to touch her, how to make her squirm and gasp. In mo-ments, she was lost in a haze of desire, arching her hips into the thigh pressing down on her mons, moaning at the way his tongue toyed with her breast, making them tingle and ache. And all the while, inside her, there was a growing tension. At first it was an ache. Then it felt like the sweetest pain.

There, where his hand stroked her woman's flesh, delv-ing gently between the hot damp folds. He rubbed and caressed until she cried out in frustration. He slipped one finger inside her, then another.

'So hot,' he murmured in her ear. 'So tight and wet and ready.'

'Yes,' she breathed in wonder at the erotic touch on her most secret place that only seemed to make the tension increase to unbearable proportions.

'Do you like this, Mary?' he breathed in her ear, swirling his tongue in that sensitive place, nuzzling into her neck, kissing and sucking until she wasn't sure which touch was driving her more mad. 'This story between us.'

'Yes,' she whispered. 'Yes,' she said louder when he didn't respond.

'Do you want to find out what happens in the end?'

'Yes.' Of course she did. How could she not? He started withdrawing his fingers and she closed her legs tight, trapping his hand and felt an astonishing rush of pleasure. She moaned at the deliciousness of it.

He muttered something under his breath. 'Relax, sweeting. Let me come over you.'

The words made no sense, but he pressed with his knee, pushing her thighs apart, then when she parted her legs he settled his hips between them, his chest rising above her like the torso of a god, bronzed in firelight, his face strained with some sort of effort.

She glanced down between them and saw that the hard ridge of flesh pressing into her mons was his male member, thick and aroused, its head gleaming darkly where the firelight caught it.

She sucked in a breath.

He didn't move.

The restless inside her, the needs he'd stoked, rose up to claw at her insides.

'Bane,' she pleaded. 'The end of the story.'

'It comes at a price,' he whispered harshly. 'Marriage.'

'What?' She shook her head, thinking to clear her hearing.

'A promise of marriage, or this ends now. I won't ruin you, Mary.'

'You can't ruin a schoolteacher,' she protested, trying to think.

He rocked his hips and sent another pulse of pleasuring ripping up from her belly. She writhed, trying to bring him closer, to ease the torment.

'If you want this, you will promise to be my wife,' he said softly. 'Agree. Or we are done here.' He started to move, lifting himself away with a grimace of pain, but there was no doubting the inflexibility of his decision.

'Yes,' she breathed. And the rush of happiness was almost as painful as his sensual torture. She would have her children, her home and her husband. She wouldn't have love. Not from him. But she had never expected love at all. And her children would love her. And she would love them. And cherish them.

'I didn't hear you,' he said, his breathing harsh and ragged.

'Yes.'

'There's no going back,' he warned. 'No changing your mind in the morning. You will be my wife.'

'Yes,' she said, proudly, more confident than she had been in years. 'Yes, I will be your wife.'

'Thank God,' he breathed and his arm shook as he held himself up on one hand as the other reached between them and guided his hot flesh into her. Large, intrusive, pushing and stretching, while his face contorted with effort as if he was holding back. And then she felt it. Something stopping him. Her maidenhead.

'This might hurt,' he warned gently.

She wanted to laugh at the thought of the pain she'd endured these past few weeks. How could this be that bad? She nodded instead.

He thrust forwards slowly with a low groan and held still.

A pinch of pain caught the breath in her throat. She froze. He froze. They stared at each other, not daring to move.

But the pain soon faded to a memory and all she could feel was him inside her body, large, hot, pulsing.

It felt good. She shifted her hips and felt a stab of pleasure.

He groaned and rocked inside her, small little movements at first, matching the pulse that beat inside them both. It felt delicious. Deliriously so. But not nearly enough.

And then he was kissing her mouth, suckling on her breasts and the tightening that had relaxed started all over again. Worse than before. His hips drew back and plunged forwards, the rhythm steady at first, then increasingly wild, and she could see darkness at the edge of her vision. Blackness beckoned.

A fall into the void.

Terrified, she resisted, her muscles clenching tight as her body strained towards it and her mind pulled her back.

'Let go, Mary,' he whispered in her ear. A devil tempting her into the abyss. 'Let it happen,' he said. 'You will be fine. I promise.'

He reached between them and pressed and circled on that tiny nub buried deep within her folds above their joining. Too much pleasure. Too much sweet pain. She could not hold on.

And she let the darkness take her.

Flew apart. Shattered. And it wasn't dark. It was brilliant with blinding light. And she was falling into bliss.

In a state of languid floating, she felt him tense. Heard his soft deep cry and cushioned his shudders with the cradle of her body. Gave him the same gift he had given her.

His lips found hers and he held himself on trembling arms. Kissing her mouth, her cheeks, her eyelids. 'So grand, lass,' he said in accented tones. 'So damned grand.'

He collapsed at her side, curling around her protectively.

Awed, she stared at the man who would soon be her husband. Handsome. Strong. Terrifying. She'd agreed to wed him based on instinct rather than intellect. He'd forced her to say yes. Even so, a sense of gladness filled her heart. It wasn't a love match. And it was better that way. Less chance for hurt. But they would each gain much of what they wanted from the arrangement.

As long as he gave her children, she could be happy. On that thought, bliss claimed her and she drifted on what felt like warm currents, only to awake a few minutes later being carried.

He lay her down on his bed.

She started to sit up. 'I can't stay here. The servants will find me in the morning.'

'We won't be the first couple to anticipate our wedding vows.' The hot, dark look he sent her way as he pressed her back down on the pillows sparked yet another round of desire. She tried to resist its allure, the pull he exerted on her body and use her mind.

'Betsy will be worried.'

He slipped beneath the sheets and pulled her into his embrace, drawing her head to rest on his shoulder, her hand to drape over his chest. His heart was a strong steady beat in her ear, his skin warm, the scent of him, all dark tones in her nostrils. And her traitorous body warmed.

He kissed the top of her head. 'And what was she to be, when she discovered you gone in the morning?'

'That was different.'

'How?'

'Because I wouldn't have to face her.'

He chuffed a small laugh. It was an endearing sound. Amusement without mockery. 'The servants know what goes on. They won't comment, I can assure you. And you are not going back to your room. Not with so many avenues for you to escape me again. I won't take that risk.'

Risk. The word was like a cold rock dropped on her chest. She gulped in air. She was taking a risk, staying here with him. 'About what happened at the mine…'

He lifted his head to look down at her. 'It's over, Mary. There'll be no more running away. You belong to me now. You swore it and I will not permit you to go back on your word.'

Something he had said didn't make sense. Idly, she placed the flat of her hand on his chest, felt the rough hair and the solid muscle beneath. Heard his quick inward breath as he sank back into the pillows. 'Don't do too much of that, sweetheart. I don't think you will be ready for me again tonight, and, as demonstrated, I don't have a great deal of control when it comes to you.'

Nor she when it came to him it seemed. But… Her brain tumbled like a well-oiled lock. 'I didn't run away at the mine.'

'Don't lie to me, Mary. I found you on the road, re-member?' The rasp was back in his voice.

She rolled on her side, pushing away, so she could see his face, watch his reaction. 'I'm telling the truth.'

He raised himself up on his elbow and pushed the hair

back from her face, staring down into her eyes. 'And I am basing my judgement on experience, sweet. You tried to buy a ticket in St Ives. You walked the path on the cliff. And then there's tonight. Why would the afternoon at the mine be any different?'

'Because I say so.' The look of doubt on his face stirred anger in her breast. 'If I am to trust you, surely you must also trust me.'

He opened his mouth to argue.

'I do not deny those other occasions, but… Oh, what is the use?'

She flopped over on her back and stared up at the canopy. He would never trust her. And she would never trust him. Because she knew what she'd heard. *You stupid little fool.* His words. Even if it wasn't his voice. People sounded different under different emotions. It could have been him. Yet what could she say? Accuse him of trying to kill her now, when they seemed to have agreed to a truce? With their wedding in the offing there was no need for him to be rid of her. He'd have his title and his wealth.

He leaned over her, turning her face towards him. 'All right. Tell me.'

She looked up into his eyes, at the frown, at the jaw already set in uncompromising lines, and knew that, having started down this path, she could not now back away. She had to say something. Come close to the truth, see his reaction.

'I went exploring and got lost.'

The frown deepened. 'How could you get lost?'

'I spoke to one of the boys, working further along one of the tunnels. Then I followed what I thought was candlelight.'

His expression lightened. 'And ended up outside?'

She nodded. 'I thought to go back to the entrance.'

'On the road you were heading downhill. Away from the mine.' He let go a deep sigh. 'As I said. It's over. Let us move forwards from here.' He looked so disappointed she wanted to cry.

'Someone pushed me down one of the old shafts,' she blurted out.

He sat bolt upright. 'What?'

Well, that certainly had his attention. She looked down at where his fist was bunching the sheets. 'Someone shoved me from behind.' Much as he had shoved her that day on the cliff, now she thought about it.

'Are you telling me the truth?'

She looked straight into his eyes, held his gaze steady with her own. 'That is what happened. That's why I was heading away from the mine.' The fear from that day rose up and tightened her throat. 'I was lucky. My bonnet strings tangled with the ladder. I was able to climb out.'

'Your bonnet?'

He sounded incredulous. He would sound that way if he was the one who had pushed her. 'Too bad for you I didn't die,' she said. 'It would have solved all your problems.'

'Too bad indeed,' he said drily. 'You tell a wild story, Miss Wilding. I am surprised you aren't blaming your disappearance on sightings of a ghost or some sort of hobgoblin.'

'A human hand pushed me, not a ghost.' *You little fool.*

He glared at her, his mouth a thin straight line. 'Clearly I should not have let you go to the mine. You are not to be trusted to behave like a sensible woman and stay with your party.'

'Interesting that you were not searching the tunnels, but rather were leaving for home.' There, she had as good as voiced her suspicions.

He frowned, his gaze searching her face. 'I found you on the road.'

'Bad luck for you, I suppose,' she muttered and was surprised when he flinched. It seemed she'd struck a nerve. 'Just like the near miss at the cliff and the lucky escape from the barrel. Marriage must seem a great deal more certain at this point.'

The words hung between them like a sword waiting to strike a death blow.

His face turned to granite. His gaze moved from hers and fixed off in the distance. When he finally looked at her, his eyes were the grey of a winter storm. 'Your powers of deduction are truly astounding.'

No denial. No claims of innocence. All her longing for one person in her life who would care about her balled into one hard lump in her throat. A burning painful blockage that no matter how hard she swallowed would not go back where it belonged in the deep reaches of her soul.

Perhaps if he would just pretend to care, it would not feel quite so bad. She forced a bitter smile. 'Even women are capable of logic when it stares them in the face.' The husky quality in her voice, the grief she hoped he would not recognise, came as a shock. Not even Sally's betrayal had left her with such a feeling of desolation.

'If your logic leads you to the understanding that marriage to me is your best chance of survival, then I am glad.'

She could not control the tremor that rocked her deep in her bones. The threat in his voice was unmistakable.

Chapter Thirteen

'Wharton will have quite a time of it, preparing your trousseau at such short notice,' Mrs Hampton said the next afternoon, as they sat taking tea in the drawing room. 'We should visit her first thing in the morning.'

His lordship looked up from the letter he was writing. 'Only a few things are required. A morning gown. A travelling dress. Send her a note. She has Mary's measurements. We will visit a proper modiste in town after the wedding.'

Mary glowered at the pair of them, tired of the way they decided everything between them. 'I don't need new clothes for a wedding no one but family will attend.'

'You will need appropriate attire for the journey to London, however,' his lordship said. He rose from his chair and went to the window to look out. It was the second time he'd done that in the space of an hour.

'Are you expecting someone?' she asked.

He looked more than a little startled and if she wasn't mistaken his colour heightened on his cheekbones. 'Templeton. He said he would either come himself or send a message. I expected him yesterday.'

'I do hope nothing bad has befallen him on the road,'

Mrs Hampton said, absently. 'What about this one?' she continued, holding up a fashion plate for Mary to see. A dark-blue military-style pelisse over a shirt with a ruffle around the neck. 'It is all the crack according to the *Assemblée.*'

'Too much frill,' Mary said. 'I prefer something simpler.'

Bane went to the hearth and rang the bell. The butler shuffled in a few moments later. His face was impassive, but Mary felt sure his eyes were curious. All the servants must be talking about them spending the night together. 'Yes, my lord.'

'Send word to the stables that I require Henry to take a message to St Ives.' He glanced over at Mary and Mrs Hampton. 'How soon can you have a list ready for the seamstress?'

Mary put her teacup on the table beside her, rose and took the magazine from Mrs Hampton. She flipped through the fashion plates until she saw what she was looking for. 'This one,' she said, showing the older lady. 'And this carriage dress.'

Mrs Hampton reviewed her choices, then nodded. 'Yes. Yes. You are right. You are a perfect height to carry these off.'

A perfect height? No one had ever called her height perfect before and yet there was no trace of mockery in the other woman's voice. 'Then the matter is settled.' She sent a glance of triumph at Bane.

He didn't seem to notice.

'If you will excuse me, Mrs Hampton,' she said, reining in her irritation, 'I find I have run out of reading material. If you need me, I will be in the library.'

'I'll come with you,' Bane said.

She smiled sweetly. 'No need. I won't be but a moment.'

He gave her a look that said he was not prepared to argue. 'No trouble at all.'

She gritted her teeth. All morning he had been at her side, as if he expected her to try to leave the moment his back was turned.

He clicked his fingers and his dog immediately came to its feet.

'That animal should not be in the drawing room,' Mrs Hampton sniffed. 'Gentlemen leave their hunting dogs in the stables.'

'My dog, my drawing room, my house,' Bane said. He bared his teeth in a hard smile. 'And no one in this house has ever suggested I was a gentleman.'

'You are the earl,' the widow said. 'So now you must act like one.'

Mary felt the hairs on the back of her neck prickle. 'He is a very well-behaved dog. I do not mind his presence at all.'

A mocking smile crossed the earl's face. 'I am pleased to hear it.'

Now what had she said to provide him with amusement? Whatever it was she was not going to ask. Not when he was behaving like a shadow. Indeed, after their exchange of truths in bed she had half-expected him to avoid her altogether, since he thought her a liar.

She strolled towards the door and he strode to open it for her to pass through. He bowed as she swept past. She couldn't help notice just how elegantly he did so, or the way her heart fluttered. Dash it all, it was hard to be annoyed when he was being so charmingly attentive.

At the library door, he moved around her to open the door, but remained, with his dog at his side, barring her way, looking down at her with those silvery eyes with an expression she could not read.

'I am sorry if you find my presence wearisome,' he said.

Was that a note of hurt she heard in his voice? She felt an unwanted pang of guilt. She pushed it away. He was playing on her emotions.

'I gave my word that I would not leave, for heaven's sake,' she said. 'But you are making me feel like a prisoner.'

His mouth tightened, and whatever amusement there had been left in his expression, it was gone now. 'You are. Until we are safely wed.'

'After that it won't matter, you mean.'

'It will matter. But not in the same way.'

'Because there is no escape, once we are wed.'

'I will do my best to make sure you do not feel the desire to escape.' His rough voice caressed her.

A delicious shimmer of desire warmed her, and infuriated her, at how easily she succumbed to his sensual wiles. 'I wonder if your best will be good enough.' She bit her lip at the flash of pain in his eyes. She had not meant to hurt him, just to maintain some distance, some control over herself, now he had taken away all her options. Petty, but necessary to her sense of self. Except it wasn't his fault she found herself in this predicament. He hadn't so much seduced her as fulfilled her every spinsterish dream and more.

She deserved whatever fate awaited her, for giving in to those fantasies.

She made to step past him.

'Wait.'

She looked up into his handsome face and once more her chest squeezed painfully with the knowledge he would never love her. She forced herself not to care. 'Yes, my lord.'

His mouth tightened as if he did not like what he was

about to say. 'I have to leave the house, on an errand of my own.'

Her jaw dropped. 'You intend to leave me to my own devices? I am honoured by your trust.'

His expression became rueful. 'You will do as I request and remain here or face the consequences. You have agreed to be mine.' He laid a heavy hand on her shoulder.

The possessive note in his voice gave her a delicious thrill low in her belly. A carnal response to the darkness in his voice she could not help. 'Our agreement is a marriage of convenience. That is all.'

'And as my affianced wife, you are mine to protect.'

'You are the one I need protection from,' she grumbled.

He grimaced. 'Perhaps. But you will not leave the house while I am gone.'

'And if I do?' she challenged.

'You won't.'

He released the door and bowed her in. 'Have a pleasant afternoon, dear Mary. I will see you at dinner.' At his side, Ranger wagged his tail, looking up at his master with complete adoration. She knew how he felt, she just hoped she wasn't quite as obvious. Not when his lordship had nothing to give her in return.

She entered the room and was surprised when the dog followed her.

'On guard, Ranger,' Bane commanded.

Mary swung around. 'You are jesting?'

An apologetic look in his eyes, Bane bowed slightly. 'I am afraid not. Enjoy your afternoon.' He left.

'This is ridiculous. Bane. Come back here.' When he didn't return, she moved to follow him. The dog issued a low growl and lifted its lip, revealing large incisors.

'Down,' she said firmly.

The hairs on the back of its neck bristled.

'Bane,' she shouted. 'Blast.' It seemed she was trapped. Again. What sort of game was he playing? She given into his demands and still he didn't trust her. It hurt. Badly. More than it should, since she certainly didn't dare trust him.

The dog watched her with pricked ears, its red, wet tongue lolling from one side of its very large mouth. She knew nothing about dogs and she did not want to put this one to the test. She moved deeper into the room and it lay down across the threshold with its head on its paws, still watching her intently.

'This is too much.'

The dog whined and thumped its tail on the carpet.

She once more moved towards the door. The dog growled.

It seemed she had no choice but to find a book and read until Bane returned to collect his wretched animal. Was this to be her future with this man? Guarded and watched?

If so, she wasn't sure she could go through with it. Yet what was the alternative?

By the time Bane strode through the door, looking wind blown and purposeful, the candles had been lit, a dinner tray provided and Mary was too furious to read a word of the novel in her lap.

Ranger bounded around his legs in joyful abandon. 'Down, sir,' he said, looking at Mary. 'I am sorry I was longer than I intended. I hope you haven't been too in-convenienced.'

'Apart from being unable to go for dinner or attend the necessary, I haven't been the slightest discommoded.'

Amusement flashed in his eyes, annoying her all the more. 'I am sorry.'

'I see nothing to laugh about.'

He sobered. 'Nor I.'

'Where were you that you must needs leave me here guarded by this animal, a source of amusement for all, especially your cousin Jeffrey?'

'He was here, was he?'

'He came for a book and left without one.'

He patted the dog's flank with a heavy hand. 'Good boy.'

A footman scratched at the door and Bane looked up.

The young man coloured. 'Mr Manners said you asked for me, my lord.'

'Yes, Henry. Please take Ranger to the stables and see him fed, would you please.'

The dog's ears pricked and he attached himself to the footman immediately.

'Cupboard lover,' Bane murmured with a mock glower.

'It's as if he can understand every word,' Mary said as the footman left with the dog lolloping along beside him.

'He does.'

'You still haven't said where you were.'

He frowned. 'Among other places, I went to St Ives to arrange a ship's passage for first thing in the morning.'

'Ship's passage?'

'To London. The sooner we are married the better. I can arrange for a special licence there.'

She swallowed. She had thought she had at least two or three weeks before they were wed. Another woman in different circumstances might have been thrilled by his desire for speed. To Mary it felt a bit like staring into a prison cell. 'Why the sudden rush?'

'I don't like this house. I never have.'

'Because of the ghost?'

'I thought you too sensible to believe in such nonsense.'

She sighed. 'After what happened at the mine, I am not so sure.'

He gave her a sharp look.

'I had the strangest feeling of someone trying to help me.'

'What? After pushing you down a shaft?'

It really did sound foolish when he put it like that. 'You know it has been a long day and I think I would like to retire now.'

'I shall escort you to your chamber.'

'It is not necessary. I can find my way perfectly well.'

'Nevertheless...' He held out his arm.

She could either take it or he would follow her. She could see the determination on his face. And something else, a kind of bitter smile, as if he expected her to reject his offer.

Had other women rejected him, knowing he was low born even though heir to a title? She could imagine they might, in the highest of circles.

She made to place her hand on his sleeve, but he grasped it and drew her close to his side, tucking her hand into the crook of his elbow. A public demonstration of intimacy, even though there was no one there to see it.

It made her feel wanted. A surprisingly warm feeling. It melted her insides, made her want to lean against his strength and let him do with her as he would. And therein lay the danger.

If she came to rely on his caring too much, she would be heading for disappointment, so she did her best to appear unconcerned. To appear as if gentlemen escorted her in such a fashion every day of the week.

'What time do you expect we will leave in the morning?' she asked, feeling obliged to break what felt like far too comfortable a silence as they strolled towards her chamber.

'To leave St Ives on the first tide, we will need to leave here no later than six in the morning. Do you think you can be ready on time?'

'I can. Are you sure we cannot marry from here? I have never set foot on a ship before.'

'Afraid, Mary? I did not think you chicken-hearted.'

'It is the middle of winter. I hear *mal de mer* can be very uncomfortable.'

They had arrived at her chamber door and he turned to face her. 'You are right. But it is the fastest way and, if it is any comfort to you, the weather is set to be fine for the next two days according to the ship's captain.'

She could see from his expression that no objection from her was going to change his mind.

He opened the door to let her in. 'Thank you, my lord.' She dipped a little curtsy.

He gave a short laugh. 'I can see you would rather hit me over the head with your poker. Thank you for not pressing your objections.'

'I can see it would do no good.'

He looked surprised. 'I think you and I will do very well together, my dear Mary.'

'As long as I do exactly as you say.' She shook her head. 'I am afraid that, as a general rule, is not in my nature. Perhaps you should think of another way out of this dilemma.'

'There isn't one.' His voice lost its teasing note.

'Then I must bid you goodnight.' She stepped into her room and was astonished when he walked in behind her.

'What are you doing?'

'Not letting you out of my sight.'

'I promise you, I am not going anywhere.'

He gave her a long considering look and then seemed to come to some decision. 'Before I went to St Ives, I went out to the mine.'

He reached into his watch pocket with two fingers and pulled forth a few strands of fabric. 'I found these.'

She frowned at them.

'Strands of ribbon caught on an iron spike in the wall at the top of one of the deepest shafts in the mine.' His voice was hard and cold.

She raised her gaze to meet his and was surprised at the bleakness she saw in those metallic eyes.

'I'm sorry,' he said in a voice as cold as ice.

She shivered. 'Sorry that I did not fall to my death?'

He grasped her arm and pulled her hard against him, looking down into her face. 'I would not see harm befall you, Mary.'

'Not now we are to be married, at least.'

He swung away with a soft curse, leaving her wishing he was still holding her and hating herself for that weakness.

'I thought your story was a lie,' he gritted out. 'Finding you on the road, heading away from the mine, was all the proof I needed that you were running away.'

Guilt nagged at her, forcing her to speak the truth. 'I was. What fool would stay and risk their life?'

'And you are not a fool.' He let go a short sigh. 'It wasn't me who pushed you.'

A rush of relief rushed through her, followed swiftly by logic and doubt. 'If not you, then who? Only you benefit by my death.'

He winced and scrubbed at his chin. 'I know.'

'Some friend trying to help you? Your friend Lord Templeton, perhaps?'

Startlement entered his gaze. 'Why would you say that?'

'You employed his help to seek information about me.'

'Templeton works for the government. He has access to information and informers. He is right now looking for your Mrs Ladbrook. I hoped she might shed some light on what it was my grandfather was up to with this will. I can assure you he was nowhere near the mine yesterday.'

'Then who could it be?'

'Jeffrey.'

'Your heir.'

'A true Beresford, despite his proclivities. A man my grandfather would have preferred over me, without a doubt.'

Proclivities? She didn't think she wanted to know. 'But how would my death benefit him, when it is you who stands in the way of the title?'

He looked at her for a long moment, as if debating with himself as to what to reveal. He took a deep breath. 'If you die and I am found guilty of your murder, he will inherit.'

The air left her lungs in a rush. If this was true, then neither of them was safe. She paced to the window and back. 'Do you have reason to suspect him?'

'I saw him near the brewer's dray moments before the barrel broke lose. Someone in this house was making those noises in the room above your chamber and he and Gerald hung around the mine as lads enough to know it better than most.'

When she looked at him, she saw there was trepidation in his eyes, as if he feared she would not believe him. Did she? Her heart certainly wanted to. But her mind was a whole other matter.

It sounded logical. But only if he had not wanted her dead. She wanted to believe it, but—

'I think news of our impending wedding made him desperate,' he said.

There was something in his tone which gave her pause. He was looking at her so intensely a hot shiver raced down her back. In two quick strides he was across the room. His fingers formed a cage for her cheeks and they were trembling. His expression was dark, almost murderous.

'Bane?' she gasped.

'I looked into the abyss, Mary. Right into the bowels of the earth. It was impossible that you did not fall to your death.'

The strain in his husky voice was a tangible thing. It swirled around them like the dark centre of a storm as if he held some deep emotion under terrible control.

'Yet here I am,' she said lightly, for it was light that was needed. Something to chase away this terrible darkness.

'Yes. Here you are.' Slowly he lowered his head, his eyelashes shielding his eyes, his mouth hovering above hers, waiting for permission.

And wanton that she was, she wanted to feel the pressure of his lips against hers, to experience the wild sensations his kisses sent rippling through her body. And why should she not kiss her fiancé?

She lifted her mouth to his and he brushed her mouth with parted lips, soft, warm, pliable, wooing. She flung her arms around his neck and kissed him back, hard and demanding, exploring his mouth with her tongue as she had learned so very recently. He growled low in his throat and her pulse jumped.

She clung to him, tasting, exploring, giving in to riotous sensations. It all felt new again. Exciting. Novel. Not different, but fresh. His hand wandered her back in slow widening circles, while her fingers tangled in the hair at his nape.

The warm caressing hand stroked her ribs, her buttocks, and the hand at her waist moved to capture her breast, the thumb gently grazing the nipple through her gown until she thought she would go mad with the tension building inside her.

He was everything she had missed in her life, though she hadn't known it was lacking. Male heat. Masculine strength. He had the power to stir up all the feminine urges she'd denied. He made her flush with heat from her head to her heels. To feel the blood pumping in her veins and her body thrum with desire was exhilarating.

It was a kiss that lasted for ever, yet was over too soon. Their lips seemed to cling and on a groan, he tasted her jaw and nuzzled into her neck.

'Once we wed,' he whispered, 'you will know nothing but pleasure, I promise.'

A promise that made her insides clench.

'Right now, though,' he breathed gently, 'you need to rest. I will sit here in the chair and watch over you.'

'To make sure I do not leave?' She could not help the bitterness in her voice.

He grimaced. 'To bed, Mary. Now. Or I cannot be responsible for what I do. I will give you five minutes to prepare and no more.'

His tone was so dark, so fierce, she undressed quickly and hopped into bed.

A scream. The sound of it echoed in his head. Filled the darkness. He couldn't see, couldn't get to her, but he knew they were hurting her.

'No,' she cried out.

He struggled wildly in the folds of his coat, which they had pulled over his head. It held his arms pinned to his sides. He was panting, struggling for breath, and the one holding him was laughing.

This was his fault. He should not have gone to the mine after she forbade him. Should not have lost his temper. Should not have made her come looking for him.

'Let me go,' he shouted. Tried to shout. The cloth muffled his voice, made it hard to breathe.

And then they were gone. He fought his way out of his coat.

Fought to find his way to the sounds of sobbing.

Free from restraint, Bane shot bolt upright. In a chair. He was watching over Mary, not searching for his mother on a cold Welsh hillside.

The damned dream had returned. Cold sweat trickled down his back. Why now, when he hadn't had it for years?

His gaze sought out Mary. She lay on the bed, still and silent, one arm flung above her head, her beautiful blonde hair tumbling around her shoulders. She looked too delicious for words. Too perfect to be true. And perhaps she was, but he wanted her. And so he would make her his wife in spite of his anger against his scheming grandfather. As long as he kept his distance, didn't allow himself to form an attachment, the marriage could work to the benefit of both. Oh, yes, he could already imagine the benefits as his body hardened.

A woman sobbed. Not Mary. His gaze shot to the chamber door. Another scream ripped through the air. His blood ran cold. Desire fled.

Mary sat up, clutching the sheets to her breasts.

'Its all right,' he said softly.

'The White Lady,' she said, her voice trembling, pointing across the room. Bane stared at the apparition floating beside the red glow of the fireplace. Behind the eerie figure was what appeared to be a gaping hole in the wall.

The ghostly shape faded into the blackness.

Mary crawled out of bed on the other side, clutching that damned poker again.

'What the devil is going on here?' he bit out.

'The tunnel,' she whispered.

'Bloody hell,' he cursed. 'You knew about that?' He pointed at the hole in the wall.

Her eyes widened. Innocence? Or something else? 'There is a passageway behind the wall,' she whispered. 'I thought you knew.'

He grimaced. 'If I had known, I would never have let you sleep here.'

He reached for his discarded coat and pushed his feet into his shoes.

'You are going after her?' Her voice shook.

Fear. She was afraid. A roiling surge of anger ripped through him. His lips drew back from his teeth in a snarl. How dare they terrify his woman? He was going to beat whoever was doing this to a pulp.

She recoiled, staring at him.

Dear God, now she was fearful of him. He fought for control. Remembered who had suffered the last time he let his temper get the best of him and put out a hand. 'We have to put a stop to this, that is all.' There, that sounded reasonable.

She put her poker down on the bed and slipped on her robe. 'The tunnel leads to the chamber above.' She hesitated. 'It also runs along behind your room.'

Horrified, he grasped her arm as she was in the process of tying the belt. She looked up at him, startled. 'Are you telling me you have been in that tunnel?'

She nodded. 'I discovered it by chance. According to the history book it leads down to the sea caves.'

'Smugglers,' he said, as it all became clear. 'The Beresfords were nothing but a pack of pirates and smugglers in Good Queen Bess's day. That's how they gained their wealth and the title.'

She nodded.

'Manners said the tunnels were closed up. Fallen in.'

'Apparently not,' she said drily.

He almost laughed. God, this woman awed him with her pragmatic little comments. 'Stay here. I am going to put a stop to Jeffrey's tricks once and for all.'

'You think it is Jeffrey.'

'Who else would it be?'

'Gerald?' She sounded tentative. 'There is something odd about that boy.'

'He went with his mother to visit friends. Jeffrey was to go with them, but changed his mind at the last, Manners told me.' He pulled on his coat and picked up a candle.

She picked up her poker. 'I'm coming with you.'

That was all he needed. A woman and, in particular, this woman to look after while he chased down a man who wanted them both dead. 'No. Wait here.'

She pushed her feet into her slippers. 'What if he comes back another way? According that history book, there are several entrances.'

The back of his neck prickled at the thought of her being found alone. His chest tightened. He ought to find someone to look after her.

Another shriek issued from the tunnel. The prankster. Or it could be someone in trouble. He didn't want Mary in harm's way. If anything happened to her—

'We are wasting time,' she said, hefting the poker with a determined look on her face.

She wasn't going to stay here no matter what he said. Something warm swelled up to fill the hollow space in

his chest. He pushed it aside. Now was not the time to examine what it meant. 'Come if you must, but stay close.'

She nodded her agreement. It would have to do. He
picked up the candlestick on the night table and ducked
through the wall.

'That way leads to the chamber above,' she whispered,
pointing.

The sounds were not coming from that direction. He
turned the other way. He could not help feeling amazed
by the extent of the structure. Whoever had built this had
done so quite deliberately. He frowned. Why had no one
told him of their existence? They had clearly been well
maintained. He would be having a word with Manners
very soon. And his steward. It seemed their loyalties did
not lie with their new earl.

He could feel Mary walking behind him, hear her light
rapid breathing. She was afraid. Of course she was. What
was he thinking letting her come with him? What if something happened and he wasn't able to protect her? A chill
crept up from his gut. It wouldn't be the first time he
hadn't been able to protect the woman in his care. Bile
rose in his throat.

He would not let that happen again. He wasn't a boy
and there wasn't a man who could withstand him. Especially not the puny, effeminate Jeffrey. Mary was safer
with him than alone. She had to be.

Ahead, the tunnel branched off in two directions.

He looked back and she hesitated for a moment. 'That
way goes down to the caves.' She pointed left.

She didn't sound sure.

He turned right. In seconds they came to a dead end.
To his surprise, Mary slipped around him and grabbed
the sconce on the blank wall facing them. As she turned
it, the wall began to shift.

So that was how it was done.

He held the candle higher, revealing a small room. 'A priest's hole.'

'I don't think so,' she whispered, stepping inside. 'Look.'

He followed her and looked around. The little room was lined with shelves—well, pigeonholes—each one containing a scroll of some kind and there were other shelves holding boxes full of papers.

'The muniment room,' he said. 'So this is where all the old papers are. I wondered why there was so little in my grandfather's study. No charters. No letters.' It had been puzzling him for days.

The sound of moaning and rattling chains came from behind them. Mary jumped. He put an arm around her shoulder and realised that for all her brave outward appearance, she was trembling.

'You should go back,' he said. 'Leave Jeffrey to me.'

Her expression turned mulish. 'I'm coming with you. I intend to give that young man a piece of my mind.'

Bane could not help the smile that formed on his lips at the image of her slicing at the little worm with the edge of her tongue. It would indeed serve him right. Once more they plunged into the tunnel and took the other fork.

At the next corner, the draught blew out his candle. He cursed softly as Mary clutched at his coat. Bane let his eyes adjust, but there really wasn't any light at all. It was pitch black. Just like the mines he loved. The only way to move forwards was by feel. 'Keep hold of me,' he whispered.

The ground began to slope steeply downwards. They were going deeper and deeper into the earth, and the sound of the sea was getting louder. After a while, the floor flattened out. The tunnel must have widened out, too. On his right he could still touch the wall, but to his left, no matter far out he reached, he could feel nothing.

Aware that Mary had a good grasp of his coat-tails, he felt his way forwards, testing the way ahead with his foot before taking a step. He had no wish to tumble down a hole or into the sea.

A light glimmered off to the left. It went out instantly. Even so, it was there just long enough to show they were in a natural cavern.

He turned to face Mary. 'How much of these caves did that blasted book show?' he murmured directly into her ear, inhaling the scent that was uniquely her.

'I didn't take much notice of the caves,' she muttered. 'But I think there was only one leading out to the sea.'

'We are going back.'

'What?'

'We have no light. No weapon. And we have no idea where we are. I am not chasing a will o' the wisp when I have no hope of catching him.' He made to step around her to head back the way they had come. His foot slipped off the edge of a rock and slid down. His heart jolted as he came to rest one leg knee-deep in water with Mary clutching his arm. He cursed under his breath, but thanked providence it wasn't any deeper. He could have pulled her down with him.

'Bane,' she cried out.

'I'm fine,' he said. 'You can let go now.' He scrambled back up the rocks to her side. 'This is why we have to go back.'

A glowing figure appeared in front of her. 'Boo!'

Mary screamed.

Bane curse as he looked over her shoulder at what was

clearly a person wearing a sheet and carrying a lantern beneath it. 'Jeffrey, you idiot. What game are you playing?'

'I am the White Lady,' the apparition moaned. 'It is your turn to die.'

Chapter Fourteen

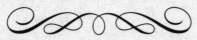

The light grew brighter, blinding Bane until his eyes adjusted. The figure behind the lantern was masked by the glare of the light, but he had no problem making out the pistol pointing at Mary. His stomach fell away.

'What the hell are you doing?' he growled. 'Put that thing down before you hurt someone.'

'Turn around and continue on.' There was no ghostly voice this time.

'Gerald,' Mary exclaimed. 'Stop this at once.'

Gerald? Now that was a surprise, but she had suspected the younger man.

Gerald laughed and it was an eerie sound that echoed off the cavern walls. 'Do as you are told. Turn around,' he said. 'Bane, you go first. Watch your step, the rocks are slippery.'

'It would be easier to see if you gave me the light,' Bane said, hoping the boy would be stupid enough to try it.

'Don't worry, you'll have plenty of light in a moment. Walk straight ahead and you will be fine.'

He lifted the lantern higher and Bane was able to make out the path ahead. They came to an outcrop of rock and the path disappeared around it.

'Stop,' Gerald commanded.

Bane did so. He reached back to where Mary was holding on to his coat and gave her hand a squeeze, offering comfort, hoping she would realise he was biding his time, waiting for an opportunity that would allow him to deal with this mad man.

His gut clenched. Fear that he would fail Mary, as he had failed his mother. No. He wasn't a weakling boy held down by a full-grown man. He just needed patience. To wait until the time was right.

'Against the wall, both of you,' Gerald ordered.

They shuffled back.

He passed by them, but since he had the pistol shoved against Mary's chest, Bane could not risk an attack. He could see that the pistol was cocked and the lightest pressure on the trigger would cause it to fire.

And then he was past them. 'Here.' He handed Bane a lantern and stepped back. 'Walk straight ahead.'

'It seems you have thought of everything,' Bane said, holding the lantern up.

'I wasn't expecting both of you,' Gerald said. 'Just Miss Wilding. But this is better. Much better. Don't try anything, Bane. Miss Wilding will confirm I have my pistol pressed to her neck.'

Mary gasped.

Bane's blood froze. He stifled a curse. He was going to make this man pay.

The skin across Bane's back tightened as they headed into yet another narrow tunnel. A draught of cool air blasted through it and when they reached the end and it once more opened out, Bane could see why. This cave led out to open water. He could see the waves washing into the mouth of the cave a few yards away.

They were standing on what looked very much like

a quay with a boat lying on its side on a narrow strip of sand. It was tied to a ring set in the rocks.

Judging from the way the seaweed grew up the walls, when the tide came in, where they were standing would be underwater.

'You weren't thinking of going for a midnight sail?' Bane said lightly. 'I don't think Miss Wilding is very fond of boats.'

'You didn't care about that when you booked her passage from St Ives,' Gerald said. 'But actually, no, the only one going sailing is me. You will be staying here.'

He waved the pistol. Bane prepared himself to jump and bring the little worm down.

The pistol steadied on Mary once more and Bane unclenched his fists. He did not want to give advanced notice of his intentions.

'Miss Wilding,' Gerald said, 'would you be so good as to take the lantern from your fiancé?' His voice dripped with sarcasm.

Bane handed it over, glad to have two free hands, but he didn't like it that it made Mary an easier target. She looked as pale as a ghost in the lamplight and her eyes, her pretty blue eyes, were large and frightened. He wanted to tell her not to worry, that he would think of something, but he could only give her an encouraging stare.

'See those chains beside your feet, Bane?' Gerald continued. 'The one with the manacles attached.'

Coldness bored into Bane's gut as he looked at the manacles. 'I see them.'

'Kneel and fasten one to your wrist.'

'No,' Mary said, her face full of horror. She'd guessed, like Bane had, the purpose of those chains. 'This is absolute nonsense. Gerald. You cannot do this. Don't you realise murder is a hanging offence?'

Gerald tittered. 'What a preachy schoolmarm you are. Just like my tutor, until I found a way to be rid of him.' He grinned. And the evil in that smiling angelic face made a shiver run down Bane's back. More than oddness resided in his cousin, he realised.

'Mary is right,' Bane said. 'You can't get away with this. And when the crime is discovered they will think it was Jeffrey.'

Gerald frowned. 'Why would they think it was him? Not that they will think it was murder. I have it all planned. They will just think you fell in the sea and drowned. You should have drowned anyway,' he said, flashing a look of hatred Bane's way. 'For years everyone thought the woman and child pulled from the sea the day your mother ran off was you.'

Bane wondered if he should threaten him with Templeton's expected arrival, but he had the feeling he needed to keep that card close for the moment. 'Any suspicious death of a peer comes under scrutiny and Jeffrey is the only one who benefits by my death.'

'Put your hand in that manacle. Now. Or I will shoot Miss Wilding.'

'And how will Jeffrey explain a bullet wound to the authorities?'

Gerald frowned. The pistol wavered. Then his face cleared. 'I'll tell them you shot her to get the money. And when I tried to protect her, you fell in the sea.'

Bane cursed. The lad might not be right in the head, but he had a chillingly cunning mind.

'Do as I say. Now. Or she dies.' He lined up the pistol on Mary's chest. Mary was looking at Bane in mute horror, expecting him to do something. Anything he could do right now would get her killed.

He did not want to put his wrist in that manacle, to willingly chain himself to a wall and leave himself helpless. He felt sick at the thought. But there was no other option, if he was to keep Gerald from firing his weapon. Gritting his teeth, he knelt on the cold hard rock and closed the iron around his wrist.

It was tight, but it wasn't yet locked.

Gerald grinned as if he'd read his thoughts. He held up the key. 'Catch it. If you drop it, I will shoot her in the head.'

Cursing inwardly, Bane caught the key and turned it in the lock. His insides rebelled at the sound.

'You can throw it back,' Gerald said. 'Be careful, I wouldn't like Miss Wilding to suffer for your poor aim.'

'Let her go, Gerald,' Bane said. 'She is a pawn in all of this.'

'She is a witness.'

Surreptitiously, Bane tugged on the chain. It seemed solidly attached, but that didn't mean one good hard tug wouldn't pull it free. 'She would probably just as soon marry Jeffrey as me. She was only doing it because I forced her.'

Gerald glanced at her.

Bane noticed she'd shifted, moved away from the wall and… Oh God, she still had the damned poker hidden in her skirts. If she tried that, he'd shoot her for certain.

'You know, Gerald,' he drawled, 'if you kill her, the money will be tied up in Chancery for years. Why do you think I didn't do it? Jeffrey won't thank you for it.'

'What?' The boy faced him. 'What are you talking about?'

'If she dies before she marries, the money goes to the Crown.'

'No. You are wrong.'

'I can assure you I know what I am talking about. Why else would I offer for her?'

The pain on Mary's face clawed at his chest, because she believed him. And it wasn't far off the truth. He would never have given marrying her a thought if it not for the money. He hadn't wanted to marry anyone. He only wanted justice for his mother.

'It's a trick,' Gerald said, glaring at him. 'Put your other hand in the manacle.'

'It is no trick.'

'Do it,' Gerald yelled, his voice rising.

The boy was getting anxious. Too anxious. Bane did not want that weapon going off by mistake and injuring Mary. His stomach lurched as he used his chained hand to close the manacle around his other wrist.

Gerald bent and locked it.

Bane lashed out with his foot at the gun as the key turned. He missed. But he managed to knock Gerald's arm, destroying his aim.

'Run,' he yelled.

Damn the woman, she wasn't listening. In awe and horror, he watched as she swung the poker. It hit Gerald's wrist. The gun flew out of his hand and skittered across the ledge. Bane willed it to fall into the sea. Dear God, the sea… While they had been bickering, the tide had been coming in. The boat was already afloat.

Gerald howled with pain and rage. He grabbed for Mary, who dodged him.

'Run, Mary,' Bane shouted, yanking on the chains, the iron biting into his wrists. 'Run. Save yourself.'

An agonised look crossed her face, then she turned and fled.

Gerald nursed his wrist for a moment, then picked up the pistol. He turned on Bane. 'I'll get her. And I'll make her marry Jeffrey. And it will be a proper Beresford who inherits the title. Not a bastard. My grandfather never wanted you as his heir.'

'I already inherited,' Bane said conversationally, judging the distance between them, trying to get under the lad's skin, to get him closer. A couple of feet and he'd have him. 'There will never be another Beresford heir.'

Gerald swung at Bane with the pistol and, chained as he was, he had no way to avoid the blow other than by turning his shoulder.

Pain exploded in a bright white light and his world went dark.

His head not only ached, but it felt like it was stuffed with wool. His ears were filled with the sound of rushing water. Was he cupshot? He opened his eyes. To blackness. And the smell of the sea. And the sound of waves. Water washed over him. Cold. Bringing him wide awake. He coughed and spat out the salt in his mouth. His mind cleared. Realisation colder than the air around him.

He'd allowed that little worm Gerald to chain him up. He shuddered as he realised he was helpless.

Fighting the insidious sensation of fear in his gut, he yanked on the chains. They'd looked rusty and old, but, no matter how hard he pulled, they didn't give.

Another wave rushed in and he fought to stay upright on his knees. This time when the sea receded, the water lapped around his legs. The tide was coming in fast. Fifteen minutes. That was all he had left of his life. Unless he could break the damn chains.

The thought of Gerald hurting Matry pierced his heart to the point of anguish. He had to get to her. Make sure she was all right. Feverishly he tore at the chains holding him fast. Pain gnawed at his flesh, but he barely felt it.

He took a deep breath, tensed every muscle in his body and pulled with all of his strength.

Pain was his only reward. He roared his anger and it echoed back at him. He sagged against the rocks, to recover his strength. To try again.

Sick horror filled his gut. Mary. He'd failed her, just as he'd failed his mother.

For days he'd tried to ignore his growing attraction. To keep himself aloof from emotions, as he had taught himself to do. After watching his mother die slowly of her injuries, because of him, he had known he could never again expose himself to the pain of losing someone else. Overcome by guilt, he had sworn he would never allow himself the privilege of another's love. He didn't deserve love.

He still didn't. But Mary, with her quick humour and courage, had made him want more than vindication for his mother. She'd made him want her, when he had known all along that he shouldn't. And now he'd failed her, too.

If only he could know she'd escaped. If he knew that for certain, he wouldn't care about the sea encroaching higher with every cold wave.

Because he loved her more than he loved his own life. He loved her.

The thought filled him with despair. He'd carelessly put her in terrible danger. Again he yanked on the chains.

A glowing figure in white floated towards him. The seawater had affected his brain, because what he was seeing was the White Lady. There was no mistaking the feminine figure outlined beneath the filmy robe and her long hair floating behind her.

His heart pounded wildly. Was this the signal that he was about to die?

'Bane,' she called out.

Not a ghost. But, oh damn, he wished it was. 'Mary,'

he pleaded desperately. 'I told you to leave. Go before he finds you.'

'I—I hit him over the head with the poker,' she said, crouching down. 'I—I think I killed him.' Her voice wavered badly. 'I have his pistol.'

Relief washed through him. Dear God, never had he met such a courageous woman or one so frighteningly resourceful. 'Do you think you can shoot at the pin holding me fast to this wall without killing me?'

She chuckled. 'Probably not. But I have something better.' She put down the lantern and reached for his hands. 'I have the key.'

The next wave was coming. He could hear it rushing into the cavern. He held his hands steady while she fumbled with the lock. 'Whatever you do, don't drop it.'

'I'll try not to,' she said, her voice grim.

The first shackle fell away. But he could see the wave rolling towards him in the light from the lantern. 'Get back,' he said, hating the idea of her moving away from him, but terrified that the next wave might carry her off.

Instead of doing as he said, she continued jiggling the key in the lock. And then it was open. He leaped to his feet and picked up her and the lantern and ran from the onrushing wave.

'Oh,' she said when he put her down. 'That was…remarkable.'

Cold and shivering, he leaned against the wall of the cave. 'Where is he?'

She took the lantern from his numb fingers. 'I hid in the muniment room and tripped him with the poker as he ran by. Then I hit him over the head and pushed him inside. I barred the door with the poker. Just in case.' She winced. 'But there was blood on his face.'

A very clever woman, his Mary. His? His heart stilled.

His mouth dried. He would be lucky if she agreed to speak to him again after the way he had endangered her life. And he wouldn't blame her at all.

He put an arm around her shoulders. 'Let us make sure he is no danger to us or anyone else, then find some dry clothes and a warm fire.'

She nodded, but her eyes were huge, her face pale and her expression fearful. He cursed the day he was born for causing such a look on her face.

Gerald was screaming invective when they reached that part of the tunnel. He'd managed to get the door open a fraction, but he barely seemed rational and was tossing papers and boxes around as if they were live things he was trying to murder.

Bane hurried Mary past and got her back to his chamber. He rang for his man and then sent him for her maid and a bath.

'I can't bathe in here,' she cried.

'You are not going back to a room that has a secret entrance,' he said. 'You can rest easy, I won't disturb you. There are many things I need to take care of before morning. But not until I am sure you are well protected.'

There was a strange look on her face. He wanted to ask her what she was thinking, but he didn't have the right. He had taken far too many liberties already.

A sleepy-looking Betsy arrived, followed by two footmen with a tin bath and another two with buckets of water.

Bane skewered the maid with a look. 'Take care of your mistress. She has been through a great deal this night and deserves every consideration.'

Betsy's mouth gaped. She dropped a curtsy and hurried through the door. Bane turned and left before he was tempted to remain, to help Mary bathe and see her safe to bed.

By letting his attraction for her overcome rational thought, he'd cause her a great deal of harm. She could have died.

And it would have been his fault.

The very idea almost sent him to his knees.

More guilt on his shoulders, heavier even than the death of his mother. Only this time he had a chance to atone.

It was almost mid-afternoon by the time Bane was able to seek out Mary. She'd slept until well past noon, he'd been told, and she was now in the drawing room.

Unable to resist looking his fill unnoticed, he paused outside the open door. She was sitting quietly gazing out the window, her hands folded in her lap, her thoughts clearly elsewhere.

So beautiful. An island of calm in a frenetic world. Only he knew the passion residing beneath the quiet exterior. Only he knew the wildly seductive woman below the unruffled surface.

Guilt assailed him. No true gentleman would have taken advantage of her innocence the way he had. He'd forced her into making a decision before he had all the facts. He'd wanted to believe she was up to some trick with his grandfather. He'd wanted to believe seduction was fair play, because he wanted her in his bed when in his heart he'd known better.

He was lowest kind of cur.

And when she found out the truth, how he had put her life in danger for his own selfish ends, he wasn't sure of her forgiveness. Nor did he deserve it.

He cleared his throat.

She jumped. Then flushed pink.

'My lord.' Only a tall, elegant woman like her could carry off that regal incline of her head.

'Miss Wilding.' He bowed.

Her eyes widened. A wary expression crossed her face. She smiled coolly. 'You have arranged everything to your satisfaction?'

'Yes. Gerald and his mother have been escorted by the doctor to York. She convinced me to allow Gerald to live out his days in an asylum there. Apparently this is not his first episode. His grandfather always put it down to an excess of sensibility. His mother suspected it was more, but didn't want to believe it.'

'I feel sorry for her. He…he won't be badly treated, I hope.'

He'd been ready to give him a quick end such was his anger at the danger inflicted on her. 'If that is your wish.'

She turned her face away. 'I hardly think my wishes are important.'

'He tried to kill you.' This time he could not keep his anger from surfacing.

'And you,' she said softly.

He waved a careless hand. 'If you can be magnanimous, then so can I.'

'And Jeffrey?'

'Like Mrs Hampton, he always knew Gerald was highly strung. He treated him with kid gloves and jollied him along. It never occurred to him that Gerald would act on his grandfather's continual complaints.'

'You believe him innocent, then?'

'I do. His horror and abject apology for not seeing what was going on were most convincing. You see, Jeffrey has money troubles. He was hoping to turn me up sweet for a large sum of money. The will made it all very difficult, as he had said to his cousin. He feels guilt for adding fuel to the fires in his cousin's head, but he would have stopped him if he had realised what he was doing.'

'So it is all settled.'

'Yes.'

He couldn't help looking at her, at the turn of her neck, at the faint pink blush on her cheeks, the bright sky-blue of her eyes. Because this might be the very last time he got to see her. She'd saved his life, while he'd done nothing but put hers at risk. Every time he thought about it his gut tightened and his blood turned to ice.

'I have to apologise to you for my behaviour these past several days,' he said.

Her gaze shot to meet his. Her chin came up. 'Your behaviour?'

His heart squeezed. She didn't trust him. She never had and with good reason. 'I have not treated you with the respect and honour you deserve.' He took a deep breath. 'I suspected you of colluding with my grandfather's machinations.'

'To what end?'

He looked at her, the heaviness in his chest almost unbearable. 'I didn't know. But I suspected there had to be something that would deprive me of my rightful inheritance. Something that would be revealed once we wed.'

A small crease formed in her brow. 'Yet you insisted we marry?'

Because he'd decided he could deal with any plan of his grandfather, once he had his instrument under his control. Liar. He'd wanted Mary in his bed.

She deserved so much more.

She certainly deserved better than a bastard for a husband who had not protected what was his. His fists opened and closed. Fear squirmed like a live thing in his gut. He pushed his roiling emotions behind a wall of ice the way he'd learned to do as a boy. At some time in the future they might bear closer examination, but not now, when it would take all his strength to do the right thing.

Squaring his shoulders, he strolled into the room. Her quick smile warmed him like the midsummer sun, but he shielded his heart in icy determination.

'What is wrong?' she asked.

Already she understood him too well. 'Word from Templeton has arrived.'

Her gaze sharpened.

'The will is undeniably flawed. He signed his father's name, not his own. Two names reversed. So small a mistake, it took ages for anyone to spot it. Whether it was intentional or because of infirmity, we will never know, even though I suspect the latter. Whatever the case, it will not stand.'

She gazed at him for a long moment, beautiful, clear blue eyes revealing the working of a bright intelligence. He could almost see the implications tumbling through her mind.

'I am not then an heiress who must marry within the year?' she finally asked.

'But we will marry,' he said. 'The settlements will be generous, you can be sure.'

He waited, his mind, his whole body, alert for some sign as to her response to his announcement. He didn't expect this to be easy, or go well.

A small crease formed between her finely drawn brows. Her gaze dropped to the still hands in her lap, effectively hiding her thoughts. He wanted to counsel her not to speak precipitously, not to rush to judgement, to consider the advantages, but he had been forcing her to his will from the moment they met. No longer. He didn't have the right.

She had saved his life.

What he wanted, what he hoped, was that she could conclude that what he suggested was the right choice, the sensible choice.

'Why?' she said to her hands. She lifted her gaze. 'Why should we marry?'

She demanded he argue his case after all.

'Surely the reason is obvious.'

A blush said she understood his meaning perfectly well. He let go of a sigh of relief. He'd feared she'd balk. Feared it badly enough to hold his breath like a schoolboy longing for a treat.

She shook her head. 'I won't do it.'

For a moment, he didn't believe what he heard. Then realisation hit with the force of a blow, shattering his soul to nothing but shards that pierced his heart in the aftermath.

He strode to stand before her, gazing down into her lovely, sorrowful face. He loomed over her, letting her see his disbelief. But not the damage. Never that. 'You are not thinking clearly,' he said.

She rose to her feet, tall, magnificent, her flashing eyes almost on a level with his. An angry goddess about to smite some lesser mortal.

And after the way he'd behaved, it was just. But he wasn't going to let her go without a fight. 'Honour demands—'

'Your honour, not mine. As I told you before, I do not move in circles that bind me to your notions of honour.' A flicker of comprehension passed across her face. 'And besides, if the will is broken, then you can no longer claim guardianship. You cannot keep me against my will, or force me to wed you.'

Oh, his Mary was indeed clever.

Only she was not his. And never really had been his. He should have known better than to think, to hope, she might yet find him of some worth. Still, he could not let her go without one more attempt to find common ground.

'Hear me out, at least,' he said.

Her eyes were as cold as the grave. 'Very well.'

'The tables have turned, yes, but it does not mean we should not marry. I am no woman's first choice of a father to their children, with my own parentage in doubt, despite my mother's denial of wrongdoing.'

'You doubt her.' She spoke flatly.

'I just don't know. She fled. If she was innocent, why would she not have stood her ground?'

'Sometimes that is the easiest way for a woman.'

He'd made her flee, too. He heard the condemnation in her voice. 'Think of the advantages. I am wealthy. I can provide for you. Protect you.' He could see he wasn't making any headway from the hard expression on her face. He started to panic. 'Build as many schools for orphans as you decide are required.'

For that he earned a small smile. It was a start. A chink in her armour. 'I'll give you free rein. Your own allowance. You don't have to see me from one year to the next, if you don't want to.' He would do his level best to make sure that didn't happen.

She took a deep breath. 'It is not enough.'

Dumbfounded, he stared at her. She turned and walked away, out of the door, out of his life.

Left him standing there feeling as if he had a hole in his chest the size of a cannonball. He looked down just to be sure he was still in one piece.

Damnation. Impossible, headstrong, wilful woman.

And he'd thought she was the only truly sensible female he'd ever met.

He ought to lock her up until she saw reason. Except he'd tried that already. He could not hold back the small smile that tugged at his lips.

Now what the hell was he to do?

Manners scratched at the door and came in, disturbing his thoughts.

'What?' he snarled, then closed his eyes and grappled his temper into submission. 'I beg your pardon, Manners, what did you require?'

Manners acknowledged the apology with a twinkle in his eyes. 'Miss Wilding has requested the carriage for first thing in the morning. I told her that our carriage was with Mrs Hampton and that the earliest I could arrange for a hiring would be the day after tomorrow. Did I do right?'

He could refuse to let her leave. Again. What would that get him, apart from her hatred? No. If leaving was what she wanted, if that would make her happy... Happy. The word painfully jiggled the shards in his chest. If leaving made her happy, he forced himself to continue, then that was what must happen. 'Arrange it.' He had one more day to find a way to change her mind.

The butler bowed himself out.

Happy. The word came back to lash him anew. She deserved to be happy. Between him and his predecessor, they'd destroyed her life. If he couldn't do anything else for her, he could help her put it back together the way she wanted.

Finding this Mrs Ladbrook might be the key. But if Templeton couldn't locate her, no one could. Then he would give her a school of her own.

Nearby. Where he could keep an eye on her. A school and a salary large enough to keep her in luxury. He would then have the excuse to ride over and see her from time to time, to inspect his investment.

His throat dried. She might not welcome visits from the bastard earl.

All right. He would have his reports second-hand. He would know she was safe, and from a distance he could protect her from harm.

The ache in his chest eased slightly.

And what if she found a man she did want to marry? What then? The thought of another man with the right to engage her wit in conversation whenever the mood took him, the right to touch her silken skin and arouse her passion... No. He would not think of his needs. This was about her happiness. Nothing else mattered.

Something burned behind his eyes.

He felt like a boy again, mourning his mother. Only this time, he knew it was different. There was no anger to balance the pain. No one else to blame.

'You sent for me, my lord?'

Bane put down his pen and looked up. How was it that when she walked into a room she made it come alive? Or was it only him who came alive?

At this moment she looked worried. Expecting he would prevent her departure on the morrow, just as he had prevented it today, no doubt. She thought him that kind of cur. And he didn't blame her.

'Please, sit.'

She did so, sinking into the chair in front of his desk with natural elegance, her long slender limbs bending to her will, when he would much rather they would bend to his, her face calm and still, her eyes a deep shadowed blue.

Perhaps he shouldn't bother her with this, but she wouldn't thank him for making her decision for her. 'I found something among the papers Gerald tried to destroy. You might find it of interest.' He passed over the piece of parchment he'd read with astonishment only half an hour before.

Swiftly, she scanned the yellowed paper. A gasp left her lips as she raised her gaze to meet his. It was filled with wonder and disbelief. 'But this is…' She looked at it again.

'From your father. It was he who consigned you to the earl's care, in payment for some earlier favour. I am assuming our marriage was what was promised.'

'Oh,' she said, her whisper husky, her eyes still fixed on the words. The paper trembled in her fingers. 'Oh.'

Tears tracked down her cheeks.

He'd made her cry. He'd thought she might be interested. Or even pleased. Tears he had not expected. He wanted to hit something. Better that than giving way to the pain at the sight of her anguish.

He got up slowly, afraid he might make things worse. 'Mary,' he whispered. He came around the desk to her side, put a comforting hand on her shoulder and was glad when she didn't pull away. He dropped to his knees, put his head close to hers. 'Mary, please. I would not have shown you this if I thought it would upset you.'

She swallowed and choked on an apologetic laugh. 'You don't understand. I'm not upset.'

With her shoulders hunched and one hand covering her eyes, she looked the very picture of misery. 'You are crying.'

She raised her head and her watery gaze met his. 'Don't you see what this means?'

'Your father undertook some sort of service for the old earl and this letter calls the favour in.'

She shook her head. 'No. I mean, yes, that is what is says. But it also says he loved me. He says *my beloved daughter.* In his last moments in this life, he thought of me, his beloved daughter.'

He frowned. 'Of course he did. You were his child.'

A tremble quaked her body. 'I didn't know. I understood he had sent me away when my mother died. That he didn't want me. To know that I was loved...' Her voice cracked and broke. She buried her face in her hands.

Bane remembered all the hugs and sweet kisses on his brow from his mother when he was young and swallowed the hot hard lump in his throat. He'd known without even thinking about it that he was loved. He'd known love in its purest form, even if he had lost it too soon. For years, he had shut himself off from its memory. Built walls of cold anger to keep the guilt at bay. The guilt for his part in his mother's death. Now those walls were shattered, leaving him with his memories and vulnerable to her hurt.

'Mary,' he whispered. He swallowed again, for the words had been so long closed off. He cradled her face in hands that felt awkward and over large. 'My darling. Look at me.' A flood of emotion washed over him. Hope. Joy. And, yes, sweet warm love. They constricted his throat as her gaze met his. 'Of course he loved you. *I* love you.'

He stilled, shocked by the sound of what he had said. Shocked by the fact that he had dared to put his feelings into words. 'I love your wit and your courage. I love your beauty. But most of all I love you.'

Her mouth trembled as her gazed searched his face. 'Please. I don't need your kindness.'

'When have I ever been kind to you?' He brushed his mouth against hers. His lips tingled at this briefest of touches, wanting more. 'It is I who needs kindness. All morning I've been plotting ways to keep you close, building a cage from which you could not escape. But I just couldn't do it, sweet. It seems I can't keep you against your will. I want you to be happy.' He groaned. 'But God, I don't want to lose you.'

'Oh, Bane.' She flung her arms about his neck and sobbed against his shoulder.

He'd made her cry yet again. He was an idiot. He'd made things worse. Awkwardly he patted her back. Forced himself not to wrap his arms around her and kiss her until she forgot his promise to let her leave. He had wooed her with seduction once, he would not lower himself to doing it again.

Slowly her sobs subsided.

He handed her his handkerchief and stood up while she dried her eyes.

'You meant what you said about letting me leave?' she asked in a shaky whisper and the glimmer of a smile.

He nodded. The damnable lump in his throat did not allow for speech, but his eyes drank her in and he realised this would likely be the last time he would ever have a chance to be this close to her.

'And if I wanted to stay?'

His heart stopped beating. He swallowed. 'Stay?' God, was that croak actually a word?

She stood up and, as always, he marvelled at how perfect was her stature, how elegant her neck, how feminine her figure. He had never seen her look more lovely, though her nose was red from weeping and her eyes still misty with tears.

To his surprise, she placed her hand against his cheek. Without thinking, he turned his face and kissed her palm before her hand fell away.

He felt its loss keenly.

'I lied,' she said so softly he had to lean closer to hear her words. 'To you. To myself. I told myself I was trapped in this house by a man I didn't trust with my life.'

'You had every reason—'

She stopped his words with a finger to his lips. 'My heart knew what my mind did not. It always knew to trust you. If not, I would have found a way to leave that very first day.' A small smile curved her lovely mouth. 'I think I fell in love with you the moment I saw you standing in the shadows like some dark avenging angel.'

Warmth trickled into all the remaining cold places in his heart. Her warmth. Her generous spirit. 'You are saying you love me in return?' he asked cautiously, fearing he had misunderstood.

Her smile broadened. 'Yes, Bane. I am saying I love you.'

He felt his way forwards with care. 'Then you mean to stay? To marry me?'

'If you truly love me and want me.'

He crushed her against his chest, feeling the pounding of his heart against his ribs. But did she really know what she was getting into with him? 'I almost got you killed. I wanted to keep you safe and I almost got you killed the way I did my mother. If I had done the same to you, I would have gone mad.'

She pushed back to look at him, a question in her eyes.

All the old guilt rushed back. 'I don't deserve your love. I don't deserve anyone's love.'

'You don't get to choose who loves you.'

'You would not, if you knew the truth.' Painful though it was, he forced himself to remember that dreadful day when his life changed for ever. 'I was ten. We had an argument. I ran off in a temper to the mine with some of the local boys. She hated me going anywhere near it, but the other boys always taunted me about being a coward and it seemed like a good way to get my own back. It got late and she came looking for me.'

He inhaled a deep ragged breath. 'We walked home in the dark, her trudging along behind me, because I was angry that she'd shamed me before my so-called friends. We were set upon by thieves. Big men. They held me down and they beat her. And there was nothing I could do. I could hear her crying out and the blows…' The sickening sound rang in his ears. 'I felt so helpless. She died of her injuries weeks later and not once did she berate me. But I knew. I knew it was all my doing. My temper that caused her death. I swore it would never happen again.'

'So that is why you always seem so cold and controlled.'

Her understanding was extraordinary. He let go a sigh. 'Always, until I met you.'

She smiled softly. But he hardened himself against his longing to kiss her. He wasn't done.

'I very nearly caused your death, too! What if you had died? I froze out the world after the death of my mother. Life would be unbearable if anything happened to you.'

'What happened to your mother wasn't your fault. Nor was what Gerald did.'

'I know that. Yet in my heart I failed my mother and I failed you. How can you trust me to keep you safe?'

'I don't need you to keep me safe, I need your love.'

The truth of it was blinding. He almost fell to his knees at the revelation. Yet even as the fear was vanquished, more doubts surfaced.

'I'll never be fully accepted in society,' he forced himself to warn her.

'I don't care about society. I only care about you.'

'What about children?'

'I want children.' She tipped up her face to kiss his cheek. 'Don't you?'

'Yes. I want your children. But…but I don't know

whose blood runs in my veins. I could be a Beresford, as my mother swore, or the son of a villain.'

'And I am the daughter of a vicar. The mixture will be interesting, I am sure.'

He looked at her beautiful mouth with longing. 'You are determined, then?'

'Am I ever anything else?'

No, thank God. He kissed her until he was dizzy with wanting her in his bed. It was all he could do not to carry her off to his chamber and make sure this was not all a dream. Make sure she could never change her mind. But there was a better way to do that.

'We will take that passage to London, first thing in the morning, and I will obtain a special licence.'

'The banns will be read and we will be married in the parish church for all your people to see, as already arranged, according to my father's wishes.'

'You don't know your father's wishes.'

She looked down at the note in her hand. 'Yes,' she said softly. 'I do.'

Tears burned behind his eyes at the tenderness in her voice. 'I don't want to wait weeks to have you in my arms, in my bed,' he groaned. 'but if that is your wish...'

Her arms came up around his neck. She kissed his lips, a small press of her lips against his, before she drew back with a smile. 'There is absolutely no reason for us to wait until we are married, is there?'

'You are a wicked woman.'

'I'm a blue-stocking, remember.'

Right then, with his blood pounding in his veins, he couldn't remember a thing except his need to be inside her. He picked her up in his arms and strode for his chamber, knowing only one thing. She was his and he was the luckiest man alive.

Epilogue

⤜⤛⤜⤛⤜⤛⤜⤛

'So Beresford, I finally get to meet your lovely wife,' Templeton drawled.

Bane narrowed his eyes as his friend, the blond darling of the *ton* and heir to the Marquisate of Mooreshead, bowed over Mary's hand. He'd given this ball at his newly renovated London town house, invited the *ton,* in order to introduce her to society. He could hardly complain that so many of them, including his oldest and most trusted friend, had come. Most of them were curious to see who the bastard earl had married, no doubt. Still, he did not have to like that his best friend and well-known rake, Lord Templeton, was eyeing his wife like a wolf who had just spotted dinner.

As usual he'd come late to the party. There were only a few more dances now supper was over and the last of the guests would depart.

Gabe caught his glare and laughed. Damn, the man was far too handsome a fellow with a smile on his lips, even if he was one of His Majesty's most dangerous spies.

'I wish you both much happiness,' Gabe said.

'Thank you, my lord.' Mary dipped a curtsy. She looked beautiful tonight in a gown of pale-rose silk, her hair arranged artfully by Betsy, her height lending her the elegance of a queen. Pride filled him, every time he looked at her, along with the desire to glare at any male who approached.

'Do you plan to return to that pile of rocks in Cornwall?' Gabe asked.

'In time,' Bane said. 'It needs some major renovations before we will feel comfortable there.' Like the closing up of passages behind the walls.

Mary nodded her agreement.

'Before you do anything to the house, would you be willing to lease it to me? For a year or so? Its inconveniences might prove very useful to my enterprise.'

Mary didn't so much as blink. They'd agreed they would keep no secrets from each other and, after receiving Gabe's permission, he'd told her all about his friend's work for the Foreign Office.

He sent her an enquiring look and she nodded. 'I owe you for finding my friend Mrs Ladbrook.'

Bane had wanted the woman to pay back the money she had salted away, but Mary wouldn't allow it. A woman alone had to do what she needed to survive. Besides, they were friends.

She turned to Bane. 'Since you will be busy making your mark in Parliament, and working for better conditions in the mines, and I have an idea for a school for miners' children I would like to raise with the denizens of the *ton,* I don't see why not,' she said. 'We will need its return when we begin our family.'

A family was her dearest hope, he knew. But he hoped it would not happen too soon. He liked having her to himself.

'Then it is agreed,' Bane said to Gabe.

'May I request this next dance, Lady Beresford?' Gabe

asked, with a sly look at Bane and a charming smile for his wife.

'Mary is promised to me,' Bane said quickly, unable to keep the possessive note from his voice.

She shook her head at him.

'You are,' he said and swept her into the waltz with a warning glower at his friend. As they moved around the floor, he was overcome by a wave of contentment.

'Are you happy?' he whispered in her ear.

'Incredibly. Unbelievably. There is only one thing missing.'

'Children.'

'Your children,' she whispered close to his ear.

His groin tightened. 'I am sure no one would miss us if it is your pleasure to try again.'

A shiver passed through her frame. 'It is always my pleasure.'

He manoeuvred her closer to the door and then whirled her out into the hallway. Giggling like children, they ran up the servants' staircase to their chamber.

'You, sir, are wicked,' she said, leaning her back against the closed door.

She looked wanton and quite delighted.

His heart swelled as he pulled her close. 'I am glad you are pleased, my dearest heart,' he breathed softly against her neck, feeling her soft swells against his length with a powerful shudder of anticipation of the love and bliss he would find in her arms.

* * * * *

MILLS & BOON®
The Regency Collection – Part 1

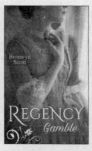

MILLS & BOON®

Why shop at millsandboon.co.uk?

Each year, thousands of romance readers find their perfect read at millsandboon.co.uk. That's because we're passionate about bringing you the very best romantic fiction. Here are some of the advantages of shopping at www.millsandboon.co.uk:

* **Get new books first**—you'll be able to buy your favourite books one month before they hit the shops

* **Get exclusive discounts**—you'll also be able to buy our specially created monthly collections, with up to 50% off the RRP

* **Find your favourite authors**—latest news, interviews and new releases for all your favourite authors and series on our website, plus ideas for what to try next

* **Join in**—once you've bought your favourite books, don't forget to register with us to rate, review and join in the discussions

Visit **www.millsandboon.co.uk**
for all this and more today!